Dear Reader,

Have you ever experienced a time when all around you others seemed happy, productive and blessed, while you felt burdened by failure, disappointment or loss?

Recently my husband and I had a delightful getaway to a wonderfully hospitable B and B in Jessieville, Arkansas. In each room was a small journal in which previous occupants had recorded impressions of their stay, describing such benefits as reduced stress, renewal of relationships, a redirection of goals—and, of course, special romantic times.

I couldn't help myself. My writer's imagination kicked in. What if (the question with which every story idea begins) someone in the depths of despair were to read such entries? The contrast between the experiences of others and one's own emotional state could be devastating. But…*what if* there was a single entry echoing that same sense of isolation?

Thus was Brady Logan born. A man who has lost almost everything and turned his back on the rest. A man without purpose and direction until he reads that one journal entry that sends him on a quest to find a woman named Nell— who may be the only one capable of understanding why he feels as he does.

It was a pleasure to send the urbane, successful Brady Logan to Fayetteville, Arkansas, a far cry from his Silicon Valley milieu. There he rediscovers the value of simple things and the healing power of new relationships, and, with Nell's help, learns that life offers an abundance of second chances if one can put the past in perspective.

May Nell and Brady affirm your faith in new beginnings!

Laura Abbot

My Name Is Nell

Laura Abbot

Harlequin Mills & Boon

Super Romance

First Published 2003
First Australian Paperback Edition 2004
ISBN 0 733 54865 2

MY NAME IS NELL © 2003 by Laura A. Shoffner
Philippine Copyright 2003
Australian Copyright 2003
New Zealand Copyright 2003

Published by
Harlequin Mills & Boon
3 Gibbes Street
CHATSWOOD NSW 2067
AUSTRALIA

Printed and bound in Australia by
McPherson's Printing Group

For my friend Jackie
with appreciation, affection and admiration

PROLOGUE

GRIPPING THE STEERING WHEEL of his Escalade, Brady Logan clenched his teeth and focused on the road ahead. The road *away*. He should give a damn. Most men would. But he felt nothing, not even relief.

When he'd made his final tour of the elaborate, expensive, now-empty house in the upscale Silicon Valley community where he, Brooke and their daughter Nicole had made their home, he'd been dry-eyed, detached. After locking the front door for the last time, he'd paused, studying the blinding white-stucco exterior, waiting for any emotion that would make him feel alive. Nothing. Only the familiar numbness.

Now, driving past the sleek four-story headquarters of L&S TechWare, nestled among the lushest landscaping an unlimited budget could provide, he still felt nothing.

Eight months ago he couldn't have imagined picking up like this and walking out. With only ingenious ideas, damn hard work and luck, he and his friend Carl Sutton had built a successful software company, now traded on the Nasdaq. He'd married a beautiful blue-eyed California blonde, purchased the gadget-laden home and cars, hired a live-in housekeeper and yard man and been accepted for membership in clubs so prestigious you didn't inquire about initiation fees, you simply wrote the check—a *large* one. In short, he had "arrived."

The best things, though, money couldn't buy. Brooke had been far more than a trophy wife. She was his other half, full of fun where he was serious, understanding of his long hours and driven work ethic. When he'd thought life couldn't get any better, Nicole had come along and grown into a loving, giggly, remarkably unspoiled preteen who'd won his heart in a way no one else ever had.

Brady gave L&S TechWare one last glance in the rearview mirror, then headed for the Interstate. It didn't matter where he was going. He should care, but he didn't. The important thing was that he *was* going.

Carl had accused him of running away. Hell, maybe he was. As he saw it, though, he had two choices. Stay and slowly, steadily, implode, or get out of Dodge and look for any spark left of the man named Brady Logan.

Here all that remained were sights, sounds, smells and memories—oh, God, the memories—reminding him that in one horrible instant, everything he loved had been wiped from the face of the earth.

Vaporized by one irresponsible drunken son of a bitch, who just happened to be driving a loaded gasoline tanker.

CHAPTER ONE

Late July, seven weeks later
Arkansas

"I DON'T SEE WHY I have to go." Abby slouched in her seat in the airport lounge, kicking at her carry-on bag. Two hanks of straight blond hair hid her features, but Nell Porter could well imagine the surly put-upon look on her thirteen-year-old daughter's face.

"You'll have a good time at your father's," Nell suggested without the faintest trace of conviction in her voice.

"Yeah, sure. Like there's so much to do in stupid Texas."

Nell sighed. This was yet another reprise of the conversation they had once a month when she took Abby to Northwest Arkansas Regional Airport to fly to Dallas for her court-ordered visit with Rick. Abby had no way of knowing how Nell dreaded the gnawing in her stomach every time she had to consign her daughter's care to the airlines—and then to Rick and Clarice, his second wife. In fact, she didn't know which was worse, thinking of her daughter all alone thousands of feet above the ground in these troubled times or picturing her in the manipulative hands of

the far-from-maternal Clarice, aka The Other
Woman. Even six years later and after professional
counseling, bitterness blindsided her, along with
those all-too-familiar feelings of unworthiness and
betrayal. She stared at her fingers, locked in a death
grip, then quite consciously separated her hands and
drew a deep breath. That was all behind her. By some
miracle, and with the help of family and friends,
she'd survived. If only she didn't have to send Abby
into the situation…

"Why do you make me go?" Abby's voice was
laced with belligerence.

"Honey, we've been over all this. It's not a choice
either of us has."

"I hate going. I don't have any friends there."

"What about your dad? He'd be disappointed not
to see you."

"Maybe." Looking up finally, Abby tucked a
strand of hair behind one bestudded ear. "But he
doesn't have a clue what to do with me when I get
there. I mean, how many times do I want to go to
Six Flags? Besides, I'm missing Tonya's birthday
party."

Abby's remarks evoked guilt Nell knew was irra-
tional. As if she could have done any more to influence the custody decision. Or changed the fact Rick
was entitled to spend time with their child. Did Abby
ever tell her father how she felt about the visits? No.
Whenever she was with him, she did a good imitation
of the dutiful daughter. Inevitably when she came
home, Nell faced the task of picking up the pieces,
putting them back together as best she could and then
sending Abby on her way the next time. Like now.
Abby needed a punching bag, and Nell was handy.

Somehow that insight didn't alleviate the hurt her daughter's petulance generated.

The mechanical drone of a commuter plane drawing up to the gate was accompanied by the disassociated voice of the loudspeaker announcing the arrival of the aircraft Abby would be taking to Dallas. "You need to go through security now," Nell said, rising to her feet.

"I guess." Abby stood, shouldered her bag and trailed Nell all the way to the short line of passengers waiting at the checkpoint.

Nell watched Abby's expression settle into affected pseudo-sophistication, the bored look of the veteran traveler. Yet when she turned and gave Nell a perfunctory hug, her clear gray eyes held not resentment, but misgiving. "Bye, Mom. See ya Sunday night."

"I'll be here," Nell said. She watched Abby pass through the metal detector and pluck her bag from the conveyer belt, then waited to catch a final glimpse of her daughter's rail-thin body as she descended the escalator and vanished from sight.

The empty feeling was always the same. It was enough to drive a person to drink.

But that was out of the question.

STELLA JANES SETTLED in the porch chair next to her daughter, then turned her gaze toward Abby, who stood at the edge of the lawn verging on an elaborate flower bed. "Do you really think that skirt length is appropriate for a middle school child?"

Nell stifled a groan. With too much idle time, her mother overly concerned herself with family. "It's what all the girls are wearing."

Stella continued staring at her granddaughter, who was herding her toddler cousin around the backyard. "I suppose, but that doesn't mean I have to like it."

"Like what?" Nell's statuesque older sister Lily, whose name fit her as well as the chic beige linen slacks and blouse she wore, approached with a tray of lemonade.

"Abby's hem length," Stella said.

Lily paused, then followed her mother's gaze. "I see what you mean."

Nell should be used to it by now, but their united front rankled. Lily and Stella tended to share a similar outlook, usually quite different from hers. They enjoyed what Nell thought of as "girly things" like quilting, home decoration and scrapbooking, while she had always preferred gardening, furniture refinishing and sports. No wonder she had gravitated to her father, finding refuge—and acceptance—in her role as "daddy's girl." There were moments, like this, when she felt like an outsider. As teenagers, her relationship with Lily had been strained, but they had grown closer as adults. Sometimes, in recent years, Lily had even dared to swim against the tide of their mother's wishes. But not often. And not today.

Lily distributed the icy glasses. "When does school start?"

Grateful for the change of subject, Nell let out a breath. "A week from Monday."

"In my day, school never started in August," Stella reminded them. "Always the day after Labor Day."

"It can't come any too soon for me," Nell said. "Abby needs a regular schedule. Time hangs pretty heavy on her hands." When she was at work, Nell worried about her daughter. Aside from helping Lily with little Chase, Abby was at the mercy of friends' mothers thoughtful enough to invite her to their houses. Otherwise she slept late and watched God-knows-what on TV.

Lily sank into the chaise and crossed her feet at the ankles. "At least next week she'll be on vacation with Rick."

"That's supposed to comfort me?"

"Why not? You'll have seven glorious days all to yourself."

"Right. Seven interminable days to worry whether Rick will pay her any attention or, heaven forbid, let Clarice take her shopping like she did last summer." Nell nodded in her daughter's direction. "You think *that* skirt's short? You didn't see the outrageous outfit her charming stepmother selected to complement the salon job she set up for Abby's hair and nails. When she came home, she looked like a prepubescent Britney Spears."

Lily giggled, restoring Nell's good humor. "Clarice always was a piece of work. Poor Abby."

Stella rolled her eyes. "If I live to be a hundred, I'll never understand it."

"It" was the topic her mother avoided. The disgrace of Rick's affair with the "younger woman," the ensuing small-town scandal and the unthinkable divorce, one more way Nell had disappointed her mother's expectations.

"Water under the bridge," Nell mumbled.

"You'll get through the next week all right?" Her mother's anxious eyes signaled her unspoken concern.

Nell clutched her lemonade. Would she forever be under scrutiny? "Yes, Mother. I'll be fine."

She couldn't fault her mother. Not really. She had only herself to blame, but it had taken her a long time—and cost her a great deal of pain—to reach that conclusion.

WHO WAS HE KIDDING ANYWAY? Nothing was better. If anything, it was worse. Brady stared into the murky depths of the thick ceramic mug he cradled between his hands, oblivious to the early morning chatter around him. These Main Street cafés were running together in his mind—each whirling, grease-layered ceiling fan, red leatherette counter stool and kitchen pass-through indistinguishable from the next. Though the spur-and-antler décor in Wyoming differed from this Arkansas country calico, the smell of bacon frying and the cloying cheerfulness of the morning-shift waitress were unsettlingly predictable.

"Decided?" The middle-aged redhead swiped a damp rag across the counter, then extracted a pad and pencil from her apron and eyed him speculatively.

"The special and a large o.j., please."

"Got it," she said and, with economy of motion, refilled his coffee.

Fortunately the adjacent stool was empty. He couldn't have tolerated another desultory conversation highlighted by comments on the weather and the market—cattle, wheat or stock, depending on where he was. Two months. He mentally ticked off the states he'd passed through—Oregon, Idaho, Montana, Wyoming, Nebraska, Missouri and now Arkansas—always avoiding the cities. He needed no reminders of the pressures of suburban affluence, rampant consumerism or commercial success. His frequent phone calls from Carl Sutton took care of that. Regardless of the artifice his business partner employed, underneath, his basic question was always the same: when would Brady get hold of himself and resume his work at L&S TechWare?

Brady didn't have the heart to tell Carl that he rarely thought of the business and gave little consideration even to the next day, much less the interminable future yawning before him. On the other hand, he knew he couldn't continue in his current mode, aimlessly wandering across the country, barely taking in the changing scenery, restlessly moving on after a few days in any one place.

The waitress plunked down a plate laden with eggs, bacon and the biggest biscuit Brady had encountered so far in his travels. "Haven't seen you around. You here for the fishing?"

Mildly curious, Brady looked up. "Fishing?"

"White River trout. We're famous for it."

Why not? "Uh, yeah. Know any good places to stay?"

"Well, there's the resort—"

The mere word *resort* reminded him of California and all that he was fleeing.

"Then there's a B-and-B, if you're into that. Quiet place with all the comforts of home. The Edgewater Inn."

All the comforts of home. Brady doubted it, but the word *home* resonated in a way nothing else had in weeks. "Can you give me directions to the B-and-B?"

"Sure." She pulled a paper napkin from the holder and drew him a rudimentary map.

Later, crossing the bridge over the White River, Brady felt a stirring of interest. He'd done a lot of fly-fishing in Colorado as a kid. Maybe he'd hole up in the Edgewater Inn for a few days, outfit himself and spend time on the river fishing—and making some decisions.

Carl had been right. He couldn't run forever.

"YOU LOOK BEAT," Reggie Pettigrew, the sixty-year-old head librarian, said when Nell reported for work Saturday after taking Abby to the airport.

Setting down the stack of books she'd collected from the outdoor depository, she shot him an I-don't-need-much-of-this look. "Full of compliments this morning, aren't you?"

"Even beat you look good. Big weekend?"

"Reggie, are you trying to get my goat or does it just come naturally? You know I haven't had a big weekend in years. And that's not all bad. They can be highly overrated." She cringed, remembering some of the "big weekends" of her past. "It's Abby. I can't help worrying when she flies to visit her dad."

"Did she give you a hard time again about going?"

"As usual. This time, it's for a week." She began sorting the returned books. "I don't know how I ended up being the bad guy in this arrangement, but she blames me for making her go."

Reggie eyed her over the top of his thick bifocals. "While Prince Charming and his lady love live happily ever after?"

Reggie had a way of seeing straight through her.

"Exactly." She glanced at the wall clock registering 9:59. "But enough about me. The hordes are undoubtedly lined up at the door racing to get to Balzac, Dickens, Faulkner, et al."

"I wish. At least we can count on Clarence Fury and his daily two hours with *The New York Times*."

Nell filled a book cart and made the rounds reshelving. When she'd hit bottom after Rick left her, Reggie had been a godsend hiring her as his assistant. Gradually her role had grown until she was now the children's librarian and coordinator of special adult programs. With the limited library budget, she wasn't able to do as much as she would've liked, but the pre-school story hour was booming and she was having sporadic success with the adult forums she'd initiated in the past year. That reminded her to prepare the flyers for the September forum. A minister from the county hospice board was speaking on death and dying. Not exactly an upper of a topic, but several patrons had expressed an interest.

Automatically reshelving two misplaced volumes, Nell fought the familiar ache in her chest. She bowed her head. It had been nearly seven years. Even so, it was hard for her to believe her father was dead. In the snap of a finger. One day, here. Robust, laughing, vital. The next, gone. Without so much as a fare-you-well.

She straightened and slowly made her way to the main desk. Maybe that was why for so long she'd resisted the death topic for the forum. What if she went to pieces during the discussion? Seemingly her mother and Lily had moved on better than she had after her father's massive heart attack, but there wasn't a day when Nell didn't think of him and miss him.

Like now, with Abby protesting vehemently about her upcoming week with Rick. Her dad would've reassured her that she wasn't the worst mother in the world, that adolescence, too, would pass, that Abby appreciated her more than she was able to let on. Although Nell could spout that kind of self-talk all day, it did nothing to ease the cramping loneliness that fused to her like a second skin.

"Has Hazel Underwood returned that new Patricia Cornwell yet?"

Nell looked up into the scowling face of Minnie Foltz, whose boundless knowledge of murder and mayhem was acquired from the numerous mysteries she devoured.

Nell searched the books lined up on the reserved shelf. "Looks like you're in luck, Minnie."

"Hmphh. I should hope so. I can't figure what takes Hazel so long. That's the *real* mystery."

Nell processed the checkout, acknowledging that at least she'd made one person happy today.

MORNING SUN SILVERED the ripples on the surface of the slow-moving river. Swallows soared and dipped above their mud nests built into the crevices of the facing cliff. Standing thigh-deep in the clear, cold water, Brady pumped his arm, flicking the fly several times before letting it settle upstream from a deep hole. He'd discovered this spot yesterday, pulling in two browns nice enough to keep. Sally, the proprietress and cook at the Edgewater Inn, had been pampering him all week, and last night she'd prepared his fish, which they'd eaten in the kitchen out of sight of the other guests. Somehow the older woman had sensed he was a troubled soul. He'd give her credit. She provided all anyone could ask—good food, soft beds, lazy afternoons in a hammock and splendid fishing.

But it wasn't enough. He wanted to share the place with those he loved. Wanted Brooke nestled beside him in the soft four-poster bed, wanted to hear Nicole's infectious laugh when she caught her first trout, wanted to watch both of them hunched over the chessboard in the inn's living room.

Wading downstream, he reeled in, then cast toward a boulder near the far bank. On either side of the river, the forested hills rose, the deep greens of the trees a contrast to the blue sky. Rounding a bend upstream were three canoes, the occupants grinning and sweating with exertion. Three men and three boys. A father-son outing, maybe. Longing, fierce and potent, stabbed him.

Would anything ever be normal again? How could it be? Not when everywhere he looked were reminders of what he was missing. Not only what he was missing now but, worse by far, what he had bypassed in the name of work when it had been right under his nose.

Too late, he felt the quick tug on his line. He couldn't react fast enough. Asleep at the switch and the big one had gotten away. He barked an ironic "Story of my life." Reeling in, he made his way to shore, removed his waders and gathered his gear.

He'd already been at the Edgewater Inn longer than he'd stayed anywhere. It was time to move on. He couldn't remain here forever, counting on Sally's hospitable and generous nature. Move on where? That was the sixty-four-thousand dollar question.

Because no place had the slightest meaning for him.

Back at the inn, he told Sally he would be leaving in the morning. That final evening he sat on the deck outside his room, his feet up on the railing, watching the sun sink behind the mountain. The occasional cooing of a pair of mourning doves and the soothing sound of the river lapping the rocky shore kept him company. In his hands he held the guest journal Sally had asked him to sign. Each room had one. He opened the paisley cover. The first entry was from 1995, the year Sally had bought the inn. ''Wonderful food, wonderful hostess, wonderful place! The slow pace was very therapeutic. Thank you.'' It was signed ''Ron and Shari Huxley, Tulsa, OK.''

Brady turned the page. ''Oh, Sally, John and I really needed this time away from the children and all our responsibilities. You've created a little piece of heaven here on earth. We can't wait to come back and be spoiled again.'' This one was signed ''Rowena.''

Then there was the honeymoon couple who cleverly implied the wedding night had been all anyone could hope for and vowed to return on every anniversary.

Couples. All of them. Made supremely happy by the Edgewater Inn. What could he possibly write? This was a place to be shared, but what was he doing? Nursing his wounds. How did he write about that?

Flicking through the book, he came to one particular entry where the margins were embroidered with small colored pencil drawings of a spruce tree, a dog-wood blossom, the rocky cliff above the rushing river, and, at the bottom, a rainbow.

Brady smoothed the page with his hand and began reading.

A sanctuary. That's what you've created here, and I will be forever grateful. I have been so alone. Unable to see a direction for my life. Not sure if there even is one. When you've loved and lost, doubt replaces hope, insecurity replaces confidence and you wonder who you are. Whether you can go on. Or even want to.

Looking up just in time to see the sun drop behind the dark curtain of mountain, Brady pondered whether he should continue reading. The words were too confessional, too emotionally raw—and threatening. Some other individual had come here full of the same thoughts and feelings.

Unable to help himself, he turned back to the graceful handwriting covering the page.

This time of quiet and contemplation has been a great gift, restoring my belief that no matter how severe the storm, rainbows can happen. Regardless of how desolate I feel right now, I have to believe that somewhere out there is someone for me. Someone I can trust. Someone I can love. When I find him, dear Sally, the two of us will come to the Edgewater Inn. Together.

Brady stared for the longest time at the signature. Simple. Bare. Exposed. ''Nell.''

He stood abruptly and walked to the railing, peering at the grove of pine trees bordering the property. Nell, whoever she was, was more optimistic than he was. As if, like Dorothy, you could click your red-shod heels and suddenly find yourself on the other side of whatever hell you were in.

God, he hated his blatant, whining self-pity. If Nell, desolate and alone, had been willing to look for something better, why couldn't he?

He leaned against a post. This attitude of his was downright depressing. He needed a plan—any plan— and at this point he didn't give much of a damn what it was.

Absently he realized he was still holding the guest book, his forefinger marking Nell's page. He opened it again and squinted in the dim light, just making out the line beneath her signature. ''Fayetteville, AR, 1997.''

He carried the book back into his room and reread the entry. Several times.

A crazy idea entered his head. But no crazier than what he'd been doing. He needed a purpose. A direction. Short-term, this would work as well as anything.

Tomorrow, after he checked out, he would drive to Fayetteville to find this Nell, a woman who still believed in rainbows.

CHAPTER TWO

TOWERING ABOVE the broad expanse of lawn in front of Old Main, the landmark building of the University of Arkansas campus, were massive oaks and maples, their leaves hanging lifeless in the heat of the late August day. Patches of shade offered only the illusion of coolness. Brady paused, gazing across the sward where members of a fraternity gathered on the porch of their house to welcome a group of rushees. He envied them this carefree time of life. College. What would that have been like?

Once, long ago, he'd assumed that was his destiny. But that was before his mother died and his father hastily remarried. Before he rebelled against his father's unreasonable restrictions and demands. Before he stood up to the old man, told him to take a flying leap and left home. On his own at eighteen. No enlightening classes, fall football weekends, frat parties or eager coeds for him.

All he had in his favor was a knack for computers, a willingness to work his butt off and a cold, simmering rage fueling his ambition.

He headed toward Dickson Street, an off-campus shopping area housing several watering holes. He needed a cool drink. He had thought his plan of starting his search with the university telephone directory

was ingenious. The U of A was the town's largest
employer, so the odds of finding Nell on campus
were better than average. However, after a day
hunched over a table in the college library, his eyes
were raw from reading endless lists of names. He'd
found several Nells. When he'd called, one had
turned out to be a secretary in the engineering department suspicious of his motives. Another was a
graduate student who knew nothing about any Edgewater Inn. A third, who sounded like Minnie Mouse,
asked him what he had in mind, then giggled co-
quettishly.

The tavern was an oasis in a frustrating day. He
settled on a bar stool and ordered a cola. In a nearby
booth, three barrel-chested young men were playing
a chug-a-lug game. Brady's lip curled. He wanted to
knock their pitcher to the floor and demand to know
if they were driving. Didn't they understand their stu-
pidity could lead to tragedy? He no longer had any
tolerance for overindulgence.

Instead of acting on his instinct, he turned to the
bartender and asked if he knew any women named
Nell. "That's kind of an old-fashioned name. Most
of the chicks these days are Chelseas or Tiffanies,
know what I mean?"

Yeah, he did. Besides, he wasn't picturing Nell as
a younger woman. More someone his age. Somebody
who'd obviously lived through hurt. Then another
thought hit him. What if Nell was older, maybe a
widow who'd lost her husband after forty years of
marriage?

He drained his glass. This was insane. Even if he
found his Nell, how could he explain his actions?

She might even accuse him of stalking. What was he hoping to find?

He signaled the bartender for another soda. What would Carl say if he could see him now, sitting in Fayetteville, Arkansas? Everywhere you looked in this town was a depiction of the butt-ugly razorback hog, the beloved mascot of the university. Yet the place had an appealing, slow-paced charm. He grinned sardonically. He had wanted to get away from the Silicon Valley. Well, he had certainly succeeded.

Nursing his drink, he noticed a local newspaper on the seat beside him. He picked it up and scanned the headlines. Zoning issues. School orientation programs. A public library forum. A controversy over pollution of the Illinois River.

As he started to shove it aside, out of the blue he recalled a seemingly vague remark Sally at the Edgewater Inn had made when he'd asked about Nell. "I can't give out personal information about my guests," she'd said. They'd been standing in the living room at the time, where one entire wall was lined with books. "Say," she'd added, gesturing to the shelves as if changing the subject, "do you like to read? I do. Libraries have always been favorite places of mine. How about you?"

At the time he'd mumbled something about not having much time for reading. He remembered being irritated that she hadn't given him any information about Nell. Now, though, he wondered. Maybe she had and he'd been too dense to realize it.

He drained his glass, then began reading the article about the library forum. In the final paragraph, he found what he was looking for. "August's forum on Arab-Israeli relations will be moderated by Nell Porter." He checked the date. Tomorrow night.

At last a genuine lead. He could blend into the audience and size up the latest Nell candidate.

He couldn't believe he was thinking like this. What would he say if he ever found *the* Nell? "Hi, I think we have misery in common?" What kind of way was that to impress anybody? Why did he care?

There was another obstacle. Her entry was dated 1997. Six years ago. What made him think time had stood still for Nell?

Despite the harsh light of reason, he felt compelled to follow his search through to its conclusion. He *would* find Nell.

"DID YOU GET Abby off all right for her vacation with her father?"

To free her hands, Nell settled the phone against her shoulder and continued searching through her office file cabinet. "Yes, Mother. As usual, she trudged through security like a condemned prisoner."

"Why can't you say something to Rick? What's the matter with that man anyway?"

"If I knew the answer to that question, I wouldn't be where I am right now." She pulled out a file folder, skimmed the contents, then discarded it. Where was that background information for her introduction for tonight's forum? "As for communicating with Rick about Abby, a cabbage is a more attentive listener. At some point, Abby is going to have to speak up for herself. She's the only one I can think of who might make a dent in his self-absorption.''

''Do you think it's wise to keep sending her, dear?''

''What choice do I have? Her visits are court-mandated. Besides, in his own way, Rick does care about her.''

Her mother's voice modulated into that concerned, faintly judgmental tone Nell had come to dread. ''Are you sure you'll be all right by yourself? It's a whole week alone. Don't you want to come stay with me?''

Rolling her eyes, Nell prayed for patience. ''I'll be fine, Mother. You can count on it. Besides, I need some time at home to clean out closets and get organized for winter.''

''That doesn't sound much like fun.''

Fun? What would that be like? ''I'll take peace and quiet over fun any day.'' She extracted two folders that had become stuck together. There it was. Her introduction. Breathing a sigh of relief, she grabbed up the phone. ''Look, Mom, I've got to go. The forum starts in half an hour.''

''I just wanted to see how you were doing.''

Nell gritted her teeth. How long would it take before her family trusted her again? ''Thanks, I appreciate your concern. I'll call you later in the week.''

With a sigh of relief, she hung up the phone and studied the bios in front of her—one for a local rabbi and another for the head of the Arab Student League. Using a highlighter, she marked the sections she wanted for her introduction.

Yet she was distracted by her mother's interfer-

ence. Was being treated like a child a price she
would always have to pay?

BRADY FOLLOWED a frumpy-looking pair of retirees
into the library meeting room and took a seat on the
aisle near the back. He looked around wondering
which of the librarians was Nell. Two stood at a side
table arranging books about the Mid-East. Another
was bent over, conferring with one of the men seated
beside the podium. When she straightened, smiled
around the room and asked for order, Brady's breath
caught in his chest. This was no old woman looking
for a dapper widower with whom to share her twilight years.

"Good evening and welcome to tonight's forum.
My name is Nell Porter and I'll be your moderator
this evening...."

Brady tuned out her words. She was a tall, slender
woman—midthirties he judged—with short straw-
colored hair cut in uneven lengths, a style that com-
plemented the casualness of her high-waisted denim
jumper. When she smiled, her eyes narrowed in delighted crinkles. She wore little makeup and he
couldn't help noticing her ringless fingers.

"...it's my pleasure to introduce..."

He became aware that a short, bearded gentleman
had stepped to the microphone. Brady's eyes, however, were glued on the graceful way Nell Porter
sank into her chair, crossing one long leg over the
other, smoothing her skirt, then fixing her attention
on the speaker.

She was not like Brooke, a sleek blonde made for
designer clothes, Porsches and expensive, under-

stated jewelry. Nell had a fresh, wholesome look, although her tousled hairstyle suggested an impish streak. She appeared thoroughly likeable. Comfortable.

He'd made his living by exercising logic. The thought in his head, however, was anything but logical.

He wanted Nell Porter to be his Edgewater Inn Nell.

"YOU'RE *WHERE?*" Carl did not sound pleased.

"Fayetteville. Arkansas."

"Hmm. I'd hoped you were on your way home."

Home. There was that word again. Didn't Carl understand. He no longer had a home. Staring at the anonymous, monochromatic motel room walls, Brady absently brushed a hand through his hair, still damp from his morning shower. "Not yet."

"I don't suppose it would hurry things along if I said we've got a lotta deals poppin' here and we need you."

The familiar clenching of his stomach gave him his answer. "Sorry, Carl, but I'd be no good to you now."

His partner's tone mellowed. "I don't mean to rush you. I know you need time. It's just—"

"When I'm ready, buddy, I'll let you know."

"What are your plans for the moment?"

Brady studied the cover of the local phone book, bearing a picture of a flowering pink dogwood. "It's nice here. I may stick around a while."

"In *Arkansas?*"

"Don't knock it till you've seen it. Natural beauty,

low cost of living, friendly people. A guy could do a whole lot worse.'' Best of all, it was a radical change from the merry-go-round California lifestyle.

He really should feel guilty about the company, but, ironically, that was the one thing about which he had no guilt. It would survive.

He wasn't so sure about himself. Two or three times a week he woke from a dead sleep drenched in sweat, the odor of diesel fuel clogging his nostrils, his heartbeat in the danger zone—and two names echoing in his consciousness.

His friends had recommended all kinds of therapists and treatments—a regular LaLa Land smorgasbord of palliatives.

Screw that. He'd find his own way. Picking up his billfold and keys, he headed for the door. Today was a day for exploring the area—and stopping by the library. He allowed himself a brief smile of anticipation. Maybe Ms. Porter could help him research area B-and-B's, particularly those along the White River.

NELL PARKED HER CAR near the square and hit her early-morning meeting at the church before heading on to work. The sun had already burned off the dew, and the temperature reading on the bank stood at eighty-five degrees and it wasn't even ten. Another scorcher. The cool of the library would be welcome.

After exchanging greetings with Reggie and the rest of the staff, she had just enough time to circle the chairs in the children's area before the toddlers and their mothers began arriving for story-time. As usual Rodney Fraim's mother could hardly control him. At every chance, he slipped out of her arms and began playing peekaboo from behind the stacks. Most of the rest, however, sat on the carpet, legs crossed, only occasionally fidgeting. Today's book was Katharine Holabird's *Alexander and the Dragon.* Halfway through the story, Nell noticed a tall, dark-haired man quietly observing the children. He looked harmless enough, but you could never be too careful. He pulled out a chair and sat at a table where he continued watching them. He seemed more pensive than menacing, an amused smile softening his strong features when one of the youngsters reacted with laughter to the idea of having a dragon under the bed.

As Nell continued reading and displaying the illustrations, she became uncomfortably aware that the man seemed to be studying her rather than the children. Did she know him? Fighting a breathless sensation, she approached the end of the story where Alexander realizes he's no longer afraid of shadows—or of his friend the dragon.

A shiver passed through Nell when the man mouthed the lines with her. Why was his expression so sad? Before she could ponder his sudden change, he stood and wandered toward the fiction section.

She shook her head to clear her mind. She must've imagined that fleeting moment of connection with him. She refocused on the boys and girls and completed the story. As she'd anticipated, it gave rise to a lively discussion of what and who lived in the bedrooms of her tiny listeners.

After helping all the children select and check out their take-home books, she straightened the area and turned toward her office. The good-looking man sat

in one of the easy chairs near the main desk, an open
book in his lap. But his dark brown eyes followed
her. Enough of this. She was uncomfortable with his
attention, even though a frisson of something like
pleasure took her by surprise.

She crossed to him. "Excuse me, sir, but do I
know you?"

He closed his book—which she couldn't help noticing was a Grisham legal thriller—and raised his
eyes, a slow smile creating a devilish dimple in his
left cheek. "No. I'm Brady Logan." With athletic
grace, he rose to his feet and now looked down on
her. "I was at the forum last night, so, in a manner
of speaking, I know you. Nell Porter, right?"

She clasped her cold hands in front of her. "Yes."
She scrambled for words. "Did you enjoy it?"

His eyes narrowed. "Discussion of conflict and
violence is more painful than enjoyable." He paused
before going on. "I vastly preferred this morning's
activities."

"You're obviously familiar with *Alexander and
the Dragon.*"

She detected a momentary steeling of his features.
He offered no explanation but simply said, "Yes."

She couldn't seem to tear herself away, but there
was little more to be said. Steering from the personal,
she grasped for the professional. "Is there something
I can help you with?"

"As a matter of fact, yes. I'm new to the area and
am interested in doing some fly-fishing, maybe lo-
cating a nice place along the White River to stay.
Have any suggestions?"

Brady Logan didn't strike her as someone so clueless about how to use a library, but then you never knew. "There are a couple of popular resorts near Flippin, or you might consider—"

"I'm more a B-and-B kinda guy."

"Well, in that case—" his eyes found hers, as if he anticipated her next words "—you might try the Edgewater Inn." More to escape his scrutiny than anything, she made her way to the travel section. "Here." She pulled out a directory of Arkansas bed-and-breakfasts. "You can read all about it."

He took the book, thumbing through it until he found the listing and an accompanying photograph. "This looks nice."

"It is." Then she found herself telling him all about her stay there.

"Sounds peaceful," he finally said.

"Very." A poignant memory came to her of ca-thartic tears shed on a lazy September afternoon rocking on a wooden porch swing overlooking the blue river.

He took her by the arm, then as if realizing he'd overstepped his bounds, he released his grip. "Thanks, Nell Porter. You've been most helpful."

She found it hard to swallow. "I'm glad."

Reggie Pettigrew bustled up alongside them. "Nell, your daughter's on the phone."

A strange look—wistfulness? sadness?—shad-owed Brady's face before he seemed to reassemble his features. He nodded his understanding.

"Excuse me," she said, then started for her office.

"Nell?"

She turned around. He smiled, then winked. "Be-ware of dragons."

On the way to her office, she couldn't explain the tingly feeling short-circuiting her body. She had the strangest sense that he'd been waiting for her. Any number of other librarians could have helped him.

Oddly, instead of making her uncomfortable, the thought filled her with the kind of anticipation she hadn't experienced in years. He was an extremely attractive man.

Any such frivolous thoughts were shattered when she picked up the phone. "Mom." Abby's voice was a harsh whisper. "I hate it here. Do I hafta stay?"

THAT AFTERNOON Brady explored the secluded neighborhoods clinging to the sides of the steep hills rimming Fayetteville, drove north on I-540, astonished at the amount of commercial development, then ended up at a marina on Beaver Lake, where moored boats of all kinds rocked with the gentle swells. As a businessman, he recognized he'd stumbled into an investor's paradise in this burgeoning northwest corner of Arkansas. He left his car and walked across the boardwalk to the marina office where he rented a small pontoon boat for a couple of hours.

Slowly edging past the buoys, he pushed the throttle forward and skimmed over the clear water, practically deserted except for a few die-hard fishermen. If this lake were in California, it would be wall-to-wall boats no matter what the day of the week or time of day. When he reached the middle of a secluded cove, he cut the motor—aware of the peaceful quality of the sudden silence.

Finally he let his thoughts return to Nell. He had been ill-prepared for her effect on him. She was a natural with the children and there was a kind of discomfiting synchronicity in her having selected *Alexander and the Dragon* to read. Nicole's favorite bedtime story. He glanced skyward, willing away the involuntary spasm of grief.

He forced himself to think about Nell again. When she'd approached him in the library, she had seemed skittish, her hands primly folded in front of her, her gray eyes wary. Her nose, dusted lightly with freckles, and her bare red-polished toes contributed to her overall sense of vulnerability. Yet she'd dared to confront him. Admittedly his observation of her had been rather obvious. *When you've loved and lost, doubt replaces hope, insecurity replaces confidence and you wonder who you are.*

The boat bobbed in the wake of a passing jet ski. Was she still all by herself? He knew now she had a daughter. Despite her ringless fingers, was there a Mr. Porter?

He devoutly hoped not.

Since Brooke and Nicole had died, he had been unable to connect with anybody—not his friends, his neighbors or his colleagues. He thought of himself as a wraith. Improbable as it seemed, though, he wanted to connect with Nell Porter.

Switching on the key, he started the motor and made his way back across the lake. By the time he reached the dock, he'd arrived at a decision.

Tomorrow he would look for rental property in Fayetteville. He was staying. And Nell was the reason.

NELL WAS REDECORATING the bulletin board in the children's area with a back-to-school motif when she became aware of a presence behind her. She finished tacking up the book cover she was working on, then turned. Hands in his pockets, Brady Logan stood there smiling a killer smile, then shrugged as if in self-defense. "I'm back."

"Not the proverbial bad penny, I hope," she said, attempting a nonchalance she was far from feeling.

"No. I have a reason for being here."

She needed something to occupy her hands. Selecting another cover from the stack on the table, she said, "Anything I can help you with?"

"I certainly hope so. I'd like you to have lunch with me."

She'd been fully prepared to direct him to the library's fishing collection or to locate the latest issue of *Field and Stream,* but *lunch?* The thought filled her with mild panic. No man had asked her to lunch in a very long time and certainly no one who made her hormones react in such an unseemly fashion. "I beg your pardon?"

He nodded his head. "You heard me right. Lunch. You know, where two people look at a menu, order and have polite conversation while they eat."

Smiling tentatively, she said, "I know what lunch is, but let's face it, I have no idea who you are, really."

"That's why I'm inviting you to lunch—to correct that deficiency." Before she could offer further objections, he went on. "I'm new in town. I'm looking for someone to fill me in on the local scene. I figure a librarian is the perfect resource. This would be completely aboveboard." He drew her to the window. "It's broad daylight, pedestrians are every-where. We could walk to the nearest restaurant, and if you decide I'm a threat, all you have to do is call for help." He touched her lightly on the shoulder. "But I guarantee that won't be necessary."

Nell fought the temptation induced by his honeyed voice and the pressure of his hand on her shoulder. Despite herself, she recalled her reaction to her mother's challenge the other day. Peace and quiet—or fun? This could be fun. On the other hand... "I don't think—"

"Don't think, just say 'yes.' You do have to eat, don't you?"

She made the mistake, then, of looking into his eyes where she found both humor and need. "I—I suppose I could—"

"Great." When he smiled down at her, she couldn't summon a single objection. "I'll wait over in the magazine section."

Then he left her. She studied the book cover in her hand, trying to think what she was doing with it. Flustered, she remembered and picked up a couple of tacks. She shook her head, wondering why in the world she'd agreed to such an improbable invitation.

Perhaps the dragon had left the bedroom and now inhabited the library.

As they sauntered along Dickson Street toward the restaurant, Brady kept feeding her questions about the town, the university, the local economy. As a native, she provided a wealth of information, but it was hard to concentrate. Her unruly hair shone in the sun, and he found amusing her self-contained way of letting him know this was purely a business appointment.

"I like what I've seen and what I'm hearing. I've decided to stick around a while."

"Oh?"

"This morning I lucked into a furnished condo. A professor leaving on sabbatical had his sub-leasing deal fall through last week. I was in the right place at the right time."

She laughed. "You certainly were. Housing is at a premium this time of year in a university town."

When they reached the brew pub restaurant, he ushered her toward a corner booth. "Hungry?"

"Starving, actually."

"Good." The waiter introduced himself while he set down their water glasses. Brady noticed Nell hadn't looked at her menu. "You already know what you want?"

"I always have the soup-and-sandwich special, but they have great burgers here."

"Okay. That's settled." He signaled the hovering waiter and placed their order. "Now, enough about Fayetteville. Tell me about Nell Porter."

"I have a better idea. You're the stranger I'm having lunch with. What about you?"

He mentally culled the details he could bring himself to share. "I grew up in Colorado. Left home at eighteen and went to work in the software industry in California, then started my own company, which, I'm happy to say, has done extremely well. I was married for fifteen years. One daughter. They, uh…" Damn. His throat was closing down.

"Yes?"

He swallowed, then managed to say, "They were both killed last year in a car accident."

He was unprepared for her hand to cover his, and even less prepared for the jolt of life it sparked. "I'm sorry."

He studied the TV mounted over the bar, then glanced out the window. "Yeah, well, these things happen."

"So what brings you to Arkansas?"

For some reason, he trusted her with the truth. "I couldn't take California any longer. Too much had changed. I've been on the road. Seeing what's out here. Getting a new perspective."

"And?" Her eyes swam with compassion. Why was it welcome from her when it hadn't been from anyone else? *I have been so alone.* Maybe because she knew.

"I like it here. Besides, I needed to stop somewhere. I couldn't go on running." There. He'd said it.

"Brady Logan, whatever it is you're seeking, I hope you find it."

Looking at her, her thin shoulders hunched over the table, her reedlike neck revealing a pronounced pulse beat, he felt a welcome surge of hope. "Me, too." He cleared his throat. "Now it's your turn. Tell me about your daughter. And husband."

Brady noticed a shutter fall over Nell's eyes. Just then the waiter appeared, set down their food and made a show of asking if everything was all right. Brady nodded. After her first tentative spoonful of the steaming soup, Nell answered Brady's question, her attention fixed on her food. "There's no husband.

I've been divorced for six years. My daughter Abby is thirteen and—'' finally she glanced up ''—getting to that stage where parents are a 'drag.' I've been told adolescence is survivable, but I'm not so sure.'' She grinned a wobbly grin.

''You have family here?''

''My father's dead, but my mother still lives here, as do my sister and her family.''

''Are you close?''

''Very, but with all the baggage, too. Since the divorce, my mother and sister are overprotective of me, which I suppose is natural, even though it can be frustrating. But I couldn't have managed without them.''

''You're lucky,'' he said, aware of his faintly bitter tone. He hadn't seen his father or his younger brother since he left home, and so long as the old man was alive, he didn't want to.

''Your ex-husband? Is he still on the scene?''

''He and his new wife live in Dallas. In fact, Abby's visiting them this week.'' Her deliberately neutral tone struck him as odd. She was holding something back. Some hurt.

''Well, since you're alone, what do you say we take in dinner and a movie? Tomorrow night?'' He watched her eyes widen in surprise, then added, ''That is if you think I've passed the test. I'm really quite harmless.'' Well, that wasn't exactly true. She'd be shocked if she knew she was his sole motive for remaining in Fayetteville.

Then she smiled, and the stomach muscles that had been taut since he first saw her this morning relaxed.

"I'd like that." The faint pink of a blush colored her cheeks. "I'd like that very much."

Her pleasure touched a chord, reminding him that he needed to proceed slowly with her. She'd been hurt enough already. And, God knows, so had he.

CHAPTER THREE

NELL HAD RACED HOME from the library, taken a quick shower and now stood in her bra and panties surveying the limited selection in her closet. Dinner and a movie? It wasn't a charity gala, for heaven's sake. Something casual. Nice. She had essentially three choices. One of her unstylish librarian dresses, a two-year-old pair of linen slacks with a matching sweater sporting a small ineradicable stain or a black Mexican fiesta dress she'd bought on a whim for International Month at the library. Wardrobe purchases had been low on her list of priorities, well beneath orthodontia and graduate school tuition.

Glancing at the clock, she stepped into a half slip, then selected the black dress and a pair of onyx and pearl earrings. When the doorbell rang, she slipped into her white sandals, spritzed some cologne in the general direction of her neck, ran a brush quickly through her still-damp hair and only then began to panic. Misgivings echoed in her mind. She didn't even know this man. Why, he could be… She filled in the blank with a number of disturbing possibilities.

All of which dissolved into a faint memory when she opened the door and beheld the flesh-and-blood object of her conjecture. Brady Logan wore crisply pressed khakis and a yellow polo shirt that accented his ruddy tan. His smile made her forget her meager wardrobe and just about everything else. "Hi," he said with a timbre that would melt chocolate. "You look gorgeous."

Perhaps he wasn't a threat after all, simply a man in need of a competent ophthalmologist. At a time like this having fair skin was a definite drawback. "Thank you." Now what? Even Abby possessed more savoir faire.

"I'll let you suggest the restaurant, but we may have to arm wrestle to decide between the new Kate Hudson chick-flick or Brad Pitt's latest."

She picked up her purse, locked the door, then started when he loosely grasped her free hand and led her toward his fancy SUV. "You've given me a tough choice. I love romantic comedies, but what woman can resist Brad Pitt?"

"We can duke that out later. For now, why don't you suggest a restaurant? Something special."

How special? She mentioned a popular chain restaurant and a locally owned bistro and let him choose.

"Let's go for the more intimate. The bistro sounds good."

The more intimate? The mere word rendered her speechless. Fortunately, that wasn't a problem because after he helped her into his Escalade, he filled her in on his further explorations of Fayetteville. At the first major intersection she gave him directions to the restaurant. She wasn't worried about dinner, or even the movie. But afterward... What if? She'd been too busy recovering from the divorce, working on her master's in library science and rearing Abby to worry about dating. After what Rick had done, men weren't subjects she viewed with optimism.

She looked over at Brady, admiring the muscles in his forearms and the way his large hands caressed the steering wheel. What did he expect from her? Was she supposed to invite him in after the movie? Did she even want to? And could she handle her own feelings, which were confusing the daylights out of her? The way they'd met should feel creepy—his coming to the forum, then appearing at the story-time the next day and, if she wasn't mistaken, observing her. Somehow, though, it didn't.

"You know that first morning in the library?"

"Yeah, what about it?"

"I had the distinct impression you were watching me."

"I was." He glanced at her, a grin forming. "You're a very watchable woman, Nell."

Defenseless, she couldn't hold back her smile. "I—I...thank you."

Fun? Oh, yes, but fun shouldn't feel so momentous.

DRIVING NELL HOME from the Cineplex, Brady reflected on how long it had been since he'd had an evening of laughter and companionship. Not since that last weekend when he and Brooke... He quickly censored the thought. Too painful. Yet he couldn't help kicking himself for taking his best friend and mate for granted while he spent twelve to sixteen hour days in pursuit of the American dream—or at least an upwardly mobile male's dream. Why hadn't he spent more time with her and Nicole? Had they known how much he loved them?

"I think that compromise worked well," Nell commented.

"What?" Lost in his thoughts, had he been rude?

"I enjoyed the movie. Believe me, casting my eyes on Mr. Pitt was no hardship."

"I'm glad." She'd scored two major points so far this evening. First, she'd declined wine at the restaurant. Second, he appreciated that she'd willingly given up the romantic comedy at the theater, because he hadn't been sure how much sentiment his unstable emotions could handle.

She grew even more quiet as they neared her neighborhood. When he pulled into her driveway, she cleared her throat and said, "Would you like to come in for coffee?"

He sensed those had been difficult words for her. Was she nervous? Merely being polite? Yet he already dreaded the return to his motel and the loneliness. "I won't stay long," he said by way of reassurance, "but I'd like that."

She settled him in the small added-on family room at the back of the modest one-story house while she bustled in the kitchen. In one corner stood a 1930s pie cabinet, doubling as a TV stand and repository for CD's and books. The sagging sofa was covered in a maroon-and-tan plaid fabric that looked as if it had seen better days. A wooden rocker painted bright blue sat at an angle to the sofa. Propped in the corner were oversize pillows next to a basket holding a colorful assortment of yarns. The combination shouldn't have worked, but instead of looking like a flea-

market display, it had a welcoming, cozy feeling.
Brady couldn't help making the comparison to the
chrome and leather big-screen viewing room in his
house.

"Here you are." Nell set a small tray on the
planked coffee table. "I hope you like oatmeal cookies."

"No red-blooded man could refuse," he said,
helping himself.

She picked up a mug and took a seat in the rocker.
"My husband always liked them."

He studied her, noting her downcast eyes. "Your
divorce? Is it amicable?"

"I suppose. It's hard work, though."

"Oh? How's that?"

"My daughter resents having to go to Dallas to
visit her father."

Brady said nothing, giving her an opportunity to
add whatever she needed to.

"She blames me."

"For what?"

"For all of it. I guess I'm a convenient scapegoat.
There was…um…another woman." He noticed her
jaw tense. "Abby apparently believes I did something to send her father away. If I had done whatever
she thinks I should have, she reasons her father
would still be here and she wouldn't have to fly to
Dallas monthly." She shrugged. "So you see, it's
my fault."

"You know better than that," he said gently.

"I'm willing to accept my share of the responsibility for the breakup of the marriage. It's rarely one-

sided, but I don't know how I failed so badly that Rick had to find another woman.''

"Aren't you being hard on yourself? I don't know Rick, but did you ever consider perhaps he has a character flaw?''

She cupped her mug in both hands. "I felt so stupid. How could I not have seen it coming? What was the matter with me?''

Her misery was evident, yet he felt helpless to address it, not without stepping over the line he'd set for himself. "Sounds as if you were devastated.''

She nodded. "Do you have any idea what that does to a woman's self-esteem? I try hard, but it's difficult not to become bitter or vindictive or to poison Abby against her father.''

"One day she'll understand the situation. In the meantime, it's got to be rough on you.'' Pain? No doubt about it, she'd had plenty of firsthand experience.

Smiling sadly, she glanced at him. "I didn't mean to get into this. It's just so nice to have a little sympathy.''

"I know what you mean.'' But did he? He hadn't been open to any himself. At least not until now.

"Look, I'm sorry. My problems are nothing compared to your loss. I can't imagine how you can carry on.''

"It's been—'' he cursed the gruffness in his voice "—pure hell.''

"How does a person ever get over something like that?''

"I'm not sure that's possible, but Brooke and Nicole wouldn't want me to give up.'' He set down his mug. ''So I do the best I can, but it isn't easy. Ever.''

''It's odd how two lost souls like us happened to get together, isn't it?''

Now was not the time to confess that their meeting had not been a result of chance. ''I'm glad I met you, Nell. Talking with you like this makes me feel half-alive again.''

''It is nice,'' she agreed.

Lost in their own thoughts, they sat quietly for several moments. But it wasn't an uncomfortable silence. Quite the contrary. Finally he stood. ''I'd better be going. You have to work tomorrow.''

Rising to her feet, she said, ''And I have an early meeting before work.'' She walked him to the front door where she paused and, still holding her mug, smiled up at him. ''Thank you, Brady. I enjoyed the evening.''

''Enough for a repeat?'' He wanted more of this comfort of home and companionship and easy affection.

In a nervous gesture, she smoothed the front of her dress. ''Yes,'' she said.

''Would tomorrow night be rushing it?''

''Not at all. In fact, that suits me since Abby will be gone until this weekend.''

He wasn't quite sure what she meant. Would Abby's presence be an impediment to their future get-togethers? ''How about renting a boat and taking a picnic with us? I'll pick up something at the deli.''

''I haven't done anything like that in a long time. It sounds like fun.''

Driving back to the motel, he reflected on his tem-

porary sense of well-being. As he had thought on first
acquaintance, Nell was an easy woman to be with.
One able to honor silence. When she spoke, it was
simply and directly. He liked that.

As for that ex-husband of hers, he'd clearly left
her feeling diminished. Brady suspected she had no
idea what a strong, resilient and lovely woman she
was.

Tossing her backpack into the overhead bin and
taking the window seat, Abby glanced nervously at
the passengers still boarding. Weekends were bad
enough, but this past seven days with Dad and Clarice had been the pits! She hoped no one sat beside
her. She didn't need any well-meaning grown-up
playing parent to her. She had enough of those in her
life even if she didn't always agree about the "well-
meaning" part. Buckling her seat belt, she couldn't
avoid looking at the geeky puke-green T-shirt en-
crusted with a rhinestone palm tree that Clarice had
bought for her and insisted she wear home. Never
mind it sucked. It had been easier to go along with
her than to argue.

A flight attendant checking seat belts walked up
and down the aisle, stopping briefly to give Abby a
warm smile and the offer of a magazine. She looked
like a nice lady, a regular person. She'd prob'ly be
a good mother, the kind who baked cookies and was
a Girl Scout leader. Not like Clarice who had made
Abby go with her to a ritzy country club for a golf
lesson. Bor-ing. Not once did anybody ask her if
she'd like to hit a golf ball. At least she might have
been able to. Not like Clarice who whiffed more of-

ten than she connected. Learning the game didn't seem to matter to her stepmother nearly as much as showing off her "adorable" new outfit.

On this visit Abby had actually had some time alone with her father, but that was for lunch at this fancy-schmancy restaurant where she could hardly eat for worrying about which fork to use or whether she'd spill on her dress. She could hardly remember when her father lived in Fayetteville and a big family outing was dinner at Applebee's and a movie. Clarice wouldn't be caught dead in Applebee's.

It was weird how she and her dad didn't have much to say to one another. He'd asked all the usual questions about school, the courses she'd be taking, her friends, at least the ones he could remember. Along the way he'd use these cutesie names on her— "Sweet Pea" and "Sugar Lump." Stuff like that. She'd rather he called her "Spud." That's what Tonya's father called her on account of how she would only eat mashed potatoes when she was a baby. "Spud" had meaning.

When the plane rolled back from the gate, Abby breathed a sigh of relief. No talkative stranger to ignore. Just her and the clouds. She would never admit how glad she'd be to get home and see her mother. She knew Mom worried about her. She really should try to be nicer—help more around the house, cut out the complaining and back-talk. But it was hard.

At least she'd escaped Dallas one more time before the ultimate embarrassment. It could happen any time now. Any place. That was the terrifying part. Tonya and Allie had already started their periods. Mom had given her the big talk when she was eleven and had shown her where the supplies were kept. Lately, like some inflatable doll, she'd felt her body shifting, bloating. She'd even imagined she had cramps.

Okay, so it was all normal, but it couldn't happen in Dallas. Not with Clarice. And no way could she tell Dad. She'd die of embarrassment. Totally.

Please, God, let it be at home. With Mom.

A lump formed in her throat and her eyes stung. She wouldn't cry. That was for babies.

All she wanted was to get back safely and hug her mother.

SUNDAY AFTERNOON after unpacking his bags, Brady surveyed his rented living room. The fusty Victorian look wouldn't have been his choice of décor, but he couldn't argue with furnished—not when all his belongings were in storage in California. There was a part of him that wondered what the hell he was doing settling for any length of time in Fayetteville, Arkansas. Although it was a decision that would make no sense to anyone he knew, it felt right.

Had he simply been ready to stop his running, or was Nell responsible? He liked her. A lot. But he could never again make someone else responsible for his happiness. He stumbled through each day trying to wrap his mind around the reality that he would never see Brooke or Nicole this side of the grave. So what was he really after?

A connection. In the here and now. Some relationship that would remind him he wasn't alone. But what would that look like? And would it be fair to

Nell? She deserved more. A lot more. Right now, though, he was giving all he could.

The evening of their boating excursion, he'd tried to keep things light. The sound of Nell's gentle laughter echoing across the secluded cove they'd found for their picnic and her tales of the characters that frequented the library had made him smile. She told him about her graduate courses at the university and her enjoyment of refinishing furniture. However, she'd reserved most of her enthusiasm for her home, relating how she'd scrimped following the divorce to make the down payment and how she'd done much of the remodeling herself. He doubted any Silicon Valley multi-millionaire took more delight in his surroundings.

He slumped into the brown overstuffed chair smelling faintly of pipe tobacco and picked up the Sunday paper. If he was going to hang around, he needed to fill his time with something productive. Otherwise, Carl would be on his case about getting back to work. An idea had slowly been forming in his brain ever since he'd explored the I-540 corridor.

When he had finished with the business section, he began studying the real estate section. Logic told him he was several years too late, but he had the gut feeling there was still money to be made in this neck of the woods, still a need for venture capital.

And if there was one thing he had a surfeit of, it was money.

"I AM *NOT* wearing this stupid top," Abby said Monday morning.

Nell looked up from the bagel she was smearing

with cream cheese. Abby stood, feet planted, holding out the blouse Nell had ironed the night before as if it were an odious rag. "You asked me to iron it," Nell said, struggling for calm.

"That was yesterday. I just talked with Tonya. Nobody's wearing flowers."

Nell knew how important it was to a junior-high-age girl to appear cool. "Suit yourself but hang that one back in your closet. Also, whatever you wear, I'd appreciate it if your navel was covered."

"Mo-om!"

"You're going to register at school. I doubt your teachers or the principal are keen on exposed body parts."

"Clarice would let me," Abby muttered as she left the room.

Great. Now, suddenly, Clarice was the patron saint of teeny-boppers. Nell knew her daughter was experiencing the mood swings endemic to adolescence, but that didn't make living with her any easier. For a brief moment at the airport, Nell had deluded herself that Abby was glad to see her. She'd even hugged her and uttered the magic words, "I'm so glad to be home."

But that was before Nell asked her to gather her dirty clothes for the wash and before the phone started ringing. Abby had been far more interested in hearing from her friends about all she'd missed during her week in Dallas than in performing any domestic duties. It was so hard to know when to cut her some slack and when to pull in the reins.

While Nell ate her bagel, Abby reappeared, picked up an uncooked Pop-Tart, took a bite, then asked for money. "After enrollment, a bunch of us are gonna eat lunch together."

"And you're promising me that your clothes will be washed by the time I get home?"

"Who cares about the clothes?"

"You do, unless you prefer going naked."

"Okay, okay. You don't need to get on my case."

Oh, really? "Fine. Don't forget to spot-treat the stains."

Abby stood beside her now, one hand held out, palm up. "The money?"

Nell dug in her purse and pulled out a five-dollar bill. "Have a good time. I'll be home around six."

Then, as if the sun had mysteriously come out in the tiny kitchen, Abby smiled. "Thanks, Mom. Love you."

Nell shook her head. There was no predicting her daughter. Up one minute, down the next. How had Stella ever managed with two daughters? More and more frequently these days she appreciated what she and Lily must have put their mother through.

Rinsing off her plate, Nell wondered what Abby would think about Brady. Would she make more of their friendship than was there? Well, that would be her problem. She and Brady were just friends. She enjoyed his company and planned to invite him to a home-cooked meal soon. Maybe as time went on, she'd introduce him to some of her friends. To Lily and her husband Evan. Even to her mother. After all, he knew no one in Fayetteville.

Mental telepathy was working as well as the phone service because just then her mother called. "Hi,

Mom. I only have a minute. I'm on my way to my meeting and work.''

''I won't take much of your time. I just wondered if you enjoyed the film?''

Suddenly the bagel became indigestible. ''Film?''

''You know, the Brad Pitt movie. Janelle Davis saw you there.'' Her mother paused to heighten the impact. ''With a man.''

''I didn't see her there.''

''Well, she certainly saw you.''

Nell paced to the window, noticing her flower beds needed watering. ''Your point?''

''Don't be obtuse, Nell. Who is he?''

''His name is Brady Logan. I met him at the library.''

''At the library? Do you think that's wise taking up with a stranger like that?''

Nell sighed. ''I've subjected him to the third degree, and he's checked out. Besides, we're just friends.''

For all her second-guessing, Stella sounded disappointed at that outcome. ''I'd rather hoped—''

''*Friends,* Mother. He's not looking for more and neither am I. But I have fun with him.'' There. The concept of fun ought to get her attention.

Stella made a tsking sound. ''Just be careful, honey. I don't want anything upsetting you.''

''I'll handle it, Mom. Thank you for your concern.'' Nell had long ago learned that the prudent policy was to keep her mother as happy as possible. ''I've got to run. Bye, now.''

Another typical start of a day, Nell thought as she drove downtown. Between Abby and her mother, she already felt like a pinball ratcheting through a maze and it wasn't even eight o'clock.

At least she had one thing going for her, she found a parking spot right in front of the church. She cracked her windows, locked her car and dashed downstairs into the large meeting room just in time to grab a cup of coffee and greet her friends. When the bell in the steeple chimed the hour, Ben Hadley, an elderly gentleman with lively, sparkling eyes who had been a lifesaver for her, opened the meeting, dispensed with a few items of business and then nodded in her direction. She laid her purse on an empty folding chair and made her way to the front of the room. Several people nodded encouragingly to her, and in the back row she noticed two unfamiliar faces. This was by no means the first time she had done this, but it never became any easier. Yet, ironically, it was freeing beyond her capacity to imagine.

She approached the speaker's stand and gripped it for support, emboldened by waves of empathy from those in the audience.

She moistened her lips, then uttered the words that at once condemned and redeemed her. "My name is Nell and I am an alcoholic."

CHAPTER FOUR

NELL SIGHED IN RELIEF after her talk was over. Therapeutic as it was to recall the lessons of the worst times, she always carried away a residue of self-disgust and fear. Sobriety was hardly guaranteed. Instead, it was a daily reprieve. Yet as she left the church, there was a spring in her step, her mood buoyed by the hollow-eyed, yet hopeful expressions on the faces of the two newcomers at the meeting.

Ben Hadley fell in beside her. "Nice job, Nell."

The quiet words of praise filled her with love for her friend, who had been through so much with so many. If anyone lived the Twelve Steps, it was Ben. His humility and selflessness were legendary. "Thank you. I don't know why, but it was especially difficult today."

He kept pace with her. "Any particular reason?"

Nell thought about his question. When she reached her car, she turned to face him. "This may sound funny, but I'm too happy. I…I'm afraid to trust it."

He nodded sagely, then smiled. "It's okay to be happy. You're worth it." He patted her shoulder. "Have a great day."

She sat in the car for several moments. That was one of the hardest lessons—liking herself. Believing she was worthy of approval, acceptance, love. It was so tempting to dwell on the harm she'd done, but the danger with that line of thinking lay in one of the "cures" for negativity. Liquor. Thank God for AA, which had given her the means to face herself and others with forgiveness and love.

Driving to work, she thought about what had made her tell Ben she was happy. She was contented with her job, her home, and, despite the normal ups and downs with Abby and her mother, her relationships. So what was different today? With unflinching honesty, she made herself utter the name. "Brady Logan." She hadn't realized how much she'd missed male companionship, the easy give-and-take of communication, even the sound of a deep voice in her home and the lingering scent of a fragrance decidedly masculine.

Given his situation, friendship was all that he could offer, which suited her fine, because anything else would scare her silly. If they ever moved into intimacy… She cringed. Memory blotted out the sun and in her mind she heard Rick again, flinging his customary accusation. "Can't you loosen up, for God's sake? Or at least try to fake it."

Oh, she'd learned to fake it all right—after several glasses of numbing wine. But it hadn't been enough to save her marriage.

She was obviously no Clarice.

Friend. That sounded just her speed. She hoped Brady never wanted more. If he did, he'd be disappointed. Sex was a thing of the past, and she'd learned there were worse things than doing without a man, particularly a sexually demanding, emotionally abusive one like Rick.

She found a parking place at the library and pulled in, but remained in the car, rendered immobile by a notion that had suddenly surfaced from somewhere in her subconscious. She was kidding herself. The truth? Brady stirred her in a way she'd never experienced and it was exhilarating.

But mostly terrifying.

ABBY'S FIRST WORDS when Nell walked in the house early that evening rocked her. "Grandma told me about your date."

Slowly Nell set down her purse, fighting the tension stiffening her neck. Stella had picked up her granddaughter, and they'd spent the afternoon together. Alike as two peas in a pod, Stella and Abby watched over her with the fierceness of mother eagles. "What date?"

Abby leaned against the kitchen counter, arms folded across her chest. "She said some man took you to a movie."

"Some man did."

"Why didn't I know about it?"

"You were in Dallas."

"So I'm not supposed to know, is that it?"

Nell crossed to the refrigerator and took her time getting out the casserole she'd prepared for dinner. "You make it sound as if I deliberately kept something from you."

"Well, didn't you?"

"It wasn't that big a deal." Nell had no idea whether she sounded convincing. She silently acknowledged her decision not to tell Abby about her outings with Brady and run the risk of upsetting her.

Now, thanks to Stella, she had no choice but to face the issue.

"Who is he?"

"A friend I met at the library."

"Grandma said you need to be careful. That he sorta picked you up."

Nell bit back an unkind retort. "Give me credit for being smarter than that." Yet, what did she really know about Brady Logan? He was a successful businessman and a grieving widower. But beyond that? "He's new in town. We're friends. End of discussion." She preheated the oven. "Now tell me about registration."

Abby eyed her dubiously, aware her mother was changing the subject, then shrugged. "Okay, I guess. Tonya's locker is in the same hall, and we both have Mr. Sanders for English. We had this dumb assembly about the rules. They treat us like babies."

Nell stifled a smile.

"What's his name?"

"Whose name?"

"The man."

Nell put her arm around her daughter, thankful Abby didn't pull away. "Brady Logan," she said in an even voice. "Abby, he's no one you need to be concerned about."

"That's a relief."

Nell turned her daughter so she could look into her eyes. "Honey, things don't stay the same."

"Duh. You think I don't know that? If they did, Dad would still be here."

Nell summoned every ounce of patience. "Someday you will have a boyfriend, go off to college, get married. And someday it's possible I might have another relationship. Life isn't about standing still. It's about taking risks. Experiencing the unusual. Meeting new people. If I've learned anything at all, it's that we must never lose sight of the potential in every person, in every day. But right now? I'm not looking for a man, okay?''

Abby looked down. ''Whatever.''

Nell turned back to the casserole, vowing not to let Abby see the tears of frustration gathering. Behind her, she heard the lid of the cookie jar being lifted.

''Mom?''

''Yes?''

Abby separated an Oreo and licked the filling off one wafer before continuing. ''If he ever comes again, can I meet him?''

''Certainly.''

''He's probably a dweeb, anyway.''

After Abby left the room, Nell slumped over the counter. She'd had no idea Abby would be so possessive of her. The last thing she needed was to upset the family equilibrium. What would she be risking if she continued her friendship with Brady?

Reflecting on the change in her mood from earlier in the day, she reached a conclusion. Fate quickly mocked anyone who claimed to be ''too happy.''

AT NOON ON Wednesday Brady attended his first Rotary meeting since well before the accident. Avoiding all unnecessary human contact on the road, he'd never given Rotary a thought, but now it seemed like a viable way to learn more about the community and to meet some business leaders. As luck would have it, seated at his table were a local bank president and Buzz Valentine, a commercial realtor. From his off-hand questions, he learned they were both high on the investment potential in the area. This optimism was further advanced by the speaker, who cited regional airport traffic figures in excess of estimated projections.

For a short time there, Brady realized later, he'd actually felt a sizzle of adrenaline at the prospects, proving his business instincts weren't totally dead. After making an appointment with Buzz Valentine for the next day, he decided to spend the rest of the afternoon at the library researching local movers and shakers.

Yeah, Logan.

Okay, and getting a "loneliness fix" from Nell, who had provided him with the only moments of contentment he'd had in many months.

NELL BENT OVER her desk, studying the book list provided by the elementary school reading coordinator, tickled to find several of her favorite titles. She picked up the list and headed for the children's area to pull some books for a shelf display.

"Nell?"

She glanced down and immediately felt her fair skin betray her. "Hi, Brady." She noted the newspapers and business magazines spread on the table around him. "More research?"

"I figure if I'm going to be here awhile, I need to learn all I can about the area economy."

She fingered a magazine cover sporting the well-known face of a nationally prominent entrepreneur headquartered in Northwest Arkansas. "This region isn't the sleepy little byway of yesteryear, thanks to people like him."

Brady cocked an eyebrow. "Hardly. Pretty impressive financials."

Nell fought the mesmerizing sensation produced by gazing into his brown eyes. "Let me know if I can locate anything for you." She held up the lists in her hands. "If you'll excuse me, I have work to do in the children's area."

He stood and started to walk along with her. "Can I help?"

"If you want." Anything was better than having him study her with that unsettling stare. "Here." She handed him the second page of the list. "You could pull some of these titles."

He ran a finger down the page. "*Johnny Tremain* and *The Outsiders*. Wow. I haven't thought of them in years."

"Books have a way of transporting us to the time and place we encountered them, don't they?"

He didn't answer. When she glanced up inquiringly, she was taken aback. Rather than the pleased smile of recognition she expected to see, his jaw had tensed and a frown creased his forehead. Odd.

Finally he said, "I suppose." He laid down a book and turned to gaze out the window. "I try not to think of the past."

He'd said the words more to himself than to her, so she continued pulling volumes in silence. She could understand why the immediate past was difficult for him, but what childhood memories had the books triggered?

She didn't know how long he stood at the window, but when he faced her again, his expression was more relaxed. "You seem to love what you do."

She smiled. "Is it that obvious?"

"Your face lights up when you talk about books. Did you know that?" His voice held a tinge of yearning. "I used to feel that way about my work."

"And now?"

"It seems meaningless. What lasting satisfaction does creating and marketing software provide? You never see the results of your efforts."

"But isn't the challenge of it fulfilling?"

"If you count the reward in dollars and cents."

"You don't?"

He stared over the tops of the shelves. "Not anymore." After an awkward silence, he took a step toward her. "At this point I have more questions than answers, but this much I know. I'm due for a change. Sticking around here for starters."

The intensity of his gaze caused her skin to tingle. "You could do worse."

"Yeah," he said thoughtfully. "There's lots to like. For instance, you're here."

Nell didn't know how to take his remark. Surely he wasn't going to make some life-altering decision based on her. That would be ludicrous. She screwed up her courage. "What's that supposed to mean?"

He gave a crooked smile. "That didn't come out right, did it? What I meant to say is that you've succeeded in helping me think about rejoining the human race."

She hugged two books to her chest, then responded thoughtfully, "Believe me, I know how hard that is to do, but, Brady, it's worth the effort. You have a lot of tomorrows left."

"Tomorrows?" Slowly he shook his head. "Yeah. I like the sound of that." He paused. "Especially from you."

Before Nell could process her reaction to his last words, she sensed the approach of someone and looked beyond Brady. Lily. Her sister's timing was as flawless as her carefully sculpted hairdo and perfectly understated makeup.

"There you are, Nell." Lily sailed into the area. "When I couldn't find you in your office, I thought I'd find you here." With an assessing smile aimed straight at Brady, she said, "And you are—"

"Brady Logan." He extended his hand and shook Lily's.

Lily turned to Nell. "Your friend?"

Lord, now Brady would think she'd been talking about him to her family. "Yes. We met here about a week ago." Nell's voice box didn't seem to be working properly. "This is my sister, Lily Roberts."

Brady nodded acknowledgment.

"The way you were talking, so seriously and all, I figured you weren't just another library patron." Lily indulged in a tinkling laugh that to Nell's ears was replete with sisterly innuendo.

Brady took command. "I am that, too. I'm trying to learn about the Fayetteville area and Nell's been kind enough to assist me."

Lily cocked her head. "In the children's section?"

Nell prayed the floor would swallow her. She

knew her sister. Beyond that flirtatious facade, Lily was determined to pump Brady for information.

Brady gestured toward the library table where he'd been sitting. "It seems I strayed a bit. I volunteered to help Nell."

"How kind," Lily said, ignoring the pleading look Nell was telegraphing her. "I understand you've only been in town a short time."

"That's right."

Lily laid a hand on his arm. "Then you need to get better acquainted, and I have the perfect solution. Evan and I are hosting a barbecue Saturday night for family and some close friends. I dropped by the library to invite Nell, but this is even better. Of course you'll come, too. All our guests will look forward to meeting Nell's new friend."

Nell couldn't be sure, but it sounded as if Lily had put special emphasis on the word *friend*. She couldn't stand by while her sister organized her life. "Lily, Brady may have other plans—"

She didn't get out any more words before she heard Brady say, "Thank you, Lily. I'd like to come."

Lily smiled triumphantly at Nell. "Well, that's settled, then. Six o'clock." Turning to Brady, she sprang her trap. "Since you'll be coming with Nell, she can show you where we live."

"Sounds great." Brady handed Nell his page of the book list. "Guess I'd better get back to my research." Smiling at Lily, he added, "Nice to have met you."

He'd gone only a few steps when Lily grabbed

Nell's arm and purred sexily, "Do many of your customers look like that?"

Nell gritted her teeth. "Do I kill you now or later, sister dear?"

"Kill me? Unless I'm mistaken, which I'm not, I just did you a big favor."

"I'll tell you what I've already told Mother and Abby. Brady and I are just friends."

Lily shot her an incredulous look. "Right."

"It's not like that."

"But it certainly could be." Lily faced her with that trust-me expression that set Nell's nerves on edge. "So you're just friends? Okay. I'll buy that for now."

"Good. He's a grieving widower, Lily. I doubt he's ready for what you have in mind."

"I didn't know. I'm sorry. But still, what's the harm in bringing him to the barbecue?"

Trapped. "Nothing, I guess." She swallowed her trepidations.

Eyeing her up and down, Lily said, "I'll be calling you to set a time to go shopping for your new outfit. You'll want to dazzle him."

Lily quickly back-pedaled toward the door, giving her a ta-ta wave of the fingers. Nell was too angry to move. Hadn't her sister understood a word she'd said?

A new outfit?

She couldn't remember the last time she'd dazzled a man.

And she wasn't about to start now.

WHEN BRADY RETURNED to his condo, the message light on his answering machine was blinking. He kicked off his shoes, padded to the refrigerator for a cold soda, then settled in the overstuffed chair staring at the offending light. It had to be Carl. Some crisis.

He swigged from the can, then rested his head against the back of the chair. He wished he could care. But he didn't. What used to be as important to him as the air he breathed, now affected him not in the least. He'd always heard you weren't supposed to make any major decisions within a year following a spouse's death. But it had been months. Shouldn't he be feeling something about his company? But pride, status, power—none of it meant a thing.

Hell, he'd worked up more energy about the idea slowly forming in his head to develop an upscale conference and resort center on Beaver Lake than he had about any of Carl's importunings. It wasn't about money, although he wasn't so far gone that he didn't want his money to work for him. It was about intangible rewards, permanence. Only with Brooke had he found that.

He closed his eyes and tried to bring her into focus—her long silky hair, her tanned shoulders, but the image kept shifting in his memory. Instead, he pictured the willowy body of Nell Porter topped by her heart-shaped face and big, knowing eyes, her arms cradling books protectively against her breasts.

The damn books. He'd been ill-prepared for the wave of nostalgia that had swept over him. *Johnny Tremain.* He'd suddenly remembered his mother's animated voice reading to him. Remembered lying in bed listening, the words transforming him into a boy in Revolutionary War times. Then, after she closed the book, she tucked the covers around him and kissed him good-night. That was before…

He cursed under his breath. For years he'd pretty much been able to fend off such memories, feeding on his resentment and losing himself in work until forgetfulness became a habit.

What was Nell Porter doing to him anyway? Whatever it was felt way too much like pecking away at his armor. Yet he was drawn to her in ways that made no sense. All he knew was that he felt better when he was around her.

He sat up, drained the soda, punched the Play button on the machine and listened to Carl's edgy voice fill him in on the latest emergency at L&S TechWare.

He should respond. Immediately. Regrettably, that wasn't a priority.

NELL HAD GIVEN IN and gone shopping with Lily. Down deep, she valued her sister's advice. Lily's taste was impeccable. The floral print wraparound skirt and filmy lavender blouse were on sale and, as Lily insisted, were Nell's "colors." Nell had to admit she'd been flattered by the lift of Brady's eyebrows when he picked her up Saturday evening.

Light from the fading sun filtered through the ancient oaks and dappled the manicured lawn as Nell led Brady to the back gate of Lily's house. Stella, Evan's mother and father, and several other couples were already there, clustered around the hors d'oeuvres table set up on the flagstone patio. In a far corner of the yard, Abby corralled Chase. Without consulting Nell, Lily had invited Abby to baby-sit with Chase and spend the night. The obviousness of her maneuver would be amusing if it wasn't so darn uncomfortable. Nell disliked being the focus of Lily's expectations.

"Here's Nell." Her mother broke away from the guests and came toward them, a fixed smile on her face. "And you must be Brady," she said, extending her hand. "I'm Nell's mother, Stella Janes."

"It's nice to meet you," Brady said. "Nell has made me feel most welcome in Arkansas."

"I'm glad to hear my daughter represents the best of Southern hospitality."

"You taught me well," Nell murmured.

Stella tucked her arm through Brady's. "Come meet Lily's husband and the others."

Trailing the pair, Nell sought to unfist her hands, aware of the tension riddling her. This was no big deal, yet she knew her family. They would make something out of nothing. She glanced across the yard and her heart sank. Oblivious to Chase tugging on her shorts, Abby was watching Brady's progress to the patio with narrowed eyes and thinned lips.

Somehow Nell made it through the introductions, ignoring the questioning looks some of the women angled at Brady and her. From the cooler Brady picked out a beer and a soda. "Which would you prefer, Nell?"

Before she could answer, Lily slipped in between them. "My sister doesn't drink."

Nell winced. Would Brady pick up on the pointedness of the remark or was she simply overreacting?

Brady handed Nell the soda, then smiled at the two women. "I don't either, except for an occasional beer."

After Lily excused herself, Brady looked down at Nell, his eyes soft. "I like your family. Nice people."

Nell tore her gaze from him and glanced around. "Yes. They are." Then she noticed Abby sitting in a swing, holding Chase in her lap. The girl's eyes were fixed everywhere but on Nell. "Brady, I'd like you to meet my daughter." She started walking toward Abby, confident Brady was following. "Abby, this is—" When she turned to include him in the introduction, he wasn't right behind her as she'd expected. He had stopped several feet away and his face had gone pale. "—Brady Logan," Nell finished lamely.

As if shaking off a trance, he ran a hand through his hair and approached the swing set. "Hello," he said in a husky voice.

Abby gave him a brief glance, then continued swinging. "'Lo."

Nell stepped forward, took hold of the ropes and brought the swing to a stop. "Brady recently moved here from California," she said in a voice full of a mind-your-manners undertone.

"I know." Abby's stony face had softened not one iota. "Grandma told me."

Nell could only wonder what other tidbits Stella had seen fit to divulge. She turned helplessly to Brady. "And this is Chase, Lily's son," she said running a hand over the toddler's curly hair.

"Hi, Chase."

The boy ducked his head into Abby's shirt. Abby continued to stare at her mother in sullen defiance.

"What grade are you in, Abby?"

Slowly Abby turned to Brady. "Eighth."

Brady's voice sounded strangled. "Hope you enjoy the year."

Nell was missing something. It was as if Brady, usually confident and assured in social situations, had become a tongue-tied adolescent himself.

"Don't you need to mingle or something?" Glaring, Abby nodded in the direction of the adult guests. Her leave-me-alone message was received loud and clear.

"I guess we should. I just wanted you to meet Brady."

"Well, now I have." Abby clutched Chase and stood. Turning to Brady, she mumbled her excuses. "I gotta go feed Chase."

"Glad to have met you," Brady said.

"Yeah." Abby marched past them toward the house.

Abby's rudeness had effectively communicated her displeasure. Nell laid a hand on Brady's arm. "I'm sorry about that. She's usually more pleasant."

Brady shook his head. "Kids. What're you going to do?" He put an arm around her shoulder, a gesture Nell found all too comforting. "I remember."

Nell looked up into eyes haunted with sadness. Then realization struck her. "Oh, Brady, how old was your daughter?"

Brady cleared his throat before answering. "About Abby's age."

"I'm so sorry."

He rested his chin on her head. "Me, too." Then in a soft echo he repeated himself. "Me, too."

There were no words. Brushing a palm across the

front of his starched shirt, Nell lingered in the curve of his embrace before stepping away. "Maybe we should rejoin the party."

He took her by the elbow and led her to a group sitting on the patio. "Brady? Brady Logan?" A prematurely balding man with glasses stood. "What a pleasure. I didn't expect to see you again so soon."

Brady shook the man's hand, then introduced her to Buzz Valentine, who, in turn, presented his wife, Sandy, who made room for her on the glider. Nell knew of Buzz Valentine by reputation. He was a successful commercial realtor and developer, and the couple were very active in the community. While she and Sandy made small talk, Nell couldn't help overhearing Brady and Buzz deep in discussion about various tracts of land. What was going on? How did Brady know Buzz? She drew a quick breath. Maybe Brady *was* serious about staying.

She studied him—earnest, handsome and incredibly virile—and tried to talk sense to herself. These awakenings in her body, involuntary as they were, were embarrassing. And way too powerful. She'd stop them if she could. He'd made his expectations quite clear. Friendship.

Just then he glanced toward her, sending a tender smile meant only for her. Her insides suddenly turned topsy-turvy, and she knew she would have to be careful. Very careful.

He was a sexy, appealing man, and despite all her rationalizations, she had noticed.

Boy, had she noticed!

BRADY WAS GRATEFUL when Nell suggested they be among the first departing guests. Although everyone

had been friendly and welcoming, this was more social interaction than he'd had since... Men and
women milling in his oversize living room, their expressions set in solemn mourning, their dark garments in stark contrast to the sunny California day
flaming beyond the floor-to-ceiling plate glass. Their
solicitous murmurs of condolence falling impotently
somewhere beyond his consciousness. The palpable
air of relief with which they turned from him and
hastened to the buffet table. He would forever see
the scene in black-and-white shattered by violent
splashes of red and yellow behind his pupils, as if
grief were being experienced through the lens of an
avant-garde cinematographer.

Now, as they approached her house, Nell brought
him back to the present moment. "Was this evening
difficult for you?"

He eased the car into her drive and shut off the
motor, surprised by her insight. "Why do you ask?"

"You've been unusually quiet on the way home."

Sidestepping the necessity of answering, he tried
a smile. "Have I been a dull date?"

"Not at all. Everyone, including me, found you
quite congenial."

"Congenial enough to invite me in for a while?"
He could've escaped, yet he wanted to talk about this
evening. All except meeting Abby. He couldn't talk
about that. Not yet. Abby's gangly legs, with telltale
razor nicks, her half-child, half-woman body, even
her braces had wrenched him back to the last time
he'd seen Nicole, modeling her new swimsuit for
him, her buds of breasts taking him by surprise, her

little-girlness metamorphosing into something alien and threatening to a father.

Nell looked up at him questioningly. "You're sure?"

"I'm sure. It's not that late."

Nell dug her house key out of her purse. "Come on then. I'll make us a pot of decaf."

She left Brady in the tiny family room, only the glow of a small table lamp illuminating the space. He put his head back and shut his eyes, letting peace wrap around him like a cocoon. For the first time that evening, he drew a deep breath and let his body relax, appreciating the fact that Nell had not chosen to press him about his reaction to the party.

When she came back, bearing two mugs of coffee, she handed him his, then settled at the other end of the couch. Yet she didn't say anything, just sat, composed, holding the mug between her hands.

Somehow the comfortable silence made it easier for him to begin. "I liked the people I met."

She smiled.

"It's been a while since I've been around so many people in that kind of situation."

"I thought so."

"I—I haven't been ready. For a long time, I couldn't understand how people could laugh freely, seemingly have so few cares. They seemed distant, superficial."

"It's painful, isn't it?"

He set down his mug and looked at her. "You understand."

"Finding yourself alone plunges you into a darkness that can seem never-ending." She, too, set aside her coffee. "When my marriage was falling apart and then my father died so suddenly, I couldn't imagine a world where the sun would shine. Couldn't begin to picture a time when I would have an ordinary day. In fact, the concept of 'ordinary' was utterly foreign to me.''

He stared into her eyes, in which was revealed intimate experience with pain and death. Yet she had found the courage to trust in rainbows. ''Do you ever look at people, like at the party, and wonder what they know of suffering?''

''All the time,'' she said quietly.

''Yet you seem to have been able to go on.''

She bit her bottom lip, then nodded. ''You will, too.''

He moved closer, then without thinking, picked up her hand. ''I wouldn't have believed that two weeks ago. But now,'' he felt his defenses begin to crumble, ''I think it may be possible.''

''Change is scary, isn't it?''

Was that part of it? Not just grief, but fear of change? ''Especially when you can't control the forces that set it in motion.''

''Control...ah, yes.'' She studied him, as if seeking some kind of answer from him. ''What is in your control now, Brady?''

It was a big question. One that deserved a thoughtful answer, but at this moment the softness of her skin beneath his fingers and the luminous quality in her eyes suggested what he desperately needed to control was the pounding of his heart. Because, more than anything, he wanted to pull her close, taste her lips, smell her skin. And that surprised him.

He steadied his emotions and answered her. ''More than there has been in quite a while. I'm staying here, I'm letting my partner handle the business until I make some decisions about the future.''

"Can you let some of it be beyond your control?''

He moved so that she was in the curve of his arm. How would she react if she knew he'd even orchestrated their meeting? "How can you already know me so well? I must come across as a controlling kind of guy.''

"You're a man, aren't you?''

He loved the teasing twinkle in her eye. "Guilty as charged.''

"Well?''

"Seriously? It's hard for me to sit back and let things happen.''

She reached up and caressed his cheek. "And you couldn't prevent the accident.''

He lowered his head, aware of the dark night lurking outside the circle of lamplight. "No.''

"That's the hardest part,'' she said. "Accepting that there are many things beyond our ability to control.''

"Were you born wise?''

"Hardly,'' she said, and he saw the hint of pain in her eyes.

He lifted his hand from her shoulder and toyed with her hair. "We sure did get serious.''

"And our coffee's probably cold.'' She leaned forward and retrieved her mug, tasted it, then smiled. "If you hurry, it might still warm your innards.''

He laughed. "Innards. Now that's the first hillbilly-ism I've heard from you.''

"But probably not the last.'' She batted her eyes and then added, "You'uns be rat fine, fer a man.''

"Rat?''

"Right," she explained.

They kept the conversation light until it was time for him to leave. In the front hall, he paused. She looked up at him, her big eyes fixed on his, and he couldn't think of a thing to say. The silence was charged with overtones of need...and control. Finally, he remembered himself. "Thank you. I had a great evening."

For the second time that night, she laid her palm on his chest, and he was sure she could feel the rapid beating of his heart. "So did I."

He covered her hand with his and then, before he could censor himself, he leaned forward and kissed her, gently, fleetingly. Not at all like he wanted to. What he wanted was to crush her to him and salve all those places where emotions had rubbed him raw, where healing had never begun. Maybe never would.

Then he was aware only of the softness of her lips beneath his, the hint of a coffee taste in her mouth and a delicious soothing warmth spreading through his body. When he released her, she gazed up at him with a question in her eyes.

Her voice was tremulous. "Friends?"

"Friends," he repeated.

"Good night," she whispered.

Later standing beside his car in the still, late summer evening, listening to tree frogs and the insistent barking of a neighbor's dog, Brady began to wonder. Was it possible simply to remain friends with Nell?

His body was demanding more. Hell, she was no longer pecking at his armor. She had pierced it.

And it was far beyond his control.

CHAPTER FIVE

AFTER LUNCH the next day, Lily and Evan dropped Abby off at home. She muttered a perfunctory "hello" to Nell before bolting to her room and closing her door. Sighing, Nell set aside the sketch book in which she'd been drawing. Friends had told her that the early teens were the worst for girls, and she had no trouble believing it. Rioting hormones had changed her daughter from a tractable, sweet child into a rebellious, insecure adolescent, who had no intention of continuing to share her inner life, at least with her mother.

Yet Nell really needed to address Abby's behavior last night. Regardless of Brady's experience with teenagers, Abby's attitude had been embarrassing. What would it take to convince her Brady posed no threat?

Nell had replayed the kiss at the door repeatedly and had concluded it was nothing more than a casual gesture, friend-to-friend. At least for him. And that was a good thing. She couldn't risk emotional involvement and the potential for falling back into the trap of failure and self-doubt.

She'd experienced plenty of that, thanks to Rick. Over and over she had asked herself where things had gone wrong. Had she been that bad a wife?

They'd met in college, a classic case of opposites attracting. She, the quiet, studious coed, drawn to the gregarious, life-of-the-party frat president. During their courtship, it was as if he drew confidence from her adoration. For her, being at Rick's side meant inclusion into social groups. Besides, his blond good looks reminded her of her father. It had been easy to say "yes" when he'd asked to marry her.

Maybe they should have left Fayetteville early in their marriage, seen something of the world, learned to depend on each other. Perhaps everything had come too easily, been too familiar. Right out of college, Rick took a job with the athletic department of the university. That meant long workdays, travel and weekends full of sporting events. And parties.

When Abby was an infant, Nell had been able to beg off most of those occasions, despite Rick's impatience with her. He couldn't understand why she didn't want to hire a baby-sitter three or more nights a week. Then, as time went on and he was more entrenched in the monied, fast world of big-time donors and alumni, it became more and more terrifying to accompany him.

It was then the drinking first began.

Just one or two to loosen up. When that no longer sufficed, she'd graduated to a quick nip before leaving home. All around her, whether at tailgate parties or testimonial dinners, there was liquor. Soothing, relaxing, *addictive* liquor.

From Abby's room issued the sound of her CD player, turned up high. Nell bit her lip, knowing it wasn't the music that had her on edge, but her memories. Rick had never understood her shyness. He'd married a homebody when he'd wanted a hostess. And a lover. Had she really been that inadequate? All she knew was a day had come when she'd panicked, sure she couldn't be what he needed her to be. Wanted her to be. And she'd self-medicated. Boy, had she ever.

No wonder Abby was concerned about Brady. She'd seen one marriage break up. Abby needed complications no more than Nell did, and she tried in her awkwardly loving way to protect both of them from change. That's why the kiss could mean nothing. Nell absolutely could not—would not—let herself become vulnerable again.

She rose to her feet, determined to reassure Abby. She walked down the hall and knocked on the bedroom door.

"What?" Abby's tone was not welcoming.

"May I come in?"

"I guess."

Abby had thrown her skirt on the floor and lay sprawled on her bed, clad in cutoff jeans and a sleeveless T-shirt, reading a teen magazine, her stuffed animals forming a phalanx around her. With an irritated sigh, she reached over to the bedside table and turned down the volume of the CD player.

"How was your time at Lily's?"

"Okay."

Count on a teenager never to volunteer anything. "Did Chase behave himself?"

"Yeah. He's cute." Abby flipped the page of her magazine.

"About last night—"

"What about it?"

"Could you look at me while we're talking?" The minute the words were out of her mouth, Nell regretted them. Accusations hardly facilitated open communication.

"Sure." Abby made a show of laying her magazine aside, sitting up, tucking her knees to her chest and staring directly at her mother. "Satisfied?"

"Oh, Abby, I'm sorry. I don't mean to come off as a shrew."

Abby quirked her mouth in disbelief.

"I, uh, was disappointed in your manners at the party."

"What about them?"

"You were not very pleasant when I introduced Mr. Logan."

Abby shrugged. "So?"

"He is my friend, and I expected better from you."

"Your *friend?* What kind of friend?" She chewed a hangnail, her sarcasm belied by the fear in her eyes.

"Abby, he's a nice man. Someone I enjoy visiting with. That's all. Why can't you just accept what I'm saying?"

"Get real, Mom."

"What's that supposed to mean?"

"He's interested in you. There. Are you happy?"

Nell stared, dumbfounded at her daughter. "Why would you say a thing like that?"

Abby threw her a disgusted look. "I saw it, Mom. Are you blind? Didn't you see the way he was looking at you? All goo-goo-eyed?"

No words came. Nell felt the heat of a blush coloring her face.

"So quit giving me that 'friend' crap, all right?" And with that, Abby rolled over, picked up the magazine and turned up the CD player.

Heart thudding, Nell slunk out of the room, flabbergasted. She wanted to protest, but she couldn't. Not without lying to her daughter—and herself.

She, too, had seen the look.

"WHADDYA THINK the mystery meat is?" Tonya set down her tray and took the seat Abby had saved for her in the school cafeteria.

"Something that may have been bologna in a former life." Abby moved her fork around her plate. "Disguised with yukky barbecue paste."

"Yummy," Tonya said, patting her bare midriff and puffing out her cheeks as if in preparation to hurl.

The sick, sweet smell of canned corn turned Abby's stomach. "I'm not hungry anyway."

Just then a freckle-faced boy walked by and, using his spoon as a drumstick, thwacked the two girls on the head. "Puh-leeze," Tonya whined to his departing back. "Grow up."

"Boys can be disgusting," Abby said, tearing off a portion of her roll and putting it in her mouth.

"*Some* boys," amended Tonya, casting a meaningful glance at a table near the food line.

Abby looked in the same direction, where a bunch of jocks sat hunched over their trays. "Dream on."

"Abby, quit putting on a big act. I noticed Alan Voyle talking to you at your locker."

Abby didn't feel like discussing him right now, even with her best friend. "So?"

"I think he likes you."

Abby couldn't suppress a thrill of interest. "No way."

"You shoulda seen how he looked at you."

Ordinarily she'd have been ecstatic. Alan was ultra cool, but Tonya had innocently reminded her of what she'd been trying to forget—the way that man had looked at her mother. She shoved away her tray, fighting tears.

Tonya studied her. "You okay?"

Abby stood. "Not really." She picked up her tray and made a beeline for the return counter.

"Wait up!" Tonya was right behind her. "You're acting weird."

"Why not? My whole life is weird."

"C'mon." Tonya grabbed her by the arm, steered her toward a floor-to-ceiling window at the end of a row of lockers and pulled her down on the carpet. Abby rested her chin on her knees and stared outside where hummingbirds flitted to a feeder hanging near the science room and a squirrel scampered across the grass. "Okay. So what's the matter?"

"What would you say if I told you my mother has a boyfriend?" There. She'd said it. Out loud. Abby watched while, as if in slow-motion, her friend's eyes widened.

"No way."

Abby was surprised by the tick of irritation. Like Tonya couldn't imagine her mother being attractive enough or something?

Tonya leaned forward, her face alive with curiosity. "Go on. Tell me. Who is it?"

"This man."

"Well, duh."

"She, er, met him at the library." How romantic did that sound?

"He must be super nerdy."

Abby shook her head. "He's not. He's actually kinda handsome."

"So what's the problem?" Tonya waited, then shook her head as if she had miraculously been given the answer to her own question. "Yeah, I guess they are kinda old."

"It's not that, it's just…weird." Abby felt stupid. What did "weird" communicate? Nothing. But she had no other words for her feelings.

"Why?"

"Mom and I have finally got it all together. We don't need anybody. Especially not him."

Tonya looked puzzled. "Yeah, but wouldn't your mom like a man? I mean, she's not *that* old, I guess."

The locker area was beginning to fill up with students getting their books for their next class. Abby leaned forward and hissed in Tonya's ear, "You don't get it, do you?"

Tonya shrugged. "I guess not."

"My mother doesn't need anybody but me. Somebody else might not understand." She gulped. "He might make everything worse."

Tonya laid a hand on Abby's knee. "Jeez, are you thinking maybe," she faltered, "like maybe your mom would—"

Abby hung her head. "Yeah. What if she liked this guy and he didn't like her? Maybe she'd—" Abby couldn't finish.

"Start drinking again?"

Abby nodded mutely.

"She prob'ly wouldn't."

"Yeah, but if she did—" Abby raised tear-filled eyes to her friend "—I couldn't stand it."

The bell for the next period rang, and both girls jumped. Tonya was the first to stand. "I gotta go. I have a test." She reached down, took Abby's hand and hauled her to her feet. "But we'll talk after school. Promise."

Oblivious to the hurried commotion around her, Abby watched her friend depart, feeling as alone as she had in a long time. She swiped at her eyes. She knew it was childish to suspect her mother would start drinking again. But there must be a reason her grandmother always reminded her to watch out for Nell. Like maybe Grandma thought her mother needed a keeper.

Brady Logan might be an okay guy. But Abby couldn't help thinking he'd end up upsetting her mother. And that would not be good.

When the second bell rang, Abby's stomach plummeted. Now she'd have to walk into math class late. Everyone would be staring at her, noticing her skinny legs, gross braces and stringy hair.

Eighth grade sucked.

Except maybe for Alan Voyle.

NELL DIDN'T HAVE TO go in for work Monday until mid-afternoon, so following her morning meeting, she went to yoga class, grabbed a quick bite and then returned home to work some more on the pencil sketch she planned to give her mother for Christmas.

No sooner had she put on some soothing music and settled at her desk than the doorbell rang.

When she answered it, there stood Lily in a powder blue shorts outfit with Chase, looking adorable in a pint-size cowboy suit. "Hope you're not busy," Lily said hopefully.

Nell stood aside and held the door open. "Just doing some drawing. Come on in." Nell hunkered beside Chase. "Hey, squirt, got a hug for your auntie?" He reached his chubby arms around her neck and planted a wet kiss on her cheek.

"Bocks," he said.

"Smart kid. You remembered, didn't you?"

Lily looked puzzled. "What?"

"Abby's old blocks." Nell led the way to the family room, where she opened the chest and pulled out a box of brightly colored wooden blocks. Chase sat down and began happily pouring them out onto the floor and then reassembling them in structures meaningful only to him.

Abby turned to her sister. "Coffee? Soda?"

"No, thanks." Lily looked lovingly at Chase. "But I could sure use a strong dose of adult conversation."

Nell laughed as they both sat down on the sofa. "I remember that phase. Believe me, when he's a teenager, you may long for diapers and wall-to-wall toys."

"Ah, the joys of parenthood. Each phase has its own set of challenges, I guess."

"Today I'm tempted to trade you mine for yours," Nell said remembering Abby's freeze-out yesterday.

Lily raised a brow. "Not our sweet Abby?"

"Our 'sweet Abby' and I are having issues."

"Rick and Clarice?"

"She's still not crazy about visiting them in Dallas, but it's more than that. At the same time she wants to assert her independence and shove me away, she watches over my every move."

Lily's expression softened. "Can you blame her?"

Nell considered her sister's question, knowing she meant it kindly, not judgmentally. "No. I put her…you…through some awful times. When I think what could've happened that night—"

"Shh. That's all behind you."

As if it could ever be behind her. Didn't her sister get it? She lived with her mistakes every day. Nell struggled to keep her tone reasonable. "No, Lily, it will never be over and done with, but I try to deal with it in a healthy way. And today I'm worried about Abby. It's as if she thinks she single-handedly has to make sure nothing changes."

Lily leaned over and helped Chase restack the tower he'd toppled. "What are we really talking about?"

"Brady Logan."

Lily's head popped up and she turned to Nell. "That's what Abby's worried about?"

Nell nodded. "Before you start in, I want to be clear here. I don't need Mother's critical take on this right now."

"And you think that's what I'll give you?"

No time like the present, Nell decided. "Do you have any idea how often it feels like the two of you gang up on me?"

Lily bristled. "Now, just a minute—"

Nell hurried on. "I realize you both mean well, but you know what I need most today? Not a mother or a sister, but a friend."

"We 'gang up' on you?" Lily seemed genuinely puzzled.

"Sometimes."

Lily touched Nell's hand. "I'm sorry. I never realized you felt that way. It's just that—" She paused as if considering her response, then gave a nod. "Okay. Today it's friends."

Nell gave her sister a brief hug. "I really want to know what you think about Brady and me. I can't make any mistakes."

"Well, I guess there are two ways of looking at the situation. Brady Logan could be an added complication in your life—"

"Which I certainly don't need."

"Or the best thing that's ever happened to you."

"Lily, it's not like that yet—"

"Your misguided, self-effacing modesty has never been one of your more attractive features. My God, the man's crazy about you."

Nell groaned. "Not you, too."

"What do you mean?"

"That's more or less what Abby said."

"Well, there. That proves it. Surely you see it."

Nell felt trapped. "I…what he needs is a friend."

Lily shot her a skeptical look. "But you're at least thinking about more. You can only use that grieving widower defense so long. Honey, what that man needs is not merely a friend, but a healthy roll in the hay and a woman to love the daylights out of him. Now whether that's a wise idea for you or not—"

Nell's stomach moved into her throat. "That would be a big problem for me."

Lily pulled Chase into her lap. "How long has it been?"

Nell averted her eyes, wishing she could pretend to misunderstand the question.

"Since Rick, huh?"

"Yes."

"And that hardly counts, I imagine."

Nell couldn't let her sister know how close to the mark she'd come with that comment. "Lily, this isn't about sex."

"Oh, I agree. It's not *just* about sex."

Chase stuck his thumb in his mouth and settled against Lily's shoulder, his big brown eyes fastened on Nell. "I don't need a man in my life. In fact, I don't need anything that would rock the boat."

"I can understand why rocking the boat wouldn't be desirable, now that you've gotten your act together. But do you think you can go through life never taking risks?"

"No. It's just—"

"That you're scared."

"Terrified," Nell managed to answer in a small voice.

"Now we're getting somewhere! So you *do* like him." Lily fingered Chase's curls. "Beyond friendship."

"Yes, I think I could."

"And the problem is…"

"He doesn't seem ready for more."

"He's still grieving. Give him time, honey. Maybe he's ready and just doesn't know it yet. Go on."

"Then there's Abby."

"Abby's a kid. She would adapt. Besides, she'll be gone in five years. What then? You don't have to be alone, you know."

"It's not that simple. I've been hurt once by a man. I don't need those problems again."

"I won't pretend I'm not concerned about the potential for Brady to upset your equilibrium. But you deserve a chance for happiness. How many obstacles are you throwing in the path? Do you plan to play it safe your whole life?"

Abby clenched her fingers. "If that's what it takes to stay sober."

Chase had fallen asleep nestled in Lily's arms. Carefully she laid him on the sofa cushion between them. "I am so proud of you, Nell, and I grant you I've never experienced what you have, but I can't believe the price for staying sober has to be the potential for happiness with Brady or someone like him. Abby will come around in time. It's easy to dream up objections, but consider the possible benefits, too. For example, Abby sees Rick so infrequently, and Clarice, well, we don't even need to discuss what kind of adult influence she is. Brady could be good for Abby, and for you."

Lily wasn't saying anything Nell hadn't thought of in the dark of the night lying awake, alone. But it wasn't that easy. Besides there was the tragedy in Brady's life. She suspected his healing would take a long time.

"You're awfully quiet," Lily said when Nell didn't respond. "Maybe the best thing is simply to follow your heart."

Nell smiled wistfully. "Promise?"

Lily reached across her sleeping son and squeezed Nell's hand. "Oh, yes, honey. I promise."

Despite the fact she could be infuriating on occasion, Lily was Nell's best friend. Her concern was evident. In the old bad days, Lily had been there for her, big time. And here she was again. Infusing Nell with support.

"What about Mother? She's as protective of me as Abby is."

"Leave Mom to me. This is one time she and I may not see eye to eye, although I understand the pitfalls she might be concerned about."

Nell thought about Brady—his husky, warm laugh, his comforting hands, his kiss so full of tenderness and promise—and wondered if he could ever be hers.

"I won't kid you. I'm still scared, but it has helped to talk about it. Now, before we change the subject, I'll finish with one last thought." She paused for dramatic effect. "I'm going for it with Brady."

"Great. Just don't dwell in fear. It isn't helpful."

Lily had that right. Fear had led Nell to the depths. She couldn't afford to indulge it again.

Buzz Valentine shifted into low gear and steered his Dodge Ram down the steep, rutted track through the woods. Brady braced his feet and hung on to the passenger handlebar.

"Interesting road," Brady remarked dryly.

"It's an old logging road. Lots of them around."

"Where's the lake from here?"

"Over there." Buzz pointed to his left. "Right

now, you'll have to take my word for it, but you'll be able to see it shortly. If you get interested in this property, you'll have to hike it if you want to explore it all.''

'·I'm surprised there's this much land left for sale.''

''Old-timers held on to it after the dam was constructed and the lake filled in the '60s. Now some of their heirs are more interested in selling. That's freed up some parcels. But they won't last long.''

Brady couldn't blame the real estate agent for his not-so-subtle application of pressure. It was prime acreage, thick with dogwoods, pine, oaks, sycamores, scrub cedars. Beautiful striated rock ledges rimmed the road.

''Here we are.'' Buzz abruptly stopped the truck. ''We'll walk aways from here so I can show you the spot with the best lake view.'' He fumbled behind the seat and pulled out a can of bug repellant. ''Spray your feet and legs.''

Taking the can, Brady raised the question. ''Why?''

''Ticks and chiggers, friend. They love me. I don't know whether they're partial to you or not, but, trust me, you don't want to find out.''

Brady stepped out of the truck, liberally sprayed himself, then stepped away and took a deep breath. The air was fresh, and all around him dew-covered vegetation sparkled in the morning sun. Brady realized he hadn't known quiet like this since he'd left Colorado those many years ago. The only sounds were bird-calls, the gentle sigh of a soft breeze through the conifers and his own breathing.

Buzz led the way through the trees until they reached a level piece of ground on a cliff high above the water, glinting blue and silver in the light. "This could be the site of your main lodge."

Brady was thinking the same thing. He could visualize a handsome log structure, nestled in the trees, with full views of the lake, meeting rooms done in rustic styles and colors, a first-class dining room with a deck overhanging the lake. Cabins and lodges scattered along the shoreline. He began pacing off the property, thinking about road easements, septic systems, wells. A lot of groundwork before construction could begin. "Politically, how difficult will it be to get the various permissions I'd need?"

Buzz pushed back his cap and scratched his head. "I won't fool you. There'll be some problems. The main one being getting a permit for a multislip dock from the Army Corps of Engineers. You'll have to have your ducks in a row."

"That's the way it is with anything," Brady said. His mind was racing with possibilities. A chunk of ground like this in California would be untouchable for most. "What are we talking about per acre?"

Buzz gave him a figure. Two million would probably get it. Brady knew he had a lot of homework to do before he committed—canvassing business leaders to see if there would be interest in a resort-conference center, talking with county officials, utility companies, the Corps of Engineers. The list was endless, yet the prospect had engaged his imagination. "If you can get me a plat map, I'd like to walk the land in the next day or two. If I like what I see, I'll consider taking an option on the property."

Buzz held out his hand. "You'd never regret that decision."

Grinning, Brady shook Buzz's hand. "Looks like I'll need to purchase my own bug spray."

On the way home, Buzz stopped at his office to pick up the map. That afternoon, Brady sat at the heavy mahogany dining table in his leased condo. *At least this piece of Victoriana has a function,* he thought, spreading out the map. Then, with a legal pad for notes at his side, he commenced studying and brainstorming. It was nearly dark before he looked up, surprised to notice the failing light.

Checking his watch, he calculated California time and put in a call for Carl. After a few pleasantries, Brady got right to the point. "I may need to sell some company stock."

Carl's reaction was guarded. "What's up?"

Brady briefly outlined the project.

Carl's next words were not encouraging. "Have you slipped a cog, pal? You're telling me you want to build a first-rate conference center and resort in the boonies of ever'lovin' Arkansas? You want a challenge? Fine. Come home and take your pick."

After Brady hung up, he sat for a moment, eyes fixed on the map. Carl didn't get it. There was no "home." Certainly not in California. Could he ever go back? He wasn't sure. That partly depended on Nell.

He groaned. Where had that thought come from? Damn it, they were friends. He stood and paced to the window, where he stared down at the concrete parking lot where two boys were skateboarding.

Hell, he'd been kidding himself. He was interested

in Nell. Her sparkly eyes and fragile, feminine body made him long to pull her into his arms. The truth resounding in his head filled him with something akin to panic. How could this be happening?

He pressed his forehead against the cool window-pane. *Oh, Brooke, I miss you and Nicole so much. What would you want me to do?* Was it disloyal to be thinking about Nell? To feel his body quickening even as he asked the question?

As if he were being sent a sign, the phone rang. When he answered, it was Nell, her voice light, animated and soothing, inviting him to dinner Friday evening.

After he hung up, he became aware he was standing in the middle of this anachronistically decorated bachelor pad, in, yes, "ever'lovin' Arkansas," wearing a sappy grin.

FRIDAY NIGHT Abby stood in the small combination living room-dining room eyeing the drop leaf table set for two. When Nell set a bowl of garden flowers in the center, Abby edged closer, glaring at her mother. "What are you trying to do? Ruin my life?"

Nell took a deep breath, then straightened. "You think I could single-handedly do that?"

Abby shrugged. "Looks like you're trying."

"All because I've invited Mr. Logan to dinner?"

"Mom, we're doing fine." Abby's voice rose in protest. "We don't need him."

"It's dinner, Abby, not a life-long commitment."

Abby's jaw tightened, and all she said was, "Oh, brother."

"You have your friends. I have mine."

Abby thrust an arm in the direction of the table. "When did you get out all this fancy junk? We never eat in here. But nothing's too good for Brady, right?" She made the word "Brady" sound like "cootie."

Rather than rising to the bait, Nell turned to the hutch and got out her crystal salt and pepper shakers. After she placed them on the linen tablecloth, she faced Abby. "What's really bothering you about this?"

She watched while Abby chewed her lip, unwilling to look at her mother.

"I asked you a question."

"What do we know about this Brady guy? Huh? So he's your 'friend' and he's from California. That's not much. What's he doing here anyway?"

"I know he is a man who lost his wife and daughter in a tragic automobile accident and he could use all the friends he can get. You included."

Color flooded Abby's cheeks. "I...I didn't know." She hesitated, as if reflecting on the conversation. "That's really sad, but, jeez, that doesn't mean I have to like him."

"No. You'll have to get to know him on your own. If you give him a chance."

"What if I don't want to?"

"I'd be disappointed in you. But that's your choice."

Abby seemed torn between resentment and acceptance. "It's just I'm afraid that—" A car horn sounded from the driveway. Abby wheeled toward the window.

"Afraid of what?"

"Never mind. I gotta go." Abby hurried toward the door. "That's Tonya's dad to take us to the game. Bye."

Like a wind preceding a storm, Abby blew out of the house, leaving Nell standing, defeated, in the living room, enthusiasm for the evening draining from her.

She knew what Abby was afraid of. The same thing she was.

But she had a choice. Living in fear or following the urgings of her heart.

Nell stepped back and surveyed the table—her good china, silver flatware, starched linens. She rubbed her arms against a shiver of anticipation.

Anything could happen when you followed your heart.

BRADY SHOVED BACK his chair. "Thank you, Nell, that was the best dinner I've had in a long time."

She smiled that crinkly smile he could look at all day. "No cook in your bachelor quarters?"

"Not unless you count the leading purveyors of frozen food." He patted his stomach. "Many more meals like that and I'll have to join a gym."

"I know the feeling. I'm stuffed, too." Nell stood and picked up their empty dessert bowls. He followed her into the kitchen. "You don't need to help."

"I want to." He took the dessert bowls from her, then nodded at the stacked dinner plates. "You load those in the dishwasher while I rinse these."

"Thanks. You're certainly more willing help than Abby."

Brady tensed. When he'd first arrived, Nell had mentioned Abby was at a football game. Since then her name hadn't been uttered. Until now. He didn't have so much trouble with the comparisons he drew between Brooke and Nell. The two were very different. But Abby was another matter. After meeting her and from what Nell had told him about her, Abby was a flesh-and-blood reminder of Nicole and what would never be his—the joy and satisfaction of seeing his daughter grow and mature. Although it wasn't Abby's fault, he wasn't sure he could open himself to the pain of a relationship with her.

"There," Nell said, filling the soap dispenser and switching on the dishwasher. "That's done." She ran her fingers through her short hair, then turned to him with a smile of invitation. "Feel like walking that dinner off?"

"Sure. What do you have in mind?"

"There's a small park down at the foot of the hill. We could make the circuit."

Her neighborhood was in an older section of town, with tree-lined sidewalks and deep front yards. When they stepped outside, the sun rested on the horizon, creating long shadows. The heat of the day had been replaced by moderate temperatures. "This way," Nell said, slipping her hand into his as naturally as if she'd always done so. He liked thinking about how they appeared to the few onlookers out watering their grass or sitting on their front porches. A couple. He was comforted by the feel of her warm hand in his, the way she matched his stride. As if they were totally in sync.

"Fayetteville is a nice town," he said. "Homey."

"I don't know if I could ever live in a big city. I'm a small-town kind of girl."

Brady pictured the traffic on the Bayshore Freeway, the commute to the mountains or the ocean, the acres of designer golf courses and upscale malls. He couldn't see her there. "Nothing wrong with that."

"I guess I sound pretty provincial."

He swung their clasped hands playfully. "City slicker meets country girl?"

She looked up, her mouth curved in a warm smile. "Something like that."

He dropped her hand and put his arm around her waist, tugging her close. "Don't you worry, dear lady, my intentions are honorable."

He'd said it in jest, but it had come out wrong. She kept walking, her pace slowing, the smile fading. Finally, she stopped and faced him. "I didn't know you had any intentions."

He stepped closer, bringing her face inches from his. He could smell the lilac sweetness of her perfume, see the question in her eyes. Energy radiated between them. An emotion—spontaneous and undeniable—filled his chest and he somehow managed to utter the words springing from pure feeling. "Neither did I. Until now."

Her eyes locked on his and he reached for both her hands, clutching them as if they were all that kept him from losing himself again. "Nell, would it be all right with you if...I wanted to be more than friends?"

He could sense her body stiffening, see the doubt clouding her eyes. But then she drew a deep breath, and as if it had cleansed the tension, a gentle expression took the place of doubt. "Yes," she said, and he no longer heard the splatter of the sprinkler system at his back nor the traffic noise. All he knew was that something important had just taken place.

"We could see—" he began.

"No expectations. Slow and easy," she said.

"And no more hurt. I promise."

She withdrew one hand and covered his mouth with two fingers. "No promises. I can't trust them."

He cradled her face in his hands. "If I have anything to do about it, you'll be able to."

Then, and only then, she moved into his embrace, wrapping her arms around his neck. "One day at a time," she whispered, before raising her lips to his.

At last.

CHAPTER SIX

AT THE PARK, Brady led Nell to a bench hidden from the street by a row of crape myrtle bushes. Sitting there, nestled in the curve of his arm, she tried to follow her own advice and live in the moment. To ignore all her nagging doubts, to bask in the warmth and strength emanating from the man beside her, to trust the step they had just taken.

To be happy. Now.

But hanging over her head was the specter of alcoholism and its potential to dash her hopes. She would have to tell Brady at some point, but for tonight? She wanted—in this moment—simply to be.

When Brady broke the silence, Nell thought he must've read her mind because all he said was, ''Happy?''

She didn't know how to answer him. ''I'm afraid of happy.''

''You're a profound woman, Nell Porter.'' He ran his hand up and down her bare arm. ''I know exactly what you mean.'' He hesitated, before continuing. ''I've asked myself over and over how I could deserve happiness after...what happened.''

''To your family?''

''Yeah. But tonight, being here with you—'' he kissed her forehead ''—it seems almost attainable.''

"I've thought about it a lot. I'm not sure anyone ever 'deserves' happiness. It just happens. The trick is to recognize it and savor it for however long it lasts. It's certainly not a permanent condition." How well she knew. There was a time in her youthful innocence when she had thought she would always be happy. In that idealized view, her father would always be there, Rick would love her forever, and she would be the perfect daughter, wife, mother.

He caressed her cheek with his forefinger. "That's why tonight is special. Being with you, I almost feel whole again. I never thought I would."

Nell leaned back, finding his words both rewarding and burdensome. "I can't make you whole, Brady. That has to come from somewhere inside of you. Healing takes time."

"So I'm told."

"You don't talk much about your wife and daughter." Nell knew she was running the risk of breaking the spell, but his reticence concerned her. "Would you tell me about them? About the accident?"

He picked up a strand of her hair and rubbed it between his fingers. "They don't have anything to do with you."

She could feel him shutting down, returning to a familiar, dark place. "But they do, Brady, if we're to have any...uh...deeper relationship. They'll always be part of you. Part of us." She felt her courage slipping. "If there is going to be an 'us.'"

Across the park at the lighted basketball court, a group of boys exchanged high fives and along the path in front of them came a lone man smoking a cigarette and walking his dog. Brady waited until he passed with a pleasant "Good evening."

"Brooke was...a golden girl. She came to work for us right out of college. In the Human Resources department. Her smile could light up my day. She was intelligent, energetic, funny. And unbelievably, she liked me."

Nell's ears perked up at "unbelievably." Had he thought so little of himself?

"I was a workaholic, driven to succeed, but she married me anyway. She never complained, at least not in any major way, and tried her best to be supportive. Then Nicole came along. I couldn't believe how lucky we were to have a good life, more money than we could ever need and a perfect daughter." His voice wavered. "Nicole was so darn cute. Bright and pretty. And she thought I was special."

"You are," Nell murmured.

Lost in his reminiscence, Brady didn't seem to hear. "I'll never forgive myself for not paying more attention to them. For letting my need for success get in the way. I told myself I was working for our family, but the truth was, I needed the ego boost."

"You couldn't have known what would happen. At the time, you were doing your best for them."

He laid both arms along the back of the bench, threw his head back, then sighed. "No, I wasn't. That night? The accident?"

When she turned to look at him, his eyes were focused on a faraway, anguished memory. "I was supposed to be with them. If I'd been driving— Aw, shit." He ran a hand through his hair.

She didn't know how to help him. He had assumed

a gigantic burden of guilt. "You couldn't have known."

"Oh, yeah, hindsight's 20/20. It was an accident. It could happen to anybody. Believe me, I've heard all the rationalizations. Hell, I'm just a screw-up. That's the story of my life."

Self-pity didn't become him, but Nell sensed there was more to it. Self-pity was indulgent, but he seemed genuinely wounded, and, if she was any judge, those wounds had origins in a time long before the accident. Out of the shadows, Abby's question, the one Nell had avoided dealing with, surfaced. "What do we know about this Brady guy?" Oh, she knew the kinds of things a résumé would include, but she sensed there was more. That he was a deep man, one with secrets.

Secrets. Again her obligation to tell him hers surfaced. But not now. Not when he had pulled her into his arms and tucked her head beneath his chin. "Sorry about that maudlin display. That's not what tonight's about. This is." He kissed her, and this time his lips moved hungrily, his tongue coupling with hers, and all she could do was bury her fingers in his hair and press her body against his, seeking to infuse him with all the pent-up longing she'd been denying.

And that continued to terrify her.

TONYA'S DAD WAS way cool. He'd taken the carload of their friends to McDonald's after the game and had sat in a booth by himself. Like maybe he wasn't even with them. Then the boys had come and taken the table across from the girls. Out of the corner of her eye, Abby noticed Alan Voyle elbow one of the guys aside so he could sit directly across the aisle from her. Maybe it didn't mean anything, but when it happened, Tonya had nudged her and whispered, "See?"

"How about that game?" Alan asked her between bites of his French fries. "Wasn't Decker awesome?"

Clueless about who Decker was, Abby fumbled for an answer. "Great. I was so nervous when the other team nearly tied us at the end."

"You like football?"

Like football? She'd never given it any thought except that games were fun times with her friends. "Yes, I mean, sure. I don't know a whole lot about it, though. You know, the rules and stuff." She prayed that admission wouldn't kill her chances with him.

Alan swiveled in the booth to face her. That sexy lock of dark hair fell over his forehead and Abby's brain turned to mush. "I could teach you. Sometime. If you want."

Gosh, maybe he did like her. "That'd be great."

"I could ride my bike to your house Sunday. Maybe we could watch an NFL game and I could explain some stuff."

McDonald's was her new favorite place in the world. This booth, special forever. "Sure, that'd be fun."

"Okay, then," he grinned, ignoring his buddies who were trying to get his attention. "About two?"

"Fine." Tonya, who had shamelessly eavesdropped, gripped Abby's knee in excitement, probably a good thing because if she wasn't grounded, she could surely fly.

On the way home in the front seat of Tonya's dad's van, Abby didn't say much, still floating in a romantic haze. Alan Voyle was coming to her house. Unbelievable. Finally she mustered her courage and leaned toward Tonya's dad. ''Mr. Larkin, what does 'NFL' mean?''

Mr. Larkin seemed surprised she wanted to talk to him, but she was glad she'd asked, because all the way home he explained to her about the leagues and franchises. Maybe she wouldn't look quite so dumb when Alan came over.

Her euphoria took a nosedive when Mr. Larkin pulled into her driveway—behind that man's car. She checked the clock on the dash. It was after eleven. What was *he* still doing at her mother's?

She should've stayed home. It was icky the way her mother put out the good dishes, wore that fancy dress, sprayed that flowery perfume all over herself. Just dinner, she'd said. Not a lifelong commitment. But what if it was? Her dad had remarried. What if her mom did?

Abby murmured a hurried thank-you to Mr. Larkin and a ''Call me,'' to Tonya before plodding to the front door.

''Abby, is that you?'' her mother called.

''Yeah.''

''Come tell us about the game.'' *Us.*

She entered the family room, where her mother and Brady sat on the sofa—close together. She looked at her mother, rosy-cheeked and smiling, then at Brady, handsome in a George Clooney sorta way, yet filling up the room like a sci-fi hulk. Abby caught a whiff of his nauseating woodsy after-shave. The cheeseburger she'd had at McDonald's revolted in her stomach and all she could think to say was, "What's he still doing here?"

An irritated frown erased her mother's smile. "Abby, did you leave your manners at the door?"

"Not really." Abby knew she was going to say too much, but she couldn't help herself. "I just wondered. Dinner was over a while ago, right?"

Brady Logan rose to his feet. "I imagine I feel like an intruder to you."

How did he know that? "Yeah, sorta."

"Abby? How many times do I have to tell you? Brady is my friend, and I didn't raise you to treat people so rudely."

Brady laid a hand on her mother's shoulder. "I don't know that she's as rude as she is truthful."

Abby looked away. First, she didn't want to see him touch her mother, but, second, she didn't know what to make of him. He seemed to understand her better than her mother did. Abby studied the coils of the braided rug beneath her feet. "I'm sorry. I guess I was just surprised."

"Understandable," Brady said, glancing at his watch. "And it is late. I should be going."

Good, Abby breathed.

Her mother shot her a look that clearly said *stay here.* "I'll walk you to the door."

Abby sank onto the arm of the sofa, digging at her cuticles. She could hear whispers, but couldn't make out the words. Then it was silent. For too long. What was he doing? Kissing her mother good-night? Gross. Then the sound of the door shutting.

When her mother came back into the room, she sat down. Abby folded her arms around herself, totally miserable.

''Brady isn't going to go away, Abby, so let's hear it. What's your problem with him? Us?''

''You like him, huh?''

''Yes, I do. But that doesn't have to change anything.''

''Change anything? It changes everything. It's embarrassing.''

''You mean I'm too old?''

Honest to God, Abby didn't know what she meant, just that everything felt weird. ''No, but—''

Her mother's expression softened. ''You're afraid. I understand. I am, too.''

''You—you are?'' That was a new thought.

''I like Brady. A lot. But that doesn't mean anything has to change between you and me.''

''But what if…he hurts you?''

''You're asking if I'm strong enough now?''

Abby hung her head. ''Yeah.'' She couldn't stand it if her mother started drinking again.

''The truth? I don't know. I think I am. But how will I ever be sure if I don't try?''

''Sometimes I'm just so scared.''

''That it'll happen again?''

Abby nodded, mute.

''Let's not borrow trouble, honey.''

''Okay.'' Abby stood, waved her arms helplessly, then said, ''I'm going to bed now.''

''I love you.''

''I love you, too.'' She started for her bedroom, then, remembering, paused and said, ''Mom, is it okay if Alan Voyle comes over Sunday afternoon?''

Her mother's smile was full of love. ''Of course.''

Abby couldn't wait to get to her room. She had too many things to think about. Her life was nothing but confusion. And Alan was only one part of it.

MONDAY MORNING Nell sought out Ben Hadley following her AA meeting. ''Do you have a minute?''

''For you? Always.'' He led her to the far corner of the room where several folding chairs were arranged in a semicircle. After they sat down, he lay an age-spotted hand on hers. ''Now what can I do for you?''

''I need to talk.''

''Then I'm happy to listen.''

She smiled. So like Ben. He always had a way of letting her figure out things for herself. ''I've met a man.''

''And?''

''I think I could fall in love with him.''

''And this is bad?''

''There are lots of problems.''

''Like?''

Briefly she told him about Brady's wife and daughter and his overwhelming grief. ''I don't know if I can take on his problems. Compete with the ghosts.''

''You can't do either one, but you *can* be the best, most loving Nell Porter in your power.''

Abby looked into Ben's wise eyes, and knew he

spoke the truth. "Then there's Abby. She's not happy about Brady."

"He threatens her safe little world."

"Yes. But it's more than that. She's afraid something will happen, and I'll start to drink again."

"That's always a possibility."

She hadn't wanted to hear him say that. She'd wanted assurance that she was "cured," even though she knew that wasn't possible. "I know," she said quietly, remembering the tailspin she'd gone into after her father's death. "Emotionally, I feel stable, but that's today."

"And tomorrow is always about the 'what ifs,' is that it?"

"I'm afraid, Ben."

"That's natural." He eyed her closely. "Have you told him your history?"

"Not yet. I know I have to, but I've been dragging my feet. Avoiding, I guess."

"It would take a pretty big man to overlook your alcoholism, is that what you're saying?"

She nodded, studying the fingers clenched in her lap.

"Are you worth it?"

She looked up, startled. "What do you mean?"

"Worth his love and approval. It sounds as if you're trying to talk yourself out of exploring a relationship with this man." He hesitated, then went on. "When you said earlier you could fall in love with him, I asked you if that was bad? All you did then was give me a laundry list of impediments. Now, I'm asking you another question. When you're with him, does it *feel* bad?"

She was aware of a sudden calm in the room. While they had been talking, the others had left and his question echoed in the silence. She didn't answer right away, recalling Brady's comforting embrace, his vulnerable heart. "No," she whispered.

"Trust the Twelve Steps. You have so much to give, Nell. If you live in fear of hurt, you'll never fully live."

She stood, then placed a hand on the older man's shoulder. "Thanks, Ben. You've given me lots to think about."

Later at her car, she stopped, took a cleansing breath and looked around. The crisp morning air held the first hint of fall, and a few trees showed early signs of color. Abby's moods, like the leaves, were as changeable as the seasons. Yesterday had been better, thanks to Alan Voyle. Giddy with excitement, Abby hadn't asked her once about Brady. The two teens had huddled in the family room, a football game the focus of their attention. Nell couldn't help overhearing Abby with Alan at the door when he left. "Thanks," she'd said. "I just love football."

Nell smiled at the memory. Since when had her daughter had any interest in football? Maybe Alan was just the distraction Abby needed. Nell hoped so because she would certainly welcome relinquishing the spotlight.

TUESDAY WAS OVERCAST, but the land was green under the pewter skies. Occasional wisps of fog flirted with the treetops. The rocky soil beneath Brady's feet was still damp from an early-morning shower, which had intensified the mossy fragrance of the woods.

Brady shouldered his pack and, holding the folded plat map in one hand, strode through the thick brush toward the shoreline. Bisecting a portion of the property was a steep ravine through which a spring-fed stream trickled. Brady studied the terrain, wondering whether it would be necessary to build a bridge to access the lodge site or whether the route Buzz had taken around the ravine would be more practical.

Yesterday he'd stopped by the local Chamber of Commerce to inquire about conventions, conferences and hotel occupancy figures. He'd been pleased with what he'd heard. He didn't want to tip his hand too soon, but every new piece of data served to make him more optimistic about his vision. Tomorrow he had appointments with representatives of two of the major industries headquartered in northwest Arkansas to get a reading on their conference needs.

He paused to caress the lichen-covered trunk of a towering walnut tree, wondering how long it had stood in this spot. He tried to temper his enthusiasm. Plenty ought to deter him from this undertaking. His lack of experience in the hospitality industry, his obligations in California, the financial risk involved. Yet with every step he took through the undergrowth, he knew this was what he was supposed to be doing.

And all because of what a stranger had written in a B-and-B journal.

He didn't believe in miracles. Not after what had happened to Brooke and Nicole. Yet he had the uncanny sense that Brooke was somehow orchestrating his future.

Listen to yourself. You're talking supernatural bullshit. But how else to explain the improbable string of circumstances that had brought him to Arkansas? And to Nell.

The snap of a twig alerted him, and he turned around. There in a small clearing stood a doe with her fawn. When she raised her head to study him in that instant before she darted off through the trees, her big, soft eyes reminded him of Nell's trusting look just before she'd kissed him Friday evening.

She'd given herself to the kiss freely. And her embrace had been as welcome as a warm shower after a grueling workout. Even as he admitted how deep was his need, he cursed himself. He swung savagely at a limb impeding his way. Could he make a new beginning when he was still riddled with guilt? He certainly didn't deserve a second chance.

But he'd promised Nell. He wouldn't hurt her.

Whether he deserved it or not, for the first time in months, he was no longer alone.

"OH, BRADY, I don't know." Excitement and fear warred in Nell. She clasped the phone in hands suddenly clammy. It was too soon.

"It would just be for two nights. I'd really like the company."

Brady had told her about his tentative plans for developing a conference center on the lake, but she hadn't been prepared for this—an invitation to accompany him to Timberview Lodge and Resort on a lake in Missouri. It was a research trip, he'd said.

Would her mother caution her, concerned with the opinions of outsiders? Would Lily encourage her? And Abby? Dear God, she'd be horrified. Nell shook her head in a liberating kind of defiance. This was her decision and hers alone. Was she prepared to go through life acceding to the wishes of others? The answer was "no."

But all she could picture was a cozy double bed in a faux-rustic cabin, complete with a stone chimney and fireplace.

"Nell? You're not saying anything."

"Uh, Abby goes to Dallas this coming weekend."

"That suits me, providing I can get reservations."

"September shouldn't be a problem." Her quivering body and rampaging imagination were not to be denied. Despite her surfacing insecurities and fears, she was actually encouraging him.

"About the quarters? I'll try to get us a two-bedroom cabin."

Never had the words *two-bedroom* been filled with such music. Yet in the midst of the deep breath she was finally able to draw, there was a hitch of regret. "That sounds perfect. Thank you."

After he told her he'd call back with the particulars, they hung up.

And panic set in.

Surely she hadn't been contemplating…*that*. They weren't ready yet. She wasn't ready. He'd find out what a fraud she was. How useless in bed.

Oh, God. Abby. She'd have to give her a number where she could be reached. There would be questions. Lots of them.

For which she had no answers.

Even for herself.

Then, to her horror, Nell recognized the thirst

claiming her body. For the first time in months, every nerve cried out for a drink. For the soothing opiate of vodka—neat.

STELLA JANES SMOOTHED BACK a lock of hair, then leaned across the table of the tea room where she'd met Nell for lunch. "I must say I don't know what to make of it. Do you really know this man well enough to take off for a...romantic weekend?"

"It's not like that, Mother. It's a business trip."

Her mother raised an eyebrow. "Get real, Nell. I know how the cookie crumbles. Why does he need you if it's business?"

Nell added sugar to her tea, stalling for time, knowing she was evading the issue. When she looked up, her mother's expression was more concerned than judgmental. "I'm rationalizing, aren't I?"

"You said it, dear. Not I."

"Mother, the truth is...I'm interested in him. And I think maybe he likes me, too."

"Well, I certainly hope so. But are you, uh, sure you're ready for—" she waved her fingers airily "—whatever this is?"

Abby's heart was pounding at jackhammer speed. She leveled her gaze, looked straight at her mother and told the truth. "No. But I'm going to find out."

"You've straightened out your life. Your problems are over. Why risk anything?"

"First of all, my problems will never be over. I will always be an alcoholic." She noticed her mother wince at her use of the word. "It is very tempting to remain passive. To let events roll past me. But Brady has come into my life. He's important to me. Of course, I'm afraid. I don't want to upset my life any

more than you want to see me do that. I have you
and Lily and Abby, but...maybe that's not enough.
I've been lonely. Brady fills that empty spot in my
heart.''

Stella covered Nell's hand. ''Oh, honey. If I could
only guarantee you wouldn't get hurt—''

''You can't, Mom. No one can. This is a step I
have to take on my own. Granted, it's unknown territory. And I won't lie. The thought of going with
Brady this weekend terrifies me so much that, for the
first time lately, I craved a drink. But I can't go
through life letting the demon rule me.''

Stella patted Nell's hand, then withdrew it to wipe
away the tears gathering in her eyes. ''What about
Abby?''

''She won't like the idea of my being with Brady,
but I'm the adult here. If I sublimate my needs totally
for hers, neither of us gains.''

''I hope it works out, dear.'' Stella sighed. ''You
need to talk with Abby.''

Nell couldn't overlook the lines of worry pinching
her mother's brow, nor the generosity of her understanding. ''I know. I will.''

''Whatever you do, darling, be happy.''

Nell's throat closed, filled with huskiness. ''I'm
trying.'' Yet the thought of that first dizzying leap
off the cliff of security made the words tremble on
her lips.

ABBY LEANED toward the bathroom mirror—horrified. Yuck. There it was—a zit the size of Colorado.
Red and crusty and pus-filled. What else could go
wrong? She ticked off the calamities in her life. This

was her weekend to go visit her dad and Clarice in stupid Dallas. Never mind Alan had asked her to meet him at the high school game and sit with him. She could've died when she had to tell him she couldn't. He probably thought she was the biggest baby in the world, trotting off to Dallas to see Daddy.

Then, worse even than that, her idiot mother was going to do it. Shack up with that man! The mere thought of it gagged her. Had her mother lost her mind? Didn't she read the magazines, watch ''Oprah'' or anything? Men like that were after one thing. Sex. Hot and heavy.

Gripping the bathroom counter, Abby shut her eyes, trying desperately not to picture her mother naked—with him—rolling around on satin sheets like in R-rated movies. She didn't care what Mom had tried to tell her in their stupid mother-daughter chat. About a woman's needs. About how she liked Brady and how you couldn't find happiness without taking some risks. That was crazy. She and her mother *were* happy. They didn't need anybody else. Despite the hot tears lurking behind her lids, Abby slowly opened her eyes.

Crap. The zit was still there like a giant neon UGLY sign blinking its horrible message to the world.

Studying it, she felt sick. She couldn't get Tonya's words out of her mind. ''I always get these huge zits right before my period.''

Her stomach did another flip-flop. *Oh, God, no. Please. Don't let it happen. Not this weekend. Not in Dallas.*

CHAPTER SEVEN

NELL HAD ARRANGED her work schedule so that she could be off by two, pick Abby up at school and deliver her to the airport for her flight. That had left her just enough time to race home, freshen up, throw the last few items in her suitcase before Brady arrived at five. She caught her breath when she saw him. His black golf shirt set off his dark eyes and tanned skin and he exuded pure animal magnetism. She might have backed out there and then except for his broad grin, deepening his dimple, that made her feel special. Tingly. Not at all the way the librarian mother of a thirteen-year-old ought to feel.

"Ready?"

She didn't know if she was reading something into his question, but it was fraught with promise—and danger. "I...I'll be just a minute."

She ducked back into her bedroom, leaned against the closed door and tried to calm her rioting emotions. Was she doing the right thing? There was an awful inevitability to the next few hours, and she knew, whatever happened, it would shift her world. And yet...

She managed a wry chuckle. She wanted this. This whatever-it-was.

She picked up her suitcase, lifted her chin and returned to Brady, a smile masking her insecurities and doubts. "I'm ready."

He took her bag from her, then led her to his SUV. He glanced skyward. "Looks like we have a beautiful evening ahead of us."

Hoping he was, in fact, referring only to the weather, she nodded in agreement. He helped her into the front seat and then they were leaving her house behind. Superstitiously she kept watching it in the passenger side mirror, as if once it was no longer visible, her security would disappear.

Apparently tuning in to her uncertainty, Brady picked up her hand, dwarfed in his, and gave it an encouraging squeeze. "You haven't done this in a while, have you?"

"What?" The word came out staccato.

"Had a weekend away. With a man."

"No." She laughed shakily. "I'm kind of rusty in the dating game."

"I know. Me, too."

Then it hit her. This must be difficult for him, as well. He'd been married a long time. Had clearly loved his wife. Oh, God. She might be his first relationship since Brooke's death, just as he was her first since Rick. She looked up shyly, studying his face. Wondering if he was as nervous as she was. In a gesture of understanding, she caressed the back of his hand with her thumb. "We're a fine pair, aren't we? I guess we'll fumble our way through this together."

"To tell you the truth, I feel like a geeky teenager on a big date with the prom queen."

She blushed. "I've never been confused with a prom queen."

He turned his head, and the look on his face reduced her to a pool of honey. "Then somebody just wasn't looking, because you're beautiful."

Nell hardly knew how to react to the compliment. Rick had called her his "funny face." Lovingly. At first. "Beautiful" was out of her league. "Thank you," she murmured. "You almost make me believe it."

He had a wonderful laugh that rolled up from deep in his chest. "You don't get it, do you? You *are* beautiful." Then he looked at her again, the humor fading from his eyes. "Somebody must've really done a number on you."

Was she that needful? That transparent? "They did. Uh, *he* did," she amended.

"Your husband?"

"I...wasn't what he wanted."

"He was a fool."

"But that's all in the past."

"Yet you haven't forgotten how he made you feel, have you?"

"Not really."

"Well, starting right now, we're going to change that."

"How?"

"For starters, repeat after me, 'I am beautiful.'"

She crossed her arms and sent him a dubious look. "Right."

"No really. C'mon. Try it."

She felt like a fool, but softly she mumbled, "I am beautiful."

Brady gave her a playful knock on the head. "Not like that. With gusto. Like this." He bellowed the phrase, then repeated it. "Join in now. One, two, three…"

And she was doing it. With him. There they were. Two grown-ups driving down the highway hollering, "I am beautiful!"

But that wasn't the most amazing part. No, it was the way he was looking at her.

For the first time ever, she believed it. She felt beautiful.

Best of all, Brady seemed to believe it.

AFTER A LEISURELY DINNER at one of the resort's highly regarded restaurants, they walked along a lighted path toward their cabin. Pausing at a picturesque footbridge crossing a gurgling stream, Brady leaned against the rail and surveyed the scene. Nell could practically hear the wheels turning in his brain. Already he'd taken in quite a bit, commenting at dinner about the check-in procedure, parking situation, signage and layout of the facility.

"I like the space and openness. Guests need to feel they have room to breathe."

Nell nodded. "The landscaping contributes to that sense. Just manicured enough, not overly cultivated, yet colorful. I've never seen such gorgeous mums."

Brady took her arm, then, and they strolled on. Maybe this really was a business trip. Maybe she'd overreacted. Seen more in the invitation than was there. Their cabin, perched right above the lake, was commodious, the comfortable pine furniture and rust and forest-green North Woods fabrics welcoming.

The two bedrooms, each with its own bath, flanked the living room with its vaulted ceiling. A lakeside deck ran the full width of the cabin. If the decor was intended to make the guests feel pampered, it was working.

When they reached the cabin, Brady turned a single lamp on low, then busied himself in the tiny kitchenette. "How about some spiced cider? On the deck?"

Nell retrieved a sweater from her room, then waited for him in the two-person wooden glider. Lights from the other cabins were reflected in the calm water of the cove, and in the sky above, stars were visible. She pushed slowly back and forth, content to rest in the moment. Before anything else happened.

"Here," Brady said, shouldering open the door, "get it while it's hot."

Nell took the warm mug and waited for Brady to join her. Soothed by the cinnamon-clove fragrance of the cider, she basked in the illusion that, for the time being, her real life had vanished and all that mattered was sight, smell and the comfort of Brady's warm body beside her as they rocked to and fro. He said nothing, perhaps, like her, caught up in the spell of the night.

Across the cove, a late fisherman motored past the No Wake buoys toward the marina, but other than that, the placement of the cabin provided seclusion.

Finally Brady broke the silence. "What do you think so far?"

"It's wonderful. I felt as if I was on vacation almost from the moment we arrived."

"I'd like to help others feel that same way. You know, it wasn't until I got to the Ozarks that I experienced any calm on this trip."

"You're not the first to say that. We like to think mystical qualities reside in these hills and waters. Early Native American tribes certainly thought so."

She nursed her cider, the scent and taste conjuring up the vivid foliage and brilliant blue skies of autumn. She felt languid, peaceful, when she supposed she should be tense and expectant.

"How did Abby feel about your coming with me?"

Pop went the balloon of self-delusion. "She wasn't thrilled, as you might expect. It's not you. She'd be the same with any man I dated."

"She worries about you."

Nell shot him an arch look. "Oh, yes."

"I wouldn't hurt you."

"But she doesn't know that." Nell hesitated. "I...we were hurt once. It's made her cautious."

He chuckled sardonically. "I guess that makes three cautious people." He took the empty mug from her hands and set it with his on the deck, then settled his arm around her shoulder. "I like being with you, Nell. You make no demands."

"We're lucky. It feels like starting fresh, doesn't it?"

When his fingers leisurely traced up and down her arm, she found it difficult to focus, lost in the sensations generated by even that smallest of caresses.

He stretched out his jean-clad legs, stopping the motion of the glider. "I have a confession."

"Oh?"

"Before...I couldn't think of Brooke without wanting to howl at the moon. But now?" The hand on her arm stilled. "Oh, hell, this is going to sound stupid."

"Not to me," Nell said quietly.

"It's as if she brought me to you. As if...we're supposed to be here. Together."

Nell turned her face to his. "I feel the same way."

For a breathless moment, neither moved. Then, with a jerk of the glider, he rose, drew her to her feet and enclosed her in a hug that made her forget the stars, the lake, everything but the musky smell and muscled body of the man she wanted—in every way. She had time only to whisper "Brady," before his lips closed over hers in a kiss so deep, so needful she was helpless with longing. Urgings and instincts she had thought dead spiraled through her. She cupped his face, the rough feel of his whiskers beneath her fingers driving her to meet his lips, his tongue, with joyful abandon.

Then, as she slid her arms around his neck, his lips sought her eyes, her temple, and again her mouth. His hands moved restlessly over her back, then clutched her closer, nestling her hips against his erection.

As if jerked from a warm pool into harsh cold, she tensed, a gasp trapped in her throat. He wasn't going to stop.

Then came an equally disturbing thought. She hadn't wanted him to. She refocused on him—his needs, his gentleness, his hands caressing her short hair, his breath smelling faintly of clove. Yes. No. A primal scream ripped at her chest, clawing for expression. Closing her eyes, she fought the olfactory comparison cruelly toying with her mind. Clove. Juniper. Gin. Clove, juniper…oblivion.

She whirled away from Brady, leaning for support on the railing facing the lake, drawing deep breaths of clean night air. He took a hesitant step toward her. "Nell?" The concern in his voice tore at her heart. "Are you all right? Did I do something…wrong?"

When she slowly pivoted, the hurt in his eyes pierced her. "No," she whispered. Laying a hand on his cheek, she prayed for the right words to somehow explain what had to feel to him like rejection, the last thing he needed. "I thought I was ready." Her throat caught. "I want to be."

He took her hand in his and raised it to his lips. "I want you, Nell, but only when you say it's all right."

If she could have changed her mind in that instant, she would have, but before she could act on that impulse, he'd put his arm around her and was leading her inside to the cozy sofa facing the fireplace. After he settled her with a fleece throw around her shoulders, he sat on the hearth, hands clasped between his knees.

"I'm sorry," she murmured.

"No apology needed. I came on too strong."

"No, it's not that. It's just—" she gave a harsh little laugh "—I'm rusty."

"We both are. And we have time." He smiled then, in a way that again made her feel beautiful. Lulled, she was unprepared for his next words. "Tell me what he did to you."

She didn't have to ask whom he meant. Her eyes

filled with tears and all she could do was shake her head.

Then Brady was beside her, cuddling her against him. "Talk to me, Nell. Get it out."

She struggled for the breath trapped in her rib cage. "He...he thought something was wrong with me. I couldn't respond like he wanted."

She felt Brady's jaw clench against her temple, but he said nothing. Just waited.

"He said I was prudish. That I, uh, wasn't woman enough to satisfy a man. Satisfy him." Hot with shame, she buried her face in his shoulder.

He tipped up her chin. "Was it always like that?"

Nell thought about his question. "No, I guess not at first. I don't remember when things got worse. Maybe after Abby came. I tried, but it didn't seem to matter what I did. Whatever it was he wanted, I couldn't give."

"So he found someone else?" Brady's tone was guarded.

"Yes." She lifted a finger to wipe the tear that trickled down her cheek.

"How did that make you feel?"

"Like I was sexless. Worthless. A failure." She couldn't believe she'd said the words aloud, after so many years of having them hurled at her—and believing them.

"That selfish son of a bitch," she heard Brady growl before he took hold of both shoulders and turned her to face him directly. "He was the failure, Nell, and I don't care how long it takes, I intend to prove it to you. What about your needs? How much concern and consideration for you did he exhibit?"

She shrugged helplessly, giving him his answer. "I tried so hard to save the marriage."

He ran his hands over her shoulders and down her arms. "I'm sure you did. You define the word *giving*." He pulled her into his embrace. "Now, let me give to you." He kissed her hair. "What you need right now is a good night's sleep."

Rewrapping her in the throw, he led her to her bedroom, pausing at the door to kiss her again with a tenderness that felt like balm. "Good night, beautiful lady," he said, then quietly closed the door as he left.

Nell leaned, weak-kneed, against the door, her fingers finding the knots in the pine. Brady's kindness and understanding, his self-denial, shook her to the core. She had not known there were men like him. Had never expected she would be given a second chance.

She'd told him. Not everything, but almost everything. She knew she owed him the rest.

She drew the throw even more tightly around herself in a futile effort to thwart the chill racking her. No. Not yet. He would hate her when he learned the truth.

Liquor had not saved her with Rick.

It could ruin her with Brady.

BRADY LAY ON HIS BACK staring at the bedroom ceiling for a good hour after he left Nell at her door. As he'd suspected, that bastard of a husband *had* done a number on her. If he was any judge, she was well out of her marriage. He'd known men like that—in locker rooms, at business meetings—for whom women existed merely as pawns in games of sexual supremacy. A my-dick-is-bigger-than-yours kind of infantilism. What her husband had done to Nell probably bordered on abuse. And she'd bought into his low opinion of her.

Damn it! He socked his pillow, then rolled onto his stomach. Nell had no idea the extent to which she'd turned him on tonight. It had taken every ounce of willpower to send her off to her own bed. Brooke had taught him sensitivity and tenderness went a long way toward satisfying a woman, so he would be patient with Nell. Gritting his teeth, he acknowledged it wouldn't be easy, though. He ached with needs of his own—to feel Nell's warm, naked flesh beneath his, to cup her small, soft breasts in his hands, to fill her until she cried for joy.

The ache in his groin was a powerful signal that after months of merely existing, he was living again and that, in time, his stormy days would pass, replaced by a vibrant rainbow named Nell.

A CLICKING NOISE, like a bird tapping on a window, drew Nell from the fuzzy depths of a dreamless sleep. She snuggled into the covers in an effort to escape wakefulness. *Scritch.* She turned toward the window, then cocked open one eye. *Scritch. Scritch.* Irritated, she rolled out of bed, padded across the floor and parted the drape. In the faint light, she saw that her ''intruder'' was a small twig scraping back and forth against the glass in a strong wind that must've come up overnight.

Returning to her bed, Nell glanced at the clock. Six. Too early to get up. She settled back in bed.

Wide awake. Lying there picturing Brady in the crisp yellow Oxford-cloth shirt he wore to dinner, sleeves rolled up to the elbows and his pressed jeans that hugged his firm thighs, she wondered what would have happened last night if she hadn't suddenly been rocketed into the past. Would they have continued, making their way slowly, or not so slowly, to a bed— reaching for each other eagerly in an effort to release that combination of lust and need propelling them both toward intimacy?

Even as she pictured it, she became aware of a pulsing low in her abdomen, a hardening of her nipples. She closed her eyes, inhaling against the message her body was sending. Now. She could go to him. All she would have to do would be get up from the bed, tiptoe through the living room, then crawl in beside him. And she would do it without liquor to blur her vision and numb her inhibitions.

Scritch. Maybe he was awake, too, waiting, as she was, for the moment they'd been heading toward since they'd first met. Yet she'd undoubtedly hurt him last night with her sudden retreat. He didn't ask for that hurt, didn't need it. On the contrary, what he needed was… Oh, God, Lily had nailed it. He needed the comfort and oblivion of love and sex.

Before she could stop to think, Nell stood, smoothed her cotton-knit gown, wishing it were, instead, a wisp of lacy silk, and walked deliberately out of her room, across the living room, pale in the predawn light, and quietly turning the knob, opened the door to Brady's room.

He lay on his back, one arm flung across the extra pillow. With a thudding heart, she studied his mussed hair and the shadow of his beard, then permitted her eyes to graze over his chest and downward where the flat of his stomach disappeared beneath the sheet and blanket.

She could turn back. Flee to the safety of her room. But a buzzing in her ears and a throbbing of her pulse robbed her of that decision.

Quietly, she drew back the cover and slipped into his bed, her gooseflesh warmed by his body heat. She lay on her side, facing him, listening to him breathe, watching his profile, smiling when he suddenly twitched in his sleep. She wanted him both to remain asleep and to wake up.

She feathered her fingers across his chest, watching with delight when his nipples puckered. Then, daringly, she blew.

Gradually she became aware of a hand on her head. She glanced up. Brady was looking at her with a wondering smile, one brow raised in question.

She nodded, then scooted nearer, raining kisses along his collarbone.

He pulled her close. ''Nell, you're sure?'' he whispered.

And, amazingly, she was. ''I couldn't sleep,'' she murmured.

''I see.'' His voice was teasing. ''Did you come for a back rub?''

''Not exactly.'' She moved her lips scant inches from his. ''I had something more in mind.''

''I'm glad to hear it,'' he said just before running a hand tantalizingly beneath her gown and pulling her even closer. When he kissed her, she forgot about second thoughts completely. But that was only the beginning.

By the time the sun rose, her gown was pooled on the floor and Brady was doing wonderful things to her—with her—things she'd only ever dreamed about. With his fingers. With his mouth. And with something else—a warm, hard something that filled her with wonder and drew from her a delighted cry that started in her womb and raced through her body, erupting at the same time she convulsed in release—total and blessed.

She hadn't known it could be like this.

Hadn't known there were lovers like him.

Brady braced himself above her, pausing to find her eyes. "I was right earlier."

She smiled lazily. "What do you mean?"

"You are a giver."

She surprised herself by laughing out loud. "If I'd known last night what I know now, I'd have given sooner."

He rolled onto his side, taking her with him. "We have all day," he said tracing her upper lip with a forefinger.

"And another whole night," she murmured, snuggling against him.

It seemed an amazing prospect provided by generous, beneficent gods.

NOT UNTIL they were on the way home Sunday afternoon did Nell permit second thoughts to intrude. In some small corner of her brain she'd known their forty-eight hours together was not the real world, that satiation of the senses was not commitment and that their obligations extended far beyond the two of them. But for these idyllic hours with Brady she would make no apologies, nor harbor any expectations. Looking out the window, she reminded herself firmly, "He's only passing through." She would forever be grateful to him for making her feel beautiful and, even more important, desirable.

He hadn't said much since they'd checked out, but then what was there to say that they hadn't already expressed with their bodies? She couldn't expect a vow of undying love. She told herself it had been a lovely weekend, a mere blip on the screen of her life, but nothing with a future. She chewed her lip. Besides, when she told him she was an alcoholic, what then? A frisson of panic stopped her breath. What if he rejected her? Oh, God, he was more than a blip on the screen. A lot more.

She studied his profile, the little nick of a scar beneath his left eye, the softness of his earlobe in contrast to his bearded cheek. He made her heart sing, her blood roar. And then it struck her. She'd already committed. She never would have gone to his bed if she hadn't.

Suddenly she had so much more to lose and the prospect scared her.

"When does Abby get home?"

Brady's question jolted her back to reality. Abby had been horrified enough that she was going with Brady this weekend. How much more critical would she be if she suspected the depth of her mother's feelings for him? "Her flight arrives at 7:35."

"Would you like me to go to the airport with you?"

''Thanks, but I'm not sure Abby's ready for that.''

He nodded. Nell wondered what he was thinking, how he saw himself fitting into their lives. Even if only temporarily. He would surely have to return to his business in California soon. If he pursued the idea for the Beaver Lake resort, he'd have to raise money from backers on the West Coast and would probably have an on-site supervisor for the building project. Oh, he'd fly in and out. They'd see each other periodically.

But she wanted more. She looked out the passenger window, barely registering the trees passing in a blur. Like a miracle Brady had come into her life and there was no hiding from the truth—she was falling in love with him.

Even though—God, Abby's question assaulted her again—she didn't know all that much about him, except that he was tenderness and consideration personified.

She faced the road again, watching the narrow two-lane highway dip around the sharp curves and steep descents. Clasping her fingers tightly in her lap, she forced the question to her lips, praying it sounded casual. ''Brady, you still haven't told me much about your growing up, about your family.''

He put a reassuring hand on her leg. ''Feel as if you've been in bed with a stranger?''

''Not exactly.''

''But women always want the complete story, right?''

She smiled. ''Guilty, sir.''

''There's not much to tell. Born in Colorado, left

home right after high school, worked in California, married Brooke. That's it in a nutshell.''

''You've told me all of that before. Would you mind filling in between the lines?''

''Like?''

''Your family. Tell me about your parents. Do you have any brothers or sisters? What are your favorite childhood memories? How often do you see them and…'' She faltered. He'd removed his hand from her leg at the word *family,* and when she looked up at him, his eyes were steely, his body tense, like a cat sensing danger.

''That's history,'' he said in a flat tone.

''*Your* history,'' she said encouragingly. ''I'm interested.''

He ignored her, negotiating a junction of two highways. She'd obviously said something wrong. But what? Her questions had been innocent. Yet she sensed anything she said now would be a mistake.

After a long pause, he spoke. ''I don't mean to be rude, Nell. Let me put it this way. My first eighteen years are off-limits. I try not to think about them and I sure as hell don't want to talk about them. Okay?''

''But surely your mother, your father—''

''Stop. My mother is dead, and if I never hear my father's name again it will be too soon. Suffice it to say, as far as I'm concerned he's dead, too. They're all dead.''

Nell winced at the raw edge of pain slicing through his words. The gentle man with whom she'd made love was gone, replaced by an angry, unforgiving one whose hurt was palpable. And what did he mean ''they're all dead''? Were there others besides his mother and father? Abby had been right. There was more to know. Brady harbored secrets.

But who was she to talk? She had one, too.

After another few miles, Brady raked his fingers through his hair, then turned to her. "Hell, I apologize for that outburst." He cleared his throat. "There are just some things I don't talk about. Not with you, not with anybody."

"Are the emotions that painful?" She knew she risked a great deal with that question, but whatever the history was, he was expending enormous energy in denial.

His expression remained stoical. "Leave it, Nell." His icy words allowed no argument. A slammed door couldn't have reverberated more decisively in Nell's head.

BRADY THREW the Escalade into gear and bolted away from Nell's house. After her pointed questions, the remainder of the trip home had been strained. Of course she wanted to know about his background. Women always did. He'd been through it once for Brooke, who, like the nurturer she was, had urged him to face his past, until she'd eventually realized she might as well save her breath. He hadn't been ready. Still wasn't. And he sure didn't need to go through the whole pathetic story again.

He shook his head, disgusted with himself. Nell deserved so much better. Hell, she even had a right to expect answers, especially after their weekend. He cared about her. He'd even felt, with her in his arms, that he might be beginning to heal.

But she was asking too much. He would not revisit

Glenwood Springs, nor those agonizing months of watching his mother gasping for every breath. And certainly not his father's betrayal of her memory. God damn him, anyway.

He swerved out of the path of an oncoming vehicle, cursing the driver, the narrow street, the stoplight that suddenly turned red and anyone, anything else he could think of.

Waiting for the light to change, he squeezed his eyes shut against the memory of his final fight with the almighty Dale Logan and the ultimatum that had made his father's choice crystal-clear. And his. Brady had stormed out of the house, leaving behind his father, his younger brother, and the stepmother who was making a mockery of his mother's memory.

The beep of a horn caused him to look up—straight at a green light. He moved forward slowly in a vain attempt to calm down. What had Nell asked? "Are the emotions too painful?"

Painful? They shredded his gut. That's why he never looked back.

What must Nell have thought? Jeez, he couldn't help himself. He'd reacted like the certified jackass he was. *Great goin', Logan. You oughta offer a class. How to ruin a romantic weekend in one easy lesson.*

He'd have to make it up to her somehow. She had been so loving. He'd hardly ever had such a delightful surprise as waking up to find her nestled against him, arousing him even before he'd opened his eyes. She had held nothing back. The wonder on her face when she came spoke volumes. She'd never known, never understood what a passionate woman she was. He couldn't hurt her.

And yet he already had.

Long shadows criss-crossed the parking lot at his condo and the smell of hamburgers on a grill caused his stomach to growl. He picked up his overnight bag and walked slowly toward the building. He had some deep thinking to do this evening. About his project, about exorcising the demons Nell's questions had raised, and about Nell herself and his feelings for her, which were growing more and more powerful.

Reaching his building, he heard a car door slam behind him. He pulled out his pass key and was inserting it in the lock, when he heard footsteps behind him, and then a familiar voice.

"Brady, man, where you been? I about went to sleep in my rental car waiting for you."

Brady whirled around. "Carl?"

His partner spread his arms in a none-other gesture. "I got tired of waiting for you to come home to California. I need to visit with you, boy."

"Problems?"

Carl nodded. "You don't know the half of it." Then he studied Brady, his eyes shrewd, despite the pleasant expression on his face. "Invite me in. Let's crack open a beer." He placed a hand on Brady's shoulder, then dropped his voice. "I'm here to talk some sense into you. What the hell are you still doin' in this burg anyway? You need to come home. You've licked your wounds long enough."

Brady stood aside to let Carl enter. No way was he looking forward to the next few hours. Carl was his oldest, best friend, but he would not like what Brady was going to tell him.

CHAPTER EIGHT

CARL SAT on the arm of the sofa, upholstered in a worn Moroccan-inspired fabric, watching Brady unscrew the lids of the beers. "Who did your decorating? Winston Churchill's mother?"

Brady crossed the thick Persian rug overlaying the institutional-tan carpet and handed Carl his brew. "Straight out of Thomas Hardy's bleakest novel, huh?" He settled in the deep leather chair. "What can I tell you? The owner's an English lit prof."

Carl grinned. "Figures. Doing his best on his meager pay to recreate Victorian England, I guess." He took a swig from his bottle, then stood and walked around the room studying the framed lithographs from old issues of *Punch*.

Drawing circles in the condensation on the glass of his bottle, Brady watched, waiting for Carl to get around to the purpose of his visit.

Finally Carl pulled a wooden desk chair closer to Brady and sat down. Leaning forward, he gestured with his beer. "Logan, what the hell are you doing here?"

"I got a good deal. Helped the old guy out."

"Bull. You could've bought the whole complex. Why settle for this?"

"It was temporary."

"Well, that's a relief. So you're coming home soon?"

"I didn't say that." Brady crossed one leg over his knee. "My plans are still up in the air. More to the point, what are you doing here? Not that I'm not glad to see you, but you kinda sprung this visit on me, buddy."

"I got tired of our one-sided phone conversations. I've been worried about you." Carl stretched, crossing his feet at the ankles. "So cut the b.s. You've had time. We've been more than patient at the office, but we need you now. The new products division has a blockbuster idea that requires development approval and the contract with the Department of Defense is at the refinement stage. We can't dick around much longer on either of these projects. And, partner, that's just the tip of the iceberg. I know you've been through hell, but work could be therapeutic, you know."

Brady had known this day would come. He and Carl had started together in a windowless basement office with nothing but dreams and a couple of computers. Once, their "overnight" success had bred further creativity and satisfaction, but even before Brooke's and Nicole's deaths, he'd felt more and more tethered to beepers and cell phones. Even a pleasure boat in the Pacific Ocean had provided minimal escape.

Brady set his beer on the moisture-ringed surface of the wooden end table. "I'll come back to California soon to help handle the responsibilities you mentioned, but I can't stay." He cleared his throat. "I, uh, may never be able to."

His partner's eyes clouded. "I guess I had to see for myself. You can't come to grips with the accident, move on?"

"I'm better, Carl. Honest. But come to grips with it? No way. Could you? I'll never understand how the trucking company could not know their driver was a drunk or how someone hauling flammable materials could be so reckless. Just my luck," his mouth filled with acid, "that he waited for my family on a day I wasn't driving them."

"Jeez, Logan, you can't blame yourself. Guilt will eat you up."

Brady held up his bottle in a mock toast. "Tell me about it." He stood then and moved to the window. "So, you ask what I'm doing here in Arkansas." A college-age couple walked hand-in-hand along the bike path circling the complex. An older man living across the courtyard was filling his bird feeders and down the street three skinny teenagers were shooting hoops. He turned. "It's Norman Rockwell, county fair, schmaltzy Americana, and I love it."

Carl joined him as he turned again to the window. "Maybe you're right. Maybe you need to get this crazy notion out of your system before you move back."

Brady faced his partner. "What if I never move back?"

"Get a grip, brother. You're scaring me."

"I've made a decision. I'm going ahead with the development project here. I'd like to show you around tomorrow, let you see what I have in mind."

Carl looked dubious.

"Please. It's the first project that's captured my interest in a long time."

Carl clapped an arm around his shoulder. "I guess I can spare a day. But there are a couple of stipulations."

"What?"

"That you agree to come home with me for a week or so to get things straightened out."

Brady felt a sigh rip open his chest cavity. "Okay. What else?"

Carl drained his beer, then grinned wolfishly. "You tell me about her."

"Who?"

"I've known you too long, pal. A business deal might interest you, but it wouldn't keep you in the backwoods this long. So I figure there must be a woman."

Brady looked into the cocksure, laughing face of his friend and felt a sudden overwhelming need to confide in someone. He smiled, a culprit caught in the act. "I'll grab you another brew. Then we'll talk. I *have* met someone."

Before he left the room, though, he paused. "Her name is Nell," he said, letting the melody of the name fill the silence—and quicken his senses.

NELL LOOKED OUT her bedroom window Monday morning and groaned. Here came Lily and her mother, marching determinedly up her front walk. The two of them at once. Why was she off work today of all days? A visit from these two was more than she could handle. Especially after the restless night she'd spent second-guessing herself about

Brady. What had she been thinking? *Brazen hussy.* With an epithet suitable for a nineteenth-century novel, she accused herself. Yet being with him had felt so good. So right.

Running a brush through her hair, she smoothed the sweatshirt over her jeans, drew a deep breath and opened the door. After exchanging greetings, she inquired after her nephew. "Where's Chase?"

"At mother's day out at the church," Lily said, leading the way toward the family room, where she perched on the sofa. Stella sat in a blue-canvas director's chair and Nell took the armchair.

"Well?" Smiling, Lily looked directly at her, her eyes inquisitive.

"You didn't waste much time," Nell said dryly.

Stella bristled. "When you didn't call last night, we were worried. Are you all right?"

Nell dug her fingernails into the upholstery. Why wouldn't she be? They would be shocked if she told them just how "all right" she was. *We spent the weekend more or less in bed. And it was g-r-e-a-t!* She wondered if her mother thought she might have soothed her nerves with the contents of a bottle. "I'm fine. Why wouldn't I be?"

An unfathomable signal passed between Stella and Lily, and Lily fielded the conversational ball she'd been tossed. "It might have been, um, stressful." Her sister, the soul of tact.

"In what way?" Seized by a fit of mischief, Nell decided she wasn't going to make it easy.

Lily had the grace to look away. "Well, you know—"

"What Lily's trying to say," Stella interjected, "is

that you don't know Brady very well, and things might've...gone wrong.''

If you only knew. ''As a matter of fact, I had a delightful weekend. The lodge was lovely, the food scrumptious. All in all, I had quite a pleasant time.''

Lily's shoulders relaxed. ''Then you didn't—''

''Drink?'' Nell took perverse satisfaction in the way both sets of eyes were riveted on her. ''No. I didn't.'' With those words, she recognized increasing symptoms of anger. She could rationalize all she wanted about how supportive and helpful they'd been, but how long would it take before they got the message? She was sober, damn it! She wasn't going to let them get away with such distrust any longer. ''Why would you think I would drink? Have I done anything recently to suggest a relapse?''

''No, but—''

Nell didn't wait for her mother to finish. ''Then, for God's sake, why can't you let me be? I'm not nineteen going to my first house party with a boy. I'm thirty-four, and in full possession of my faculties.''

Spots of color appeared on Lily's cheeks. ''I'm sorry, Nell.'' She looked contrite.

Sulking, her mother joined in. ''I had no idea our concern wasn't welcome.''

Nell grimaced. Look where too little sleep and too much worry could get you. Leaning forward, she reached for her mother's hand. ''It's not unwelcome—'' she paused, wondering how to put it ''—it's just sometimes I feel like a specimen under a microscope. I know you're both acting out of love for me, but you need to quit trying to protect me.''

Crossing the room, Lily knelt at Nell's feet and took her hands. "I see what you mean. Maybe we do gang up on you. We love you. The last thing we want to do is hurt you."

"I know," Nell murmured.

Lily looked up. "So you had a good time, then?"

Nell included her mother in the smile she pasted on her face. "Yes, I did. A very good time. Brady is a nice man."

Stella let out a sigh. "How is Abby doing with all of this?"

"About as you might expect. It's threatening to her that I could be interested in someone. We've been alone a long time."

"That's only natural, dear. She was just a little girl, but she remembers your drinking. Maybe she's worried about what would happen if this man hurts you. Maybe she can't help expecting the worst."

"Surely she doesn't equate the presence of a man in my life with the temptation to drink?"

Nell crumpled in the face of her mother's implication. She had laid a heavy burden on Abby. Instead of dissipating, had her daughter's concerns only deepened over the years?

She closed her eyes in a vain attempt to erase the picture forming in her brain—Rick's humiliating accusations, the cold, snowy night, the fear in six-year-old Abby's screams, the icy blur that was the road in front of her car, the warmth of the alcohol zinging through her veins. Oh, God, did the struggle ever get easier?

Her stomach knotted, and it was taking every last

iota of will not to head directly for the nearest liquor store. The irony of it. Her mother and sister had come out of concern and love to check on her, and that very act of concern, had sent her mind down that dangerous spiral from which there were few avenues of escape.

"Nell?" Lily squeezed her hands.

"I'm fine. Please, quit worrying. I can handle whatever happens." She trembled with sudden doubt.

Stella stood, then moved closer and placed a hand on Nell's shoulder. "I'm sure you can, darling."

But uncertainty lingered in her voice.

After they left, Nell went outside and tried to calm her ragged emotions by concentrating on the beautiful day as she watered her newly planted chrysanthemums. But no good intentions could keep her mind off Brady. Or off Abby and what would be best for the two of them.

The unwelcome question battered her. Could she really handle whatever happened? She was falling in love with a man scarred by a past he refused to speak about. A man who had warned her he liked the fact she made no demands on him. A man perhaps incapable of commitment.

Yet this same man had awakened her to the knowledge that she could be responsive, desirable. Even beautiful. She smiled wistfully, remembering.

She had been wrong that evening when she'd said being with Brady was like starting fresh. She could never start fresh. Brady had understood about Rick, about her hurt. But would he understand when, at last, she told him the truth? There would be no way to prepare him for the words "My name is Nell and I am an alcoholic."

FIRST THING AFTER he and Carl got back to the condo after tramping the land Monday, Brady ordered flowers delivered to Nell. Not roses. That was predictable. No. A bird-of-paradise with a card that read *Like this flower, you are one-of-a-kind beautiful.*

He and Carl had just time to eat a quick dinner of Memphis-style barbecued ribs before he took his partner to the airport, where an insistent Carl had stood by while Brady purchased his own ticket for a Thursday flight to San Francisco. He owed Carl that much. The man had been more than patient. Although the money the company had been making these past months meant little to Brady, he could no longer afford to be so cavalier about his responsibilities to L&S TechWare.

When he returned home after sitting at the airport discussing business with Carl until he had to go through security, Brady called Buzz Valentine and asked him to get the paperwork ready for taking out an option on the Beaver Lake property. Earlier Carl had asked him if he was sure he knew what he was doing. Brady had laughed, shocked to discover that, indeed, he was sure, the first thing about which he could make that claim since the accident.

Next he called Nell and invited himself over. He wanted to explain in person about his California trip and his decision to go ahead with the development. Her voice rippled with pleasure when she thanked him for the bird-of-paradise. She suggested he wait until after nine to visit since she would be helping Abby with a school project until then.

When Brady put down the receiver, he found himself wandering through the condo, a vague sense of dissatisfaction marring an otherwise perfect day. What was bugging him?

He pictured Nell and Abby bent over the dining room table, newspapers, popsicle sticks, glue and pipe cleaners spread over the surface. His gut churned. God, the fort. As if suddenly winded, he sank into a chair. Giggles, smears of brown paint, Nicole's blond head bent, her concentration intense as she formed the stockade fence. Brooke coming into the room with her contribution, a tiny American flag and a colorful cavalry guidon she'd stitched. It was one of those rare nights when Brady was home, when he'd brought a huge grin to Nicole's face by offering to help.

Abby. Sooner or later if he continued his relationship with Nell, he'd have to face his conflicted feelings about her daughter. She was part of Nell, as Nicole had been part of him. Maybe if it weren't for the uncanny resemblance, their being nearly the same age, he could handle it.

He groaned. He wanted Nell. Could maybe even consider commitment. But Abby? She was part of the package and deserved his unconditional affection and acceptance, but he didn't know if he would ever be ready to claim another child as his.

California. He didn't want to go. Wanted to avoid the inevitable onslaught of memories and emotions. God, just when life had seemed, at last, to hold promise, reality was grounding him with a vengeance.

He didn't know how long he sat there lost in thought, but when he looked up it was nearly nine. He ran a hand through his hair. Maybe Nell could restore the elusive peace he'd experienced with her this weekend.

But that was asking a lot of her.

"HE'S HERE AGAIN," Abby hissed into the phone. "You'd think a whole weekend would've been enough."

"That's kinda gross when you think about it," Tonya said.

"What?" Abby rolled over on her bed, then stuffed a fat feather pillow beneath her chest.

"You know. The weekend. I mean, like, uh, do you think they did the big nasty?"

Abby clutched the phone, afraid she might puke. It was bad enough she'd asked herself that question, but to hear it come out of Tonya's mouth was disgusting. "Jeez, Tonya, that's sick."

"Well, ex-scuze me, but think about it for a minute. Why else would they go away for a weekend? Especially one when you were in Dallas?"

Abby didn't want to admit it, but she'd had the same thoughts. "I dunno," she mumbled, then added, "but I don't like it."

"Well, maybe you could go live with your dad."

"Not in my lifetime." Abby knew Tonya was just trying to be helpful, but the idea of being holed up with Clarice for any length of time was something she didn't even want to think about. Besides, maybe her mother wasn't so hot on this guy after spending a weekend with him. But, then, what was he doing here tonight and why had her mother looked so happy? Crap.

"How *was* your weekend?" Tonya asked. "I didn't get a chance at school to hear about it."

"Boring. Like always. The big woo this time was going to a Cowboys' game." Abby wouldn't admit that the only thing that had made the outing bearable was that she could tell Alan about it. And she had. After sixth period. He'd given her this big, sexy smile and told her he thought it was cool she liked football.

"That could be okay, I guess." Tonya hesitated and Abby could hear a GameBoy bleeping in the background on the other end of the line. "Did you get home without a visit from our crimson friend?"

Abby flopped over on her back and stared at the ceiling. "Is something wrong with me, Tonya? I mean practically everyone I know has started."

"What does your mom say?"

"That it's normal for it to vary with different girls. But I guess I'd rather be weird than have it start in Dallas." She cast around for a change of subject. She was tired of looking in the mirror every morning wondering if this was the day. "I told Dad about Brady."

"You *did*? What'd he say?"

"He frowned and asked me if I was all right with that."

"And you said?"

"I lied and told him I was happy Mom had a boyfriend." Abby remembered the skeptical expression on her dad's face. "I think he knew I wasn't telling the truth."

"What are they doing now?"

"Who?"

"Your mom and that guy. Is he still there?"

Abby rolled off the bed, tiptoed to the window, parted the blinds and spotted the Escalade parked in the driveway. "Oh, yeah." She glanced at her alarm clock. "Jeez, it's almost eleven."

"Maybe they're like, you know, in love."

Abby's throat was raw with unshed tears. "Yeah, maybe. Look, Tonya, I still gotta study the vocab words for science. I'll talk to you tomorrow." Before Tonya could say anything further, Abby clicked off the phone.

What was the matter with her? She swiped at her eyes. These days every little thing made her cry.

But Brady Logan was no little thing.

BRADY SHOOK HIS HEAD, baffled about how the conversation could have taken such an unpleasant turn. Up to this point, everything had gone smoothly. He'd shared his excitement with Nell over going ahead with preliminary steps to develop the resort and conference center. Even though she'd gripped his hand more tightly when he explained about returning to California for a few days, she'd understood that it was time he shouldered his responsibilities. He'd reassured her that he would be coming back, that he would be spending most of the next few months right here in Fayetteville. So where had things gone wrong?

One little question, that's where. *Do you always run away from your problems?*

They'd been talking about his "sabbatical" from

work and somehow the conversation had segued, once again, to his distant past. To Colorado. "Why haven't you ever been back?" she'd asked.

So he'd told her he'd left right before his high-school graduation. Nothing about the way his father had betrayed his mother's memory or about that last violent argument. That's when she'd asked the question, accused him of running away from his problems.

All he could do was stare at her. "Is that what you think?"

She sat facing him on the sofa, her feet drawn up beneath her skirt. "I think you're a sensitive, kind man who will never be free until you face your past."

"Who appointed you counselor?" He hated the bitterness lacing every word, but, damn it, she was getting too close.

"Is that how it seems?" She hesitated, studying his expression. "I thought we cared enough to begin sharing with each other. That the weekend meant something—"

"It did!"

"But there is a point, Brady, where you shut down. It's as if you only have part of yourself to give. As if you have erected walls you won't permit anyone to breach."

"I can't talk about it, Nell. You'll just have to understand that. I've spent years trying to move beyond the anger and hurt I experienced. Nothing good could come out of revisiting that time."

"I see."

"You'll have to take me as I am. Like it or not."

He longed to touch her, to reassure her, but he owed her this time of reflection. She sat, self-contained, studying her hands, clasped in her lap. He could hear every beat of his heart, every tick of the wall clock.

At last she looked up. "You've made me very happy," she said huskily, "been tender and gentle with me. And now you're asking me to give you your space." She laid a soft hand on his cheek. "It's the least I can do."

He pulled her into an embrace, then kissed the top of her head. "I'll miss you."

"Me, too, you," she murmured.

"I can't make any promises, yet," he whispered.

"I know."

"I wish I could show you right now how much you mean to me."

"Abby—"

"—wouldn't approve."

She nuzzled his neck. "Are we wicked?"

He chuckled. "I hope so."

Then he kissed her, again and again. Wanting to prolong the moment. Wishing he didn't have to leave. Wondering if he could possibly be falling in love again.

It was a stroke of luck when Ben Hadley came into the library Tuesday afternoon. Nell had been intending to call him. It was time, past time, to talk with him about the topsy-turvy direction her emotional life was taking and to admit she'd done more thinking about a drink in the past few weeks than she had in many months. She recognized the danger signs and they scared her.

Addictions served to define identity for some, so it was all too easy to cling to them, to nourish them. To excuse one's actions because of them. But if ever there was a time she needed to be responsible for herself and for Abby, it was now.

She approached Ben and asked if he had a few minutes. When he allowed that he did, she ushered him into her office and closed the door.

He took the seat across the desk from her. "Something bothering you, Nell?"

She explained to him how important Brady was becoming to her, even about their weekend and how he'd restored her faith in her femininity. "I don't want to hurt Abby in the process, but—"

"You have needs of your own," he finished for her. "Do you love this man?"

"I think I do, but there's a problem." Then, haltingly, she told him about Brady's resistance to revealing his past and what she perceived to be an unhealed wound.

Ben steepled his hands. "He has to tell you when he's ready. On his timetable."

"But what if he never does?"

Ben smiled, as if he'd seen it all. "He must be carrying a pretty heavy burden. He'll lay it down when it's important enough to him to do so."

"Meanwhile?"

"You go on loving him. As he is. If you can."

Nell recognized the wisdom of his words. After all, she'd asked her family to love her as she was.

And they had, despite the fact that at times their love felt suffocating. She nodded. "I want to."

"Good." Ben made no move to leave, as if he intuited she hadn't finished.

"There's one more thing." She grasped the arms of her chair for support. "I...I haven't told him."

Ben cocked his head in question. "Why is that?"

Her mouth felt dry. "I'm afraid."

"So honesty is only a one-way street?"

"What do you mean?"

"You want his whole story, but you're unwilling to risk yours."

"We both fear rejection, is that it?"

Ben waited, saying nothing, letting the truth sink in. After a moment he said, "And, more than once, you've thought about a drink, haven't you?"

"How did you know?"

"I'm well acquainted with fear, Nell."

"I've resisted."

"I thought so. You know you don't have to go through this alone."

"Thanks to AA, I do know. I'm trying really hard."

Ben's eyes were heavy with the toll of experience. "One minute, one hour, one day."

Nell's palms felt moist on the arms of the chair. "I have to tell him, don't I?"

Ben leaned forward. "You know the answer to that question as well as I do."

"Soon?"

"Now, Nell."

Long after Ben left, Nell sat at her desk arranging and rearranging her pencils and pens, knowing she should have been open with Brady from the beginning. And fighting her fear. She'd had enough rejection and humiliation to last a lifetime. But Brady's judgment mattered more than she'd ever thought possible.

Please, God, let him see who I've become, not who I was.

CHAPTER NINE

IT WAS ONE OF THOSE idyllic California Saturdays travel agents and Chamber of Commerce executives dream about—cloudless skies the soft blue of a baby's blanket, the whisper of a breeze rustling through palm fronds, temperatures in the low 70s. Golf courses smelled greener, tennis balls bounced higher, swimming pools glistened Caribbean-turquoise in the morning sunlight.

Brady hated it.

At every turn was a reminder that years of his life amounted to no more than discarded film on the cutting room floor. He hadn't meant to drive by Nicole's school or the beauty salon where Brooke had her hair done. Nor could he understand how he found himself slowing his rental car in front of their former home, now occupied by strangers, trying to ignore a girl's bicycle lying temporarily abandoned in the yard.

Stone-faced, he rolled on through his old neighborhood. Already the house at the corner had been repainted a different color and, in two yards, grass had been replaced by crushed rock and desert plantings. Hell, why should he expect anything to remain the same when his entire world had been blown apart?

Yet as he drove farther past Starbuck's, streetside

cafés, wine boutiques and other upscale merchandis-
ers, memories of the Arkansas landscape dimmed,
the way a vivid dream fades like wisps of fog in the
early morning sun. He'd phoned Nell Thursday evening after he got settled at the hotel. Since then, however, he'd realized he wouldn't feel right about calling her again until he dealt with the heartache he
experienced everywhere he looked. From the first
moment he'd walked into his corner office at L&S
TechWare and seen the familiar photographs on his
credenza—Nicole at her first horse show, Brooke in
a stunning cocktail dress at a charity gala, the three
of them, suntanned and grinning, on the deck of their
sailboat—he'd known Nell was right. He had run
away.

But that knowledge didn't make coming back any
easier. He'd gone through the motions with Carl,
making decisions, signing documents, nodding his
head sagely. He'd exchanged greetings with old
friends and colleagues without remembering ten
minutes later what he'd said. Today, he'd driven
down memory lane with the premeditation of a sa-
domasochist.

Bottom line? He wanted to run away again.

But he owed more than that to Nell. To Brooke's
and Nicole's memory. And to himself.

The funeral was long over. Now he'd arrived at
the moment of truth. It was time to bury the dead.

With clear-eyed detachment, he made an abrupt U-
turn and headed for the cemetery.

BECAUSE OF THE NUMBERS of older patrons who had
wanted to attend the adult forum on death and dying,

Nell had rescheduled it for late Saturday morning when more of them would be able to drive to the library. The speaker had done a sensitive job of anticipating the questions and assuring the audience that death was a natural process.

Nell envied those who had been given the opportunity to say goodbye to their loved ones. She had tortured herself after her father had died so suddenly. Had he known how much she loved and appreciated him? What were her last words to him? She couldn't remember and that missing link plagued her. He'd seemed so jolly at Christmastime that year, making his traditional toasts, greeting everyone with a bear hug, laughing uproariously at Abby's antics. Then, a mere three days later, he was dead.

As the speaker responded to a question about medical directives, Nell found herself reliving the days that followed. Rick had been out of town for a New Year's bowl game. When she'd finally reached him at the team hotel, a woman had answered. In the background, a party was clearly in full swing. Just before Rick picked up the receiver, she heard him give the punch line of an off-color joke, followed by raucous male laughter. No matter how many times she looked back on the next minute, she could never explain what had caused her to ask the question, why she hadn't immediately told him about her father. Instead, her first words were, ''Who was that woman?''

''What woman?''

''The one who answered the phone.''

''Hey, babe, lay off, will you? We're just having a little fun down here, that's all.''

And in that moment, she knew. She didn't know how. It made no sense, but she'd never been surer of anything in her life. When she'd called their travel agent the next morning, any lingering doubt had been removed. Rick had left town with a Clarice Townsend.

"...decide whether you want a Do Not Resuscitate order." The speaker was giving valuable information, but Nell couldn't concentrate.

In a single week she had lost her father and learned of her husband's unfaithfulness. In hindsight, she should have kicked Rick out then, but for Abby's sake, they had tried to salvage the marriage. Or rather she had. Rick gave mere lip service to the effort. Over the long months, his vacant stares, secretive phone calls and late nights "at work" took their toll on her self-esteem. Weary with disillusionment, a sense of abandonment and self-hatred, she sought solace in the soothing depths of a bottle. A little vodka in her orange juice to get her going in the morning, rum in her soda to see her through midday, a pick-me-up to lighten her mood before Abby came home from school, two martinis to get through the awful twilight hours when husbands and fathers traditionally returned home from work, and, of course, a nightcap before bed.

At first she'd made excuses, claiming the stress of her father's death, playing the betrayed wife to the hilt, but after a while she didn't worry about excuses. Her only concern was where she would get the next drink. And the next.

God knows what she'd missed, whom she'd hurt. Poor Abby. She'd lost both father and mother in that cruel time. As long as she lived, Nell knew she could never make up that loss to Abby. All she could do was make each new day a good one.

Nell raised her head when a burst of applause indicated the conclusion of the question and answer period. She made her way through the departing patrons to thank the speaker, then as soon as she gracefully could, headed for home.

It was a gorgeous late September day, mild, but with the hint of a cool breeze. The dogwoods and some oaks already sported their autumn finery. Maybe Abby would want to go for a walk with her.

She entered the house through the kitchen door and immediately spotted the note on the counter. *Gone with Tonya and her mother to the mall. Back about four.* So much for a companionable walk with her daughter. She put a kettle on to boil for a cup of tea and rummaged in the pantry for a can of tuna to make a sandwich.

In the quiet of the house, she could no longer avoid thinking about Brady. He'd called Thursday to tell her of his safe arrival, but it had been a short, unsatisfactory conversation. She'd second-guessed herself ever since Monday night. What on earth had made her accuse him of running away from his problems? It didn't take a professional psychologist to know that act was akin to throwing the gauntlet where a man was concerned. He'd made the boundaries very clear. Why had she crossed them?

When the answer surfaced, she sank down on a kitchen stool. She loved him. She wanted to spend the rest of her life with him. To do that, she needed to know everything about him, just as he needed to know all about her.

The shrill whistle of the teakettle intruded on her thoughts, and she poured water over the tea bag in her cup and slapped some tuna, mayonnaise and lettuce between two bread slices. As she chewed on a bite of sandwich, she wondered for the umpteenth time since yesterday, why she hadn't heard from Brady again. He'd promised to call back. Was she fooling herself? Did California hold a bigger attraction for him than he'd let on?

She was cleaning up the kitchen when the phone rang. Finally. It had to be him. She dashed to the wall phone and picked it up, her voice alive with expectation. "Brady?"

A sardonic laugh she'd know anywhere was the first thing she heard, followed by, "Not hardly, Nell. It's Rick."

"Oh." Why had she done a dumb thing like assuming the caller would be Brady? Was she that far gone?

"Not who you were expecting, I gather."

"No."

"Who is he, Nell?"

"Who?"

"The man Abby told me about."

Glancing out the kitchen window, Nell wasn't at all surprised to see a dark cloud glide past, obscuring the sun. It figured. She fought panic. What had Abby told her father?

"Cat got your tongue? I gather his name is Brady."

Nell willed herself a solid backbone. "Yes. What concern is that of yours?"

"That's rather obvious, isn't it? My 'concern' is Abby. I hope you're being discreet."

That was rich! It was all she could do to bite her tongue. "Abby's welfare is uppermost in my mind, and you can rest assured I'm not doing anything you need to worry about. After all, I am entitled to a social life, aren't I?"

"I want Abby to be happy, and if circumstances there are uncomfortable for her, I'm sure we could agree on other arrangements."

Was the man saying what she thought he was? Nell's blood boiled. He was actually suggesting Abby live with him and Clarice. Gritting her teeth, she carefully made her voice neutral. "We share in common the goal of Abby's happiness. I don't expect either of us to jeopardize that again as we once did."

"Clarice and I will be looking out for her welfare."

Nell blinked away angry tears. "So will I, Rick, so will I."

After she hung up, Nell bolted out of the house, oblivious to the gathering storm clouds. Fury propelled her down the street, through the park and up the steep hill on the other side. When she reached the top of the ridge, she stopped, lungs heaving, gasping for breath.

Dear God, what had Abby told her father?

Worse yet, what was he prepared to do?

THE GRAVES WERE on a slight rise, sheltered by a flowering bougainvillea. A prime spot, the cemetery director had said. At the time, the remark had irritated Brady. Even in death, for materialistic Californians, location mattered. Brady kicked at a tuft of grass. Well, it certainly didn't matter now.

He studied the inscriptions on the headstones—the bare facts, the ineffective hints of who Brooke and Nicole had been. What they had meant to him. He wanted to feel something. In this place, surely, he would find a connection with them.

But the scene was too perfect to have any relevance. Manicured grass, carefully trimmed shrubbery, discreet directional markers sectioning up plots of ground. An elaborate filing system for ghosts that didn't take into consideration the all-too-human imperfections—the mole at the base of Brooke's neck, Nicole's funny, long toes and chipped front tooth.

He knelt, hands on the ground, bracing himself, hoping the sensation of grass and earth beneath his fingers would awaken raw emotion. He needed to feel their presence, damn it.

Nothing. Far in the distance he could hear the hum of traffic on the freeway. Here, aside from the occasional trill of a bird, it was quiet. Too quiet.

Ultimately, with an urgency he couldn't explain, he found himself talking. Telling them about the blur of days following the accident, about selling the house, taking time off from work, leaving California. About his desperate cross-country odyssey, his loneliness, his hopelessness. About the gaping hole surrounded by the bone and tissue that was his body.

He placed a hand on each grave, still slightly rounded beneath his palms, and poured out his anger and grief, not even pausing to wipe away tears he was helpless to control.

After a while he rocked back on his heels, drew a handkerchief from his pocket and blew his nose. From the bell tower, a carillon chimed the haunting notes of "Amazing Grace." Unsummoned, the words came to him from a time long ago when his mother, in her soft, true alto, would sing the hymn to him at bedtime. Yet even as the familiar words formed in his mind, he wondered what could possibly save a wretch like him.

When the final note echoed in the silence, he heard in his heart the answer. Nell.

Then, in a hoarse whisper, he told Brooke and Nicole about Nell. About the chance for a new life with her in Arkansas. "I will always love you, my darlings, but I have a decision to make. To live or merely go through the motions. I didn't look for this to happen, didn't seek it exactly, but I think I'm ready to love again. Please understand."

Slowly he stood, knowing he wouldn't receive a response, yet craving one anyway. He waited, hands in his pockets, reluctant to leave. Avoiding a parting that *he* would initiate this time.

Then, without warning, a strong breeze blew across the open space and pink rose petals from a nearby gravesite settled at the foot of Brooke's and Nicole's markers. Whether it was a sign or not, he couldn't say.

All he knew was that he felt their presence—and their blessing.

Drained of emotion, yet more peaceful than he'd been in months, he nodded in acquiescence.

He would choose life.

And Nell.

ABBY SQUIRMED. The way her mother was looking at her made her feel funny. Like she'd done something wrong, but she didn't know what. "I didn't spend any money at the mall, if that's what you think."

Her mother glanced at the kitchen table where bills were spread out in neat piles as if that explained everything. "I'm not angry, Abby. Just preoccupied." She set down her pen and with a weary sigh said, "Did you have a good time?"

"I guess. Mrs. Larkin treated us to lunch and a movie."

"That was nice of her."

Her mother's worry lines grew more pronounced. Whenever she paid bills, it made Abby nervous. Like maybe they were having financial troubles. Abby nodded at the invoices. "Do we, uh, have enough money?"

"Don't you worry about that. We always make do, don't we?"

Well, yeah, but there sure wasn't a lot extra for stuff like getting a new school wardrobe the way Tonya did every year. "I suppose."

"Do you have a minute?"

Oh great. "I was going to my room to read my book for English."

"This won't take long."

Realizing her escape route had been cut off, Abby settled on one of the kitchen stools. "What?"

"First of all, understand I'm not trying to pry."

Right.

"It's about your last weekend in Texas at your dad's."

"What about it?"

"You're aware, of course, that Brady Logan's friendship is important to me. Can you remember exactly what you told your father about that?"

Crap. She'd known the minute she'd said anything to her dad that she should've kept her mouth shut. He'd acted outraged. Like he was threatened or something. Which was a crock because he had Clarice, so what did he care about Mom? He'd left them, not the other way around.

"All I said was that you were up in Missouri with your boyfriend." Bad answer. Her mother's shoulders drooped like they always did when she was disappointed in Abby. "Did I do something wrong?"

"Telling the truth is never wrong. It's just I wouldn't want you making too big a deal of my relationship with Brady."

"But you like him a lot, right?"

When her mother answered, Abby almost had to look away. The longing in her mother's eyes scared her. "Yes, honey, I do."

"Okay, then." Before her mom could go on about stupid Brady, Abby jumped up and fled, only stopping for breath when she reached the refuge of her room. She was no dummy. She'd seen that look before. In the movies. Or sometimes when Tonya's mother looked at Mr. Larkin.

Cripes. She didn't care what her mother said about Brady Logan. It was clear as anything—she was in love with him. Gross.

TONIGHT COULDN'T come soon enough. All day Tuesday at work, Nell walked on air. Brady had called her early Saturday evening from California. With an openness that caused her heart to soar, he'd explained his experience at the cemetery and assured her he was eager to get back to Arkansas—and to her. With low chuckles and playful innuendo, he'd reminded her that their trip to Missouri was only the beginning. She had stopped short of confiding that her newly awakened body had reminded her more than once since that she missed and needed him. Sometimes, out of the blue, she found herself giggling like a schoolgirl. She'd had no idea lovemaking could be so satisfying or so addictive.

She glanced at the clock over the checkout desk. Three more hours and he'd be home. More than once, Reggie Pettigrew had teased her about her daydreaming. If he only knew.

Finally the minutes crept by and it was time to leave work. Driving home, she pictured Brady deplaning, arriving at his condo, maybe taking a shower. Blushing, she lingered over that image. His body was leaner, firmer than Rick's and, with a single caress, could make hers hum. She wanted tonight to be about reunion and easy affection.

Beneath the surface, though, lay a deeper concern—telling him, as she must, about being a recovering alcoholic. She never wanted him to accuse her of duplicity. So now she must face the consequences of her choices and actions. She would tell him. When the opportunity presented itself.

She just hoped that wasn't tonight. She didn't want anything to spoil his homecoming.

BRADY COULDN'T STOP grinning from the moment he left Northwest Arkansas Regional Airport. The air was rich with a hint of wood fires, and the unending foliage took him by surprise after California. Traffic was so light, compared to the coast, that he shook his head in disbelief. It took him all of thirty minutes and a mere three stoplights to reach his condo. He'd told Nell he'd arrive at her place about eight. That would leave him just enough time for a shower and a quick sandwich.

As he let the hot water pour over his shoulders, he sang lustily, feeling happier than he could remember being in a long time. How could he have guessed that the simple act of reading an entry in a guest journal at an Arkansas bed-and-breakfast would change his life? Nell had given him so much. She was gentle and kind and fun. And just unpredictable enough to keep life interesting. He'd bet his last dollar she had no idea the extent to which she turned him on. Well, time would certainly take care of that little problem.

On the way to Nell's, he made a quick stop to pick up a bouquet of daisies. The choice had been easy. They reminded him of her—dainty, yet perky. A natural, refreshing kind of beauty. When he reached her house, he stood a moment on the front porch studying the seasonal wreath, a circle of grapevines decorated with plump, purple artificial grapes and dried leaves. That simple touch left him misty-eyed with a vision of what he could have with Nell.

Yet even with those thoughts, he was unprepared for the wave of feeling that flooded him when she opened the door, her face glowing with a welcoming smile, her slender body reedlike but appropriately rounded in places his fingers itched to explore. "I missed you," he choked out.

When she laid the flowers on the hall table and walked into his waiting arms, he knew this truly was home. "I thought eight o'clock would never come," she whispered.

He looked beyond her, then back into her eyes.

She read his mind. "She's in her room."

"Good," he said just before leaning closer to capture her sweet, full lips and show her with the power of his kiss just how much he'd missed her. That's all it took before his body reacted. He groaned.

"Oh, my," she breathed when she finally managed to step back. "We could be in trouble."

"Bring it on," he growled.

"I'd love to oblige, but there is Abby to consider. What kind of example would we be setting?" Her eyes were playful, but the boundaries had been made clear. She picked up the daisies and nestled them to her chest. "Thank you," she said, then took his hand and led him into the family room, where a plate of brownies and an insulated carafe were waiting. "I thought you might be hungry after your flight."

No way would he tell her he'd just eaten. "Don't mind if I do," he said, helping himself to a brownie.

She busied herself getting a vase for the daisies, then sat beside him on the sofa and poured two cups of coffee.

He took his coffee from her and grinned. "So all we can do is talk?"

"There's nothing wrong with that. It gives me a chance to tell you you're spoiling me. First the bird-of-paradise, and now daisies. A girl could get used to such treatment.''

He set down his cup and moved closer, wrapping an arm around her. "I certainly hope so." He ran a finger down the slope of her nose. "You're worth it."

He couldn't believe it. There was genuine doubt in her eyes, when she faced him. "You think so?"

"I know so," he said, planting a kiss on her forehead.

She relaxed against his arm. "Tell me about your trip."

She was a good listener and he found himself elaborating about his disenchantment with the pretentious and competitive lifestyle he'd once cultivated. "The contrast with Fayetteville is mind-boggling."

In a careful tone, she said, "This isn't paradise, Brady."

"No place is. We make our own heavens and hells."

She tensed, looked at the ceiling, then finally spoke. "Brady, maybe now is a good time to tell you—" But before she could go on, the phone rang, shattering the silence. From her bedroom, Abby hollered, "I'll get it."

Nell seemed somehow...relieved by the interruption. "Cross your fingers that's the new boyfriend calling. She's been agonizing all weekend. There's a school dance this coming Friday and she's dying for him to ask her."

"And he's all of thirteen, right? Trust me, he's scared spitless to invite her for fear she'll turn him

down. Asking a girl for a date is the torture of the
damned for a guy that age.''

''And this is the voice of experience speaking?''

''Yes, ma'am.'' Although the scene forming in his
mind was hardly as innocent as one from *Happy
Days*. Sheryl Clay. He hadn't thought of her in years.
A ninth grader with tits that were the talk of the
junior high locker room. His eighth-grade teammates
had dared him to ask her to a school barn dance and
hayride. ''Screw off, runt,'' she'd said in response to
his stammered invitation. Just one more in the series
of rejections that were the rule rather than the exception when he was growing up.

''Where'd you go just now?'' she asked.

''Nowhere.'' He didn't want to tell her and run the
risk of opening the door to his past again. She'd just
have to understand. That area was hands-off. It
wouldn't do her any good, and it sure as hell
wouldn't benefit him.

''Mom?'' Abby burst into the room with a smile
that made it clear the kid had screwed up his courage.
''It's Alan. He asked me!'' She shrieked with
delight. ''Can I go?'' She went down on one knee.
''Please.''

Nell moved away from Brady and affected mock
sternness. ''Before I give my answer, haven't you
forgotten something?''

Abby looked confused, then turned to Brady. A
light bulb went on. ''Oh, hi, Mr. Logan.''

''It's nice to see you, Abby.'' When he uttered
those words, he realized it really *was* nice to see her.
That he was enjoying the adolescent drama being
played out before his eyes.

Abby wiggled with impatience. "Mom? Can I?"

Nell relented and smiled. "Yes, darling, you may."

"I love you," Abby offered her mother before running down the hall.

"Thank God," Nell breathed. "I wasn't sure how she would handle rejection."

"She's your daughter. She'd have survived." He pulled her closer and played with a lock of her hair. "You know, I just realized something important."

"What's that?"

"When I left California after the accident, I made mental shrines to Brooke and Nicole, not allowing myself to see them as anything other than paragons. Somehow I was able to move beyond Brooke when I met you, but I have to confess Abby was giving me serious difficulty."

"What do you mean?"

"She and Nicole are, uh, were so close in age. Nicole had long blond hair, too. Every time I was with Abby or heard you talk about her, all I could focus on was Nicole. On what I was missing. Being a father was very important to me." He paused to collect his thoughts. "I wasn't totally sure about us, Nell, because I didn't know if I could accept Abby. I knew I needed to, but it wasn't happening."

"And now?"

"Saying goodbye to Nicole and then seeing Abby tonight, so upbeat and excited...I finally realized I can't blame Abby for not being Nicole. And if I shut Abby out, then I lose not only you, but the opportunity to enjoy watching another girl grow up." He could hardly go on. "I don't want to miss out on that. On any of it."

Nell laid a soothing hand on his cheek. "I hope you won't have to."

He nestled her closer. "We're pretty lucky, aren't we?"

"Maybe we have the chance to make our own heaven out of the hells we've been through."

He waited for the pounding of his heart to slow before cupping her face and searching her eyes. "I'm counting on it."

"Brady," she breathed, pulling his head closer and lifting her lips to his.

With the diabolical timing of a twisted film director, the phone rang again. Nell pulled back. "Abby'll get it."

Reluctantly, he moved away. "Guess I'll have to behave. We wouldn't want to be caught in the act."

Nell chuckled. "How does it feel being chaperoned by a thirteen-year-old?"

Before he could answer, true to form, Abby yelled down the hall. "It's for you, Mom. It's your sponsor from AA."

Brady could feel blood eddying in his ears. Surely he hadn't heard Abby right. But the stunned look on Nell's face verified that nothing was wrong with his hearing. "AA?" He stood. There had to be some mistake. Something he was missing. As his gaze homed in on Nell, he was helpless to curb the anger twisting his gut. "What is she talking about?"

Nell turned away to pick up the phone, leaving him alone in the silence of what might well be the second worst moment of his life. "Nell?"

Nell murmured something into the receiver, clicked it off and set it on the coffee table, then faced him, her head bowed. "I was going to tell you."

"Tell me what exactly?"

Threading her fingers together in anguish, she lifted her ravaged eyes. "Brady, I am an alcoholic."

CHAPTER TEN

HIS FACE DRAINED of color and his chest heaving, Brady stared at her, awareness slowly replacing shock. "You've got to be kidding."

Nell summoned her voice somehow. "No, Brady, I'm not."

From his distorted mouth came the ragged parody of a laugh. "Some secret you've been keeping from me." He shook his head in disbelief. "Give me a minute." Then, drawing a shaking hand through his hair, he went to the window where he stood, his back rigid.

Nell had expected him to be surprised and had wondered if he would have trouble accepting her once he knew. But this felt like total rejection. And she had no tools to combat it.

Her forehead beaded with clamminess, and she was afraid she was going to throw up. Swallowing hard, she wiped her damp hands on her slacks, then began speaking, her voice a low monotone. She had no idea whether he would listen, but she had to try. To explain—and confess.

"I know I should have told you sooner. I tried to. Earlier, before Alan called. But it's not the sort of thing you go around announcing to people."

He hadn't moved, except to thrust his balled fists into his pockets.

"For what it's worth, I've been sober for six years."

She could barely hear him mumble, "You want a goddamn prize?"

Her face reddened and her heart pounded double-time. "No, but I wouldn't mind a little understanding."

"That's asking quite a bit."

What had happened to the sensitive, gentle man she'd fallen in love with? This icy stranger was someone she didn't know.

He whirled around. "All right, tell me about it. Tell me how you justify it."

"I don't justify it. Alcoholism can happen to anybody. No one is immune. And it happened to me. It's not something I'm proud of, but it's a fact I live with every day."

"Why?"

Nell recoiled. That one anguished word was as much of a concession to understanding as he was going to make. She wanted to pace, to work out the explanation through movement. But she stayed where she was, rooted in an agony that went beyond any AA testimonial. And so she began—with her history of social drinking, her insecurity, the liquid escape she had sought from her father's death and Rick's unfaithfulness. When she finished, she stared into Brady's implacable eyes. "I'm not asking you to condone what I did, but I'd like to think you could understand. Forgive?" The last word came out tremulously as a question.

He shrugged disgustedly, and in that moment Nell knew they were doomed.

"While you're at it, you may as well tell me the rest."

"The rest?"

"How in some moment of glorious revelation you decided to go to AA."

"Glorious revelation?" She snorted. "I wish. Then I wouldn't have come close to losing Abby."

He stepped toward her, his face even grayer. "What are you talking about?"

"The night Rick delivered the divorce papers, we got into a huge fight. He walked out. Abby overheard us and was semi-hysterical and kept crying 'I want my daddy, I want my daddy.' No amount of vodka numbed her protest, so I decided to take her to Rick and let him see just what a mess he'd made of our lives."

She paused, wishing she didn't have to go on. Brady leaned on the arm of the sofa and waited, his jaw working.

"It was a snowy night. The roads were icy. I...I didn't care." Her voice broke. Clearing her throat, she went on, knowing she had to finish, had to accept every measure of damnation from him. "We got to the car, and I strapped Abby in the back seat. She wouldn't stop howling. I dropped my keys in the snow. How I wish I'd never found them." She stopped, unable to continue.

Brady's eyes were locked on his laced fingers. From down the hall Nell could hear the pinging of pipes. Abby was taking a shower.

"Go on," Brady said like a man condemned to hearing the worst.

"But I did find them, and I started driving toward Clarice's apartment. On these hilly streets, ice is treacherous," she said in grotesque understatement. "I never could remember exactly what happened, which wasn't surprising since I was drunk. I woke up in the hospital." Her eyes moistened with emotion, but she struggled for control. "Abby could've been killed in the accident. Only a matter of inches saved her."

A strangled moan erupted from Brady and he strode again to the window.

Determined to finish, Nell went on. "That's what got my attention. AA saved me."

"How convenient for you."

Shocked, Nell rose to her feet and took a step toward him. She'd never encountered such indifference. "What's that supposed to mean?"

Slowly he faced her, his own cheeks tearstained. He looked devastated, and when he spoke, she had the impression he didn't know or care that she was there.

"That your story has a nice, tidy ending. Happily ever after." He practically choked on bitterness. "Brooke and Nicole weren't so lucky. Their particular drunk driver failed to stop at a highway intersection and he hit them broadside."

"*Their* drunk driver? What do you mean?"

"Just what I said. Don't you get it? The tanker driver had a blood alcohol level well above the limit. Brooke and Nicole weren't as lucky as Abby. As if 'luck' had anything to do with it. People like you and that truck driver never consider anyone else, do you?''

She deserved it—every last ounce of his scorn and fury. Everything he valued in life had been lost because someone else, someone like her, had a consuming thirst that blinded him to anything but his own needs for self-gratification or escape. What could she say? Finally, she heard herself mumble, ''I'm sorry. I'd undo it if I could.''

''You can't, Nell.'' He started for the front door, then hesitated and turned around. ''I'm sorry, too. I thought we had something magical. I guess I'm not as good a judge of character as I thought.''

After he left, emptiness echoed throughout the house. She should've known better than to trust that she'd be given a second chance. Reentering the family room, she looked wildly around, trying to beat back a desperate craving for alcohol. *Brady, Brady, Brady.* She couldn't stop repeating his name or gasping with the painful knowledge of the wound she'd opened up in him tonight. And in herself.

For something, anything, to do except grab her keys, dash to the liquor store and drown the fear lodged in her throat, she picked a daisy from the bouquet Brady had brought her earlier, when things had been happy, promising.

One by one she plucked each petal. ''He loves me, he loves me not, he loves me…''

Finally one last petal remained. Why was she surprised? ''He loves me not.''

She collapsed on the sofa, stifling her wrenching sobs with the overstuffed pillow, knowing she had hurt him beyond repair.

But that didn't mean she'd stopped loving him. She couldn't.

CLUTCHING THE STEERING WHEEL like a lifeline, Brady threaded his way through the light traffic on Fayetteville's main drag. Flashing neon lights were nothing more than a haze in his peripheral vision. *Goddammit, goddammit!* With the flat of his hand, he pounded the wheel. He wanted to kick a wall, drive his fist through a pane of glass, anything to obliterate the pain holding him captive.

He still couldn't believe it. He forced himself to repeat Nell's words over and over in his brain. *I am an alcoholic.*

Before, he'd only wondered if God had a malicious streak, now he knew for sure. Enraged, he shook his fist. "You listening up there? Okay, you win. I cry 'Uncle.'"

Of all the things Nell could have done to destroy him, this was the worst. Had it been only a few hours ago he'd considered her unpredictability interesting?

What an ass he was! Thinking that by reading some sappy entry in a B-and-B journal he could find true love. Happiness. Oh, yeah, happiness. Like there was any such thing.

I am an alcoholic. Why hadn't he seen it coming? She didn't drink, her husband had walked out. All the pieces had been there, but he'd painted her as he'd wanted her to be, as he'd needed her to be. The sweet, fun-loving Nell he thought he knew was merely the projection of his own lonely imagination.

He'd thought he was doing a great thing by loving her, restoring her damaged sense of her desirability.

But what was that all about? Had she been using him? He'd read somewhere that alcoholics could be manipulative. Had she been playing him?

Beneath his anger, he knew he was raving. That he was doing Nell a disservice with such cynicism. But he had no outlet for the force of his anger and disillusionment. For…name it…his desolation.

First Brooke and Nicole. Now Nell and Abby. Lost.

Eventually he became more aware of his surroundings. He was in the old-fashioned town square, symbolic of everything he'd come to love about the town—the slower pace, friendlier people, simpler lifestyle.

But was it all based on an illusion? Wishful thinking? Without Nell, could he be happy here?

He grunted. He couldn't be happy anywhere.

That being the case, what did it matter whether it was California or Arkansas? Neither could be *home*.

It was well after midnight when he finally gave up and returned to his condo. The forlorn, repetitive hoot of an owl accompanied him as he walked from his parking space to his door. The musty smell of stale pipe smoke assailed him when he stepped inside. In the moonlight streaming through the windows, he made out the boxy forms of the antique furniture his landlord prized.

In that moment, he was seized by an intense aversion to the place. What the hell was he doing here? From the Edgewater Inn until tonight, had he been living in a fantasy world? Damn, it was as if he had no grip on who he was anymore.

He flicked on the desk lamp and pushed the Play button on the answering machine.

"Hey, buddy, it's Carl. You should be back in Arkansas by now. Since you've been home to California, maybe Fayetteville won't look so good. I know you. You can't stay away. Lemme know when you're comin' back. Bring your Nell if you want to. She'll love it here."

Your Nell. He couldn't blame Carl. That's how he himself used to think of her, dream of her.

The machine played the second message. "Brady, Buzz Valentine. Good news. The option on the land went through fine, but beyond that, I had a call from one of the company executives you spoke with about the conference center. He not only thinks it's a great idea, but his firm wants to consider investing in it. Looks like you're on your way."

Brady hit Rewind and listened to the chuckling of the tape feeding through the mechanism.

Malicious or not, God had a great sense of humor. Now Brady had two choices for his future.

Neither held any appeal.

In the core of his heart, he knew why.

Neither involved Nell.

OBLIVIOUS TO the late afternoon sun filtering through the giant oak and maple trees, Abby pedaled as hard as she could down the hill, through the park and up Tonya's street. She hadn't risked talking to Tonya at school. Someone might have overheard. But she had to tell somebody. The lump in her throat just kept growing. In algebra, when the teacher called on her, she'd been afraid she'd burst into tears and make a complete fool of herself.

This morning her mother had tried to act like everything was normal. Abby didn't have to be a genius to know it wasn't. Red-rimmed eyes, pale skin, a fake laugh, trembling fingers. In a shaky voice Mom had explained that Brady hadn't known about AA until she'd shouted it down the hall. Well, how was she supposed to know it was still a big, dark secret? Even so, she had tried to apologize, but her mother had waved her hands and said in a broken voice, "Let's not talk about last night. Or about Brady. It wasn't your fault." Then Mom had hugged her and whispered, "It was my responsibility, not yours." But that hadn't made her feel any better.

Abby drew in deep lungfuls of air as she skidded to a stop in the Larkins' driveway. She could kill that Brady Logan!

It took five minutes of chitchat with Tonya's mother before the girls could escape to Tonya's bedroom. Mrs. Larkin had forced a sugar cookie on Abby, but she could hardly choke it down. Now she sat curled up in Tonya's beanbag chair, while her friend settled on the floor, leaning against the footboard of her bed, her legs stretched out in front of her.

"Okay, Abby. What's up?"

Abby hugged her knees to her chest. "Oh, God, Tonya, I'm so scared."

"Scared?"

Abby could feel the soft denim of her jeans beneath her fingers, smell the faint scent of fabric softener. "It's Mom."

"What happened?"

All day she'd been waiting to tell Tonya, but now that the time had come, she had trouble beginning. "It's all my fault."

"What is?"

"Mom and Mr. Logan."

Not unkindly, Tonya said, "Earth to Abby. Come in, please. You're not making any sense."

Abby told Tonya about the phone call from Ben Hadley and how she'd mentioned AA in front of Mr. Logan. About how her mom hadn't told him she was an alcoholic.

"What happened then?"

Abby shrugged. "I don't know exactly."

"So what do you think?"

"They must've talked a while, 'cuz I heard him leave later. I waited for Mom to come to bed, but she never did. At least not before I fell asleep. You shoulda seen her this morning. She looked like somebody with a bad case of the flu."

Tonya scooted forward and crossed her legs. "So whaddya think happened?"

"Nothing good. I think maybe he broke up with her."

"Jeez."

"What if she was in love with him?"

"Do you think she was?"

Abby laid her chin on her knees and considered the question before saying, "Yeah, I'm pretty sure. And I messed it up. Totally."

"It wasn't your fault he didn't know she's an alcoholic. A recovering one," Tonya hastily added.

"She was prob'ly going to tell him."

"Sure."

"She was really unhappy this morning. I'm so afraid, Tonya. What if she starts to drink again?"

"You gotta do something."

Abby felt like she might be sick. "What?"

Tonya raised her hands helplessly. "I dunno. Something to fix it."

Like the answer to a prayer, an idea began to take shape in Abby's head. "Maybe she wouldn't drink if—"

"If what?"

Abby continued, thinking aloud. "If she loves Brady, she needs to get him back. Then she'll be happy. When she's happy, she doesn't drink."

"Yeah, but—"

Abby leaped to her feet and began prowling around the room. "I could, like, find out where he lives and go visit him. Tell him how miserable Mom is. How it was all my fault. How she would've told him herself if only I hadn't opened my big mouth."

"It could work."

She stopped in the middle of the room. "How'll I find out where he lives?"

"I guess you'll have to ask your mom."

Abby felt deflated. She didn't want to watch her mother's reaction when she mentioned Brady Logan to her. "Crap. I guess it's not such a good idea after all."

All the way home on her bike, she felt queasy. She ought to be able, somehow, to make things come out right. She arrived home before her mother and went straight to the trash can to see if there were any empty bottles. None.

She should be relieved. Instead, she felt this tight-ness like the whole situation was about to get worse.

She went to her room and lay down on her bed. She unbuttoned her jeans, wishing the full feeling would go away, but knowing it wouldn't until she did something.

Okay, what would it hurt? She'd ask her mother about Brady Logan.

NELL CHASTISED HERSELF on the way home from work. She'd been barely functional, and it hadn't es-caped Reggie's watchful eye. He'd seemed more concerned than upset, but she couldn't risk disap-pointing her boss. She loved her job. She'd need it now more than ever. To keep her sane. To keep her from jeopardizing her sobriety.

More than anything, she'd longed to lose herself in an alcoholic blur. To have a few blessed hours when she could forget the anguish and judgment written on Brady's face. To block out the awful knowledge that his family had been killed by a drunk driver. By association, she was as guilty in his mind as if she'd been in the cab of that rig.

As she turned in her driveway, she sucked in a sob. She'd lost Brady, and it was a pain even deeper than Rick's defection, which, if she was honest, had contained an element of relief.

She sat for a moment summoning her acting skills. No way did she want to inflict her disappointment and pain on Abby. But this morning that's exactly what she'd done. Bless the girl's heart. It hadn't been her fault. Ben often called. Abby knew him. It had been a natural thing for Abby to say. Besides, in her heart Nell knew she should have told Brady long ago.

She'd been living in violation of the Twelve Steps. She was back to Step Four—''Make a searching and fearless moral inventory.'' Bottom line, she'd been both self-indulgent and dishonest. She'd call Ben later tonight, talk about the situation—and about her temptation to drink.

Now, though, she had to face Abby. Reassure her.

She found her daughter in the kitchen in the throes of trying to make spaghetti, her efforts clearly a peacemaking gesture. Boiling water had splattered over the stove top and Nell noted the red trail from the empty can of tomatoes to the pot of simmering sauce. ''Hi, honey, have a good day?''

''Not really.'' Like the countertop, Abby's gray Razorbacks sweatshirt sported splotches of red.

Nell tried a joke. ''Was Alan absent?''

Abby threw her a get-real look. ''No. He was fine.'' She ducked her head, stirring the pasta with a vengeance. ''I was worried about you. You know, about what I said. I just figured Mr. Logan knew.''

Nell moved to the stove and put her arm around Abby's waist. ''No, honey, he didn't. But that was a natural assumption. I should have told him long before last night.''

''Was he mad?''

''Disappointed.'' Nell sighed internally. Above all, she didn't want Abby assuming ill-placed guilt. ''There was something I didn't know about the accident that killed his wife and daughter. Something that explains why Brady couldn't accept that I am a recovering alcoholic.''

Abby moved to the spice rack, as if to avoid proximity to her mother. "What?" she asked, reaching for the oregano.

"The accident that killed his wife and daughter was caused by a drunk driver."

Abby clutched the spice jar, her face draining of color. "How?"

"The man was driving a loaded gasoline tanker. He ran a stop sign at a highway intersection and he broadsided them." Nell swallowed several times, the words assuming even more horrible proportions when she uttered them herself.

"That's awful!" Abby's eyes were wide. "His daughter, how old was she?"

"About your age."

Nell watched Abby process the information, the enormity of it sinking in. Finally, Abby returned to the stove and sprinkled oregano over the sauce.

Nell struggled onward. "Brady wasn't prepared for me to be an alcoholic. Neither of us would have been as hurt if I'd been honest from the beginning. So, in a way, you did me a favor last night." She paused, then tilted her daughter's chin so she could look into her eyes. "Never for one minute should you blame yourself. This is my fault, mine alone."

"I guess." Abby tested the pasta, then nudged Nell aside as she carried the steamer pot to the sink. Carefully she poured off the water and slid the spaghetti into a bowl. Neither of them said anything until after Abby had added the sauce. Then Abby turned to face Nell. "I haven't treated Mr. Logan very well. I didn't know about how it happened. I think I'd like to write him, like, a sympathy note or something."

Overcome with relief and pride in her daughter, Nell smiled. "I think that would be very thoughtful."

"Okay. Could you give me his address, then?"

"Sure." Nell pulled a sheet off the grocery list pad and wrote down the information. Maybe writing Brady would give Abby a sense of closure.

As for herself? She didn't believe anything could ever do that.

SHORTLY AFTER SCHOOL the next afternoon Abby and Tonya met at the picnic pavilion in the park. Abby straddled her bike while Tonya sat on the top of a picnic table. "I can't believe you got his address so easily."

"Me neither. The idea just came to me." Abby couldn't admit to her friend how low she felt about saying she'd write a sympathy note. Her mother had made out like she was some sort of junior saint.

"What are you going to say to him?"

"I dunno. What if he isn't even there?"

"I guess you'll have to keep trying."

The pain in Abby's stomach gripped her. Trying this once was bad enough. She couldn't imagine having to do it again. "Maybe he won't even talk to me."

Tonya tossed her head. "He will. Adults always try harder with kids. Makes 'em feel good."

"You won't tell?"

"Of course not." Abby started to interrupt, but Tonya kept right on. "I know, if your mom calls, I'm supposed to say you're in the bathroom or something, right?"

"Right. She'd kill me if she knew I was going to his apartment."

"But you gotta try."

Abby hunched over the handlebars. "Yeah."

Tonya stood up and put a hand on Abby's shoulder. "Well, go on then. You haven't got all day."

Abby straightened and blew out a breath, wishing the panicky ache would go away. She was afraid. What if she failed? "Okay." Bracing herself on one foot, she put the other on the pedal.

"Call me the minute you get home."

"I will." Then Abby shoved off, hoping she could get this whole ordeal over with in a hurry.

Ten minutes later, she sailed down a hill and coasted into the parking lot of the Devonshire Village condominiums. The third building displayed the number she was looking for. She slid off the bike, set the kickstand and looked around. Her heart sank. His SUV was there. In the parking lot. In a way she'd hoped it wouldn't be. Hoped she wouldn't have to face him.

But then she thought about her mother. She needed to be happy. And if Brady Logan was what it took for that to happen, Abby was prepared to help things along. No matter what had happened since, she couldn't forget the way her mother and Mr. Logan had looked at each other when they thought no one was watching.

Wiping her hands along the sides of her jeans, she tried to ignore the scared feeling she had. *Just do it,* she said under her breath, the slogan providing her with the motivation she needed.

She lifted her fist and knocked on his door, convinced he would be able to hear her heart thudding as well.

When the door opened, he seemed taller than she remembered, wearing a navy T-shirt, gray sweatpants and running shoes. His eyes, like her mother's, were bloodshot and his hair was all rumpled. "Abby?" He stepped back. "What can I do for you?"

"We need to talk," she said, sounding even to herself like a character in some dumb soap opera.

He tried to smile, but she could tell he wasn't quite succeeding. "Okay. Come on in."

He ushered her into a living room with all this weird grandma furniture and these crazy framed drawings all over the wall. It wasn't what she'd pictured at all.

He'd apparently observed her reaction because he said, "Looks like a room straight out of Harry Potter, doesn't it?"

She ran a hand across a sofa upholstered in this scratchy fabric that felt like a buzz cut. "Did you pick it out?" That was as polite as she could think to be.

He chuckled then, a sound that filled her with relief. He wasn't going to be mad. "No way. I'm leasing the apartment from one of the professors at the university."

"It smells funny in here."

"Hard not to notice, isn't it?" He gestured to a chair, and she sat down, perching on the edge of the seat. "Could I get you a soda?"

She needed time to think. "Uh, yes. Thank you. That would be good."

"Root beer okay?"

"Sure."

While he was in the kitchen, she studied the creepy condo, noticing all kinds of blueprints and plans spread out on a big table. Should she talk about his family's accident first? About her mother? She rubbed her stomach, worry sitting there like a barbell.

He was smiling when he came back into the room. "Here," he said, handing her a can of root beer. For himself, he had a mug of coffee. He sat across from her in an ugly recliner. "Does your mother know you're here?"

Abby shook her head. "No."

"Shouldn't she?"

"She might not like why I came."

He cradled his mug between his fingers. "Why is that?"

She stared at the steam rising from his coffee. "Because she says it's not my fault, but it was." This wasn't coming out the way she'd intended. She'd meant to start with how sorry she was about his family, but now they were already into the hard part.

"Spilling the beans, you mean?"

"Yeah." Abby squirmed. "I mean, she was going to tell you. She would have. I know she would. But—" She felt an uncomfortable shift in her abdomen.

"She didn't. I hope you understand how that news hit me."

"Mom told me about the accident." She hurried the next part. "I'm so sorry about your wife and daughter. I guess you have a reason to hate alcoholics, but Mom isn't like that.'' She slurped some root beer, trying to moisten her dry, gritty mouth.

He looked up over the lip of his mug, raised his eyebrows and simply said, ''Really?''

Abby fidgeted, feeling all gooshy inside. ''No, she's not. She's worked so hard to stay sober. She's a wonderful mother and people like her and she's trying so hard never to drink again. And you make her happy. If you're not there, I don't know what'll happen and—'' Abby stopped, her face flushing. Something damp was between her legs. Had she spilled the root beer? Slowly she looked down. Nothing. ''I wanna fix things. Please don't hold AA against her. Please don't leave her. She really, really likes you. A lot.''

She ran out of breath and only then did she fully focus on the realization that she might have wet her pants. How embarrassing!

''Abby, I appreciate your defense of your mother and the courage it took to come see me, but—''

Abby jumped to her feet. '''Scuze me, Mr. Logan. Where's the bathroom?''

He stood. ''Are you all right?''

She crossed her legs in anguish. ''I don't know.''

''There. Down the hall on the right.''

''Sorry, I'll be right back,'' she said, scuttling to the bathroom.

She closed the door quickly, then unbuttoned her jeans and started to sit on the commode. What she saw on her panties majorly grossed her out—and humiliated her. Slowly she sank down. She wouldn't be coming right back. She couldn't. She would be spending the rest of her life right here in this bathroom.

Angry tears coursed down her cheeks. No way! Not here. Not now. What was she supposed to do?

All her mother's lovey-dovey reassurances about becoming a woman were nothing but a crock. She buried her head in her hands.

No way had her period started at Brady Logan's.

CHAPTER ELEVEN

BRADY WAITED, uncomfortably aware that several minutes had passed. He hoped to God nothing was wrong. The poor kid. It took guts to come here and assume the blame for what had gone wrong with his and Nell's relationship. Abby must really be worried about her mother. The urgency in her voice as she appealed to him made him feel like a cad. Yet Nell wasn't the one wronged. He was.

He swallowed the last of his coffee. It was already cool. He glanced at his watch. How long had Abby been in the bathroom anyway? She didn't wear much makeup, so odds were she wasn't spending all this time primping.

Maybe she was sick. He stood and paced around the room. He should probably check on her. Make sure she was all right. He walked down the hall and paused outside the bathroom door, listening. Nothing.

Then he heard a sound, like a muffled giggle—or sob. A sense of impending dread filled him. He rapped on the door. "Abby, are you okay?"

The silence was pregnant. Then in a small voice he heard her say, "No."

"Are you sick? What do you need?" He was in way over his head here. He remembered taking care of Nicole when she was tiny, but as she grew older, Brooke was always the one who dealt with illness.

"I'm not sick."

"Did I say something to upset you?"

"No. Could you, uh, could you call my mother? Ask her to come get me?"

"I could take you home, honey."

"No!" Her reaction was sharp and immediate.

It was then he knew. Girl stuff. He closed his eyes, remembering Brooke's recounting to him her mother-daughter talk with Nicole. Nicole had thought becoming a woman sounded "icky," but she could see it might be worth it if someday you could have a baby. He shut down the memory and spoke encouragingly through the door. "It's all right. I'll call your mother. I'll be right back."

He didn't want to do this. Didn't want to hear Nell's voice again. Didn't want the interaction that must follow. He needed their connection severed cleanly. But like everything else in Abby's life, this wasn't her fault either. He picked up the phone and dialed the familiar number.

Their conversation was mercifully businesslike. Holding his emotions in check, he explained the reason Abby had come on her own to see him. Before Nell had time to react, he went on to tell her he suspected Abby had started her period and that she needed her mother. Nell told him this was Abby's first time and promised to come right over.

He set down the phone, feeling totally at sea. What could he do for Abby? If she were Nicole, what would he have done? Said? Finally he went back down the hall and hunkered outside the door. "Abby?"

"Yeah?"

"Your mother's on her way. You're sure you're all right till she gets here?"

Abby's voice sounded forlorn. "Yes."

He'd never been female, of course, but it was likely the kid was scared to death. Probably no amount of sex education could prepare an adolescent girl for this moment.

"Good. I'm going to stay right here with you until she comes." When she didn't answer, he started talking, saying anything he could think of to soothe her. "I believe I know what's happened to you today, and it's the most natural thing in the world, although I can imagine it's a bit scary, too. If you were Nicole, that was my daughter's name," he explained, "I'd be so proud and yet I'd feel kind of sorry for myself at the same time because it would mean my girl had begun to grow up. That's an awesome realization for a father. We dads think we're the only ones who can protect and care for our daughters. And next thing you know, some guy's come along and married our little girl."

"Could you, I mean would you, tell me about her? Nicole?"

He rocked back and sat on the floor, his head in his hands. He had to clear his throat twice before he could begin. "You remind me of her. She had long blond hair like yours, but her eyes were brown, like pancake syrup. She enjoyed swimming and boating. Best of all, she loved horseback riding." A momentary image stabbed him. Nicole clearing her first jump in a horse show, the grin that creased her face even as she concentrated on the next barrier.

"Did she have her own horse?"

"Sure did. Belle was a honey of a chestnut mare."

"I've never been horseback riding."

He started to say they'd have to do something about that, then checked himself. He was merely getting Abby through these next few moments. After that, he'd never see her again. "It's a lot of fun. Nicole was just beginning to like boys, too. Do you have a boyfriend?" He knew she did, but figured he needed to get her mind off her problem.

"Kinda."

"What's his name?"

"Alan. He plays football." She hesitated. "I'm going with him to the school dance tomorrow night."

"Well, he must be a bright young man to choose you."

She stammered, "I...I, uh, thanks, Mr. Logan."

"Brady," he corrected. "Are you feeling better?"

"A little. I'm so embarrassed."

"Please don't be. I feel kind of privileged to be here with you. I was robbed of that opportunity with my own daughter. It feels right to be celebrating this milestone with you."

"Really?" Her voice seemed stronger.

"You bet. I like you, Abby. If Nicole had lived and you two had met, I think you would have been friends." He hesitated, debating his next words. "You know, I used to resent you."

"You did?"

"You reminded me so much of Nicole I couldn't stand the pain. But I was wrong. Instead of bad times, you remind me of good times with her and of new things she and I might have shared.''

"I'm glad," she said softly just as he heard a knock on the door.

"I think your mother's here.''

"Good.''

He had just risen to his feet when he thought he heard her speak again. "Did you say something, Abby?''

"Yes. I've been so scared, but you talking to me really helped. Thanks for understanding.''

Hell. His eyes grew filmy. He took a handkerchief out of his pocket and blew his nose. The girl had touched a chord no one had reached since Nicole. Nell should be very proud of her daughter. She was quite a young lady.

He grinned crookedly. Given today's events, that described her exactly.

ARRIVING AT THE CONDO, Nell had greeted Brady with cursory thanks, attended to Abby, then whisked her out to her car. Brady had offered to follow in his SUV with Abby's bicycle.

But he wasn't in any hurry now as he approached Nell's street. He didn't want to be sucked into this family event. Didn't want to endure the torture of looking at Nell with his newly opened eyes. An alcoholic. Worse yet, one who had nearly killed her daughter. Well, he hoped she knew how damn lucky she was.

Something about Abby had touched deeply buried paternal feelings. She'd had her share of loss along the way, too. Considering her parents' divorce, her father's remarriage and Nell's drinking, the kid was actually pretty well adjusted. Helpless to make things right for her today, he'd felt sorry for her and disappointed in himself. She'd been so sincere in her defense of her mother. So vulnerable in her distress and embarrassment. Before she left with Nell, he'd had to fight the impulse to gather the girl in a fatherly embrace. How funny. Now that he could accept Abby, a relationship with Nell had become unthinkable.

He pulled into Nell's driveway. He'd given them a half-hour head start, figuring they needed a little mother-daughter time. He turned off the ignition, went to the back of the vehicle and extricated the bicycle, carrying it into the garage, which Nell had left open, probably for that purpose.

He could leave now. Let it be over. But maybe he owed Nell a further explanation of Abby's visit. He didn't want the girl getting into trouble. Not on his account.

Reluctantly, he strolled to the front door and knocked.

"Come in," Nell said when she answered the door. "I guess we need to talk about this." She started toward the family room.

He trailed behind her, wishing he were anywhere else but here. "How is she?"

She shrugged, then gestured for him to sit on the sofa. "Embarrassed, excited, scared."

He took the indicated seat and watched as she deliberately moved to the other side of the room. Silhouetted against the last light of the setting sun, Nell, perched on the edge of the rocker, sat in shadow.

Her cheekbones stood in sharp relief, accentuating dark smudges under her eyes. She wore a pink boat-necked sweater that revealed her collarbone, rigid beneath her soft, pale skin. Brady was having a hard time remembering what she was to him. "Abby's not in trouble?" he finally asked.

"She was too upset about starting her period at your place, although she said you were very understanding. I decided there would be time later to talk about why she came to see you."

"She feels responsible, Nell."

"What do you mean?"

"She thinks if she hadn't assumed I knew your history, that everything would be all right between us. She was trying to fix our relationship."

Nell rubbed the arms of the rocker with her palms, then sighed, a forlorn sound that stabbed Brady in the gut. "No chance of that, I guess."

He forced himself to think about Brooke and Nicole and the agent of their deaths. "No. How could I ever trust you?"

She looked stricken. "You couldn't unless you could forgive not only me, but others who have wronged you."

He stood. "Well, you can forget that."

She raised her eyes. "How far back does your bitterness go, Brady? Isn't it hard to keep slamming doors on people just because they're human and they've failed you?"

A blood vessel in his temple throbbed. "What's that supposed to mean?"

"There's got to be a reason you won't talk about your upbringing. Your family."

"Look, how many times do I have to tell you? That is none of your business."

"Maybe not. But since it no longer matters what I say, I'd like to suggest you can't control the world, especially one in which other people occasionally make a mistake."

"Mistake? Is that what you call nearly killing your daughter?"

Nell, face aflame, rose to her feet. "Don't you think I relive that horror every day of my life? That I haven't spent years acknowledging that fact and attempting to make amends? At least I don't try going it alone in this world."

"What's that supposed to mean?"

"Brady, believe it or not, you're not in charge. I'm not in charge. There *is* a higher power in our lives. When we accept that reality, troubles don't disappear, but life can become more bearable."

If she wasn't a woman, he'd have decked her. He could remember few times he had been so angry. "How dare you spout that AA crap to me?"

"At this point, I have nothing to lose with you. And what I see is this. You, my friend, are every bit as addicted as I am."

"The hell you say. I'm not the one who solves my problems by swilling down booze like it's water."

She clutched herself around the waist, as if restraining herself within some emotional boundary. "No. You solve problems by running away. First from your home and family in Colorado. Then from California. Now, from me." She moved a step closer, her eyes glittering with tears. "Oh, yes. You're addicted. To anger and resentment and guilt."

She stopped to catch her breath, then went on. "You can make fun of AA if you want to, but living those Twelve Steps has saved me and, pray God, will continue to save me. You know, you just might try them yourself."

"Slim chance of that."

"What's the worst thing that could happen? Would it be so terrible to admit to God and someone else the nature of your wrongs? To ask God to help? To make amends to those you've hurt?" She paused, her tone softening. "To find peace through a spiritual awakening? That's what the Twelve Steps are about, and, trust me, they'll work for you, too."

Brady had stood there throughout her lecture, jaws aching from gritting his teeth in anger and denial. Now he loomed over her. "Are you quite finished?"

"Yes, I believe I am. Except for one thing."

He made a mocking out-with-it gesture. "Well, please give me the benefit of the entire spiel."

She laid one small hand on his chest and looked up at him with brimming eyes. Her whisper was barely audible. "I love you, Brady."

He stared at her, his facial muscles paralyzed. What a cheap shot. "Sorry, Nell, you can lay that on me if you want, but no way am I going to assume that guilt on top of all the others you accuse me of." He moved toward the door. "Tell Abby she's a beautiful young woman." He grasped the doorknob, then let go of it to face her one final time. His tone was steely. "Goodbye, Nell."

At his car, he braced himself against the cool metal of the driver's door and sucked in deep breaths of air. He couldn't believe it. By accusing him was she trying to justify her own actions? And what was that last bit about? *I love you, Brady.*

He seethed. *Too damn bad, lady.*

He climbed in the SUV and started toward home, furious with her and with his stupid eyes that insisted on watering. Lady. He laughed derisively. Oh, yeah. Lady. His rainbow lady, who believed in miracles.

Well, Nell could continue to dwell in fantasy land if she chose, but he was totally out of miracles. Love was nothing more than an illusion. No steps, not twelve or twelve hundred, could fix that.

THE DEFINITIVE CLICK of the door shutting behind Brady reminded Nell of the sound of a cork being pulled from a wine bottle. Leaning her back against the door, she rubbed her face with the palms of her hands. *Please God. Don't let me think like that.* It was bad enough he'd walked out of her life, but why was wine—that deep, rich, mellow palliative—her first thought as an antidote for the hollow ache gnawing at her?

Quaking with an onslaught of emotions, she walked back into the family room and sank onto the sofa, holding a pillow against her chest for comfort. He hadn't blinked an eye when she'd told him she loved him. Why had she thought that would make a difference? Yet it was the truth. And for too long she'd withheld truths from him.

The room, nearly dark now, matched her mood. He would never be able to accept her. Even if she remained sober the rest of her days. He was a hard man.

A hurting man.

Sinking her teeth into her fingers simply to experience a pain she could control, she tried to hold back the flood gathering in her throat. She'd said awful things. Hurtful things.

A sob erupted. Then another. Finally she gave in and let the storm come. Her body shook with the force of her loss.

All she wanted was to love him. He needed love so badly.

But she was an alcoholic.

Like a tide, all the old feelings of worthlessness and despair swept over her. She would never be good enough. Sober enough.

Through her tears, she licked her lips, picturing the outlines of a fine bottle of wine, the contents beckoning her with cobralike charm. She pulled up her legs, gripping her knees, then rocked back and forth. *Don't do it. Don't do it.*

Suddenly she heard Abby's bedroom door open. Nell scrambled in her pocket for a tissue and quickly wiped her eyes.

"Mom? Aren't you late for your meeting?" Abby flipped on the lights.

Nell blinked at the onslaught of brightness. The meeting. The nighttime women's AA group she attended every week. The one she'd also missed last week. She was getting careless. Dizzy with fear, she set the pillow aside and looked up at her daughter. "Yes. I...I thought you might need me tonight."

"Mo-om. I'm okay. It's not that big a deal. Like you said, I'll get used to having periods. Anyway, you know how worried I've been. Like maybe I was a freak or something."

"Oh, honey, you're not a freak."

"It was kinda weird, though, being at Brady's." Amazingly, her face lit up. "He told me to call him that. He's really pretty cool, you know."

Nell didn't trust herself to speak.

"Did you guys get everything fixed up?"

Nell felt as if all the air in her lungs had disappeared in a single whoosh. She patted the seat beside her. "Sit down."

Abby wrinkled her nose questioningly, but sat beside her mother. "I'm not gonna like this, am I?"

"Probably not. For what it's worth, honey, neither do I." She tried to clear the frog in her throat. "I don't think we'll be seeing Brady anymore."

"But I thought if I told him how much you like him and everything…"

"I appreciate what you tried to do. But it was too late. He can't accept the fact that I'm an alcoholic."

Abby glowed with indignation. "But you're not really."

Nell put her arm around her daughter and drew her close. "Oh, but I am, Abby. And you must never forget it. I have a disease, just like people who are victims of high blood pressure or tuberculosis. My body cannot tolerate alcohol. Not even one drink. How Brady chooses to react to that fact is his business."

Nell saw the pain in Abby's eyes. "But, Mom, you love him, don't you?"

Nell kissed the top of her daughter's head. Then after a few moments of silence, she said, "Yes, Abby, I do."

"So what're you gonna do?"

With a finality that turned her to stone, Nell said, "There's nothing I can do."

Straightening so she could look squarely at her mother, Abby said, "You won't start drinking again, will you?"

Nell took a deep breath. "I won't have a drink tonight."

"But that's not good enough. What about the rest of the time?"

"Tonight is as much as I can promise, Abby. You know how it goes. One day at a time."

If Abby only knew how hard it was going to be these next few minutes, hours. This one night. Brady's rejection had left a hole in her heart no amount of liquor could fill.

But the wine remained a temptation. One she had to overcome. Somehow.

ABBY CLUTCHED Tonya's arm the next morning as they stood outside the school waiting for the warning bell. "I thought I was gonna die!"

"I would have," Tonya said. "They'd have had to carry me outta there feet first."

"It's funny, though. You know, in a way, it was easier starting my period there than being at my dad's and having Clarice flutter around like I'd broken one of her precious pinkie nails."

"But what did you say to Mr. Logan?"

"I didn't have to say anything. He guessed. Then he was cool and talked about his dead daughter almost like I was a grown-up."

"But what about why you went there? Did you

have a chance to tell him about how your mom likes him?''

Pulling Tonya along with her, Abby moved into the shadow of the building, avoiding a group of preppy girls who loitered nearby, almost as if they were eavesdropping. ''I thought everything was gonna be cool when he came over to our house afterward.'' She swallowed hard. ''But it wasn't. Mom told me later he wouldn't be coming to see us anymore.''

''Why not?''

Abby warmed slightly with her friend's empathetic indignation. ''Um, he can't deal with Mom.''

''Whaddya mean?''

''Her being—'' Abby squirmed, hating the word ''—an alcoholic.''

''But she doesn't drink now.''

''I guess he thinks she could, though.''

''Well, could she?''

Abby clutched her book bag like an anchor. ''I don't know. She was pretty upset after he left. It scared me.''

''What are you gonna do?''

Feeling helpless and very alone, Abby shrugged. ''I don't know.''

The warning bell interrupted their conversation and they joined other students entering the building. Tonya took off down the hall toward the art room. Abby headed for social studies, wondering what, if anything, she *could* do.

Halfway through the first-period discussion of forms of government, an answer came. She dug in her purse to see if she had the right change. She could make the call at noon.

Grandma and Aunt Lily needed to know about her mother. Surely they could cheer Mom up, keep her from drinking.

Only, if she phoned them, then Aunt Lily would prob'ly talk to her, like she always did, about going to Alateen meetings.

What was the matter with adults anyway? It was hard enough being a kid and worrying about boy-friends and zits and stupid homework without having Brady and her mother screw up not only their own lives but hers as well!

NELL HAD NOT BEEN happy when her mother called at work and asked her to stop by the house on her way home. She'd hardly slept at all last night and they'd had a frantic day at the library. She looked like a walking ad for an insomniac's convention. The last thing she needed was to fall under maternal scru-tiny. But there had been no putting Stella off, and truth to tell, she hadn't seen her mother lately. She couldn't even use Abby as an excuse. Before she'd left for school this morning, Abby had told her there was an after-school chorus rehearsal and that Mrs. Larkin would pick them up afterward. Nell needed to be home in time to help Abby get ready for her big date with Alan, but that wasn't for a couple of hours.

Nor did she have any excuse for missing her morn-ing AA meeting. Yet facing all those knowing people and having them see right through her was more than she could handle on top of Brady's final words.

The carefully landscaped Victorian home sat on a deep lot near downtown. As Nell walked up the steps and onto the wrap-around porch, she remembered her dad and his teasing comments. ''Your mother talked me into this drafty old barn. Lord, we could've bought three houses for what it's cost to fix up this place.'' And yet he'.d loved the project. Nell smiled wistfully, remembering happy hours she'd spent helping him in the garage workshop, where sawdust and radio coverage of the Razorbacks kept the two of them company as they worked.

Nell gave a quick rap on the front door, then walked on in. The music system was playing a soft classical piano selection, and from the library, she heard voices. Two of them.

Lily was here, too.

All Nell wanted was to get this ordeal behind her as quickly as possible. ''Anybody home?''

''In here, Nell,'' Stella called.

Entering the richly paneled room, Nell noticed that both her mother and sister had goblets of…surely soda or tea, not wine. She couldn't face the temptation of wine. Lily rose to her feet and spread her arms in the invitation to a hug. Nell stepped into her arms, relieved by the faint lemony scent on her sister's breath.

Stepping out of Lily's embrace, Nell dropped a kiss on her mother's head. Stella smiled, then asked, ''Coffee, tea or a soda, Nell?''

She didn't want anything. At least none of what had been offered, but she needed something to hold on to. ''Is the coffee made?'' When her mother nodded, Nell said, ''I'll get it.''

In the quiet of the kitchen she leaned for a moment against the counter, summoning the strength to get her through the next few minutes. After pouring a cup of coffee, she pasted a smile on her face, returned to the library and sat in the wingback chair facing the leather couch where the other two sat.

"The yard looks nice, Mother."

Stella set down her drink. "Nathan does a good job with it. Not as good as your father did, of course, but widows can't be choosy."

"We should all be so lucky as to have a Nathan," Lily said, with a chuckle.

"How's my granddaughter these days? I haven't seen much of her lately."

"Very relieved."

Lily sat forward. "Why's that?"

"I'm sure she won't mind my telling you. Her period started yesterday. She'd been so afraid she was never going to catch up with Tonya." Nell tried a little laugh. "In hindsight, it's nothing I would have been in a hurry about."

"Bless her heart. I'll have to get her a grandmotherly present to mark the occasion."

"It's certainly a rite of passage," Lily said, picking up her iced tea and taking a sip.

"It seems like only yesterday she was a baby and tonight she has a date to the eighth-grade dance." Nell shook her head. "My how time flies," she said wincing at the truth of the old chestnut.

"Speaking of that," Lily said, "we haven't seen much of you lately. Too busy with Brady Logan?"

"That won't be a problem any longer." She took

a swallow of her coffee, black and bitter. "As the kids would say, 'He's history.'"

Stella cradled her goblet, caressing the stem with her slender, manicured fingers. "Oh, honey, what do you mean?"

"Just that. We…didn't work out."

"But you cared for him, right?" Lily's gaze was sympathetic. Both her mother and sister waited for her to say something. "Yes." Nell wanted to scream.

"You must be upset," her mother said.

"I've had better days."

"Abby said you couldn't promise you wouldn't drink."

Nell whirled on Lily. "'Abby said'? What do you mean?"

Lily blushed and ducked her head guiltily. "Abby called Mother. She's worried about you, Nell."

Great. As if she didn't know that. The last thing she needed was a triumvirate of female relatives observing her every move.

"Did you tell her you might drink?" Stella asked.

Very deliberately, Nell set down her cup. "No. I told her I wouldn't drink last night."

Stella's eyebrows peaked. "Well, that wasn't very encouraging for her."

"But it was honest. That's all I can ever promise. One day at a time."

"Maybe Abby thinks this upset over Brady Logan might make you…vulnerable." Lily glanced at her mother as if to secure concurrence. "We think you need to be especially watchful. Of course, we're both here for you whenever you need support."

Abby flushed with anger. "Do you have any idea

what it feels like to have you looking over my shoulder all the time, waiting for the next blunder, the next fall from grace?''

Lily's head snapped back. ''Easy, Nell. We're only trying to help.''

''I've appreciated everything you've done for me, but I need some space. And how about showing a little confidence in me?''

''You don't need to get huffy.'' Stella placed her goblet carefully on the coffee table. ''You'll have to excuse us, but we remember those months when we were terrified for you and for Abby. When we'd call you at ten in the morning and find you still in bed, hardly coherent. When we were all on tenterhooks at family gatherings wondering if you'd make a fool of yourself. When I could hardly bear to think of what would happen if you were driving after you'd been drinking. I guess we got the answer to that one, didn't we?''

Nell stood abruptly and walked away from their accusing eyes, their long memories. The silence in the room was painful.

Lily broke the tension. ''Nell, Abby was little then. She's not now. Don't put her through something like that.''

Nell clenched her fingers, trying to drown out the words and the images the words evoked. Her voice came out cold, metallic. ''Don't six years count for anything?''

Lily's voice was practical. ''You said it yourself. Six years or six days. It's this one day that counts. We just don't want to see you mess up because you're upset about Brady.''

Nell faced them then. "I love Brady, okay? It was devastating when he left last night. I'll admit it, I was tempted to drink. But, guess what? I resisted. I plan to resist tonight. And, God willing, tomorrow night. But this is *my* life, *my* decision. Not yours. And there comes a time when your solicitude is not helpful. I need to be treated like a fully functioning adult, not some morally handicapped person whose own mother, sister and daughter can't trust her."

Lily stood. "Nell, we didn't mean it like that."

Picking up her purse, Nell headed for the door. "I'm sure you didn't. I love you both, but you have to let me go. Let me be my own person. Not you, not Abby, not anybody can keep me from the next drink if I really want it. So, please, if you wish to be helpful, quit assuming weakness and start trusting me."

Just as she turned to leave the room, her mother's voice rose in concern. "But you will be careful, won't you, darling?"

Incredulous, Nell stared back at her mother for a moment, then left. She couldn't wait to get outside. She was breathing heavily when she reached the haven of her car. How dare they? Her hands shook when she tried, unsuccessfully the first time, to insert the key in the ignition. Why would they automatically assume she would take a drink just because Brady had walked out on her?

Trembling all over, she started the car and backed slowly out of the driveway. Heartache was just something you lived through. There would be no Brady in her tomorrows.

And she had to remind herself over and over that

there would also be no liquor in her tomorrows. No warm soothing of the loneliness yawning inside her. No blissful, blurred vision of reality.

And yet...

CHAPTER TWELVE

NELL STOOD behind Abby watching her in the bathroom mirror as she painstakingly applied the merest hint of blush. "Is this about right?"

"Looks perfect. Too much would make your skin look harsh and you have such a pretty complexion."

Abby shot her a skeptical look. "Mom, get a grip. I feel weird when you say things like that."

Nell fell silent. Her daughter wanted reassurance, just not too much. Figuring out the correct dosage was a maternal challenge beyond her powers at the moment. She sighed softly. That delicate line between approval and interference. The one her own mother had crossed earlier in the day. Were mothers and daughters forever doomed to get on each other's nerves? "What are you wearing tonight?" Surely that was a neutral change of topic.

"I haven't decided. Maybe my khaki skirt and that new green top I got at Old Navy or that purple flowered T-shirt and my black skirt. What do you think?" She wrinkled her brow and leaned closer, picking at a pimple on her cheek.

Nell wasn't about to involve herself in that issue. "No matter what you decide, you'll look great."

Abby turned around and leaned against the basin. "I'm so nervous."

"That's natural. I remember the first date I had. Lester Royer took me to the skating rink and all evening I was convinced he was noticing how sweaty my palms were."

"Gross. Lester?"

"Believe me, Alan Voyle is a stud, compared to poor Les. You'll have a great time."

Abby flung her arms around Nell's neck. "Thanks, Mom. I love you."

"And I love you."

After the brief hug, Abby drew back, then turned to catch one last glimpse of herself in the mirror before starting down the hall. "I'll be in my room. I've gotta call Tonya and see what she's wearing."

Watching until Abby reached her bedroom, Nell shook her head, baffled at where the years had gone and praying that Alan Voyle was as nice as he appeared to be. There was no Rick or Brady to string him up by the heels if he wasn't.

Did Abby miss having a father? In recent years, they'd never really talked about it, but she had to feel a void. Nell's father had been the hero of her life. She couldn't imagine growing up without him.

Suddenly the events of the past twenty-four hours caught up with her. Her own tardy confession about her alcoholism, Abby's coming of age and Brady's subsequent kindness to her daughter and then his angry departure. And that didn't even take into account today's sneak attack by Lily and her mother.

Then there was the other problem—the one she refused to think about. Rick. Abby's next visit to Dallas was coming up soon. What if Rick said something to Abby about living with him?

She wound her arms around her waist and hurried to the kitchen. She needed to keep busy. She pulled out a cookbook and began assembling the ingredients for devil's food cookies. Chocolate. The universal pacifier. *I'm a big girl,* she kept telling herself. *I can get through all of this.* Mother and Lily hadn't done anything they didn't normally do. Hover. Rick and Clarice wouldn't really want Abby, would they? She would certainly put a damper on their high-flying lifestyle.

Instead of getting out the mixer, Nell used a spoon to cream the butter and sugar, transferring her frustration to the batter. She could rationalize those problems all she wanted, but what about Brady? How would she ever get over him?

Damn it, I will not cry. I have no more tears. She'd been pretty rough on him last night. Had she been motivated by defensiveness or by a genuine desire to help him? What did it matter? In either case, he'd stormed out of her life. He'd had a right to be angry. But what about all those good times? The two nights they'd spent in each other's arms? For the first time in her life she had felt—in the fullest sense of the word—womanly, adored.

Dropping the spoon into the bowl with a clatter, she bent over the counter. Or had he merely been using her? She was convenient and willing. Boy, had she been willing!

No, it wasn't like that. For better or worse, she loved him.

And loving him, she couldn't help picking up on the hurt he still carried around with him. He might have come to some kind of peace about Brooke and

Nicole, but it was clear he still had demons to wrestle, and that was something he had to do alone.

So now she had no choice, none at all, except to let him go and somehow, some way go on with her life. She stared at the eggs and flour and vanilla as if she'd never seen before. She didn't want chocolate. What good could it do? She wanted Brady. Without stopping to think, she scooped up the ball of creamed butter and sugar and threw it in the garbage, then put away the other ingredients, slamming cupboard doors as she went.

A huge sob racked her. God, she couldn't go on. Not without him. Before, she hadn't known what she was missing. Now she did.

But he had made his decision. He had walked out of her life. The sooner she reconciled herself to that fact, the better.

But even as she stood wiping her eyes with the corner of a dish towel, there remained a glimmer of hope. Maybe he would come back. When he wasn't so angry. When he'd had time to think.

When he could trust her. Forgive her.

Hope died at the same moment the doorbell rang. Nell glanced at the kitchen clock. It was too early for Alan to be arriving. She folded the towel, placed it on the counter and headed to the door. "I'll get it."

"Who is it?" Abby called, her voice panicky.

When Nell opened the door, a delivery man handed her a bouquet of rosebuds, carnations and baby's breath. "For Abby Porter," he said.

Nell thanked him and started down the hall to deliver the unexpected gift.

"Is it him?" Abby hissed from behind her door.

"No, honey. It's flowers. For you."

Nell entered the room and placed the vase on the dresser.

Abby's eyes rounded with delight. "Who are they from? Nobody's ever sent me flowers before."

"Here." Nell unpinned the small envelope attached to the pale pink bow and handed it to her daughter.

Abby pulled out the card and read it silently. When she raised her head, tears stood in her eyes.

"What?" Nell asked, concerned.

"Oh, Mom, he remembered."

"Who remembered?"

"Brady." She offered the card to her mother.

Nell hesitated. She didn't want to take it. Didn't want to read it.

"Mom?" Abby prompted.

Nell took the card and lowered her eyes to the strong masculine pen strokes. "Abby, you are a beautiful young woman. I hope tonight's dance is special for you. I'm leaving Arkansas early in the morning. Even though I won't be seeing you again, please know that you will always have a special place in my heart."

The letters of Brady's signature swam. Even though Nell had anticipated he would leave, seeing it written by his own hand had a finality that shattered her.

"Hope is a thing with feathers." From nowhere came the lines of Emily Dickinson's poem.

And things with feathers flew away.

Somehow she managed to hold herself together until Alan arrived to pick up Abby.

Then the darkness came.

And the thirst.

THE OVERCAST SKIES matched Brady's mood as he slung his bags into the back of the Escalade late Friday afternoon. He glanced back at the bland exterior of the condominium where he'd spent the past few weeks. He'd had such high hopes when he'd made the decision to sublet the unit. He shook his head. Had he been so desperate for stability in his life— for companionship and acceptance—that he'd sacrificed his reason?

In business that would have been disastrous. He mocked himself with a derisive chuckle. Just goes to show what happens when you abandon the practices and principles that resulted in success.

He headed down I-540 on his way to I-40, which would lead him west to sunny California and work— the only security in his life right now. He'd bury himself in the damn projects lined up and waiting for him.

Carl had been ecstatic, of course, when Brady had called to announce what felt like craven surrender. He hadn't had time today to do more with Buzz Valentine than tell him he'd make some decisions about the optioned property in the next few weeks. So what if he lost his earnest money? It was, after all, only money—the one thing he had plenty of.

Rain accompanied him all the way from Ft. Smith to Oklahoma City, where he planned to spend the night, but he didn't care. The swish-swish of the windshield wipers had a comforting, metronomic quality that helped soothe his churning stomach.

For the thousandth time since Tuesday night, he repeated the words. *Nell is an alcoholic.* In his mind, he'd tried to argue that she was not an alcoholic, but a *recovering* alcoholic. Tried to believe that insight made a difference. Hell, from her actions, he never would have known. She might go on for years without taking a drink, if ever. But how could he be sure?

Even if he could accept her, he couldn't accept that desperate accusation she'd flung at him, as if turning the tables on him excused her. *You're addicted.* Right. He wasn't the one drowning his sorrows in a bottle, was he? But that wasn't what she'd said. Even though he remembered her words exactly, he didn't want to consider her indictment. Addicted to anger, resentment and guilt?

Hell, yes, who wouldn't be? His old man hadn't even waited until his mother was cold in the grave before bringing Velda home and having the nerve to suggest Danny should call her "Mother." Her chipper smile and the way she clung to his dad, looking up at him as if she'd taken home the blue-ribbon hog from the county fair, were an insult to his mother's memory. Had he been the only one who'd mourned her?

He'd never forget the day he'd come home from school the week after the funeral and found all traces of his mother removed—her hairbrush no longer on the dresser, the framed photograph of her parents that had always sat on the mantel gone, her prized cut-glass serving bowl missing from the china cabinet, her closet empty of everything except the lingering scent of talcum and lavender. Even now, his jaw clenched in anger. What kind of man removes all traces of the woman he's supposedly loved, who has borne his children?

Danny had been too young, of course. What did a seven-year-old know? Especially when for most of his life their mother had been sick. He'd fallen right in with the plan, snuggling up to Velda from the beginning. It had sickened Brady, who had managed to get through most of his senior year before his father kicked him out, days short of graduation. Thank God for Coach Elbert, who'd somehow sweet-talked the superintendent into awarding him his diploma anyway. They'd mailed it to him in care of General Delivery in the town where he'd gotten work as a roofer.

He turned on the radio full blast, in the futile attempt to block out his memories and the gut-wrenching realization that Nell had nailed it, whether she knew it or not.

He hated his father.

NELL SAT on the rug cradling the wine bottle she'd pulled from the paper sack. Her frantic trip to the liquor store was a blur. All she knew was that after Abby left, the walls of the house had crushed her with their mocking silence. She'd ended up—again—abandoned and alone. The bright lights inside the store had hurt her eyes, but she was drawn instinctively to the racked bottles, lined up row after row, their ambers, crimsons and roses seductive in their appeal.

Now, running her hands up and down the smooth,

cool glass, caressing the curve leading to the slender neck and the rubbery seal over the cork, she focused on her palate, tingling in anticipation. Imagining that first euphoric swallow, the feel and taste of it coursing down her throat, warming her chest from the inside.

She closed her eyes and leaned against the sofa. It would be so simple. The corkscrew lay within easy reach on the coffee table. Her favorite rounded goblet, which nested perfectly in her palm, stood beside the corkscrew—waiting. Could she stop with one glass? Would she?

Nothing and no one else offered her the immediate comfort of the merlot resting heavy and promising in her hands.

Opening her eyes, she grabbed the corkscrew, studying it as if it represented the tempter—and the deliverer. *Remember.* The word jolted her, causing her to drop the corkscrew. *Remember your last drunk.* The words of every AA sponsor stopped her. *Before you take that first drink, relive your last drunk.*

She set the wine bottle beside her on the floor and buried her head in her hands. Did she have to? It would be ever so much easier to open the bottle and have a drink. People did it all the time.

Your last drunk! The idea grew insistently, clawing at her, refusing to let her go. Rick. The fight. The images beckoned, demanding to be revisited.

She jumped to her feet and paced to the window, remembering their spacious but homey living room, decorated with antiques she and Rick had restored, the fire crackling in the fireplace, the lambent glow of the new brass table lamp she'd purchased only that day. She'd meant only to have one little drink before Rick got home, but one had turned into three. She'd carefully rinsed her glass and put it in the dishwasher before he came in, hiding the evidence.

That evening had started out no different from every other evening in the months before, when she'd begun to dread his arrival. The cool, polite distance he kept as if she were tainted. Long gone were the welcoming kisses, the tell-me-about-your day ritual. Instead, he moved straight to the bar and fixed himself a bourbon and water. She never protested when he fixed her one, too.

Protest? She lapped it up, hoping it would inoculate her from his obvious aversion to her. That night he'd perched on the hearth, holding his drink between his knees. He looked fuzzy to her, the fire backlighting his body turning him into a fiend. She had blinked, but the image remained hazy, sinister.

His words, like a razor slice, had cut through her alcoholic haze. *I've filed for divorce. Here are the papers.* She'd sloshed her drink as she carried it to her lips and drank thirstily. He wasn't finished. *I'm moving out tonight. To Clarice's.* He set the legal-size envelope on the bar.

She could never remember if she'd flung the glass before or after he mentioned Clarice. All she knew was that suddenly she was standing in their decorator-beautiful living room, surrounded by shards of broken glass, staring at a stain created by bourbon and melting ice darkening the thick cream-colored carpet. Screaming an obscenity, she had launched herself at Rick, now standing, his face gray with disgust. She had called him names she didn't even know were in her repertoire, all the time pounding her fists against his unyielding chest. Finally he had grabbed her arms in a viselike grip. *You're a drunk, Nell. What did you expect?*

Bile and phlegm had risen to her mouth, and tears, maudlin and self-pitying, had dripped down her cheeks, off her nose and chin. He couldn't do this to her!

Nell laid a hand on a cool pane of glass, grounding herself in reality. That was then. This was now. She could stop this horror film in midreel. *You want to stay sober? Force yourself. Remember the worst.*

Somehow, she'd staggered through the shattered glass to the bar, where she drank directly from the bottle of Jack Daniel's Rick had left out. She couldn't get enough to douse the flames licking at her psyche. She'd whirled around then. *What are we supposed to do? Abby and I?*

My attorney will be in touch. Meanwhile, call your mother to come get Abby. In this condition, you're not a fit mother.

He'd been right, of course, Nell thought bitterly. How could she have lost sight of Abby? No matter how diminished Rick had made her feel, how could she have been so irresponsible a mother?

Her reaction that night had been violent. She'd screamed one word at him. *Bastard!*

That's when Abby had appeared, her eyes wide with fright. *Mommy?* she'd cried, her bottom lip trembling. Nell had scooped her up and faced Rick, barely able to control the venom threatening to spew out of her. *Get out,* she'd spat. He'd given her one last look of undisguised repugnance and said, *Call your mother. Now.* And he'd left.

Nell paced to the center of the family room, staring at the wine bottle, the corkscrew, the glass. All urging her to a decision.

But memory insisted. Confront the worst. She'd stood, rooted, six-year-old Abby clutching her around the neck, asking over and over, *Mommy, who spilled the drink? Where's Daddy going?*

She remembered carrying her child to the bar, setting her on her feet and downing the remainder of the bourbon in great gulping swigs straight from the bottle. Finally Abby had nudged her. *Why did you yell at Daddy. Where is he? Why did he go?*

Nell picked up the merlot and studied it. Tempting, with its tasteful label and graceful, understated script. She nestled it to her chest, wondering why on earth she had ever answered Abby as she had. *He's left us, Abby.*

The howls had erupted then. Seeming to grow louder, more intense, as Nell drunkenly tried to explain. How could Abby ever have forgiven her?

I want my daddy. I want my daddy. I want my daddy.

Nell hadn't been able to stand Abby's screams. She'd grabbed her purse, buttoned Abby's coat around her, thrown on her own and dragged Abby to the car, her stomach revolting with every gasp of breath. After she'd buckled Abby in, she remembered fumbling on her hands and knees, searching for the ignition key she'd dropped in the snow, all the time craving another drink to calm her nerves.

Well, her prayers had been answered thanks to the

county liquor laws. On her way to confront Rick she'd pulled into a drive-thru liquor store and purchased a pint of vodka. At the next stoplight, hands shaking, she'd stripped off the seal and swallowed a third of the bottle.

Abby had become strangely quiet. Snow drifted dreamily from the sky, landing on the windshield. Headlights blurred together like a soothing watercolor wash. The combination of the car heater and the vodka warmed Nell, relaxing her as she started down one of Fayetteville's steep hills toward Clarice's. Rick needed to see what he'd done to them. To her, but especially to his daughter.

At first it had seemed like a graceful glide toward a fleecy white backdrop, but then, in a moment of sudden clarity, Nell saw the brick wall rising to meet them, her car in a sickening spin she was helpless to control. She gripped the wheel. The last thing she heard was her own voice screaming *Abby, Abby!*

That was all she could remember until she woke up in the hospital, her bandaged head full of anvils. The elongated human faces peering down at her came and went, then dissolved completely, leaving nothing but darkness and stabbing pain.

Nell turned on the lamp beside the armchair and sat down, still holding the bottle, menacingly familiar in its shape. As long as she lived, she would never forget the words of the police officer who'd visited her in the hospital. *You had a close call, Mrs. Porter. Another six inches and your daughter wouldn't have been so lucky.*

Nell's mouth soured. Who was that woman who

had so carelessly risked her child's life? Who had preferred a bottle to her own daughter?

Was she prepared to put Abby through that hell again? Worse yet, was she deliberately going to become that woman she loathed?

Still cradling the bottle of wine, slowly, deliberately, so she would never forget this moment, she stood, picked up the corkscrew and walked into the kitchen. She flipped on the light, peeled the sealant from the neck of the bottle and then, with deadly aim, impaled the center of the cork with the tip of the corkscrew. She levered the arms of the corkscrew, then heard the soft pop of the cork, smelled the faintest, tantalizing hint of grape before she lifted the bottle, upended it over the sink and watched as every last drop spiraled down the drain.

Afterward, she threw the bottle in the wastebasket, then leaned against the sink, drawing ragged breaths.

Finally she went to her purse, removed a small metallic object and clutched it in her hand, as if it possessed magical powers. Opening her fist, she placed the AA chip on the counter, rubbing her finger over the Roman numeral six etched there. Six years of sobriety. She was not willing to sacrifice that for anyone. Anything.

Picking up the chip, she bowed her head, humbled by the grace that had brought her to this moment. In the quiet kitchen, her prayer of thanksgiving, strong and healing, rose from her heart.

Never losing her grip on her six-year chip, she opened her eyes to overwhelming relief. She was back on track again.

In the morning she would call Ben, seek his counsel, but for tonight? She had triumphed over the enemy—for yet one more day.

That didn't mean she wouldn't miss Brady. Worry about Abby. Feel stifled by her mother and sister on occasion.

It simply meant she valued Nell again.

WHEN SHE HEARD Abby at the front door, Nell muted the TV. "I'm in here, honey."

"Okay."

She looked up when Abby entered the family room, her eyes sparkling. "Did you have a good time?"

Abby sank into the rocker, hitched her legs over one arm and then sighed dramatically. "Oh, Mom, I'm in love. He's *so* nice."

Nell permitted herself a concealed sigh of relief. "Tell me all about it."

And, unbelievably, Abby did, so caught up in what a good dancer Alan was, how dreamy his brown eyes were, how polite he'd been that she must've forgotten she was speaking to her mother. But then, Nell mused, Abby was like that. When she wanted to share her feelings, she could be completely up front. But when she didn't? You couldn't pry a single tidbit from her.

"Tonya was green with jealousy. Her date was a total jerk, all the time trying to make people laugh with these lame jokes and pigging out at the refreshment table."

"Tonya's day will come. We all have to kiss a few frogs in the process."

Abby twisted a strand of hair around her finger.

"I guess I was just lucky to get a prince the first time."

Nell smiled at her daughter's innocence. Yet stranger things had happened than meeting The One in eighth grade. "Alan knew a good thing when he saw you."

"Mo-om, you're prejudiced."

"Guilty."

Abby hopped up. "I'm gonna get a cola. Want one?"

"No thanks. The caffeine would keep me awake."

Nell watched the final couple of minutes of the movie while Abby was in the kitchen, then flipped off the TV.

"Mom?"

A coldness in her daughter's tone caused Nell to glance up. Ashen, Abby stood clutching the empty wine bottle. Nell cringed. Why hadn't she emptied the wastebasket before Abby got home?

"What's this?" Abby demanded. "Have you been drinking?"

Nell rose to her feet, crossed to her daughter, took the bottle from her and set it on the table. Praying for the right words, she laid her hands on her daughter's shoulders and found her troubled eyes. "No, honey, I haven't been drinking. I'll admit I was tempted, but instead, I poured all the wine down the drain."

Abby hung her head. "I should've been here."

"No. It doesn't work like that. If an alcoholic wants a drink, she'll make it happen. You don't have to keep watch over me, sweetie. I'm the one who must do that for myself. Tonight I did."

"It's Brady, isn't it?"

Nell lifted a hand and smoothed back her daughter's hair. "It's lots of things, but I'm determined never again to let alcohol become more important than the people I love. And, yes, Brady is one of those people. But how can I demonstrate that love unless I give him his freedom?" She hesitated, struck by another truth. "And honor my feelings for him by remaining sober."

Abby hugged her then, an embrace that warmed her far more than any amount of liquor could ever have done. "I'm so proud of you, Mom."

"I love you," Nell barely managed to say before her throat clogged with tears of gratitude.

The struggle would be ongoing, but what reward could be sweeter than Abby's forgiveness and love?

CHAPTER THIRTEEN

BRADY STOOD at the window of his corner office, eyes fixed on the vermillions, bronzes and sun-bright yellows of the chrysanthemums planted artfully around the L&S TechWare flagpole, imagining how the fall foliage in the Ozarks might look at its height. He cursed under his breath, wondering how long it would take before he could focus totally on the here and now. *Here* was California and his work. *Now* was not then and certainly not the tomorrows he couldn't bring himself to contemplate.

He turned around to face his desk, where a computer monitor demanded his attention. He stood for a moment, massaging the back of his neck, ropy with tension. He'd snapped at his secretary this morning, alienated a longtime client and fouled up a set of important computations. And it wasn't even ten o'clock.

He slumped into his leather desk chair and started through the letters requiring his signature. Carl and others in the front office had been great about bringing him up to date after such a long absence. He wished he could care about the new projects they'd shepherded since he'd been gone. He threw his pen down in disgust. What the hell was the matter with him? Where was the energy and excitement the company had engendered in the past?

He'd been back a month now. Why couldn't he stop thinking about Arkansas? About Nell? Picturing her in the library. At home. And tousled and sweet-smelling in a warm bed still rumpled from love-making.

On an impulse he picked up his suit jacket and headed to the outer office. "I'll be gone for a few hours," he said to his startled secretary as he breezed out the door.

He had some thinking to do in a quiet place.

And he knew Brooke and Nicole would be good listeners.

BEN HADLEY WAVED from the back booth where he sat nursing a cup of coffee. Nell threaded her way between the tables and chairs and then sat down. "Sorry I'm late. I had a frantic morning. More children than I'd counted on showed up for story hour."

Ben smiled. "Sounds like a good problem to have." He passed her his menu. "Take your time. Catch your breath. I've decided to indulge. Barbecued pork sandwich and fries. My wife would kill me."

Nell winked over the top of the menu. "My lips are sealed."

They made small talk about their Thanksgiving plans and the fate of the Razorback football team until the waitress set their food down. Nell sniffed the air. "Hmm. That barbecue smells heavenly." She appraised the salad in front of her. "Wouldn't it be nice if lettuce had a tantalizing aroma, too?"

"But don't you feel virtuous?" Ben asked, teasingly.

"I don't know that I'd go that far, but my bathroom scales will be proud of me."

Nell studied Ben as she ate. A man with a ready smile, kind, knowing eyes and years of wisdom he graciously shared. Not only with her. With anyone in need.

Yet she knew his history. It wasn't pretty. If Ben could rise from the pit of alcoholism, anyone could.

With his napkin, he wiped a trace of barbecue sauce from his lips, then looked straight at her. "How long has it been now since your Brady left?"

She flinched at the *your*. "Five weeks."

"Have you had any further episodes like the one with the wine?"

"No, and with God's help, I won't. I've done quite a bit of thinking, and I realize Brady has to live his own life. When I accused him of being addicted, I meant it as a constructive comment. But I can't change him. It's not my place even if I somehow had that power. He's the only one who can do that."

"You told me once he had a history of running away."

Nell set down her fork. "I remember."

"Do you think he ran away from you this time?"

An interesting question. Nell sat back in the booth and gathered her thoughts. "In part. I blindsided him with news that had to be an awful shock. Truth is, I wasn't who he thought I was. He was entitled to walk away from me."

Ben waited. "But?"

"In reality, I think he ran away from himself."

"Go on."

"Like all of us, he has issues to resolve, but he doesn't want to. Is maybe afraid to. After what I said about his being addicted to anger and resentment, if he'd stayed, I'd have been a constant reminder of all that he's spent years fleeing."

"Can you live with that?"

Nell reached out and touched the older man's hand. "I'll have to, won't I?"

"What is this doing to you, Nell?"

"I'll be honest, Ben. That night, before I lived through my last drunk, I thought the world had ended. That losing Brady was going to be insurmountable. But somehow I made it. And I will continue making it. I have to. For Abby, of course. But, more important, for me."

"You have a lot of people pulling for you."

"I know that. The Serenity Prayer has never been truer for me. I can't change what's happened or who I am. I've had to accept that Brady is gone. Now I'm praying for the wisdom to keep my life in balance." She patted Ben's hand before withdrawing her own. "Thanks for getting together with me outside the group. We both know I had gotten lax about regular attendance at meetings. That left me without sufficient resources when Brady couldn't deal with my alcoholism." She smiled. "I won't let it happen again."

"Good," Ben said, picking up the check and shooing her off when she attempted to pay. He fumbled with his billfold and almost as an aside, tossed out, "What would you do if Brady did come back?"

"I don't think he will. Not until and unless he deals with his past. I'm not holding my breath."

After laying down some bills, Ben found her eyes and held his gaze steady. "But if he did?"

Nell's heart raced, even as she tried to control the impulse. "Oh, Ben, I'd love him with every fiber of my being."

Ben chuckled. "Then it looks like I better start praying for miracles."

"Can't hurt," Nell murmured as she slid from the booth. But it was too much to ask. She was grateful for her sobriety. She had no right to ask for more.

CARL AND HIS WIFE Jill had invited Brady to dinner. A delicious game hen with plum sauce, risotto, fresh broccoli, chocolate mousse. Hardly bachelor fare. Now, sitting on his host's patio holding a mug of coffee, Brady should have felt comfortable, relaxed. But the sight of Carl's and Jill's easy domesticity, the silent signals they sent practically without knowing, the ways they absently touched each other filled Brady with a loneliness he was powerless to banish.

The autumn sun was setting over the hills, fiery and spectacular. Jill had left to pick up their son from soccer practice. The pungent aroma of Carl's after-dinner cigar spiced the night air. How many times had he and Brooke enjoyed the Suttons' hospitality? Sat on this very patio, laughing, telling stories, dreaming big dreams?

Carl blew a puff of smoke into the air, then stretched out his legs. Brady gently sloshed his coffee, then took a small sip, willing it to relax him. It didn't.

At first, preoccupied, he didn't take in Carl's words. Then, like a delayed broadcast, they filtered through his reminiscences. "This isn't working, is it?"

Brady wanted to pretend he didn't know what his friend was asking. But he couldn't. "No," he said quietly.

"We've been friends a long time, Logan. I've tried my damnedest to be patient. To wait for you to speak up." He rolled the cigar between his thumb and third finger. "I want what's best for you. But you're gonna have to tell me what that is and somehow I don't think it's in California. Not anymore."

Brady was choked with emotion and his head felt as if it could crack open any time now. "It's like my whole life is in limbo."

"Work?"

"I don't know, Carl. I want to care. Get revved up, you know, like I used to in the old days. And yet…" He trailed off, wishing he could see a clear path, craving normalcy.

Carl took another puff of his cigar, then turned to Brady. "You can't?"

Brady shrugged impotently. "I'm letting you down. I know that. Hell, I can't expect you and the others to put up with my whatever-you-want-to-call-it. Midlife crisis, for lack of a better term."

"You've experienced a great loss. We understand that. But at some point—"

"I need to carry my weight." He paused. "Or sell." Before, it had been only a vague idea. Now the words were out, lending a resolve that hadn't been present before.

Carl didn't seem terribly surprised. "If you sell, what then?"

What then, indeed? "I don't know."

"I think it's time you told me about Nell."

Brady drank from his mug in an effort to mask the emotions generated by Carl's unexpected question. What was there to say? "It's over."

"Bull!" The word exploded from Carl's mouth. "You can talk all you want. But I know what I see. What's the story?"

Brady sighed. What the hell, he might as well get it over with. "She's a card-carrying member of AA," he said bitterly.

"So?"

"*So?* Is that all you have to say?" Brady set down the mug, then leaped to his feet and paced to the house and back. "My wife and daughter were killed by a drunk and I'm supposed to forget that and take up with an alcoholic?"

"How long has she been in recovery?"

"Six years."

"Jeez, pal, half the people you know are either borderline alcoholics or in recovery. Are you going to condemn them, too?"

Brady stopped his pacing. "What's your point?"

Raising the cigar, Carl inhaled its bouquet, apparently considering his answer. "My point? This— you're sounding pretty damn judgmental to me. Have you never made a mistake, Logan? Give her a break. Holding grudges is exhausting work. Transferring blame is doing a disservice to a lady who just might be the lifeline you need. So what's the worst thing that could happen?"

"She could start drinking again."

"Yeah. And you could continue being a self-absorbed, rootless jerk. What's the difference?"

Brady turned his back, his teeth clenched. First, Nell. Now, Carl. They both seemed to think he thrived on resentment. Slowly he pivoted to face Carl. "Is that what you believe I am?"

Carl shrugged. "If the shoe fits…"

"What is it you think I'm supposed to do? Go ahead, let me have it."

Carl stubbed out his half-smoked cigar and rose to his feet. He approached and clamped a hand on Brady's shoulder. "I love ya, buddy. You know that. But you seem determined to self-destruct. Much as I hate to say it, Arkansas was the best thing that's happened to you since Brooke and Nicole were killed. Your Nell must've had some rough times, but it sounds to me as if she's fought back. Her sobriety record is pretty darn good. Most important, she was enough of a woman to breathe life back into you. That's rare. If I were you, I'd think twice about walking away from her."

Brady stared out beyond the patio and the pool, overcome with conflicting emotions. He didn't like the reflection of himself he'd seen in Carl's words. "How do I just ignore her alcoholism?"

"You don't. You hang in there with her, giving her every reason to find joy in life. You love her, dumb-ass. It's plain as the nose on your face. You act like being an alcoholic is all she is. Sounds as if she's much more. For starters, the woman you love."

Brady was speechless. He couldn't dispute what

Carl had said. For one simple reason. Every word he had said rang true.

Carl engulfed him in a bear hug. "Go back to Arkansas, Brady. Go home."

Jill's return prevented Brady from blubbering like a baby. He would miss Carl, he realized.

But he had things to do.

WHEN THE PHONE RANG one evening late in October, Nell muted the PBS program she'd been watching and picked up the receiver. When she heard the voice on the other end, her heart sank. Rick. She'd been laboring under the illusion that no news from him was good news. What if he'd called to talk about custody? Would it matter to him that Brady was no longer in the picture?

His tone was more unctuous than usual. "Nell, I hope this is a convenient time. There's something I need to discuss with you. About Abby."

Nell could hardly manage a response. "What's that?"

She hadn't realized how tense she'd been until she heard his answer and felt her entire body turn to rubber. "I'm afraid it's not going to work out for Abby to come here next weekend."

"Oh? Why is that?"

"Well, you see, Clarice was able to score some tickets for the big Texas game in Austin."

"Couldn't Abby go with you? I know she'd enjoy seeing the campus."

"I'm not sure that would work. We've been invited to go with some friends in their motor home, er, you know. Not exactly a child-friendly environment."

Understatement of the year, if she knew the type of friends Rick customarily attracted. "Abby will be disappointed," she said, although she wasn't at all convinced that was an accurate description of Abby's likely reaction.

"I'd appreciate it if you'd pass the news on to her. Oh, and tell her we'll be looking forward to her November visit."

Oh, no, you don't! Nell summoned her sweetest, most neutral tone. "You can tell her yourself." Before Rick could protest, she started for Abby's room. "She's right here studying. I'm sure she'll want to hear the news from you, rather than me."

"But—"

She didn't hear the rest of Rick's protest, because she'd handed the phone to Abby. "Here. It's your dad."

Then she beat a hasty retreat. It was high time Rick quit using her as the middleman, assuming she would compensate for his shortcomings. With a shock of recognition, she realized that had been the role she'd always assumed back when she'd thought their marriage was working. She'd been the peacemaker, the one who ran interference for him, smoothed over any problems. Well, she was through with that. She allowed herself a chuckle of satisfaction as she settled back into the sofa. He was on his own now.

The television program had just concluded when Abby came into the room to return the phone. When

Nell looked up, she was surprised to find a scowl on her daughter's face. "What's wrong?"

"I don't get to go," Abby said, banging the receiver into the base unit.

Something in her tone alerted Nell. She'd assumed Abby would be relieved. "Would you have enjoyed going to the Texas game with a group of your father's adult friends?"

Abby stood with one knee bent on the arm of the sofa. "No."

"Help me, honey. I don't understand what the problem is."

Abby twisted the tail of her University of Arkansas T-shirt. "They don't want me to come."

"I don't think that's it at all," Nell said, although she wasn't convinced herself. "This may be a one-time deal."

"They could've stayed home from the stupid game," Abby persisted stubbornly.

"Yes, I suppose they could." Nell felt as if she were on shaky ground. It would be all too easy to say the wrong thing.

Abby gave a dramatic shrug. "Oh, well, me and Tonya can mess around this weekend, I guess."

"Tonya and I," Nell corrected automatically, sensing there was something important that hadn't been said. She took hold of Abby's arm and dragged her down beside her. Abby slouched over, her head hanging. Nell tipped up her chin. "Your dad loves you."

"Right." Abby's eyes burned with resentment.

Out of the blue, it struck Nell. "You're disappointed."

"Duh. He's my dad. I hardly get to see him at all."

Once that remark would've threatened Nell, but now all she could focus on was her daughter's pain. "It's been hard for you, hasn't it? Being without a dad in your life all the time."

"It's not your fault. Or his, I guess. But Tonya's father is so cool. Sometimes I'm really jealous of her, you know?" Her eyes were moist with unshed tears.

"I'm sorry we haven't talked about this recently. It must be hard on you."

"I thought for a while that it would be okay. When Brady was here, I mean. He kinda reminded me of Tonya's dad."

Nell winced. Was it possible Abby had actually entertained the idea of Brady as a stepfather? No wonder she was upset. She'd been betrayed on every side by the adults in her life. "It's okay to feel let down. Hurt. But sometimes things don't turn out the way we'd hoped they would. This is one of those times."

"I know that. I'm not a kid anymore."

Nell reached around Abby's shoulder to draw her near. "I've got news for you, kiddo. You'll still be my child when you're sixty-five. My grown-up child. That's the way it works." She dropped a kiss on Abby's hair, redolent with the strawberry fragrance of the latest fad shampoo. "But that growing-up part is hard, isn't it? When you learn that adults have feet of clay, that people don't always behave the way you'd like and that sometimes they disappoint you big time."

"Do you think Dad loves me?" Abby asked, her voice quivering.

"Without a doubt, honey. Without a doubt."

It was only later when she was getting ready for bed that Nell realized what Rick had *not* said. Not one word about custody or visitation. Somehow, she now understood, events like football weekends with friends would play an increasingly important role in her ex-husband's life. He would love Abby, all right. When it was convenient.

BRADY HAD CLEARED his desk, packed up and was finally able to leave California at the end of the week following his conversation with Carl. Although he had contacted his attorney about the repercussions of cashing out of the business, he still had not made a decision about his future—for one simple reason. He couldn't look ahead until he confronted his past.

He'd spent the hours behind the wheel barreling across the wide-open spaces of Nevada and Utah considering Nell's and Carl's judgments of him. For much of his adulthood, he had deliberately compartmentalized his life, dealing with his immediate family and his work and keeping the past locked away behind a barrier constructed of bitterness.

Nell had breached his defenses and Carl had stormed on through. The tight control he'd always exercised over his memories and emotions had slipped away, leaving him vulnerable. And scared. The closer he came to the Colorado border, the more like a lost boy he felt. He didn't want to go back into that world where his every action had been berated, where no one had bothered to mourn his mother, where he had no place.

But his self-respect demanded it. He had to move on and this step was the key.

He spent the night in Green River, Utah, tossing fitfully, falling asleep sometime after three. He showered, shaved and had breakfast in the motel dining room, wishing all the time he could delay the inevitable.

What would he find in Colorado?

The mileposts blurred as he continued east on I-70. His thoughts turned to the two-story early twentieth-century house he'd called home. His small bedroom had overlooked the barn and the mountains beyond and shared a common wall with his parents' room. He remembered balling his fists over his ears in the futile attempt to block out the squeak of the mattress as she pushed herself higher on the pillows, followed by her relentless cough. In vain he would wait for his father to help her. On the infrequent occasions when he did, he could hear his mother say, "That's all right, Dale. There's nothing to be done." Like an echo that single word had resounded in his head. *Nothing.*

Through the years he'd kept tabs on his family through data collected via the impersonal vehicle of the internet. Both his father and Velda were still alive. Still living on the ranch. His brother Danny taught and coached at the local high school.

Brady adjusted the car heater. Danny. There was a source of shame. When Danny was born, Brady had been eleven, far more interested in sports and horses than in a demanding baby brother. Then for a time when his mother's condition deteriorated, Danny had been farmed out to his grandmother. Brady had never been close to his brother. For years after he left home, he had felt guilty. On two occasions he'd tried to contact Danny, but by then it was too late. Danny wouldn't even talk to him. Perhaps Velda and his father had successfully turned his brother against him—or he'd built up his own case of resentment. After Nicole's birth, he had made one last attempt to contact his brother. When he'd received no answer, he'd said the hell with it.

He'd been angry for a long time. Then anger had turned to apathy. But beneath the surface, boiling like hot lava, lay the resentment. And, damn it, the guilt Nell had recognized. He'd been a teenager in turmoil—cocksure, defiant, hurt. He'd bargained with the gods, then raged at them. How could they have done this to his mother? To him?

Then had come his father's unthinkable betrayal, moving Velda in mere weeks after they'd laid his mother in her grave.

Even now, as he slowed for the Grand Junction traffic, his stomach churned with the injustice of it all.

He gnashed his teeth. So what was he doing anyway? What could he possibly accomplish?

Yet deep inside he knew he had to go through these next few hours if he was ever to move on with his life.

It was noon when he pulled into Glenwood Springs. The town had grown some and new motels and franchise restaurants bordered the highway, but once he reached the center of town, he noticed familiar landmarks. He pulled into a service station and filled his gas tank. As he was paying his bill, a wizened little man with a Denver Broncos ball cap punched him on the arm. "Say, aren't you Brady Logan?"

Brady flushed. "Yes. I'm sorry, but—"

"Oh, I wouldn't expect you to recognize me. I'm Buster Fowler's dad. I only recognized you because you were such a jock in high school. Buster always wanted to be just like you."

Brady covered his confusion with a laugh. "Well, I hope he turned out better than that." Then he changed the subject to Buster, whom he barely remembered. "What's Buster up to these days?"

The man visibly swelled. "He has a great job with the *Denver Post*. Selling advertising."

Brady signed the credit card receipt, hoping to put an end to the conversation. "Good to see you."

He had made it halfway to the door when the man called out, "Say, we're sure proud of that brother of yours."

Brady wheeled around. "Oh?"

"Yeah, helluva basketball coach. Took us to state last year, you know."

No, he hadn't known. It had been a while since Brady had checked out Danny on the internet. "I hope he's as lucky this year."

Only after hearing about the four returning starters and a six-foot-six sophomore did Brady manage to extricate himself from the conversation.

On a whim, he detoured past the high school before heading for the ranch. He didn't know what he expected to see. Yet Mr. Fowler's words had brought to the surface memories of his own high school days. Memories that had lain buried for years. He was tempted to go inside. Find Danny. Get that part of his visit behind him.

But it wasn't the time. Or the place.

Or was he simply procrastinating? Avoiding the worst? The ranch. Velda. His father.

Near Carbondale he turned off the highway and traveled a few miles to the familiar dirt road. The mailbox, battered by time, looked as it always had, the "Logan" painted in crooked white letters.

As a matter of course, Brady didn't consider himself a praying man, but he was conscious of forming a word in his mind—over and over again. *Help.*

He pulled around to the side of the house and parked. On the back of the house was an addition. Maybe a family room. On the sidewalk, a golden retriever lifted its head, then ambled to its feet and approached his vehicle. Brady climbed out of the SUV and leaned down to pet the dog. "Easy, pal. I'm a friend."

Straightening, he took a deep breath and walked to the kitchen door. *Help.* He knocked.

He could hear a radio playing soft music, then the sound of someone moving to the door. He hadn't known what to expect, but not what he saw when the door opened.

Before him stood a roly-poly woman with soft reddish-gray curls and beautiful brown eyes partially concealed by a pair of granny glasses. The welcoming smile on her face faded and she raised trembling fingers to her lips. When she spoke, her voice cracked. "Brady?"

Only then did he recognize faint traces of the woman he had known years before, with her well-endowed body, long auburn hair and the flirtatious dark eyes that ate his father in one gulp. The woman who had called his mother *friend*. Nursed her. Then betrayed her by marrying his father in record time. "Velda?"

She stared straight at him, sadness and shock in her gaze. "It's been a while," she said.

"Eighteen years."

"I suppose I should be killing a fatted calf or something," she murmured dryly. "Instead, I'll just ask a simple question. What do you want?"

Damn good question. What *did* he want? Then the answer came. "It's time to make peace. If that's possible."

Cocking her head, she studied him for a few seconds before standing aside. "Come in."

When he stepped over the threshold, smells and sights inundated him, carrying him back to days when he couldn't wait to get off the school bus, run up the lane to the house—and into his mother's arms. "Thank you."

Velda gestured to the kitchen table. "Have a seat. Coffee?"

"Sounds good." Neither of them said a word until she'd poured the coffee and sat down across from him. He needed to pose the question burning in his gut. To stall, he took a swallow of the coffee, thinking about what he had to ask. "Where's Dad?" he finally said.

She nodded toward the pasture. "Over there. Mending fence."

"Do you think he'll talk to me?"

She shrugged. "That's entirely between you and him."

"You're not going to give me any help here, are you?"

"Seems to me you never wanted any, if I recollect right."

"You've got me there."

Velda lifted the lid of the sugar bowl, then dipped out a teaspoonful. Stirring it into her coffee, she went on. "You never cared much for me, either."

"There were reasons."

She nodded. "Yes. There were. But there was a lot you didn't know. Didn't want to know, I imagine."

Was she trying to prepare him for something? Her tone was neither hostile nor welcoming, but she was hardly the home-wrecking siren he'd imagined her to be. "We all made some mistakes back then."

For the first time she allowed the wisp of a smile to cross her face. "Is this a new Brady Logan? One actually willing to listen?"

He had to give her credit. She wasn't backing away from painting an accurate picture of him as a teen, no matter how unflattering.

"I don't know if there's any way to deal with what happened."

"Listening's a step. The main thing is—you're here. Dale needs to know." She took hold of his hand. "Why don't you wander out to the pasture. Find your father."

Fear, oily and hot, sat in his stomach. "That's what I came to do." He stood, then paused, looking down at the small woman. Harmless. Honest. "I'll listen, Velda."

"Good," she said behind him as he walked out the kitchen door.

A cold wind blew down the valley as he made his way through the gate and across the pasture. In the distance he could see a figure in a sheepskin rancher's coat bent over a fence post. It required an effort of will to take each step that closed the distance between them. Finally, when Brady was about twenty feet from his father, the man looked up.

His body stilled and his gnarled hands closed around the fence stretcher he held. His weathered skin bore deep wrinkles and his chapped lips formed a thin line. His eyes, still steely blue, narrowed.

The man was...old. How had that happened? Somehow Brady had always pictured the father he'd known as a teenager—ageless, rock-hard, unyielding. He braced himself, awaiting his father's judgment.

But Dale Logan surprised him. He dropped the implement in his hand, then approached Brady. As if no time at all had elapsed since they'd seen each other, he simply said, "Let's go to the house, son."

The vise constricting Brady's chest loosened and he could breathe again. He'd called him *son*. That didn't erase the pain of the past, but it was a start.

Maybe that's all they needed. A start.

CHAPTER FOURTEEN

NEITHER MAN SPOKE as they walked toward the house, its white frame silhouetted against the distant mountain range now shadowed by dark clouds. Expecting to feel detachment, Brady was ill-prepared for the memories, long submerged, which rose to his consciousness or for his sense of connection to this place.

And certainly not for the impulse of something akin to affection he felt for his father.

He plunged his hands into his pockets, fighting his weakness. Or would Nell call it forgiveness? He'd been wronged, damn it. He couldn't afford that luxury.

He *would* think of Nell at a time like this, her gaze tender even as she accused him of addiction. Resentment and anger had fueled many of his actions, but, by now, they were familiar companions. Could he give them up? Was she asking too much?

Inside the house, his father took off his coat and slung it across the back of a kitchen chair, then hung his Stetson on a peg near the door. Brady, likewise, draped his coat over a chair while Velda filled his coffee cup and another for his father. Then she looked inquiringly at Dale, sending one of those messages that pass between a man and a woman that requires no words.

His father sat down in the place across the table from Brady. "Stay, Velda. You're part of this, too." Without a word, Velda slipped into the chair beside her husband.

Dale lifted his cup and blew on the steaming liquid. Finally he fixed his eyes on Brady. "Why now?" was all he said.

Brady considered his answer. "Because someone I care about accused me of being addicted to the anger and pain of my past. She suggested it would be therapeutic for me to face my demons."

His father's eyes were cold. "Is that how you think of us?"

Brady felt defensiveness kick in. "I never understood. I still don't."

"What? Spill it, son."

Brady fingered the distressed wood of the kitchen table, remembering the long-ago times he'd gripped the edge of this same table as an anchor in the sea of his rage. "Didn't you care about Mom at all?" He was surprised to hear the crack in his voice.

"Is that what you think? That I didn't care?"

"You tell me." He nodded at his stepmother. "Sorry, Velda, but, Dad, you certainly didn't waste any time moving on, did you? Did you ever stop for one minute to think how that made me feel? It was as if you didn't care. You planted Mom in the ground and then, within two months, remarried. You expected me to just accept that. To forget all about my mother." The coffee in his stomach soured.

Velda's eyes darkened with concern. "We didn't let you grieve, did we, Brady?"

"I've grieved for years." He stared at his father. "You're the one who never grieved."

His father slumped in his chair. "You couldn't be more wrong."

"Well, excuse me, if I fail to see it."

"You're still angry." His father made the words a statement.

"Damn right."

"I tried to talk to you back then. So did your mother. You wouldn't listen."

"To what?"

"The plans we made for what would happen when—" his father stumbled over the words "—when she died. You refused ever to hear us out. You'd stomp out of the room."

"What plans? What are you talking about?" It was all Brady could do to remain seated.

Velda covered Brady's hand with her own. "Your mother picked me."

"Picked you for what?"

Dale raked a hand through his thinning hair. "Let me start at the beginning. Your mother knew about Velda."

Surely he wasn't hearing correctly. "Knew what?"

"That she was a godsend during the last weeks of her illness. That she was a kind woman and a good friend. Your mother had been sick for so long, but she was always loving. Always thinking of others. She didn't want me to be alone. Didn't want you boys to be motherless. She'd known Velda for years.

Liked her. I was torn up with grief and, well—'' he patted his wife's arm ''—Velda was there for me.''

''But you married so quickly.''

''I'd grieved for years before your mother died. I couldn't do it any more. It was either lose myself or start a new life. I had your mother's blessing. I didn't see any reason to wait.''

Brady leaped to his feet. ''What about me? Wasn't I reason enough to wait? Danny?''

''Like I said, there was no talking to you. You were determined not to hear.''

Brady paced the floor, finally bracing himself against the counter, his back to his father. ''Hear what exactly?''

From behind him came the explanation, told in a labored voice by the man he'd spent years hating. The shock of his mother's diagnosis, her long illness, his parents' agonizing over the future, over what would become of their sons. Even as her health declined, his mother's insistence that her husband get his rest, her refusal to let him do for her what she could still do for herself.

Brady closed his eyes. That explained those awful nights when his mother's relentless coughing spells went unattended by his father.

''I begged her to let me help,'' his father continued, ''but she knew I needed my strength for the ranch.'' There was a long silence broken only by the furnace blower and icy raindrops flicking at the kitchen window. ''Toward the end, she began talking about what would happen to us—you, me, Danny. She understood how heavily I had come to depend on Velda, the one friend I knew I could count on day or night.''

Stirring in Brady was a vague recollection of coming home from school to find Velda reading to his mother.

''It was your mother who first suggested that I take another wife. Quickly.'' He cleared his throat. ''She wanted it to be Velda.''

Brady turned to face them. ''Still, you didn't waste any time.''

''I had loved your father and mother for a long time,'' Velda murmured. ''We would never have proceeded without your mother's blessing.''

''I hated you,'' Brady said, addressing his father.

''I know. And in a way I hated you. You wouldn't listen to us when we tried to explain, not to me and not to your mother. It was as if you didn't want to hear the truth—that your mother was terminal. Then, afterward, you took all your grief and anger out on me.''

''If you understood that, why did you treat me so badly?''

He raised his eyes and expelled a deep sigh. ''I was wild with the pain of losing your mother. Worried sick about the future. Anger was my outlet, I guess, and you gave me plenty of cause to unleash it.''

''You were like two wounded bears,'' Velda said.

''You'd grown physically big and strong, Brady. I thought you could take it. You were my whipping post. I forgot you were still just a kid.''

''You made some pretty unreasonable demands.''

''I did some things I'm not proud of. I couldn't

deal with my emotions where you were concerned. Maybe I was afraid of letting you get too close. Afraid what it would do to me if something happened to you or Danny." He snorted at the irony. "Pretty screwed-up thinking when you consider what I did was drive you away."

Brady saw himself at eighteen, standing in the doorway, his backpack slung over his shoulder, facing his father. *I hate you for forgetting about Mom. For marrying that slut. If I never see you again, it'll be too soon.* And his father's cutting reply. *Get out!*

"Why didn't you ever look for me?"

"I could ask you the same thing."

Brady sat back down, studying his coffee cup.

Velda smiled sadly. "You're two of the stubbornest men I know."

Brady quirked his lips. "Must run in the family." His father seemed lost in thought. Brady took a swallow of the tepid coffee, then set the cup down before continuing. "What now?"

"Are you still so angry?" his father asked.

Brady looked up, aware of an inner calmness he hadn't felt…maybe ever. "No," he said with wonderment.

"Could you…would you tell us about these missing eighteen years?" The hardness in his father's eyes had disappeared.

Brady sat back in his chair. "Yeah," he said, "I think I can. But first, Velda, I owe you an apology."

She smiled. "Accepted."

He nodded, breathed deeply and then began speaking. Neither his father nor Velda said a word during his recitation—the odd jobs that had led to a junior

260 MY NAME IS NELL

college computer course, losing himself in the world of cyber-technology, meeting Carl, moving to California, setting up the company.

But then, a huge lump formed in his throat. He struggled to talk about Brooke, then Nicole and, ultimately, the accident. At that point his father reached across the table and grasped his hand in an iron grip. Brady fell silent after telling about the collision.

"I understand that kind of grief," his father said.

When Brady looked into his father's eyes, he knew he was hearing the truth.

"And after that?" Velda prompted.

It was almost six when Brady finally finished. Unbelievably, he'd found himself telling them about Nell and Abby, about the chance for a new life he'd walked away from.

"You have a history of turning your back, son. Any idea why?"

His brain buzzed and his chest went hollow. "No," he said. But he *did* know. It wasn't something he felt like sharing now with others. He reviewed his boyhood, his youth, the recent months. The answer lay before him. Clear. Uncompromising. He hadn't felt worthy of love. Not after his mother died—and then Brooke and Nicole. He had convinced himself he deserved punishment.

Velda stood. "I better get us some supper. But before I do, I want to tell you something, Brady. I remember you as a teenager. You always felt things deeply and not always temperately. Your emotions were intense. I don't imagine you've changed much. Take that intensity and turn it to good. Love your Nell and Abby."

Brady pondered her advice. After leaving here all those years ago, he'd thought he could insulate himself from hurt. He'd let down his barricades with Brooke and Nicole. And then had come the accident followed by his self-inflicted emotional imprisonment. Until Nell. If he were to go back to Arkansas, it would have to be with openness and trust, and he didn't know if that was possible.

His father, too, rose to his feet. When Brady looked into his eyes, he saw something astonishing. Approval. "Reckon we better phone Danny and get him over here," he said.

"Yeah," Brady said, clenching his hands. "I guess I have some explaining to do. I abandoned him."

"He idolized you," his father said quietly.

"I, uh, tried a coupla times to get in touch with him. He never responded."

Velda arched an eyebrow. "Any wonder? He inherited that stubborn gene, too."

Dale laid a hand on Brady's shoulder. "Lucky thing, I guess, that it's not too late. Right, son?"

Brady swallowed hard, then nodded, his voice lost somewhere in the vicinity of his heart.

NELL WAS LATE getting to her mother's house for Lily's birthday party. She'd had to stop at the store, then pick up Abby at Tonya's.

Abby sat beside her in the front seat, cradling Lily's wrapped gift. "How old is Aunt Lily anyway?"

"Thirty-six."

"Yikes. I didn't think she was that old."

That old. Nell managed a bitter smile. At thirty-four, she, too, must be totally over the hill in her daughter's estimation. "Next thing you know we'll both be using walkers."

Abby glanced up at her. "I didn't mean it like that."

"I know, honey. We must seem ancient to you."

"I guess you can't be too old if you and Brady could fall in love."

What was it with the girl? She wouldn't leave it alone. Almost daily she found a way to insinuate Brady's name into the conversation. "Why do you keep talking about him?"

"I miss him, I guess."

Nell pulled to the curb in front of her mother's house and parked the car. "It's unrealistic to think like that. Brady is gone."

"But I just keep hoping—"

"What? That he'll mysteriously reappear? That we'll get back together?"

Head down, Abby studied the package in her lap.

"We have to move on, honey. I'll be fine. I *am* fine."

"Grandma doesn't think so."

Nell rolled her eyes. When would her family quit second-guessing her? "Could we please just get out of the car and go to the party?"

Abby shrugged. "I guess."

All the way up the walk, Nell concentrated on reducing her pulse rate. This was supposed to be a festive occasion, she reminded herself.

"Darlings!" Her mother threw open the door and

held out her arms in greeting. "We were worried when you were late."

Nell grimaced. Worried about what? That she'd started drinking? That she'd been in an accident? "The grocery store was crowded. My shopping took longer than I thought."

"Nell, is that you? At last?" Lily, dressed in a stunning mauve pantsuit, joined them in the hall. "I kept telling Mother you'd be right along."

"Happy birthday," Nell said, kissing her sister on the cheek.

Lily beamed, then dropped an arm around Abby's shoulder. "And how's my favorite niece? I understand you have a boyfriend. I want to hear *all* about him."

They made their way into the living room, where Evan was sprawled on the carpet playing trucks with Chase. He looked up with a smile. "Hi, Nell, Abby."

Abby added their gift to those stacked on the coffee table, then joined Chase and Evan on the floor.

"So what exciting things have you been doing on your birthday?" Nell inquired.

"Let's see. The florist delivered roses from Evan about ten, then I met my book club for lunch and this afternoon I had the most divine massage."

"Sounds heavenly."

Narrowing her eyes, Stella studied Nell. "You could use a massage. You look tense. Stressed."

"Now that you mention it," Lily leaned closer, "you do look a bit pinched."

A bit pinched? A line straight out of Jane Austen. "I'm fine," Nell said.

"You haven't heard from that Brady person?"

"No, Mother. I didn't expect to."

Lily intervened. "Mother, Nell doesn't need this."

Ignoring Lily, Stella laid a hand on Nell's leg. "And you're sure you're all right with that?"

Nell tried to be fair. Her mother had every right to be concerned, just as she would be if Alan Voyle broke up with Abby. "No, but that's the reality, like it or not. Aren't you actually asking something else?"

"What, dear?"

Lily's eyes rounded in sudden understanding.

"Whether I've been drowning my sorrows, so to speak."

"Nell!" Stella covered her bosom with the flat of her hand. "Why, we never—"

"Yes, you have. But I'm beginning to understand what you've been telling me. It's because you love me and want the best for me. I can't argue with that." She leaned forward and went on more calmly. "I need you to trust that I will persevere and remain sober because *I* want to. This is *my* problem and I'm the only one who can address it.

"We all know there will be difficult times. But, look. I made it through this episode with Brady without a drink. I don't intend to let anybody down. Especially myself."

"Oh, honey," Stella whispered, her eyes shiny with tears.

"I simply have to take each day as it comes."

Abby, who had clearly been eavesdropping, scooted across the floor and rested her head in Nell's lap. "I'm proud of you, Mom."

Lily looked fondly at Nell. "Me, too."

Stella hesitated, then added her endorsement. "And Mother makes three."

Nell ran her hand over Abby's silky hair, the ball in her stomach dissolving. "Thank you. I feel better already."

"We all do," Lily said.

Stella stood and waved her arm at the birthday presents. "Well, for heaven's sake, ladies, let's get this celebration underway. Lily's birthday and Nell's new tomorrows."

Then her mother winked at her, a gesture that included only her. Not Lily. Not Abby. A gesture that made Nell believe she'd finally gotten her point across—and was still, and always, loved.

BRADY HAD STAYED three days in Colorado before hitting the road. Now, headed toward Arkansas, he had the leisure to reflect on his visit. It had not been an easy time. There had been too many years and too much history to overcome in one brief visit. Too many misunderstandings. Especially with Danny, who had seemed unable to give Brady the same benefit of the doubt his father had.

How could he have been so oblivious at the time to his brother's sensitivity and grief? Had Brady thought he had a corner on the market?

Sure, Danny had been living with their grandparents during that last year, but why hadn't he kept in better touch? Gone to see him? The kid had to have been scared shitless.

So how could he blame his brother for his lack of enthusiasm when he learned Brady had returned?

Danny hadn't been rude, exactly. Just indifferent. As if he didn't trust Brady to maintain the relationship they'd started.

Hell, why should Danny trust him? Much as Brady hated to admit it, Nell had been right. He'd fed on his own bitterness and let far too many years pass without confronting himself and what had happened during that awful senior year. When Brooke had challenged him to face the past, he'd shut her out, just as he had anyone who'd ever questioned him. Until now.

The highway climbed steadily toward Vail Pass, and Brady idly wondered how far he could get today. How long before he reached Arkansas? The intervening miles stretched painfully in front of him. Miles he needed for some deep thinking.

What awaited him when he arrived? He had to be sure about his intentions before he approached Nell. This time he couldn't question her.

Look what had happened because he'd failed to listen to his parents. But trusting Nell was different. It meant forgiving her and giving up his unfair association of her with the man responsible for the deaths of his wife and daughter. It meant living in the present, not the past.

He'd never seen her drunk and he didn't want to. Ever. But he needed to be prepared for that eventuality—and for his role in supporting her sobriety. If he made a commitment to her, he would be in it for the long haul, warts and all.

By her honesty, she'd given him back his life. Was he willing to help do the same for her?

"C'MON, ABBY, just once around his block."

Abby, astraddle her bicycle, threw Tonya a disgusted look. "What're you gonna do if we see him?"

"Swoon." Tonya sped off down the street.

Reluctantly, Abby followed, knowing she'd die of embarrassment if Mr. Sanders, their English teacher, spotted them. She had to admit he was adorable and way cool, but she didn't understand why Tonya was wasting her time on somebody that old. Why didn't she find someone her own age, like one of Alan's friends?

Besides feeling geeky about Mr. Sanders, it was kinda sad being in this neighborhood. She couldn't help remembering that day she'd come down this same street on her way to Brady's condo. How nice he'd been. Kinda like a father.

Her mom had really, really liked him. She was trying to act brave now, but Abby could tell she was sad. Sorta like the light in her eyes was set on dim.

Ahead of her, Tonya pumped her fist and pointed toward a small house wedged between two three-story apartment buildings. It had all these cars in the front yard and looked like a hangout for college guys. But she guessed that's sorta what Mr. Sanders was. He was a first-year teacher, just out of the U of A.

Loud stereo music boomed from an open window, but even going past slowly, they couldn't see anyone. Tonya stopped at the corner, then shrugged when Abby drew alongside. "Crap. No stud spotting today."

Abby gazed beyond her friend and saw in the distance the entrance to Brady's condominium complex. It was getting dark, but surely it wouldn't hurt to ride by. She could show Tonya where Brady had lived.

"Follow me," she said, pulling into the intersection ahead of Tonya.

"Where're we going?" Tonya called, but Abby just kept pedaling toward the condominium, all the time feeling queasy with regret. He was never coming back.

She stopped at the edge of the lot, where Tonya caught up with her. "What're you looking at, Abby?"

"There." She pointed toward Brady's unit. "That's where my mother's boyfriend lived."

"He's gone, though, right?"

Abby's toes curled inside her sneakers. "Yeah," she said quietly. Why was she about to cry? This was stupid. She hardly knew the man. It wasn't like he had ever planned on being part of their family or anything. But she was convinced he'd really cared about her. She loved her dad, of course, but sometimes she felt like he didn't know much about daughters. Not like Brady did. You could tell how much he'd loved Nicole.

"Hey, dorkess, what are we standin' here for? I gotta get home."

"Okay," Abby said. She straddled her bike, then paused for one last look at the condo.

What she saw caused her to grip the handlebars so tightly her knuckles whitened. *Oh, please, oh, please* she found herself imploring, her breath coming in tiny gasps. *Let it be him.*

An Escalade had turned into the far entrance to the parking lot. Abby motioned Tonya to follow as she concealed herself behind a hedge.

"What are you doing?" Tonya demanded.

"Shh." Abby narrowed her eyes, waiting to see if it could possibly be. The Escalade parked, then a man wearing a ball cap climbed out—a tall man with broad shoulders. Abby crossed her fingers, continuing her mantra, afraid to trust her eyes. What if she was wrong? He opened the tailgate, gathered some luggage and, unbelievably, made straight for the right condo unit.

"Omigod," Abby breathed.

"What?"

"It's him. Brady. He's back."

Tonya moved closer, squinting through the branches. "Wow," she breathed. "For an old guy, he's a hunk."

They watched until he closed the front door and then slowly pedaled back the way they had come. Tonya tried to talk to her, ask her all these nosy questions, but Abby didn't have anything to say.

Was he back for good? Or just coming to pick up some stuff he'd left?

Maybe it didn't matter. The important thing was that he *was* back and that gave her mother a chance.

And a chance was better than nothing.

All the way home Abby plotted her strategy. She was just a kid, but this time she wasn't going to mind her own business. Or was she? Maybe this was her business, too.

NELL SHOOK OUT the towels as she moved them from the washer to the dryer. Tearing off a sheet of fabric softener, she passed it under her nose before adding it to the load. The manufacturer had come darn close to the scent of fresh spring air.

Spring. Her favorite time of year. With fortitude and patience, in April she would get her seven-year chip. Few outside of AA had any understanding of the significance of these milestones. She was proud of each of her chips and, after her recent close call, had made a vow to relive those high points, which could be equally as motivating as the low moments.

Humming to herself as she turned on the dryer, Nell reflected on the change in her mother since the night of Lily's party. She no longer prefaced comments with "Lily and I think..." and her recent phone calls had been chatty rather than thinly veiled inquisitions.

Nell turned to the laundry table and began folding the underwear she'd taken out of the dryer earlier, acknowledging the relief she felt now that things were back to normal, or whatever passed for normal. After Brady had left, she'd settled back into the routine of work, meetings and family. Maybe she'd only imagined that brief window of opportunity when she'd glimpsed a future that had included Brady. Even then, though, she had understood he wasn't ready for commitment—not until he made some kind of peace with what had happened to his wife and daughter. And with his early years in Colorado about which he refused to speak. However, she'd been hopeful that with time...

Nell smoothed a half slip, then folded it in thirds. Part of what she'd loved about him was the very fact that he cared so deeply. There was nothing superficial or contrived about his emotions. He was a man capable of loving passionately.

Damn. She wished she hadn't used that word with

its painful reminders of warm, soft lips, exploring fingers and eager, aching flesh. She ran her hands over the slip, wondering if she ever would've dared to wear something exotic, tantalizing...maybe one of those see-through teddies or....

"Mom! You'll never guess what!"

Nell started. She hadn't even heard the front door. She grinned, wondering what late-breaking development in Abby's life led to the mega-decibel volume of her voice.

"Where are you?" Abby's exasperated tone was hard to miss.

"In the utility room." Nell gathered the folded clothes to her chest and stepped into the kitchen.

Breathless, Abby stopped in the doorway, her face red from exertion, her eyes snapping with excitement. "I rode home as fast as I could. I couldn't wait to tell you the news."

"What news, honey?"

"He's back!"

Had she missed something? Had Alan Voyle been on a trip? "Who? Alan?"

Abby spread her arms in triumph. "Duh, Mother. Brady!"

She clutched the laundry more tightly. "What do you mean?"

"I saw him, Mom. He didn't see me, but I know it was him. He drove that same kind of car and went into that same building."

Nell felt sick. She made it to the table, laid the clothes down and sank into a chair. He was here. In Fayetteville. But he hadn't called. Hadn't come by.

"Are you all right?" she could hear Abby asking.

"Yes," she said, aware she was flat-out lying to her daughter.

Abby pulled a chair from the table and, drawing one foot up under her, sat down. "Don't you see? Everything's going to be all right."

"Abby, calm down, it's—"

"All you have to do is go see him. It's simple."

Nell wished with all her heart that she could view the world from such an idealized perspective. "No, I can't. If he wants to see me, he'll call."

Abby blew the hair off her face. "Mo-ther. That's so retro. It's the twenty-first century. You don't have to sit around waiting for a man."

"If he'd been interested, he'd have called by now."

Abby glanced at her watch. "Give him time. He only just got to town."

Nell's heart shifted into triphammer speed. "How do you know?"

"When Tonya and I spied on him, he was unloading bags from his car."

Nell wouldn't, couldn't get her hopes up. He'd just come to town to finalize his move back to California. Nell reached over and patted her daughter's hand. "You have to get used to it, honey, as I have. Brady is a wonderful man, but he won't be part of our lives."

"Bull!" Abby leaped from her chair. "He loves you. You love him. All you have to do is march over there and tell him. I betcha he feels the same way."

"It wouldn't be proper."

"Adults!" Abby rolled her eyes before putting her hands on Nell's shoulders. "You're the one always talking to me about taking risks. About how you have to be willing to stick up for what you believe. To go after what you want.''

If the subject hadn't been so serious, Nell would've been tempted to smile. Abby was right. She had preached all those lessons—and now they were coming back to haunt her. ''I can't.''

Her daughter shook her gently and gave her a skeptical look. ''Don't turn chicken on me, Mom. If you don't go for it now, you'll look back and always wish you had.''

Nell shrugged in defeat. When the kid was right, she was right!

CHAPTER FIFTEEN

BRADY PULLED OFF the rutted road at the edge of the resort property and sat in the Escalade, amazed at the way the view had opened up now that many of the trees had shed their leaves. In the early morning cold, condensation off the lake created clouds of mist that moved, specterlike, across the blue surface of the water. On the far hillside a few trees still displayed vivid colors.

His option was nearly up. It was decision time. Good sense dictated he should abandon his foolish dream, but, then, good sense had nothing to do with the excitement he'd been helpless to prevent when he crossed the state line into Arkansas. Nor with the sense of well-being generated by the scene before him.

He stepped out of his vehicle, shouldered a day pack and started off through the woods, awed by the scent of pine and the chatter of birds darting from limb to limb. He didn't want to think about the power this land exerted over him. It was either a major weakness or a sign. And he didn't believe in signs.

Or did he? What else to call his stumbling across Nell's message at the Edgewater Inn?

Nell had called the bed-and-breakfast a sanctuary. Was that what he had been seeking? He halted, his attention arrested by several buzzards wheeling over-head. Nature. Predator. Prey. Cyclical. Ever the same, ever different. A far cry from Silicon Valley.

As he tramped on, he was able to name what this place meant to him. Freedom from the past. New beginnings. Serenity. Yes, even a sanctuary.

But part of that sense of connection and belonging rested with Nell. More of her words came back to him. *I have to believe that somewhere out there is someone for me. Someone I can trust. Someone I can love.*

He had hurt her with his condemnation of her drinking. With his self-righteous judgment, his leap to make her the scapegoat for his own anger. Before going to Colorado, he had never thought of himself as a black-and-white thinker. Yet he had painted his father and Velda with the monochrome of rancor, when, in fact, the situation had been far more complex.

Reaching a large limestone outcropping, he dropped his pack and sat on the edge, his feet dangling. A squirrel skittered past, intent on gathering his store of winter acorns.

He had been unfair to Nell. He'd put off calling her or going to see her. This time he had to be sure. She was deserving of the best a man could give her—and for her that meant trust and love. No matter what.

If he was truthful, it was the "no matter what" that scared him. Yet no one knew better than he that life doesn't come with guarantees. Certainly he'd never imagined Brooke and Nicole's accident. Maybe it was the things you didn't worry about that caused the gravest problems, so what was the point of borrowing trouble?

Some things were in his control. Facing his fears. Loving Nell for the wonderful woman she was, not the desperate one he'd never known. Trusting her.

He leaned back on the cool rock, pillowing his head in his linked hands. A sudden thought came to him—powerful and affirming. His personal storm had passed, and in its aftermath, he now realized, was his rainbow—Nell.

He laughed aloud, a sound joyous and free. He, too, was a believer in rainbows.

NELL SAT at her office desk trying to read book reviews in the *Library Journal*. Yet her concentration was shot and she found herself rereading every three or four lines.

Two days had passed since Abby's announcement, and Nell still hadn't heard from Brady. She'd thought a lot about Abby's suggestion that she go to him, but ultimately it had to be his choice whether he could live with an alcoholic.

Yet even as that thought surfaced, her inner demon—or angel?—accused her. *So you're willing to leave it all up to him? You've lived "safe" a long time. What about taking a chance? How else will you know what might have been? Why settle for "safe" when you might have "fulfilling?"*

She threw down the magazine and plunged her hands through her hair. She didn't need voices like that haunting her, eroding her carefully constructed world, exposing her loneliness.

What about Abby? Oh, yes, her guardian spirit had

to bring that up. Somehow, in a very short time, Brady had become important to her daughter. Could she overlook that? Especially when the girl's own father found parenting difficult?

Get off it, Nell. Give up the rationalizations. You love the man. You think that comes without risk? But there's no prize without risk. You want rainbows? Okay. They come at a cost.

Nell stood up and looked around her office, where she'd accomplished absolutely zilch in the past two days. This state of affairs simply couldn't go on.

All right, she would do it. She would see him. She would go prepared for anything—even rejection.

And with her heart in her hands.

NELL SHRUGGED INTO her red all-weather coat, waved goodbye to Reggie Pettigrew who was manning the checkout desk and slipped out of the library. A hard freeze was predicted for tonight and the air was already sharp with cold. Head down against the strong north wind, she hurried toward her car. She would get this over with this afternoon. Abby had a late basketball practice and it was the Larkins' turn to pick the girls up. If Brady was at home, she would have the ordeal behind her before dinner. Then she could settle things with Abby once and for all.

Tripping over a crack in the sidewalk, she nearly fell, saved only by a strong arm around her waist. "Careful."

When she looked up, her breath stopped. "Brady?" His serious expression put her on guard.

"I've been waiting for you."

"Oh?" She could think of nothing further to say,

the awkwardness between them an impediment to rational thought.

"We need to talk."

When she stepped back and raised her head, the wind whipped strands of hair into her face. "You're right. Abby told me you were back."

"How did she know?"

"She saw you."

Putting his hands in his pockets, he studied her, his expression difficult to read. "I should've called."

"I wasn't expecting it."

He nodded, as if she'd confirmed something he already knew.

It was now or never. "I agree that we need to talk. In fact, I was just on my way to see you."

"I said some awful things to you."

"And I withheld the truth."

He moved closer and it required all her self-control not to reach up and brush her fingers over his cheek. Her breath came raggedly. She was even more attracted to him than she'd remembered. More than anything, she craved the comfort of his embrace.

Then his gaze caught hers and in it she saw a flicker of yearning. He lifted his hand and smoothed the hair out of her eyes. "Do you have time now?"

Not trusting herself to speak, she nodded.

"Could you come to my place? I want to show you something."

"I'll follow you," she said.

He walked her to her car. Once she was behind the wheel, he held the door just long enough to murmur, "Be careful. I don't want to lose you now."

Nell's hand shook as she turned the ignition key.

She couldn't read too much into those words. He was just being polite. Or maybe he was talking about losing her in traffic.

But what if he meant he didn't want to lose *her?* What if she could permit herself hope?

Nell discovered something as she followed Brady to his condominium. Time passes more easily when you're praying.

HEEDLESS OF THE strong wind, Brady waited outside for Nell, knowing that the next hour or so would determine his entire future. He'd been unprepared for his reaction when he'd first seen her outside the library. All other considerations had evaporated in the rush of love that had swept over him—followed by fear, empty and cold. What if he was too late?

Yet when she'd said she had been on her way here, he'd relaxed. Maybe there was a chance. He'd already lost so much. He couldn't lose her.

She turned into the parking space next to his and he hurried to meet her. "Come along inside. I'll brew us a hot cup of coffee."

She smiled and his heart thawed. "I'd like that."

He took her by the arm and, once inside, took her coat, then ushered her to the ugly oversize sofa. "Make yourself at home, or as much at home as possible in this mausoleum. I'll be right back."

He carefully measured the coffee, added water and flipped on the switch, rehearsing in his mind what he would say to her, how he could convince her of his change of heart. From the pass-through he could see her head bent over a magazine she'd picked up from the coffee table. His throat thickened. He didn't want to talk. He wanted to pull her into his arms and carry her down the hall to his room, where the one redeeming feature of this furnished condo waited—a feather-soft, king-size bed.

She looked up expectantly when he entered the room. "This ought to warm you up," he said, handing her a mug, then taking a seat at the opposite end of the sofa.

"Thank you." When she carried the cup to her lips, her downcast eyelashes reminded him of the morning she'd covered his bare chest with butterfly kisses that drove him wild. "It's very tasty."

He smiled. "My specialty."

She looked at him. He looked at her. It was a silence suspended between hope and fear. Finally she said, "What now?"

He couldn't stand the waiting a second longer. "Why were you coming here this afternoon?"

Leaning forward, she set down her coffee before turning toward him. Her eyes glittered and when she spoke, her voice was raspy. "To see if there was a chance." She hesitated. "And to tell you I love you."

Dizzying waves of relief washed over him. In a flash he had moved beside her and pulled her into his arms. "Nell, sweetheart, I love you, too." He buried his mouth in her hair, smelling of sunshine, wind and green, growing things. He framed her face between his hands and looked into those deep eyes he'd dreamed about every single night they'd been apart.

Her hands tightened on his shoulders. "I haven't changed. I...I'll always be an alcoholic."

"You're much more than that." He kissed each eyelid, then her nose. "You will always and forever be the woman I love."

"I've been so afraid."

"Of what?"

"That you wouldn't come back." She seemed to struggle to go on. "Or that you'd reject me."

He chuckled. "Funny. I was afraid of the same thing. After the ugly things I said, I knew I'd blown it with you."

"So why did you come back?"

"I had to take the chance it wasn't too late."

"But I said some pretty awful things to you, too."

"All of which were right on target." He leaned back against the sofa, pulling her with him. "I *was* addicted."

She lifted her head. *"Was?"*

"How much time do you have?"

She shrugged. "I don't know. How much do you need? I should leave before six-thirty. Abby gets home from basketball then."

Two hours. It had to be enough. "That should do it. I need to tell you some things."

Somehow unburdening himself was easier with her by his side, the warmth of her body soothing years of pain. He started with his childhood, the mother he'd adored, her lingering illness and death, then the abrupt change when his father had married Velda. His unwillingness to listen. His anger and rebellion. His abandonment of Danny. The decision to put the first eighteen years of his life behind him. She already knew about Brooke and Nicole, but he found he needed to go through it all again. Even the accident. He ended with his recent visit with his father and the beginning they'd made. It was nearly six when he finished. "I can't live any longer with anger, resentment and grief."

"Acceptance," she whispered. "It isn't easy."

"No," he agreed. "It isn't."

"You loved your mother very much. Perhaps it's only lately that you've mourned her, along with Brooke and Nicole."

He looked at her. "I'd never considered that, but I think you're right."

"No wonder you were in such pain."

"Until I met you." He traced her hairline with a finger.

"You're sure?" The question in her eyes revealed fragility and vulnerability and conveyed far more than the words suggested.

He knew this was the defining moment. He had to be certain. Anything less would be a disservice to her and a betrayal of himself. This meant commitment. Unconditional love. Still clasping her, he stood up, drawing her with him. He held her, then, at arm's length, studying her beloved face. "Dearest Nell, I am absolutely, positively certain."

"Oh, Brady." She sagged against him and before he knew what he was doing, he found her lips, his body fiery with need. She met his tongue thrust for thrust, her mouth warm and sweet. "I've missed you so much," she whimpered.

"I'm not leaving," he said. Then, pulling back and taking her by the hand, he led her into the spare bedroom, which he'd converted to a makeshift office.

"Remember, I told you I have something to show you." He ushered her through the door, then stood behind her, his arms circling her waist. "What do you think?"

He heard her tiny gasp, before she pivoted in his arms. "Brady, is that what I think it is?" Her eyes were shining.

"It's the architect's initial rendering for the Vista Inn and Resort." Before he'd left for California he'd commissioned this preliminary step. He could have canceled out. He could have let his option lapse. But he hadn't. Deep down, he'd always known why. He was destined to come home. To Arkansas. To Nell.

"It's beautiful," she breathed, the admiration in her eyes humbling.

"No," he corrected. "It's nice. You're beautiful." He held her lightly, sliding his hands down her back, over her rounded hips. "What time did you say you had to be home?" He nuzzled her neck.

"Soon," she murmured langorously. "Too soon."

He bent his head and began unbuttoning her blouse, rimming the top of her bra with his forefinger. "Sure you couldn't stay a little longer?"

She thrust her hands inside the back of his trousers, the pressure on his buttocks increasing the urgency threatening to send him over the edge. "Maybe I could call the Larkins."

"Sounds like an inspired idea," he said, easing her blouse over her shoulders and partway down her arms.

"I need to use the phone," she managed to say between kisses.

"No problem," he said, propelling her down the hall. "There's one in the bedroom."

An hour later, sated and spent, he cuddled Nell's satin-smooth body into his, thanking his lucky stars for the Larkins' flexibility and his landlord's bed that had more than lived up to its promise. Way more.

"Omigod, ohmigod." Abby burst through the front door mere minutes after Nell arrived home. She had just stepped out of the shower, having cleansed from her body the traces of lovemaking that made her weak in the knees just thinking about it. She'd even decided maybe she would dare to buy that sheer teddy she'd fantasized about.

Gathering her terry-cloth robe around her, she knotted the sash and stepped into the hall. "What's the matter? Did something happen at practice?"

Abby was practically jumping up and down with excitement. "You'll never believe it."

What now? "I'm all ears."

"I've gotta show you. Come into my room." Abby dumped the contents of her backpack on the floor, then rifled through books, pens and notebooks until she came up with a rumpled piece of computer paper. "In computer class today we had an assignment to look up someone we knew on the internet to see what information was there."

"So?"

"I picked Brady." She thrust the paper into Nell's hands. "Go ahead. Read."

She looked down at a print-out of an article from the *Wall Street Journal*. The title meant nothing to

her. "Silicon Valley Creates Instant Millionaires."
She let her eyes scan the sheet until she found
Brady's name, followed by the words, *entrepreneurial genius, estimated worth $50,000,000.* Nell collapsed into Abby's desk chair. For a minute, she was
afraid she was going to pass out.

Abby bounced from one foot to the other. "Isn't
that exciting?"

Nell thought about it. No wonder he could afford
to hit the road for months following the accident,
take an option on the Beaver Lake land, drive an
expensive vehicle. Why hadn't he told her? This
sounded like some crazy imitation of a reality TV
show. She couldn't help herself—she erupted in
shaky, manic laughter.

Abby did a double take. "Mom, are you all
right?"

"I think maybe your news changes everything. No
way is he going to stay in Fayetteville, Arkansas."

"Mom, don't you get it? It's like he's Prince
Charming."

Nell hiccupped, caught between laughter and tears.
"Be that as it may, but I have a feeling this Cinderella is back to scrubbing pots and pans and cleaning
the fireplace."

"I don't believe you."

"Why on earth not?"

"Because you've seen him, haven't you? You've
told him how you feel."

Abby was way too sharp. "How on earth would
you know that?"

"Well, duh, Mother." She pointed to the collar of Nell's robe. "Look at your neck. You've got a hickey the size of a headlight!"

NELL WENT AROUND the next day at work adjusting the silky scarf wrapped around her neck, hoping no one besides Abby would detect the all-too-visible signs of an enchanted hour of lovemaking. The smug grin had not left Abby's face since. This morning before she'd left for school, she'd shot Nell a knowing look, then said, "Lookin' good, Mom."

But the hickey blooming at the base of her throat was the least of her worries. Fifty million dollars! An unthinkable amount, almost obscene. She couldn't begin to wrap her mind around that information. How could Brady have withheld such a vital part of himself? There was no way he would turn his back on his lucrative business. And no matter how much she loved him, she couldn't uproot Abby and leave her family. California was glitzy and foreign. This was her home, the place where she'd wrestled with addiction, where she felt safe, secure.

She stood at the copy machine, lost in thought. The truth was, his wealth scared her to death. Just like her alcoholism had to scare him.

She gathered up the flyers and returned to her office, eyeing the clock. Half an hour to go. Then home. To Brady. Before she'd left him yesterday afternoon, she'd invited him to dinner tonight. Knowing Abby would be at the high school football game, Nell had originally envisioned an intimate evening— soft, romantic music, flickering candles, good food.

And, just in case, she'd thought about putting fresh sheets on the bed.

But Abby's bombshell had changed all that. Now instead of a flirtatious smile, she'd greet Brady with a huge question and butterflies in her stomach.

BRADY HAD BEEN euphoric all day. Everywhere he looked was something to like—the smogless blue skies, the hometown-friendly store clerks, the harvest decorations bedecking most front porches. Yet the hours until he could be with Nell again had passed too slowly. His heart warmed every time he thought about her sweet, spontaneous responses to his love-making. She had no idea what a sexy, desirable woman she was. Rick must've been an idiot.

Or the wrong man. The next thought brought a grin to his face. Heck, maybe all along she'd been waiting for him. Well, her waiting days were over. Now that he'd come back to her, he would never let her go. Life, he'd learned, was too short to be eaten up by grudges and pain.

Yet sitting here at the dining room table after her delicious pork roast dinner, with the light from two tapers the only illumination in the room, he sensed something was out of kilter. Nell had been abnormally quiet, the silences filled by the mellow strains of dinner music. When she had talked, it had been about work, Abby and AA. Especially AA. As if she was trying to warn him off. She'd confessed to her bout with temptation when he'd left to return to California. He recognized that she needed to tell him the worst, so he let her relate each detail of the night of her accident and of her recent struggle.

As she talked his stomach churned, both with memories of Brooke and Nicole and the all-too-real eventuality she painted for him. No more kidding himself. Her sobriety was hard-earned. Always there would be the fragile balance between will and temptation. Yet he'd told her he was certain about his feelings and about his commitment.

He studied her across the table. Her skin was pale above the soft robin's-egg blue sweater she wore. Her serious gray eyes spoke volumes about her struggles—and her fears.

Yet in that moment he loved her more than he could ever have thought possible. Whatever the future held, they would face it together. He waited until she finished talking. She sat, hands folded in her lap, head bowed.

"Okay," he said. "That's out of the way."

She looked up. "What do you mean?"

"The attempt to run me off. It didn't work, Nell. So now, how about the truth?"

"The truth?"

"Yes. Why are you so hell-bent to put obstacles in our path?"

"Obstacles?" Her mouth flattened to a thin line. "Since you're so into the truth, why don't you come clean, too?"

What was she talking about? "I don't know what you mean."

"The little detail about yourself you forgot to mention."

He hadn't a clue. "Detail?"

She reached into the pocket of her skirt and drew out a folded piece of paper. She handed it to him. "Were you ever going to tell me?"

He unfolded the sheet of paper and scanned the contents. That damn *Wall Street Journal* article. Why was she looking at him with such resignation? Such sadness? "What about it?"

"Brady, my God, you're a millionaire."

"So?" What in hell was the problem?

"You didn't tell me."

"No, I didn't. You know why? Because it isn't important. It's just money, most of it on paper. I hardly ever think about it. Yes, I can live well and that's nice, but the money itself is meaningless."

"How can you say that?"

"Because my success was never about money. It was about proving to my old man that I'd amount to something after all."

"Oh."

"Does it matter?"

"I can't live in California, Brady. I'm a home-body."

Now he understood. She thought he was going back to California, that he expected her to adapt to his lifestyle, when in fact it was just the other way around.

He circled the table and knelt beside her chair. "You're too late, Nell."

She bit her lip, then spoke. "When do you go?"

If she hadn't looked so forlorn, he'd have chuckled. Instead, he rose to his feet, took her by the hand, then pulled her into his arms. "I'm not going any-where, especially not without you."

Her voice quavered. "What do you mean?"

"I bought the land today."

"You did?"

"And that's not all. I've rented office space, hired a project architect and am in the process of setting up an Arkansas corporation. I like Arkansas—the land, the people, everything. Above all, I love you. Money and success mean nothing if you don't have someone with whom to share them. You and Abby are my 'someones' and you'll have one heckuva time getting rid of me."

She trembled in his arms and he wrapped her even closer. "So you're an alcoholic and I'm a million-aire. Big deal. I can put up with you if you can put up with me." He tilted her chin and smiled down at her. Her face was alight with hope, a flame he wanted to tend for as long as he lived. "Marry me, Nell."

No sooner were the words out of his mouth than the front door banged and Abby came barreling into the room. Talk about timing.

"Oops, sorry," she said, doing a theatrical about-face.

"No, wait, Abby," Brady said, still holding Nell in his arms. "Help me out here."

Abby turned around, cocked her head and studied him. "Sure. Whaddya need?"

He nodded down at Nell. "Convince the woman to marry me."

"Mo-om—" Abby sprinted across the room and

joined the hug. ''Are you crazy?'' Then Abby grinned at him. ''Of course she'll marry you.''

The two of them stepped back and looked at Nell, who turned from one to the other, her eyes glistening, her cheeks pink. ''Are you ganging up on me?''

''If that's what it takes,'' Brady said.

Nell seemed about to speak, but hesitated. Brady's heart was in his throat. She moved to put an arm around Abby. ''Are you sure, honey? You know what this means?''

Abby stood up tall. ''Yes. It means you'll have a husband who loves you and I will have a way cool stepfather.''

Nell gazed at her daughter for a long moment. The love in her eyes almost hurt Brady to watch. Then she turned those same eyes on him. ''I would be honored, Brady.''

He enclosed his new family in his arms, home at last. A chuckle rose from deep in his belly. ''It's not every day a fella gets two lovely females for the price of one.''

NELL DETAINED Ben Hadley after her Saturday morning meeting the next day. ''Walk me to my car?'' she asked.

''It would be my pleasure,'' he said gallantly taking her by the elbow.

It was a gorgeous November day, sunny and cloudless with the kind of chill that brings roses to the cheeks. ''I have news,'' Nell said as they exited the church.

Ben kept walking. ''And what would that be?''

"I'm getting married."

He dropped her arm, took off his hat and, with wild abandon, threw it into the air. "Hallelujah and amen!" After he retrieved his hat, he faced her, beaming with unadulterated joy. "How did that come about?"

Her eyes danced. "Let's put it this way. I accepted some things I couldn't change, had the courage to change some things about myself and finally had the wisdom to know the difference."

Throwing her arms around the older man who had always been there for her, she whispered, "Oh, Ben, my name is Nell and I am loved."

EPILOGUE

NELL STEPPED OUT of the bathroom, pulling her satin peignoir closer around her. Brady, in plaid flannel pajama bottoms, lounged on the striped love seat in one corner of their cozy bedroom in the Edgewater Inn. A floor lamp cast soft light across the room. She could feel the pulse in her neck quickening as her eyes fixed on his bare chest. Despite having been married before, this felt like her first honeymoon. Like a real honeymoon.

He held out an arm, beckoning her to join him. She snuggled against him, reveling in the sea-fresh aphrodisiac of his cologne. "It was a great wedding, wasn't it?" he said, fondling her shoulder.

"It couldn't have been better. I hadn't realized how moved I would be by having our family and friends all together." She smiled, remembering her mother beaming from her first-row pew; Lily, radiant in a deep purple dress; Chase prancing up the aisle as ringbearer; her co-workers and many of her AA friends gathered to wish her well. She would never forget the moment when the organ swelled and she took Ben's arm as he led her toward her handsome groom.

She continued, "How special it was that your dad and Velda could be here." Although the situation had been somewhat awkward, Stella had taken the matter in hand and made his parents welcome. "Did you mind about Danny?"

A shadow fell across his face. "I would've liked him to be my best man. But I guess our relationship will take time. At least he answered my last e-mail."

"Well, Carl filled in beautifully. I enjoyed meeting him and Jill."

"They're great people." He sat quietly for a moment, then went on, "Abby was a gorgeous maid of honor. If you hadn't been such a beautiful bride, I'd have had a hard time keeping my eyes off my new daughter."

"I was so proud of her."

"Do you think she'll be all right in Dallas while we're gone?"

"Now that she's accepted you as part of her family, I think she's realized she has to make more of an effort with her father and Clarice. She told me the other day that maybe there were some things she hadn't understood. That maybe she hadn't given them much of a chance."

Brady chuckled as he played with her hair. "Sounds like she's growing up."

Nell sighed. "Too fast."

"But just think," he said, moving his hand to part the collar of her peignoir, "that'll leave all the more time for us."

Nell nestled her head into his neck and rubbed gentle little circles over his chest with her fingertips. "That could be good," she agreed.

"Say, before you get me too hot and bothered to think straight, I have a confession to make."

Her hand stilled. Not another one. She had had it with surprises. She lifted her head. "What?"

"You think I brought you here to the Edgewater Inn because you told me about it in the library that time, right?"

"Of course."

"That's not why."

"It isn't?"

"Nope." He leaned across her to retrieve a small journal from the lamp table. "You've stayed in this very room before."

The inn wasn't that big. She'd thought it mere coincidence. "How did you know?"

He thumbed through the book, flattened it to one page and handed it to her. "Recognize this?"

Nell read her entry in disbelief. *I've been so alone. When you've loved and lost, doubt replaces hope, insecurity replaces confidence and you wonder who you are. Whether you can go on. Or even want to.* She had actually been that woman, sent off to the restful bed-and-breakfast by her mother and sister following her final divorce hearing. She read on, her eyes filling with tears as she remembered that Nell. *This time of quiet and contemplation has been a great gift, restoring my belief that no matter how severe the storm, rainbows can happen. Regardless of how desolate I feel right now, I have to believe that somewhere out there is someone for me. Someone I can trust. Someone I can love. When I find him, the two of us will come to the Edgewater Inn. Together.*

When she glanced up, Brady was studying her, his

eyes bathing her with love. "I came looking for you."

"I...I don't understand."

"I didn't care about anything. I'd lost hope. And then I read your entry. You understood how I felt, but with one difference. You believed in rainbows."

"And?"

"I decided I wanted to meet the rainbow woman." He picked up her hand, urging her understanding. "That's why I came to Fayetteville."

"Brady, that's wild. I can hardly believe it."

"Believe it." He took the book from her and flipped through more pages, then settling on one, handed it back to her. "Read."

He moved closer, putting his arm back around her, his warm breath stirring the hair at the back of her neck. Whispering the words aloud, she began to read the firm, clear handwriting. *For most, this place is a sanctuary. I would like to believe it could be. I read in these pages of celebration, new beginnings, old joys revisited. Only in one entry have I found another who understands pain. Nell, whoever you are, if there are such things as rainbows, help me find them. Then maybe, just maybe, we* will *come back here together.*

She drew a stuttering breath. If it was possible to feel more love for another, to be more loved by another, she couldn't imagine it. "I never knew," she murmured.

"The only thing that matters is that I found you, my beautiful Nell."

When he pulled her against him and lowered his

lips to hers, she didn't even realize her robe had fallen open revealing the lacy see-through teddy she'd bought especially for him. For her rainbow man.

Dear Reader,

As a child I spent many hours with a length of clothesline in my hand. My friend Susie would be on the other end and our friend Joanie would be in the middle, jumping as we twirled the rope and sang one of the many ditties created especially for skipping rope. Our favorite was the one that ended with "First comes love, then comes marriage, then comes Joanie pushing a baby carriage."

It's a refrain that echoed often in my head while I wrote this book because my heroine, Krystal—like a lot of women—believes she's going to fall in love, get married and have a baby—in that order. Then she does a favor for a friend and discovers that her plan has suddenly been thrown out the window. Now she finds herself wondering if it's possible to have a baby first, then get married and then fall in love.

As you read this story you'll find the answer. You'll also meet the women who live at 14 Valentine Place, a wonderful old Victorian house where love has a way of sneaking up on its tenants when they least expect it. I hope you'll enjoy your visit with them.

If you'd like to write to me, I love to hear from readers. Send your letters to Pamela Bauer, c/o MFW, P.O. Box 24107, Minneapolis, MN 55424, or you can visit me via the Internet at www.pamelabauer.com.

Warmly,

Pamela Bauer

A Baby in the House
Pamela Bauer

**Harlequin
Mills & Boon**

*Super
Romance*

First Published 2003
First Australian Paperback Edition 2004
ISBN 0 733 54865 2

A BABY IN THE HOUSE © 2003 by Pamela Bauer
Philippine Copyright 2003
Australian Copyright 2003
New Zealand Copyright 2003

Published by
Harlequin Mills & Boon
3 Gibbes Street
CHATSWOOD NSW 2067
AUSTRALIA

Printed and bound in Australia by
McPherson's Printing Group

For the baby in our house,
Aedan Paul.
What a joy you are!

And a special thank-you to
Michelle Rudolph for sharing her
professional insights with me.

PROLOGUE

KRYSTAL GRAHAM SPOTTED Garret Donovan across the ballroom, briefly locked her eyes with his, then glanced away. She waited only a moment before allowing her gaze to slowly wander back to his, giving him a smile that said, *You know what I'm thinking and it's a bit naughty.*

The flirtatious move hinted at an intimacy that didn't exist and was part of a plan to make Samantha Penrose jealous. It worked. Samantha couldn't keep her eyes—or her hands—off Garret.

As Krystal stared at Garret, she could see why. He was cute. Not exactly her type, but still cute. And sexy. That realization rocked her for a moment. She hadn't thought of him in that way before. He'd always been her landlady's son. A friend. But tonight he looked good enough to send a little jolt of pleasure all the way down to her toes.

She shook her head. There was no point in thinking of Garret in that way, because she was making a new start with Roy.

She glanced at her watch, wishing she were with him now. As if Garret could read her mind, he came toward her and suggested they leave.

She slipped her arm through his as they said goodbye to his colleagues. Seeing Samantha across the room watching their movements, she whispered to

Garret, "If you kiss me now you can make your old girlfriend very jealous."

He looked her in the eye and said, "As tempting as that offer is, when I kiss a woman it's not for someone else's benefit. It's because she wants me. Do you want me to kiss you, Krystal?"

She did, only she wasn't about to admit that to him. It was a startling discovery and one that kept her quiet as they walked through the hotel corridors to the front entrance. When they were waiting for the parking lot attendant to bring his car around, she knew she needed to say something about the sexual tension that seemed to have come out of nowhere between them.

"Garret, the reason I came with you tonight…" she began.

"I know why you're with me, Krystal. My mother asked you to be my date, but contrary to what you—or my mother—may think, I don't need help when it comes to my relationship with Samantha Penrose."

It wasn't the first time she'd heard those words. When his mother had suggested they go to the hospital ball together, Garret had objected to the idea, but it had been a good-natured objection. Now he sounded angry.

"Look, it's still early. Why don't you go back inside and I'll take a cab home," she suggested.

"You aren't taking a cab anywhere. I brought you here and I will take you home."

His tone made her sound like an obligation. "I wasn't planning to go home. I thought I'd go to Roy's place."

"Old unfaithful, huh?" He slowly shook his head.

As her friend, he knew about her on-again, off-again relationship with Roy Stanton. Until tonight, however, he'd kept his opinions of the other man to himself.

"He's changed." She felt the need to defend her decision to give Roy another chance.

"I'm glad to hear that," he stated. She wished she knew if he truly meant those words, but as usual, his face revealed nothing of what he was thinking.

The parking lot attendant had brought the car around, and he held the door open for her. Reluctantly, she climbed inside. Garret didn't speak as he drove except to ask for directions. She should have been used to it by now—his penchant for silence. It had been that way since the first day she met him. She'd never known a man who could get so lost in his own thoughts.

When they reached Roy's apartment complex, he said, "Wait. I'll walk you to the door."

He was the dutiful escort, making sure she arrived safely inside the dimly lit lobby. "Thanks. It's right here." She motioned to the lower level apartment. "Someone's home. I can hear music."

"So can half the neighborhood," he said dryly.

"You can leave. I'm fine."

He surveyed their surroundings with a critical eye, then said, "I'll go back to the car, but I'd appreciate you signaling when you've made it inside."

She nodded and watched him walk away before pounding on Roy's door. She knew it wasn't likely he'd hear her. The music was too loud. She figured he was probably stretched out on the sofa, watching videos on MTV and missing her.

Krystal dug deep into her purse for a key she'd never returned after one of their earlier breakups. She inserted it in the lock and pushed open the door.

"Surprise! Party was over sooner than I expected," she announced as she stepped into the room.

Only the party wasn't over in Roy's apartment. He

was indeed on the sofa with music videos playing on his big-screen TV, but he was definitely not missing her. Next to him was a woman. A naked woman whose limbs were entwined with his.

The blood rushed to Krystal's face and pounded in her temples. For a moment she was too stunned to speak, but then her anger erupted.

"You scumbag! How could you do this to me?" She screamed at him. "You told me being in the military had made you realize how important I was to you, that you were never going to look at another woman again. You...you..." she stammered, struggling to get her breath, so great was her fury. "You are a disgusting pig, Roy Stanton, and I can't believe I was stupid enough to believe you could ever change!"

"Wait, I can explain," he began, but she wasn't going to listen to one more word he had to say.

She threw the key at him, bouncing it off his bare chest. She turned and ran out of his apartment, sickened by what she'd seen. To her surprise, there were no tears flooding her eyes.

As she stepped outside she saw that Garret's car was still at the curb. He saw her coming toward him and got out to open the door for her. She slid inside.

He didn't say a word to her until he was behind the wheel. Then he said, "Change of plans?"

"Yes, change of plans," she managed in a voice that was surprisingly calm.

"Where to now?"

When she looked at him she didn't see her landlady's son. She saw the man who'd looked at her with desire in his eyes. "Did you mean what you said earlier this evening?"

"You ought to know by now that I don't say things I don't mean," he answered in a voice that sent a shiver of awareness through her.

"Then take me to your place."

CHAPTER ONE

"I'M SORRY YOU HAD TO WAIT, Angie," Krystal said as she escorted her eleven-o'clock appointment to her workstation.

It was an apology she issued often in a typical work-day. No matter how hard she tried to stay on time, she usually failed. Not because she was slow, but because she regarded styling hair as an art form and one that shouldn't be hurried. Creating the right look for a client was more important than staying on schedule.

Angie brushed away her apology with a flap of her hand. "No problem. I needed the downtime and your reception area provided a very nice distraction. That construction site across the street is crawling with men in tight, dusty jeans. Have you seen the size of the arms on some of those guys?"

"I try not to look," Krystal told her, shaking out the black plastic cape before draping it over Angie's shoulders. "A guy I used to date works there. A real zero. Cute with a great body but—" she pointed to her head "—nothing up here."

"Yeah, I know what you mean. A good personality can make a guy look attractive, and you can always drag him to the gym and work out together to get his body in shape, but if he's dumb as dirt, what's the point?"

"There isn't one. So what are we doing today? The usual?"

"Uh-uh. I need a change. Chop it off."

"Oh-oh. If you want me to cut it, you must be having guy trouble."

She grinned. "You know me well, don't you?"

Krystal knew most of her regular clients very well. She regarded them as friends and she often found herself privy to information some of them hadn't even shared with their closest family members. She knew that before this woman left, she'd know all about her breakup with her boyfriend.

"Any ideas as to what you want me to do?" she asked, running her fingers through the blond tresses.

"Take it up to about here." She used her hand as a measure, raising it to just below her ear. "I'll let you decide how you want to style it."

Krystal studied the hair from all angles, lifting and rearranging strands as she mentally sculpted a new style. She loved it when a client gave her carte blanche. Creating the right look for someone was a challenge and she took great satisfaction in knowing that if she did her job well, she would make a woman feel better about herself.

While Krystal shampooed and rinsed the woman's hair at the sink, the client filled her in on her troubled love life. Krystal didn't mind. She was a people person and enjoyed hearing what was happening in their lives—the good and the bad. It was one of the aspects she loved most about her job—interacting with others.

"So how are things with you?" the young woman finally asked Krystal when she was once more sitting facing the mirror.

It was a question Krystal expected to hear from all of her regular clients at some point during their visits. And usually her life was an open book, with many of her customers knowing as much about her personal life as her friends did, but not today. A page had been written she wasn't ready for anyone else to read. At least not yet.

"Things could be better," she said, tossing the wet towel into the bin behind her.

"Does that mean you and Roy have split up again? The last time I was in you told me you were giving him one more last chance to make things work."

"I did and that was a mistake."

"It didn't work out?"

She chuckled sardonically as she reached for a comb. "It lasted all of three days. I wanted to believe that serving in the military had changed him. I was wrong."

"You don't sound brokenhearted over it," Angie observed.

"Because I'm not." It was the truth. Looking back now she could see how foolish she'd been when it came to her relationship with Roy, seeing only what she wanted to see. She'd wasted her time trying to recycle an old love—only it hadn't even been love, just a misplaced devotion. She wished it hadn't taken her so long to realize that.

"I suppose you've already found one...or two...or three guys to take his place," she said with a sly grin.

"Uh-uh. My juggling days are in the past. Gone for good," Krystal said on a note of finality.

"You're kidding!" Wide eyes met hers in the mirror. "You are like the queen of the dating scene."

"Not anymore I'm not. I need a break from dating."

"You and me both," she seconded, then went on to lament the lack of decent men in their age group, concluding with the statement that life would be less complicated without men.

Krystal knew that *her* life certainly would be if she hadn't let one particular man into it. When she'd finished styling her client's hair, she handed her a mirror. "What do you think?"

"It looks fabulous." As she climbed out of the chair, she pulled a folded ten-dollar bill from her pocket and gave it to Krystal. "Thank you so much for the great cut."

"Thank *you*. I'm glad you like it."

"Oh, I do. And I appreciate you letting me whine about guys," she said as she straightened her skirt.

"Hey—we all need to do it now and then," Krystal told her.

"Yes, we do, and especially with someone who understands what it's like out there in the dating world. You, Krystal, are one smart lady when it comes to men," she told her, then, with a grateful wave goodbye, headed for the front desk.

A few minutes later one of Krystal's co-workers approached her with her lunch—an order of take-out barbecue ribs. "Want some? I'll share." She held up the package invitingly.

The aroma hit Krystal the way heat blasted her face when she stepped outside from cool air-conditioning, causing her stomach to revolt. She uttered, "No, thanks," then bolted for the bathroom. She barely managed to get there before she was sick.

As she washed up at the sink, she stared at her reflection in the mirror and thought, *Oh yeah, I'm real smart when it comes to men.* She clicked her tongue in disgust, dried her hands and went back to work.

GARRET WAS TIRED. He'd spent most of the night at the hospital with a patient and after only a few hours of sleep on a cot in the doctors' lounge, he'd had to make his morning rounds, fill out a mountain of paperwork and attend a staff meeting. Now he'd promised one of the nurses at the clinic that he'd stop in and check on her mother who was a patient in a nursing home.

Garret knew that if Dolly Anderson still lived in her house on the east side of St. Paul, she'd be outside in her large floppy hat tending her vegetables. But at eighty-nine, a broken hip had marked the end of her days as a home owner and landed her in the nursing home not far from her old neighborhood. Although her bones had healed, she'd never regained the strength and agility to return home. That hadn't stopped her from gardening, however.

When Garret arrived at the nursing home, he found her outdoors tending to the plants on the tiny patio outside her room. One hand rested on a cane helping her stand, the other clutched a plastic watering can.

"Got any pumpkins in that patch?" he called out as he made his way across the lawn toward her.

She looked up at him. "It's a good thing you're a brilliant doctor. You'd stink as a farmer. Pumpkins need room to spread." As he drew closer she added, "You look tired. You'd better go easy on the women for a while and catch up on your sleep." She gave him a crooked grin.

"Oh, Dolly, you ought to know you're the only one for me." He'd never been much for flirting with women, but with her he couldn't resist. "How come you're not wearing your sun hat?"

"Don't want to mess up my hair." She turned back to watering her plants. "Just had it styled. I always get it done on Tuesdays."

He didn't correct her and tell her it was Wednesday.

"What brings you here?" she wanted to know.

"I was in the neighborhood and thought I'd stop and see how you're doing."

She slanted a look at him. "Liar. I know Mavis called you."

He didn't deny the accusation. "She's worried you might have a cold."

She harrumphed. "Can you believe it? My daughter is fifty-nine years old and she still doesn't know the difference between a cold and allergies. If I cough, it's because the pollen count is high. It tickles my throat. It's been that way ever since I was a child."

"That's why I told you to stay inside in air-conditioning this time of the year," he said with a gentle wag of his finger.

"Can't. Have to take care of my garden."

The garden to which she referred was comprised of large pots holding a variety of vegetable plants on her patio. To his amazement, she had cherry tomatoes, radishes, green peppers and even a bean plant, which she'd staked with a yardstick.

"Don't they feed you here?" he asked.

"Of course they do. That isn't why I have my vegetables and you know it," she scolded him.

Yes, he did. On more than one occasion she'd told him that she'd planted her first garden during World War II when Americans were encouraged to grow their own vegetables as a sign of support for the troops. When her husband had been killed in the war, she'd decided to continue the tradition in honor of his memory. She'd been planting her victory garden for over sixty years.

"I brought you something," he told her.

"Not more pills to swallow, I hope."

"No, something sweet."

That had her setting her watering can down and

giving her attention to him. "Ooh. Gingersnaps," she cooed, when he pulled a box of cookies from his bag and handed them to her. "What do I have to do for them? Take off my clothes?"

He saw the twinkle in her eye and smiled. "You know me well, Dolly." Not many of his patients did, but he had a soft spot for this octogenarian with her sharp mind and keen wit.

"You're not going to take my word for it that it's only the pollen, are you, Dr. G.?"

"I'd like to, but I'm afraid if I don't give you a clean bill of health, Mavis won't get any sleep tonight. How about it? Should we put her mind at rest?"

She hesitated momentarily, then said, "All right. To please Mavis." She moved slowly but with a gracefulness few women her age possessed. He slid open the patio door for her and followed her inside.

"You're not going to make me get back into bed, are you? Once I'm up and dressed, I don't like to even look at that thing," she told him with a wave of her hand in the direction of her bed. "Someone around here is always trying to get me to nap. I'm not a nap person. Never was, never will be."

He patted the leather chair. "How about sitting right here."

Sitting had never been easy for someone as active as Dolly and today was no different than any other time he'd visited her. She squirmed and fidgeted, but he managed to complete the exam and was relieved when he found there was no cause for alarm.

"Okay, that'll do it," he said, stuffing his stethoscope back into his bag.

"I'm as right as rain, aren't I?"

"You are. How's the hip?"

"The only thing wrong with my hip is that it kept

me from getting my hair done yesterday because I had to go to physical therapy,'' she grumbled.

He looked at her white curls. ''I thought you said you had your hair done today?''

''I did. My gal came back this morning. Made a special trip for me. Isn't she just the sweetest thing?'' She didn't wait for an answer but continued on. ''I think you'd like her. She's pretty. Really pretty.''

''Now don't go getting any ideas, Dolly,'' he warned.

''I know better than to do that,'' she said with a flap of her wrinkled hand. ''Kryssie's got too many boyfriends the way it is. She gets flowers all the time from this one or that one. They usually end up here…the flowers, that is. She doesn't want reminders of a bad date.''

Garret didn't comment and she continued on, ''You wouldn't be interested in her anyway being you're not looking to settle down just yet. You have too many things to accomplish.''

''Yes, I do,'' he agreed.

''Are you still thinking about the Doctors Without Borders program?''

Because Dolly's husband had been in the Red Cross, Garret had told her about his interest in doing relief work. She'd shown him journals her husband had kept during his tour of duty overseas and shared stories of what it had been like to be a doctor's wife during the 1940s. Besides being a very interesting woman, she was easy to talk to and encouraged Garret to use his medical training in whatever way he felt was best.

''I don't think I'll be leaving until after the first of the year,'' he told her.

''I'll miss seeing you, but I'm happy to share you

with the rest of the world," she said with a gracious smile. "You remind me so much of my husband. Dedicated. Passionate about helping people. A true gentleman."

"Thank you. I wish I had known him."

"You would have liked him. He was a good man." A wistful expression came over her face as she talked about him. "We only had a few years together, but they were wonderful years. It's too bad everyone can't have a love like ours. There'd be a lot fewer divorces."

"You were lucky."

"Yes, we were. No amount of time can erase what we had together. True love is like that. It'll go on forever..." She trailed off, her eyes glassy with a distant expression in them. "Even after all these years I still have so many clear memories. And of course I have Mavis. There is no greater reminder of a love shared than a child. Don't you agree?"

"I certainly do. And your daughter should sleep well tonight. Your lungs sound fine, Dolly."

"I told you it was only my allergies causing me to cough."

"Yes, you did," he said, snapping his bag shut. "Do you have any questions before I go?"

"Oh, you're leaving so soon?" she said, suddenly sounding very childlike. "I was hoping you could stay and talk."

"I wish I could, but I have appointments this afternoon. I'm sorry." His apology couldn't have been more sincere. It was one of the aspects of his job he wished he could change—there were never enough hours in a day. He regretted not being able to spend more time with his patients and it frustrated him that he had to spend so much of his workday doing paperwork. He wanted to be helping people, which was why he was interested in doing humanitarian work.

She nodded her head in understanding. "Mavis said you're the hardest-working doctor at the clinic."

"I don't know about that. All doctors work hard, Dolly."

She sighed. "You don't need to tell me. When you do finally settle down, you'd better make sure it's with someone who understands that."

"Of one thing you can be sure, Dolly, and that's when I do finally get around to doing just that, you'll be the first to know." With that statement, he left her with a smile.

THE FIRST TIME KRYSTAL HAD walked into 14 Valentine Place she'd felt at home. If houses had personalities—which Krystal believed they did—this one's was warm and inviting and definitely female, just like its owner, Leonie Donovan.

Contentment resonated in the polished wood floors and mahogany-trimmed walls. Krystal noticed it every time she stepped through the front door. Her landlady said it was because it had been home to a happy family. Three generations of Donovans had lived in the house and there'd been no divorce, no bitter battles over who owned what, no kids coming and going in split-custody arrangements.

It was only after Leonie's husband had died unexpectedly that the big old Victorian structure had been converted into a boardinghouse. Everyone understood why Leonie had decided to rent the rooms to women. She'd raised four sons and had reached a point in her life where she wanted to connect with the feminine side of life.

Krystal had been one of the first women to rent a

room and, like everyone else who would live at 14 Valentine Place, was treated like a member of a family. It was an extended family that included Leonie's sons, her daughters-in-law and her grandson. It was a family rich in history, just like the house, and hearing the Donovan brothers talk about their childhoods reminded her how very different their lives had been from hers.

That's because home to her had been a series of house trailers, none of them double-wide. What little furniture they'd had was either rented or purchased at a garage sale or flea market. There had been no family heirlooms handed down from generation to generation. While Leonie's home often smelled of lemon-scented furniture polish, the mobile homes where Krystal had lived had reeked of stale cigarette smoke.

Not that Krystal had been unhappy with her childhood—she hadn't. It was just very different from the one the Donovan boys had experienced, and not just because they lived in a house with a concrete foundation and plaster walls.

She'd grown up in a house of women. She'd never known her father, she didn't have a brother and she seldom saw her grandfather. If her mother had men friends, she and her sister Carly never saw them.

Krystal knew it was because she was trying to be a good role model for her daughters. To Linda Graham, the most important lesson she could teach her daughters was not to make the same mistakes she had. She'd had not one but two teen pregnancies, and she'd made it clear that she wanted her daughters to have a different life than she'd had. It was why she had imposed such strict rules when it came to dating.

No matter how hard Krystal and Carly had tried to convince her they were teenagers who could be trusted, their mother had refused to allow them to date until they were seniors in high school. Both had thought their mother was unfair, but only Krystal had rebelled against her authority, willing to risk punishment for a chance at romance.

The strict rules may have been a good parenting tactic in Linda Graham's eyes, but to Krystal they had only created distance in their mother-daughter relationship. Her love life became a frequent source of conflict between them that continued into her late teens and early twenties.

It was one of the reasons Krystal had been eager to move out of Fergus Falls. Besides the limited employment opportunities, the town was small enough that it was difficult to keep her personal relationships private. And as long as she lived there, she felt as if her mother was looking over her shoulder into her love life.

Until she moved into 14 Valentine Place, she'd thought most mothers were probably like hers—critical of whomever their children dated. Then she met Leonie. Even though her landlady was a romance coach, she seldom interfered in her sons' love lives.

Leonie rarely gave anyone unsolicited advice, yet she was always there for moral support when it was needed. Not only did she encourage the young women who rented rooms from her to feel free to come to her if they wanted to talk about relationships, she designated the living room in the house as the great room where discussions of men and romance became a regular occurrence. It wasn't long before Krystal came to regard Leonie as a second mother, only with this mother she could talk about everything and anything.

At least she had been able to until a few weeks ago. Now that aspect of their relationship had changed. Krystal had made a mistake. A big mistake. And it was one she was reluctant to admit to anyone, and especially to her mother and Leonie.

Instead she would keep it secret. Not easy for someone who usually blurted out whatever was on her mind. Worried that Leonie would be able to detect that she was keeping something from her, Krystal did her best to avoid seeing her landlady.

Today, however, was Tuesday, which meant Leonie wouldn't be at home. She'd be teaching a class on the dos and don'ts of dating at the community center and that meant the only other person in the boardinghouse would be Dena Bailey, since the third-floor apartment was still vacant.

As she expected, Dena was in the kitchen. When she saw Krystal she said, "Oh good! You're home. I was hoping I'd see you." She motioned for Krystal to come sit beside her. "Come join me for a glass of lemonade."

Krystal shook her head. "I'll pass on the lemonade, thanks." She did go over to the refrigerator, however, to get a bottle of water. When she opened the door, the aroma of the leftover parmesan chicken she'd had the night before nearly caused her to bolt toward the bathroom. She didn't understand how something could taste so good warm yet smell so bad cold that it made her wish she'd never gone near it.

But then so many things made her stomach queasy. Like when she was in an elevator and someone stepped in wearing perfume. Or the pungent smell of gasoline at the service station. Or the tiny bit of oatmeal left in Leonie's bowl each morning.

Krystal shuddered and willed her stomach to settle itself. When she sat down at the table, she saw Dena had a bridal magazine spread open in front of her.

"What's up with that? I thought you and Quinn were going to elope."

"I thought we were, too, but then we sat down to make plans and before I knew it, we'd reserved the church and booked the reception hall. It's amazing what that guy can talk me into."

"Must be the power of love," Krystal remarked, noting the glow on Dena's cheeks. "So when's this big day going to happen?"

"September sixth." Seeing Krystal's jaw drop open, she quickly added, "I know, it doesn't give us much time, but we've hired a wedding coordinator who assures us it's possible. Still, I feel as if I have too much to do."

"I would think so. Is there anything I can do to help?"

"Actually, there is. You could be one of my bridesmaids."

The invitation caught Krystal by surprise. "You want me to be in the wedding?"

Dena nodded and looked at her expectantly, waiting for her response, only Krystal didn't know what to say. "That is so sweet of you to ask me, but…" She paused, searching for the right words to decline without hurting Dena's feelings.

"But I shouldn't have asked because we haven't been friends all that long," Dena finished for her, looking embarrassed. "I'm sorry, Krystal. I didn't mean to put you on the spot."

Krystal reached for her hand. "You didn't. I'm honored that you asked me. The fact that you did says a lot about our friendship."

"But you still don't want to do it."

"I want to, but…" She hated to bring up the subject, but knew she had no choice. "You know I'm pregnant."

Dena gave her a blank look. "Yeah, so what?"

"So all eyes are supposed to be on you, the bride. By September sixth I'm going to be just far enough along that people will be wondering if I'm having a baby or if I'm just getting fat. You don't need that kind of distraction at your wedding."

"Have you been talking to Maddie? She's worried about the same thing and I'm going to tell you what I told her. It doesn't matter if your belly sticks out like a watermelon, which it won't. I want you to be in my wedding."

Maddie Donovan was a dear friend to both of them. Although she'd already married Leonie's son Dylan and moved to France before Dena had moved into 14 Valentine Place, her friendship with Dena went back to their college days when they'd been roommates. Had it not been for Maddie, Dena wouldn't have rented her old room at the boardinghouse and she and Krystal wouldn't have become friends.

"Is Maddie going to be in the wedding?" Krystal asked.

"Yes. I convinced her that I had found the perfect dress to cover what she refers to her as her walrus-shaped body, although I can't imagine Maddie looking anything but gorgeous no matter how much weight she gains."

"Are there dresses that can hide pregnant tummies?"

"Actually, there are." She thumbed through the magazine until she'd found the page she wanted, then shoved it toward Krystal. "Look at this plum one. See how high the waistline is? It's perfect for you and Maddie...and my sister-in-law, Lisa, too. She's going to be my matron of honor, and having had three kids, she also wants to hide her bulges.''

''Don't dresses in these magazines take months to order?''

''Not a problem. Quinn's sister has a friend who works in a bridal shop and she says she can put a rush on them and get them in time, but I do need to get moving on this, which is why I really need an answer from you…like today.'' She gave her an apologetic grin.

Krystal wanted to say yes. Dena had only lived across the hall from her for six months, yet in that time they'd become good friends. She also liked Dena's fiancé Quinn, who was the only man Leonie had allowed to live upstairs. A close friend of the family he had become like a brother to Krystal, as well.

''Would it make it any easier for you to say yes if I said you could bring Roy as your date?'' Dena asked when she continued to deliberate.

''Good grief, no!'' Her response was forceful enough that Dena apologized.

''I guess that means you haven't worked things out.''

''No, and we aren't going to.''

''I'm sorry. I thought…with the baby…'' She trailed off, looking a bit self-conscious.

Krystal reached across and gave her hand a squeeze. ''I'm the one who should be apologizing. I should have told you before now that Roy isn't the father of my baby.''

Dena tried not to look shocked, but Krystal knew she was. Although she'd dated many men, Roy had been the only serious relationship she'd had since living at 14 Valentine Place. It was only natural that people would expect that she was carrying his child. Krystal knew it was what most of her friends would think when they learned of her pregnancy.

"Have you told the father?" Dena asked in a quiet voice.

Krystal shook her head. "Not yet. I want to, but it's complicated." She wished she could tell her just how complicated it was, but she couldn't. Not with the wedding only weeks away.

"Well, if there's anything I can do to help, you'll let me know, right?"

Krystal nodded. "Thanks for caring, but I'm afraid the only thing you can do is not mention to anyone that I'm pregnant."

Dena held up her hand. "That goes without saying. I won't say a word."

"What about Quinn? He was the one who found my home pregnancy test in the bathroom," she reminded her.

"Yes, but I'm not sure he even realizes it was yours. At the time I told him it could belong to any one of a number of your friends who'd stayed with you. Don't forget. He's lived upstairs so he knows how popular you are."

"I usually do have people coming and going, don't I?" she said, hoping Dena was right about Quinn.

"Yes, but if you're worried, I can speak to him about it."

"Would you mind?"

"No, not at all. Now, back to my request," Dena said with an endearing smile. "Will you be my bridesmaid?"

As tempting as it was to decline her request, Krystal could see by the look on Dena's face how important it was to her. "If you're sure you want me, then yes, I'd love to be in your wedding."

Dena leaned over to give her a hug. "Thank you. It'll be so much easier for me to do this whole wedding thing knowing you and Maddie will be there."

Easier for Dena maybe, but more difficult for Krystal. "How many people are coming?"

"We wanted to keep it small, but that's not easy to do when your fiancé is a professional hockey player." She flipped open her day planner. "Here's what's been decided so far."

They spent the next two hours discussing everything from what music should be played at the church to what lingerie Dena should take on her honeymoon. It was exactly the kind of girl talk Krystal needed and she appreciated the fact that Dena made no other references to her pregnancy.

"So now you know why I'm so nervous," Dena said as she stacked her day planner on top of the bridal magazine. "By the time this wedding is over, I'm going to be a basket case and you are going to be happy to be rid of me."

"I most certainly will not be. I hate the thought of you leaving," Krystal said sincerely. "I'm glad you decided not to move out until after the wedding. Do you know if Leonie has found someone for the third floor?"

"You haven't heard?" When Krystal gave her a blank look, she continued. "I thought you would know all about it. You see more of Garret than I do."

Krystal frowned. "Know what?"

"Your plan worked."

Krystal was puzzled. "What plan?"

"Going with him to the hospital ball to make his old girlfriend jealous. It must have worked."

Krystal had a bad feeling in her gut and it had nothing to do with morning sickness. "He's seeing Samantha again?"

"He must be. Why else would she be moving in here?"

Krystal gasped. "No! Oh please, tell me it isn't true!" she begged.

"Isn't she the one you said had so many ruffles on her dress at that party that she looked like she could set sail if a gust of wind came up?" Dena asked.

"Yes, and it's too bad it didn't," Krystal retorted.

"Wow! You really don't like her, do you?"

Krystal could see the curiosity in her eyes and knew she needed to give an explanation. She would have liked to have told Dena the real reason she hated to see Samantha Penrose move into the house, but the bride-to-be didn't need to get drawn into the melodrama her life had become.

So instead she said, "Don't pay any attention to me. I'm just in a witchy mood. This early stage of pregnancy is like having PMS 24/7." She brushed the hair from her forehead and sighed.

"It's all right, I understand," Dena assured her.

"Will you please just forget I made a fuss, because I shouldn't have said anything. That night of the hospital ball I hardly spoke to Samantha. For all I know she could be a very nice person."

"I don't think Leonie would have rented the apartment to her if she didn't think she would fit in here. You know how she is about her tenants," Dena pointed out.

Krystal nodded. "I'm just surprised she gave her Quinn's old place. I didn't think Leonie liked her because of what she did to Garret. You do know that she was the one who left him."

Dena nodded. "If Leonie had any hard feelings toward her, they're gone. She spoke very highly of Samantha when she mentioned her to me. Said she was lovely and that she thought we'd get along with her just fine."

Krystal had to stifle the laughter that nearly spilled out of her. Fortunately Dena's cell phone rang at that moment.

"I'm sorry, Krys, but I have to take this. It's Quinn. You don't mind, do you?"

Krystal shook her head, excused herself and went up to her room. As she climbed the stairs, her legs felt like undercooked pasta. The first thing she did when she got inside her apartment was to collapse on to her bed and stare at the ceiling, stunned by what Dena had told her.

Samantha Penrose would soon be living above her.

If it weren't so tragic it would be funny, Krystal thought. She threw her shoe at the ceiling and groaned in frustration. This couldn't be happening to her. Was fate so cruel or had her life suddenly become a black comedy?

She could only wonder what the lovely Samantha was going to say when she found out her new neighbor was pregnant with her boyfriend's baby.

CHAPTER TWO

"What do you think? Wing collar or lay-down?" Quinn Sterling held two pleated shirts up for Garret's inspection.

Before he could answer, Shane Donovan leaned close to them and said, "Whichever one doesn't make you feel like you have a rope around your neck." He made a choking gesture with his hands.

"He *does* have a rope around his neck," Dave Duggan was quick to add with a cocky grin.

Shane's and Dave's kidding brought back memories of their teenage years when the four of them had been the best of friends and someone was always making a wisecrack. Garret pointed to the shirt on his right. "Go with the wing collar and don't pay any attention to these guys. Marriage is going to be a good thing for you and Dena."

"So speaks my brother, the bachelor," Shane drawled sarcastically.

"Hey—his turn will come. Some woman will get her hooks into him sooner or later," Dave warned.

Quinn put one of the hangers back on the rack of starched white shirts. "My money's on later."

"I'd say sooner, judging by the way women eye him once he puts on that white coat," Dave teased.

"Quinn has you on this one, Dave. Come the first of the year, Garret's going to be overseas practicing medicine," Shane said.

"That doesn't mean he can't get married," Dave pointed out.

Garret would have preferred not to have his bachelor status be the topic of discussion, but he knew you couldn't put a group of men in a wedding wear shop and not have the usual banter involving women and marriage. Since the only other single guys in the wedding party were hockey players and everyone apparently expected them to be bachelors, Garret was the prime target for their quips.

"Just for the record, as happy as I know married life can make a man, I think I'll stay single for a while…like five or ten more years," he added with a huge grin.

"I hope you told that to Samantha Penrose," Dave remarked.

That had Quinn asking, "Who's Samantha Penrose and how come I haven't met her?"

"She's just a colleague," Garret answered.

Dave elbowed Shane. "Did you hear that? Just a colleague? Is that any way to talk about your old girlfriend who's hot for you?"

Quinn shot Garret an inquisitive look. "All right, out with it. What did I miss?"

"Nothing important," Garret answered. "Samantha and I dated while we were in medical school. Then she left to do her internship, but recently she moved back to take a position at a hospital here."

"She's not the doctor who's taking over my apartment at 14 Valentine Place, is she?" Quinn asked.

It was the first Garret had heard of it. He turned to his brother. "Has Mom rented the third floor to Samantha?"

"Yes and I can tell by the look on your face she

didn't ask you about it before she did,'' Shane answered.

No, she hadn't, and it annoyed him. He wondered what his mother was up to. First she'd finagled him into going to the hospital ball so that he would see Samantha again, now she was moving her into the boardinghouse. It wasn't like his mother to meddle in his personal life, so just what was going on?

Dave slowly shook his head and whistled through his teeth. "It's not a good sign, Garret...your old girlfriend moving into a house where there's a matchmaker.''

"She's not a matchmaker," Garret corrected him. "She's a romance coach.''

Dave shrugged. "Same difference. She hooked Quinn up with Dena, didn't she? And Dylan with Maddie. Has she had any tenants move out who weren't getting married? I mean, they move into that place single and the next thing you know...'' He clapped his hands. "Bang. There's a wedding in the works.''

Shane shoved his hands to his hips. "I hadn't thought about it before, but you're right. All of her previous tenants are married.''

When Dave began to hum a funeral dirge, Garret stopped him with a raised palm. "You can cut the music. *If* I ever get married, it will be to someone of my choice, not my mother's. And I say *if* because I'm telling you guys, my plans at this time don't include marriage.''

It was the truth. Right now all he wanted to think about was his career. To finally have the freedom to choose what he wanted to do with his medical training was exhilarating. It made all the struggles he'd been through the past ten years worthwhile.

"Come on, buddy. Are you going to say you don't have any time for women in those plans?" Dave asked him on a note of disbelief.

"Women yes, marriage no," Garret said with a sly grin.

Quinn clapped him on the shoulder. "That's exactly what I said right before I met Dena."

Garret was relieved that a wedding specialist chose that moment to arrive, and for the next half hour, talk was of tuxedos and accessories. While they were measured and fitted for the formal wear, they discussed their roles as ushers and groomsmen at the wedding and reception.

When a question arose regarding which groomsman would be escorting which bridesmaid down the aisle, Quinn said, "I'm not sure. That's Dena's territory."

"I'll take the hot redhead who lived downstairs from you," one of the hockey players offered with a huge grin.

"You mean Krystal."

Upon hearing her name Garret's blood stirred. It had always been that way, even before he'd spent the night with her. Someone would mention her name and he'd be aroused. He blamed it on the fact that the first time he'd seen her she'd been half-naked. He could still remember the look of surprise that had been on her face when he'd pushed open the laundry room door at 14 Valentine Place and found her sorting her dirty clothes clad only in a lacy bra and pants.

Ever since that day he had fantasized about what it would be like to see all of that delectable body unclothed. Never had he expected it to happen, and certainly not on the night of the hospital ball. Only it *had* happened and now he was having trouble forgetting how she had looked lying naked in his bed.

"Is she seeing someone?" the hockey player asked.

"Are girls that hot ever not seeing someone?" Dave wanted to know. "She probably has guys lining up halfway around the block to take her out."

"I bet I could get to the front of the line," boasted the hockey player.

Garret didn't doubt that he could. He looked like the kind of guy Krystal would find attractive. She liked men who looked as if they spent more time at the gym than they did at a job and dressed as if they were on their way to a *GQ* photo shoot.

He wondered what everyone would say if he announced that he had been to the front of the line. That he'd spent the night with her and she was everything a fantasy should be and then some.

He chuckled to himself. They probably wouldn't believe him. Not that he could blame them. He and Krystal were as different as night and day. No one would expect that someone as fun loving and outgoing as Krystal would be attracted to a man who spent most of his free time reading medical journals.

"Knowing Krystal, I bet she already has a date lined up for the wedding," Quinn commented.

Garret suspected he was probably right. There was no shortage of men in her life. He only hoped that the man she did bring wouldn't be Roy Stanton. After the way Roy had betrayed her, Garret didn't want to think she would ever let the creep back into her life. Yet he knew the possibility existed. History had proved that she'd forgive him for almost anything.

"Will you be bringing this Samantha as your date to the wedding?" Quinn interrupted his thoughts.

"Ah...I'm not sure," he said evasively. Until now he hadn't considered taking anyone, but if he needed a date, Samantha would be a sensible choice. She was, after all, more his type than someone like Krystal.

Again his thoughts returned to the beautiful, impulsive hairdresser. He wondered if she ever thought about their night together, or had she simply written it off as a night she wanted to forget. Judging by the way she'd avoided him whenever he'd stopped in at 14 Valentine Place lately, he guessed it was the latter. He knew he should do the same. Forget about her, forget about that night.

Only he couldn't. He'd messed with a fantasy and his life would never be the same.

"I'M SO GLAD YOU WERE OFF today and you could help me move," Samantha told Garret as she filled a shelf with books.

Because she'd hired professional movers, there was little to do except help her unpack boxes. To someone as organized and as efficient as Samantha, it was a task that didn't take long to accomplish.

"I believe that's the last of it and just in time," she told him as she dusted her hands off on her blue jeans. "I'm ready for lunch. Where do you recommend, since this is familiar territory to you?"

"Dixie's is good and it's close."

"Great, I'll just make a couple of phone calls and we'll go." She leaned over to grab her phone from her desk.

"I'll wait for you downstairs. It'll give me a few minutes to talk to my mom," he told her, then headed down to the first floor.

He found his mother in the kitchen seated at the large round oak table. She wasn't alone. Krystal sat across from her, a pair of scissors in her hands. Her expression was one of concentration as she cut clippings from a magazine.

Dressed in a T-shirt and jeans with her hair pulled back from her face and held in place by a barrette, she looked like an innocent and very different from the woman who'd seduced him the night of the hospital ball. She'd been all glitter and glamour and his body tightened as he remembered what had happened after they left the party.

"All finished?" his mother asked when she noticed him.

"Yes." He didn't miss the way Krystal kept her eyes lowered and focused on her task. Usually she greeted him with a grin and started a conversation, but not today. He'd expected that after the way they'd parted the next morning, things would be awkward between them, but not this awkward.

As he moved closer to her he saw what had her attention. Spread out on the table were what looked to be paper dolls, only they were all men wearing swimsuits and none of them had heads.

"What's up with that?" he asked, gesturing to the clippings. "Are you venting your frustration with the opposite sex?"

"We're working on a game for Dena's wedding shower," his mother answered.

"What kind of game has headless male swimsuit models?" he asked.

"A fun one," Krystal answered, cutting around a pair of men's legs.

His mother used her scissors to point to a small stack of paper heads. "The object is to match the celebrity's head with the body. Each match is worth a point. The person with the most points wins. It's as simple as that."

"But Quinn is five points," Krystal corrected.

"Quinn? You have his body in here?"

"Of course. He *is* a celebrity," his mother reminded him. "Although it wasn't easy finding him in a swimsuit. He's usually photographed in his hockey gear."

Garret peered more closely at the headless paper men on the table. "Which one is he?"

"You can't tell?" his mother asked.

He chuckled. "No, Quinn has clothes on when I'm with him." That comment caused Krystal to smile, but she didn't look up at him. "Won't this give Dena an unfair advantage? She's probably the only one who's seen that much of Quinn's skin."

"That's part of the fun…seeing if she can identify her own fiancé without his clothes," Krystal answered.

She glanced up at him then and, from the look in her eyes, he knew she was remembering what he looked like without *his* clothes. If his swimsuit-clad body was in the game, he wondered if she would be able to identify it.

She looked away and he knew that what had happened the night of the hospital party had definitely changed how she felt toward him. The old Krystal would have flirted with him and made a comment regarding the two of them sharing a secret. The new Krystal looked as if she wished he wasn't in the same room with her.

Just then Samantha appeared in the doorway to the kitchen. In her usual take-charge manner, she strode in and greeted his mother.

"I'm glad you're all settled," Leonie said. "Have you met Krystal?"

"Yes, at the hospital ball," Samantha extended a hand, but Garret could see her smile was forced. "It's nice to see you again."

Krystal stiffened and for a moment Garret thought she might bolt right out of her chair, but to his surprise, she smiled brightly, shook Samantha's hand and said, "You're right. You had on the dress with all the ruffles."

The two women made small talk about the food and music at the party. Garret tried to remember Samantha's ruffled dress, but all he could recall was the slinky dress that Krystal had worn. It had been a bright blue and cut to a vee in the front revealing a generous cleavage that had drawn the eyes of every man in the place. Then there had been the slit up the side that had spread whenever she walked, revealing a thigh that was ever so...

"Garret, I asked if that's all right with you?" Samantha sounded a bit impatient and he realized he'd missed what she'd been saying.

"I'm sorry, what did you say?"

"Your mother offered to show me how to use the laundry facilities. You don't mind waiting a few minutes longer, do you?"

She didn't wait for his response but headed out of the kitchen.

Leonie followed her out and suddenly he found himself alone with Krystal for the first time since the party. She didn't look at him but continued cutting out the paper dolls. Before today it would have been unusual for there to be quietness between them. But then it would have been unusual for anyone who was in Krystal's company. She could talk enough for two people and often did.

Only she wasn't talking now. She wasn't even looking at him. And he knew why. They'd had a one-nighter and nothing would ever be the same between them again.

"I'm glad we have a few minutes alone," he finally said, breaking the awkward silence. "I wanted to talk to you about Samantha living here."

"If you're worried I'm going to slip up and let the cat out of the bag that I wasn't a real date that night of the ball, you can relax. I'm not going to say anything," she told him, her concentration on the trimming of a brawny chest. She must have made a mistake because she crinkled the paper and tossed it aside.

"It was a real date, Krystal...or have you forgotten?" He deliberately made his tone seductive, wanting to get a response from her and he did. Her cheeks turned a light pink. "Besides, the cat's already out of the bag," he added.

That brought her head up with a jerk. "You told her the truth?"

"Is there a reason why I shouldn't have?"

"Yes! What happened between us was private," she said, her eyes sparkling with emotion. "I didn't think you'd tell anyone."

"I meant I told her the truth about why you went with me to the ball. She doesn't know what happened after we left and I don't plan to tell her. Or anyone else for that matter."

She looked relieved. "Then she thinks we're just friends."

"We are friends, aren't we?"

"Yeah, sure."

He wasn't so sure she wasn't simply agreeing with him because she didn't want to get into a discussion about what had happened between them. "Is it going to be awkward for you having her living upstairs?" he asked.

She rolled her eyes. "I'm not going to lose any sleep over it, if that's what you're thinking."

"You have no idea what I'm thinking."

She looked directly into his eyes and said, "Then why don't you tell me?"

He couldn't because, if he did and his mother and Samantha were to walk back into the room, they'd hear that he'd made love to her. Because that's what was running through his mind right now—the memory of that night they'd spent together. How incredibly good sex had been with her. How he hadn't been able to forget that it had happened—or that the only reason it had happened had been because she was trying to ease the pain of Roy Stanton's betrayal.

But he couldn't tell her any of those things so he said, "You know Mom likes to think that everyone who lives here is one big happy family."

She set down her scissors and stared at him. "So that's it. You're not worried about things being awkward for me. You want to make sure I'm nice to her."

"That's not what I meant at all," he denied firmly.

"Isn't it?" She jumped up from the table. "I've got to go. I have things to do."

"Krystal, wait," he called out to her as she hurried out of the room.

She kept walking, saying, "You don't need to worry, Garret. I'm not going to be mean to your girl-friend."

"She's not my girlfriend," he said, but she was already gone.

KRYSTAL AWOKE TO the feeling of something not be-ing quite right in her world. It didn't take her long to remember exactly what it was. Before even lifting her head from the pillow, she reached for the soda crack-ers on her nightstand. After several bites, she gingerly rolled out of bed, relieved that the home remedy for nausea worked for her.

As she did every morning, she showered then examined her naked body in the mirror, looking to see if it had changed enough that other people would notice she was pregnant. So far it hadn't. Except for the slight thickening of her waist, which wasn't any different from the bloating that usually accompanied her PMS, she looked the same as she had ten weeks ago. She wondered how much longer that would be true.

She hoped to keep her pregnancy secret until after Dena and Quinn were married. Weddings were supposed to be happy occasions and with so many Donovans involved in this one, the news that she was expecting Garret's baby could make things uncomfortable for people she cared about, including Dena. She wasn't going to take that risk. A pregnancy lasted forty weeks. Whether she told Garret now or in four weeks wouldn't change that. Postponing the news would, however, make Dena's wedding a more joyful celebration.

Which was why, after dressing in a pink polka-dot chiffon skirt and a white tailored blouse, she went straight to her car instead of stopping for breakfast in the kitchen. She felt confident that she could keep her secret from Leonie, but Samantha was a doctor, trained to diagnose such things as pregnancy. She didn't want to be around her any more than was necessary.

On her way to the mall, she stopped at a convenience store for a bottle of orange juice and a container of blueberry yogurt, which she ate in her car. Next she tackled the shops with her usual zest for shopping.

When she'd purchased everything on her list, she glanced at her watch and saw that it was past noon.

Her stomach growled in hunger, reminding her that, although she was plagued by morning sickness, there was nothing wrong with her appetite during the middle of the day.

She drove home expecting she'd have the kitchen to herself. Only as she pulled into the alley, she saw not only Samantha's car but Garret's, as well.

"Is it going to be awkward for you to have her living upstairs?" Garret's question echoed in her mind.

She couldn't believe he'd even ask such a thing. Of course it was awkward. She'd slept with the woman's boyfriend. The only thing that made her even more uncomfortable was seeing him, which was why she didn't want to go inside when she knew he and Samantha could very well be having lunch together in Leonie's kitchen.

For the first time since she'd moved to 14 Valentine Place, the boardinghouse did not feel like home. And after everything that had happened the past few weeks, if there was one thing she needed, it was the comfort of home.

As she sat staring at the big old Victorian house, she realized this wasn't the only place she called home. Lately she hadn't been back to Fergus Falls, but ever since she'd moved to St. Paul she'd gone back to her hometown when she needed to be with people who loved her unconditionally.

Today she felt that need. Carly already knew about her pregnancy, but she'd been avoiding telling her mother about the baby for fear of what she'd say. Maybe the time had come for her to trust in that unconditional love and ease the burden of her secret a little.

So instead of parking her car next to Garret's and

going inside for lunch, she drove right on through the alley and out on to the city street. Within a few minutes she was on the interstate and heading west. She made one stop on the way—to pick up a chocolate milk shake at the drive-through window of a fast-food restaurant.

When she reached the city limits of Fergus Falls, it was the middle of the afternoon. As always when she returned to her hometown, she felt a rush of nostalgia. Nothing had changed since the last time she'd been back, except lawns that had been green were now brown from the extended hot spell.

The mobile-home park where her mother lived was on the north end of town. It, too, looked the same. A row of long metal boxes parked close together. Her mother was outside her pink-and-gray box home sunning herself on the small patio next to it. A woman Krystal recognized as her neighbor, Edie Fellstrom, was in the reclining lawn chair next to hers. Both wore two-piece swimsuits that were tinier than any Krystal had ever owned. White cotton balls covered their eyes.

They looked oblivious to everything going on around them. Country Western music played loud enough to drown out the sound of her tires crunching on the gravel. It wasn't until Krystal slammed her car door that her mother removed the cotton balls and lifted her head.

"Well, look what the cat dragged in."

Krystal was used to her mother's sense of humor and didn't take offense to the greeting.

"Hi, Mom."

"What's wrong?" she demanded to know.

"You make it sound as if I never come to visit you unless something is wrong."

Her mother swung her legs to one side of the reclining lawn chair and sat up. "Why aren't you at work?" she asked suspiciously.

"When I work Saturdays I get a weekday off. This week it's Tuesday." She watched her mother spritz arms already a deep bronze with cold water. "You should watch how much you sit in the sun, Mom. Too much isn't good for you. It can cause cancer."

"Everything causes cancer. Smoking, drinking, eating, breathing…" She shook her head. "I might as well just crawl into a box and wait to die."

Krystal knew it was useless to argue with her, so she didn't.

Edie said, "You don't have to worry about your momma, Krystal. She takes good care of herself," she assured her. "She uses sunscreen. We both do." She held up a bottle for Krystal's inspection.

Krystal forced a weak smile to her lips.

Her mother said, "Are you hungry? There's chicken salad in the refrigerator."

Only a few hours ago she would have jumped at the chance to eat. Now her appetite had deserted her again, replaced by an indifference to any food. She was learning that when it came to eating, as a pregnant woman she had a short window of opportunity.

"It's too hot to eat," she told her mother.

"It's cool inside."

Still Krystal shook her head.

Her mother rattled off several more food options before finally giving up. "Suit yourself. I hope you have more of an appetite by dinnertime. There's a new Mexican place just up the road I'd like to try. Are you going to stay the night?"

She hadn't thought that far ahead. She shrugged and said, "I suppose I can. I don't have to be at work until noon tomorrow, but I didn't bring any clothes."

Her mother's brow wrinkled. "You didn't call to tell me you were on your way, you didn't bring a change of clothes…what's up with you? There is something wrong, isn't there?"

Edie saw the questions as a sign for her to leave. She reached for a terry-cloth beach wrap draped over the back of her chair. "I gotta get going."

"You don't have to leave because of me," Krystal told her.

"I'm not leaving because of you, sweetie. I'm leaving because I'm getting toasted." She pushed the strap on her bra aside briefly and said, "See?" Then she downed the remainder of her beer, picked up her sunscreen lotion and slipped her feet into a pair of flipflops. Posed to go, she asked Krystal's mother, "Are you planning to go to the candle party at Jilly's tonight?"

"Not with Krystal here I'm not. Tell her to bring the booklet to work and I'll order something there."

"You don't have to miss it because of me, Mom," Krystal insisted.

Her mother flapped her hand in midair. "It doesn't matter. I didn't really want to go."

"Me, either. I was just going to see Jilly's new place."

Krystal turned to her mother. "I think you should go, Mom. I'll visit Carly while you're gone."

"If you're sure you don't mind…it would be kinda fun…" She trailed off.

"Then it's settled. You're going," Krystal stated firmly.

Edie waved goodbye and called out as she left, "I'll pick you up at seven-fifteen."

As soon as Edie was gone, her mother turned to Krystal and said, "Okay, so what's wrong?"

Despite the fact that Krystal knew it was impossible to lie to her mother and get away with it, she said, "Nothing. Really."

Her mother gave her a look Krystal had seen often. It said, *I'll let you think you're fooling me, but we both know you're not.* She motioned for her to come inside the mobile home. "I want to show you what I've done to the place."

Because her mother had told her she'd made some changes, Krystal expected to find new curtains on both the kitchen and living room windows. To her surprise, however, the entire inside had been paneled in white, replacing the dark walnut walls.

She did a three-sixty and spread her hands in wonder. "You did all this yourself?"

Her mother nodded. "Edie and I went to a couple of those classes they have at the home store in Alex. It's not the most professional-looking job, but it's good enough for this place."

"It looks nice, Mom," she told her, noticing she'd made a new slipcover for the sofa. Instead of the blue-and-green-plaid fabric that she and Carly had soiled on many an occasion, there was a polished cotton floral print. "I like what you did to the sofa. It adds a lot of color to the room."

"And look. I finally got air-conditioning." She pointed to a window unit humming quietly as it blasted cold air into the small home. "I had to. This summer is a killer. If you want it colder, just turn the knob."

"No, it's fine," Krystal said, still looking around in amazement.

"Sit down. I'll put on some clothes and then we'll catch up."

Krystal knew it wasn't going to be easy to tell her

about her pregnancy, not considering their history when it came to talking about sex. She hoped that, because her mother had been a single mom, she'd understand that what she needed most of all was a mom who was there for her.

"Even if you're not hungry you must be thirsty. There's beer and soda in the fridge. Help yourself," her mother said as she moved through the tiny kitchen area.

"I'll just have some water, thanks."

"I don't buy that bottled stuff. What I have comes straight out of the tap," she warned before going into her bedroom and closing the door.

Krystal pulled a tumbler from the cupboard and filled it with water. Before sitting down at the table, she went over to the wall to look at the pictures hanging there. Most of them were of her and Carly when they were kids. She wondered why her mother didn't have pictures of them as adults. She'd gone to all the trouble of replacing the paneling in the mobile home, yet she'd hung the same old pictures on the wall.

She looked to the far end of the living room and, as she expected, there hung the watercolor of the Eiffel Tower—a gift from one of her mother's friends who'd been to France. It had to be close to twenty years old and had survived several moves in which many of her mother's possessions had been carted away to the dump. Linda still hadn't given up on her dream of someday visiting Paris.

When her mother returned, she had on a pair of capri pants and a scoop-neck top that made her look much younger than her forty-five years. "You look good, Mom."

The compliment brought a smile. "Why thank you, dear."

Again Krystal looked around. "I really like what you've done with the house."

"It looks good, doesn't it? I should have spruced up the place years ago, but there were always other things that needed my money."

"Yeah, me and Carly."

She chuckled. "One of you was always needing something." She grabbed a bottle of beer from the refrigerator, twisted off the cap and took a sip. "Are you sure you don't want a beer?"

Krystal shook her head. "No, I'm fine."

Her mother sat down across from her. "So why are you here on a hot summer day when you should be at the beach on one of those beautiful lakes they have down there in the cities?"

Krystal looked at her glass and shrugged. "You know I'm not a beach person."

"No, but you're a city person. You didn't have any trouble making that transition, did you?"

"I like the fact that there are so many people. There's an energy there…always something going on, always something in motion."

"You don't miss your hometown?"

"I miss you and Carly."

She could feel her mother's eyes on her. "Everything going okay at work?"

She nodded. "Yeah, work's going good."

"You must be putting in long hours. You look tired."

She was tired, but not because of extra hours at work. "I've been busy and then it's been so hot. You know the heat always drains me." Even with the new window air conditioner, she felt warm and swiped at her brow with a napkin.

"Maybe you want to take a nap before dinner," her mother suggested.

She nodded. "I would, but first I need to talk to you about something."

Her mother's brow furrowed. "So you didn't just come because you wanted to see me. I should have known."

"Mom, that's not fair. I come up here all the time and very seldom do I ever ask for anything."

Her mother reached for her hands and gave them a squeeze. "I'm sorry. I shouldn't have said that. Oh, before I forget." She jumped up and went over to the tiny bookshelf in the corner. "I have a new book for you."

Krystal read the title aloud. *"How to Marry Your Soul Mate in One Year Or Less."*

"I heard the author talking about it on TV," her mother said, her voice full of excitement. "She knows her stuff, Kryssie. Take it home with you and read it."

She nodded and murmured a thanks, knowing perfectly well that she'd take it home and add it to the pile of self-help books her mother had given her over the years—most of them about how to find a mate for life. She knew it was important to her mother that Krystal find her soul mate. Really important. Which made it all the more difficult for Krystal to tell her she was pregnant, yet it had to be done.

She set the book aside. "Mom, I need to talk to you."

Her mother frowned. "Something's bugging you. What is it? Are you having money problems? Is that it? If you need to borrow some, I have a little put away," she told her.

Krystal pushed a stray red strand of hair back from her face. "I don't need money, Mom."

"But you need something. I can see it in your face."

Krystal took a deep breath and clenched her fingers, aware that the moment she'd been dreading had arrived and there was no turning back. "I do need something, Mom. I need your understanding."

"About what?" she asked slowly.

Krystal tried to get the words out, but they stuck in her throat. She swallowed with difficulty, trying to stop the emotion that threatened to make this even more difficult than it already was. When moisture pooled in her eyes, she knew she'd lost the battle.

Her mother saw her distress and demanded, "What is it? What's wrong?"

A tear slipped down her cheek and she swiped at it with the back of her hand. "I messed up big time, Mom."

"Messed up how? You didn't get fired, did you?"

She shook her head. "It's not about work, Mom. I already told you that."

"Then tell me what it is about. You're sitting there looking as if you've lost your best friend. Is that it? Did you and Shannon have words?"

Krystal reached into her purse for a tissue and blew her nose. She knew there was no easy way to tell her mother and blurted out, "I'm pregnant."

In the blink of an eye her mother's hand slapped her face, stinging her cheek. For a moment, Krystal was too stunned to move. Then she jumped up from her chair, grabbed her purse and headed for the door.

She expected her mother to come after her, to tell her she was sorry, that she'd reacted emotionally and she regretted it.

But she didn't. For all Krystal knew she could still

be sitting at the kitchen table. She certainly wasn't making any effort to stop her daughter from leaving.

With tears streaming down her cheeks, Krystal climbed into her car and started the engine. And for the second time that day she felt as if she were running away from home.

CHAPTER THREE

WHEN KRYSTAL PULLED IN TO Carly's long driveway she saw her sister sitting on the porch swing. Beside her was Emily, her four-year-old daughter. As soon as they saw Krystal's car, they came running across the lawn to welcome her.

"I'm glad you came here," Carly said, wrapping her in a sisterly hug.

It was the only place in Fergus Falls Krystal could go. Since she'd moved to St. Paul she'd lost touch with many of her friends. Most of them had moved away, but of the ones who remained, none could give her the emotional support that Carly provided.

As children they'd been like other close siblings, rivals one minute and best friends the next. Being older by fifteen months, Krystal had often played the role of protector, looking out for the smaller, more innocent Graham girl. It wasn't until the emotional turbulence of adolescence that their roles reversed, with a calm Carly being the one who kept a watchful eye on an impetuous Krystal.

"Did Mom call?" she asked, although she already knew the answer.

Carly nodded. "I'll tell you about it in a minute."

Emily tugged on Krystal's hand saying, "Auntie Krys, guess what? I get to go with Grandma."

Krystal stiffened as she looked to her sister for an explanation.

"Relax. She means Joe's mother," Carly explained.

"I get to eat supper at Grandma's, then go get ice cream at church," Emily boasted.

"It's an old-fashioned ice-cream social." Carly then said to Emily, "Go get your backpack from the house. I think I see Grandma's car coming." As she skipped away she said to Krystal, "You didn't tell me you were planning to tell Mom you're pregnant today."

"I didn't know. I just got in the car and came up here on the spur of the moment." She shook her head. "Boy, was that a mistake."

Carly placed a hand on her arm, her eyes full of compassion. "Are you okay? You're trembling."

"I know. I should probably eat something. I haven't had anything since breakfast except for a milk shake," she told her, not wanting to begin a discussion with Carly's mother-in-law in the driveway.

"I'll make you something as soon as Joe's mom leaves with Emily," she said with a comforting pat on Krystal's arm.

Krystal nodded and tried to act as if nothing was wrong as the three women made small talk. It was a typical August afternoon with the humidity making it feel much warmer than the temperature indicated. By the time Emily and her grandmother finally left, perspiration tickled the back of Krystal's neck and she felt light-headed.

Carly noticed her paleness and looped an arm through Krystal's. "Come. We're going inside where it's cool and I'll get you something to eat."

Carly's house was definitely cooler than her mother's, but then it was nothing at all like the homes in the trailer park. It was two stories of brick with tall ceilings, lots of windows, and a design that was as elegant as any of the model homes she'd seen in the cities. It had everything she and Carly had dreamed about as children, including a swimming pool in the backyard.

"Would you rather sit outside by the pool?" she asked when Krystal glanced through the patio door.

"No, this feels good." As she passed the family room she saw a piano. "Where did that come from?"

"Joe's parents bought it for Emily." She nudged her toward the kitchen. "You sit while I make us some tea and get you something to eat. What sounds good?"

"Nothing," she answered honestly.

Carly grinned. "I know that feeling. How about if I toast you an English muffin? I have some fresh raspberry jam."

Krystal shrugged. "That's fine." She took a seat at the breakfast counter on one of the tall stools and watched her sister move about a kitchen that looked like something out of a magazine.

"So tell me what happened at Mom's," Carly ordered as she set two china cups on the counter.

"What did she tell you?"

"Not very much," she answered, filling the teakettle.

Krystal knew her sister was being diplomatic. "You don't need to worry about my feelings, Carly. I know Mom's upset. I'm sure she sees my being pregnant as just another one of the many things I've done to disappoint her."

"We both know she has high expectations of us," she noted.

"Yes, well her expectations were met when it came to you. You have a beautiful house, a great husband, and an adorable daughter." She sighed, not out of envy but because she knew it was the truth. Carly had fulfilled their mother's dream for her. She, on the other hand, hadn't even come close.

Carly frowned. "She didn't drag my name into it, did she?"

"No, she didn't say anything at all. There was no time. I blurted out, I'm pregnant, she slapped me and gave me this wounded look, then I left."

Carly gasped. "She slapped you? She didn't tell me that!"

"It's probably not something she wants to admit." The memory was enough to make Krystal's eyes misty. "If there was one thing Mom never did to us when we were growing up it was hit us."

"No, which means she must be really upset to strike you now," Carly concluded.

"*She's* upset? What about me? How does she think I feel?" They were rhetorical questions she didn't expect her sister to answer. "The one time in my life when I could really use her understanding, she treats me as if I've shamed her."

"You haven't shamed anybody."

"Tell that to her."

"I already did. I'm on your side, Krys. You ought to know that. I always have been." She reached for Krystal's hand and gave it a squeeze.

"Thanks, but I don't want to put you in the middle between me and Mom."

"Isn't that where I am anyway?"

Krystal nodded soberly. They both knew that their mother had put them in that position by setting "married with children" as a standard by which she judged her daughters. Krystal knew it made Carly just as uncomfortable as it did her, but there was really nothing they could do about it.

"Part of the problem is she takes everything so personally,'' Carly continued. ''As if every mistake we make is her fault.''

''You mean every mistake I make,'' Krystal corrected her. ''Let's face it. I'm the one who was always getting into trouble. And she hasn't liked one single boyfriend I've brought home.'' Her voice broke as she struggled not to cry.

''I can sure tell you're pregnant.'' Carly handed her a tissue.

Krystal blew her nose. ''I thought I was emotional before I got pregnant. Now it's ten times worse.''

''Maybe it's better if we don't talk about Mom. Let's talk about you.''

''Then for sure I'll be mopping up the tears,'' she warned her.

''Aw, come on. It can't be that bad.'' Carly came around to Krystal's side of the counter and put her arm around her. ''Where's that 'the glass is always half full' sister of mine?''

''She discovered her glass is almost empty,'' she said miserably.

''No, it isn't,'' Carly contradicted her. ''You are going to be a mother, Krystal. That in itself is a miracle and a blessing.''

''I know, but right now I'm having trouble seeing the blessing part,'' she confessed.

''Of course you are. It's too early in your pregnancy for you to see this as anything but unexpected and scary. But you have a little person growing inside you. Someone who's going to be so happy to have you for a mom.''

She sniffled. ''Someone's who going to wish I also had a husband.''

''Listen to me.'' Carly grabbed Krystal by the shoulders and forced her to look into her eyes. ''You don't need a husband to be a good mother. And your baby has a father—a man you've told me is a good guy and one you know won't turn his back on his child.''

Krystal nodded. ''I know. I'm trying to stay positive about all of this, but it's just such a big mess.''

''A mess that can be straightened out,'' Carly stated reassuringly. ''I know you want to wait until after Dena's wedding to tell Garret about the baby, but I wish you'd do it now. You need to know what he plans to do. His reassurance that he's going to be a part of the baby's life would ease some of the stress you're feeling. Plus then you wouldn't have to keep this big secret from everyone.''

''You're right. I will feel better once Garret knows, but I have to wait to tell him, Carly,'' she insisted. ''Do you realize what it's going to be like at 14 Valentine Place when everybody hears of this pregnancy? Leonie's the unsuspecting grandmother who lives downstairs, Samantha's the unsuspecting girlfriend who lives upstairs, and Dena's stuck in the middle trying to plan a wedding, one in which most of the Donovan family has a part. In a few weeks she'll be married and it won't matter what's going on in the house, but for now I don't want my problems spoiling what should be a happy time for Dena.''

''All right.'' Carly hopped down off the stool to tend to the teakettle that whistled on the stove. ''I won't bug you about it again. Let's talk about something fun. Tell me about the wedding. I want to know all the details. It's not every day my sister's a brides-maid in a professional hockey player's wedding.''

Krystal told her about the wedding shower and just about everything she could think of that Dena had told her about her plans, including the list of celebrities and professional athletes who'd be attending. It was the diversion Krystal needed to forget about the scene with her mother.

When Joe didn't come home for dinner, Carly ordered a pizza for the two of them. By the time they'd finished, they were laughing and they'd forgotten the tears that had been shed earlier in the day. Even though she'd had the scene with her mother, Krystal was glad she'd driven to Fergus Falls for the day. Carly gave her something no one else could—a sister's love and understanding.

When it came time for her to leave, she wasn't surprised when her sister said, "I think you should go back to Mom's. She cares about you, Krys."

"Don't you ever get tired of playing peacemaker between me and Mom?"

"Uh-uh. I love you both. And I know she loves you. And if you had heard her on the phone today, you'd know she does, too."

Krystal sighed. "I'm not sure she's ever going to speak to me again."

"Of course she will."

Krystal looked down at her fingers. "You didn't see the look in her eyes when I told her I was pregnant."

"You broke the most important rule she ever set for us. Do as I say, don't do what I've done."

"That's why I thought maybe she'd understand where I'm at emotionally right now. I don't need another critic. I have enough of them, but I could use a mother." She hated that her voice faltered.

Carly placed a comforting hand on her arm. "Then don't go home angry. Go back over there," she urged her. "Mom will have had some time to think about this and to get over her initial shock."

"You really think I should?"

Carly nodded. "The two of you need to talk."

"I'm not sure we can. You know what Mom's like. Did she show you the latest book she bought for me?" When Carly shook her head, she said, "It's *How To Marry Your Soul Mate in One Year or Less.*"

Carly grimaced. "She just wants you to be happy."

Krystal groaned in frustration. "She wants me to be married. How are we going to be able to have an honest discussion about my being pregnant?"

"You've got to try, Krys. For your sake and for Mom's," her sister pleaded with her. "You should listen to me on this one. I don't have pregnant hormones messing with my emotions. You do."

As difficult as it was, Krystal took her sister's advice and went back to the trailer park. When she got to her mom's, there was no one home. Krystal figured she'd gone to the candle party with Edie after all.

She found the spare key under the clay pot with the red geraniums and let herself in. Feeling a craving for something sweet, she opened the freezer, grateful to see that her mother hadn't changed. Inside was a half gallon of her favorite ice cream—mint chocolate chip. It was Krystal's favorite, too.

She ate two scoops, then stretched out on the sofa. She turned on the TV, trying not to think about what lay ahead when her mother returned.

Only her mother didn't return. At eleven Krystal looked up Jilly's number in her mother's address book.

"Hi, Jilly, it's Krystal. I heard you were having a candle party tonight. My mom isn't still there, is she?"

"No, Kryssie," the older woman replied. "She never came to the party. Edie said she went with a friend to hear some band play over in Alex."

Friend meaning *man,* Krystal deduced, since if it had been one of her girlfriends Jilly would have said her name. It didn't matter. She wasn't going to wait and find out, because with her mother it was always the same old story.

Krystal got in her car and drove back to St. Paul. The house at 14 Valentine Place was in darkness when she arrived. She was glad. What she didn't need was to find Samantha and Garret in the kitchen at two in the morning. She used the side entrance and quietly climbed the stairs to the second floor, relieved to find her room was once again the haven it had always been. She shed her clothes and crawled into bed.

KRYSTAL AND HER MOTHER HAD argued in the past, but never had they gone for more than a day or two without talking to each other. Now more than a week had passed without any communication between them. Krystal had called and left several messages after returning home, but now with each passing day, it became more difficult for her to pick up the phone, especially when she wasn't sure if her mother would hang up on her.

But it wasn't only the possibility of her mother rejecting her that kept her from calling. Pride stood in the way of her making a peace overture. Normally Krystal wasn't one to hold a grudge, but lately nothing seemed normal when it came to her emotions.

That's why, when she arrived home from work on the day of Dena's bridal shower and found her mother sitting in Leonie's kitchen, she found herself angry. She struggled to keep her feelings in check, unsure what had transpired between her landlady and her mother, who sat with their heads together over coffee.

They looked as comfortable as if they were the best of friends, which shouldn't have surprised Krystal. Leonie had a way of making guests feel at home in her kitchen. Krystal could only hope that Leonie's empathetic nature hadn't evoked any great urge on her mother's part to pour her heart out on the subject of her daughter's pregnancy.

"Mom! I didn't expect to see you here." Krystal could feel Leonie's eyes on her and she hoped she didn't sound as uneasy as she was feeling.

"Isn't it a lovely surprise?" Leonie asked with her usual cheerful grin.

Lovely was not the adjective that came to mind for Krystal. *Scary* was more like it. In less than two hours the house would be filled with people showering good wishes on Dena, and her mother had chosen today to visit. Since she rarely drove to the city, Krystal wondered if she'd come to scold her or to reconcile with her.

"We've been getting to know each other better," Leonie said as she rose to get a refill of coffee.

Krystal eyed her mother suspiciously, wondering what she'd said to her landlady. Had she told her they'd been fighting? Or worse yet, had she revealed the reason for the tension between them? Judging by Leonie's jovial expression, Krystal didn't think she had.

"Leonie told me you're giving Dena a bridal shower tonight," Linda commented.

Krystal nodded. "Yeah, and I have a lot to do before the guests arrive, so I should go upstairs."

"Maybe I can help," her mother offered.

It was her peace offering and Krystal knew she should behave like a grown-up and accept, but she'd discovered that during pregnancy her moments of maturity had a way of escaping when she least expected it. "No, I'm fine. I can manage."

She could see she'd shocked Leonie. Her landlady

leaned over to her mother, patted her forearm and said, "That's very sweet of you to offer to help, Linda. We can always use an extra pair of hands in the kitchen."

Only Krystal knew that her mother's smile was forced. "Just give me an apron and tell me what to do."

To Krystal's dismay, that's exactly what her landlady did. Her mother listened intently as Leonie launched into a description of the melon baskets and vegetable crudités they were going to serve. Krystal felt as if the rug was being pulled out from under her feet. She needed to talk to her mother and she needed to do it soon.

"Mom, maybe before you get started down here you could come with me upstairs. I have the party favors in my room and we still need to decorate the great room, too."

"No, you don't," Leonie told her. "Lisa was over earlier today and took care of the decorating. Wait until you see what she's done. She has white paper streamers everywhere and lots of balloons."

"Oh, that sounds lovely," Linda beat her to a response. "I'd love to take a look."

"Go ahead," Leonie instructed with a wave of her arm. "It's just down the hall and around the corner."

Krystal suppressed her sigh of frustration. "We can take a look when we bring the party favors down from upstairs." She motioned for her mother to follow her out of the kitchen.

She planned not to say another word until they were in her room, but at the top of the landing her mother said, "Your landlady's a nice person. She's very easy to talk to."

Krystal turned to face her. "Just what did you tell her?"

"Nothing about—" she paused, then lowered her voice to a near whisper "—your condition."

Krystal heaved a sigh of relief. "Thank God. My life is enough of a mess without having Leonie upset with me."

"Oh, I see. It's okay for you to have your mother upset with you but not Leonie?" she snapped.

"No, it's not okay, but I'm not the one who hasn't been returning phone calls this past week," she shot back.

"I had my reasons."

"And they would be…" she prodded.

"This hasn't been easy for me, Kryssie."

"And you think it has been for me?" She didn't want to sound defensive, but that's exactly how she felt. "You know, this really isn't the best time to be having this conversation. I'm supposed to be getting ready for the shower. Why did you come down here today of all days?"

"Because I don't want the next week to be like this past one has been. This nontalking has got to stop."

"I'm not the one who hasn't been talking!"

Aware that Dena could come home at any time and find the two of them arguing on the landing, Krystal pulled her mother by the arm into her room. She didn't bother to ask her to sit down, but stood facing her, her hands on her hips.

Her mother stated the obvious. "I know you're angry with me."

Krystal folded her arms across her chest. "How do you expect me to feel? You wouldn't even listen to me when I came to see you." She hated the way her voice quivered when she spoke.

"I know and I'm sorry. It was just such a shock

hearing that you'd done the one thing I'd prayed you'd never do. I thought I'd raised you to have values."

"I do have values. I'm pregnant, not morally bankrupt, and if the only reason you came here was to tell me I've done a bad thing, I got the message loud and clear last week." She wished she could express herself without getting so emotional, but she was dangerously close to tears. "A stinging palm on my cheek, not coming home, not returning my calls... I believe I know exactly what you think of me, Mom."

"No, you don't, and I am sorry. For everything, but especially for slapping you. You know how I feel about mothers hitting their children. I've always taken pride in the fact that I raised you and Carly by myself yet I never laid a hand on either of you. I was ashamed of what I did."

Krystal could hear the regret in her voice, see the sadness in her eyes. "Then why did you do it?"

Linda shrugged. "I don't know. Maybe it was because I saw myself in you."

"Mom, I'm not a teenager who got caught having sex."

"No, you're a grown woman who should have known better."

It wasn't anything Krystal hadn't said to herself a hundred times, but she didn't need to hear those words from her mother. "You know what, Mom? I should have known better but I didn't. I messed up." She threw up her hands. "There. I've admitted it. Are you happy?"

"No, I'm not happy."

"Well, that makes two of us because I'm not happy, either. I'm scared. Damn scared. And it would be nice if I could talk about that with my mother instead of feeling like I'm the world's biggest loser of a daughter.'' There was no stopping the tears. They flooded her eyes, shook her shoulders and wrinkled her face. She turned away, but within a few moments she felt a pair of arms around her.

Her mother pulled her close, soothing her with the same words she'd used so often when she was a child. ''There, there, now. It's going to be all right.''

''I don't think it is, Mom. I don't know what I'm going to do,'' she sobbed into her shoulder.

''You'll figure it out,'' Linda said reassuringly. ''And I'll be there to help you.''

''Do you mean that?'' Krystal asked on a hiccup, straightening.

''Of course I do.'' She handed her a tissue. ''That's why I'm here.''

Krystal tried to smile but failed. She swiped at the tears with the back of her hand. ''We shouldn't be talking about this now. I have to get ready for the shower.''

''Then we won't talk about it anymore,'' her mother said with a maternal authority. ''Now stop crying so those splotches go away.''

She glanced in the mirror and moaned. ''Oh great! My eyes are all puffy.''

Her mother scrutinized her swollen lids. ''Do you have any cucumbers?''

''I'm sure Leonie has some, but I don't think I have time to sit with them on my eyes. I've too much to do.''

''Then we'll have to think of something else.'' Linda gave her a gentle shove. ''You go get in the shower and let me get started on your to-do list. What should I do first?''

''The party favors have to be taken downstairs.'' She gestured to the tray on her dresser that was covered in tiny champagne cups filled with candies. "Mom, you have to promise me you won't mention my pregnancy to Leonie or anyone else you meet tonight."

Linda made a sound of indignation. "Of course I'm not going to say anything."

"Good. This is Dena's night. I can't seem to even mention the baby without getting weepy and if there's one thing I don't want to do, it's spoil the bridal shower by being a wet rag."

"Doesn't anyone know about the baby?"

"Dena does, but she's the only one. Are you planning to stay the night? You can sleep on my futon if you want," Krystal offered.

"Why don't I wait and see how late it is when the festivities end?"

Krystal nodded. Some of her apprehension must have shown because her mother said, "You can take that worried look off your face. I'm not going to reveal your secret. I've walked in your shoes and I know what you're going through."

"Then help me get through it. Please," she begged, again getting weepy.

"I will, sweetie. I will," her mother said, giving her another hug.

"And please whatever you do, don't say anything to Leonie about the baby," she repeated.

Linda sighed impatiently. "I've already told you I wouldn't."

Yes, she had and Krystal needed to trust her.

During the bridal shower, her mother spent most of her time in the kitchen. When it came time for the food to be served, however, Leonie insisted that she join the party and eat with everyone in the great room. It was a long night for Krystal, not because she worried her mother would slip and mention the baby, but because of the look in her mother's eyes as she listened to Dena talk about the wedding. It was what she'd always wanted for her daughters—the white dress, the elegant reception, the romantic honeymoon.

Later, as they cleaned up the kitchen, she knew she hadn't imagined the wistful look in her mother's eyes. "Bridal showers are such happy occasions, aren't they?"

"Mmm-hmm," Krystal agreed, rinsing plates in the sink before putting them in the dishwasher.

"It sounds as if Dena and Quinn are going to have the kind of wedding most folks only dream about."

"I'm sure it'll be nice."

"She showed me a picture of her dress. It's gorgeous."

"I know. I was with her when she picked it out."

"They've hired a live orchestra for the reception. It's at the country club," Linda told her, as if it were news. "It's amazing what they've planned in such a short time, isn't it?" She didn't wait for Krystal to comment but added, "Which just goes to show you that you can have a beautiful wedding on short notice."

"I suppose you can...if you want one," Krystal said on a weary note.

"Every girl wants one."

Krystal didn't say a word, but continued working in silence until her mother said, "You want one, don't you?"

"No, I don't think I do."

"Krystal!"

Without glancing at her mother she knew the look on her face. It was the shock and disappointment that always accompanied that tone of voice. When Krystal did finally look at her she saw that she was right.

"Are you telling me you're giving up your dream of a wedding with all the trimmings?" Again she didn't wait for an answer. "Just because you're—" to Krystal's relief, she stopped herself before saying the word *pregnant* "—doesn't mean you can't have a wedding."

Krystal had heard enough. She wiped her hands on a dish towel and tossed it aside. "I'm going outside for some fresh air."

She should have known her mother would follow.

"You can have as big a wedding as you want, Krystal." Linda stood beside her, pleading her case. "You just need to do it quickly and, if that's what's worrying you, I can help with the plans. Dena is proof that it doesn't take long to set the plans in motion. Look at what she's accomplished in just a few weeks."

Krystal was tired, too tired to be having this discussion, but she had to say, "I don't have any plans to set in motion."

"Not right now, maybe, but you're going to have to make some soon. Time is not on your side. You need to think about this."

Think about getting married was what she meant. Her mother had jumped to the conclusion that because she was going to have a baby she was going to get married.

"Now if it's money that has you worried, I've got a little put aside. You know I helped Carly with her wedding and I want to do the same for you."

"You can keep your money. I don't want to get married, Mother," she stated firmly.

"What do you mean you don't want to get married?"

"Just what I said. I don't want to get married," she repeated, enunciating each word slowly.

"Of course you want to get married. Do you know how many times you and Carly played brides when you were kids?"

"Well, I'm not a little girl anymore so can we please not talk about this?"

"I'm only trying to help."

"I don't need that kind of help," she said with exasperation.

Her mother shook her head in resignation. "I don't know what you want."

"Neither do I, Mom. Neither do I," Krystal mumbled, but her mother had already gone back inside.

As GARRET PULLED HIS CAR INTO the small parking area behind 14 Valentine Place he noticed two figures on the steps. Even though it was dark, the door cast enough light for him to see they were women. It wasn't until he climbed out of his car and heard their voices that he realized one of them was Krystal.

From what was being said, it wasn't difficult to figure out that the other woman was her mother. Or that they were arguing. To his surprise, it was over the subject of weddings. When the screen door slammed shut, he knew one of them had gone inside.

As he rounded the corner of the house he saw that Krystal sat on the steps staring up at the sky.

"Are you keeping the crickets company?" he asked as he walked toward her.

She jumped to her feet with a tiny shriek. "Where did you come from?"

"I'm sorry. I didn't mean to startle you. I thought you heard me pull up." He jerked a thumb toward the parking lot.

"No, I didn't hear anything but my mother's screaming," she answered candidly.

"I wouldn't say she was screaming exactly."

She eyed him suspiciously. "Then you heard what she was saying?"

He shook his head. "Not really. Just the sound of voices—not what was actually being said."

"I think you're saying that to be polite."

"And if I am?"

"Thank you." She smiled at him and reached out to touch his hand. It was as if that night of the hospital ball had never happened and they were friends again.

But just as quickly as she reached out to touch him, she snatched her hand away. "I should go back inside. We had Dena's shower tonight."

The awkwardness was back and he hated its presence.

He guessed it was probably inevitable, considering everything that had happened. But he'd caught a glimpse of that spontaneous smile of hers and he wanted to see it again.

As she started for the door, he stopped her. "Krystal, wait."

When she glanced at him she wore a look of vulnerability and for one brief moment he was reminded of the way she'd looked that night when she'd come running out of Roy Stanton's apartment building.

"I'm hungry and I could use some company," he said quietly.

"I'm sure there's food left over from the shower if you want to come inside," she told him. "Some of the guests are still here."

"I brought my dinner," he said, lifting the delicatessen bag. "And that's not the kind of company I had in mind."

"I don't think Samantha's home yet."

"I didn't come to see Samantha," he told her, although it wasn't exactly true. They had arranged to meet for a late supper, but she'd been detained at the hospital. Instead of eating alone, he'd decided to stop by 14 Valentine Place. He was glad he did.

He walked over to the picnic table on the patio, hooked a leg over the bench and sat down. "I have enough for two if you want some."

"No, thanks."

"You could keep me company. I know I'm not exactly your favorite person lately, but I won't scream at you," he promised. When she didn't say anything he added, "You don't really want to go back inside, do you?"

She unfolded her arms and walked over to the picnic table and sat down.

"So who won the game?" he asked. She gave him a puzzled look and he added, "The headless paper dolls."

"Oh, that." A smile played at the corners of her mouth. "One of Quinn's sisters."

"I guess she would know what he looked like in swim trunks, wouldn't she?" he said with a half grin.

"Oh, she didn't get Quinn's right. No one did, which made Dena quite happy."

He glanced at the bright lights shining through the windows. "Is the party over then?"

"Mmm-hmm. Your mom and a few of the guests are still in the great room with Dena talking about the wedding."

"So was it a good shower?" he asked.

"It was great. I think everyone had a good time."

"What about you? Did you have fun?" He knew

that was like asking if the sky was blue. Krystal made her own fun wherever she went.

She smiled. "Yes. We had a few surprises for Dena that had everyone laughing."

That didn't surprise him. He unwrapped a sandwich and asked, "You sure I can't tempt you with one of these? I have an extra one."

She shook her head. "No, but you go ahead."

"What about an Evian?"

"Sure, if you have one."

He pulled a bottle of water from the bag and unscrewed the cap before handing it to her. "If I'd remembered the bridal shower was this evening I wouldn't have come over."

"Why? Do they give you the jitters or something?"

"Or something," he confessed with a half grin. "So what were you and your mother arguing about?"

"I thought you heard," she said with a lift of one beautiful eyebrow. She took a sip of water, then said, "Bridal showers put her in this mood where she wants to talk about weddings—and mine in particular, or I should say the lack of there being one in my immediate future."

"It must be something that comes with the territory of being a mom. They want to see their children married with children."

"Some moms. Leonie isn't like that."

He chuckled sarcastically. "That's what you think."

"She wants you to get married?"

"She hasn't come right out and said as much in so many words. I suspect she's a lot like your mom only much more subtle. I know she'd much rather see me married than have me go overseas with Doctors Without Borders."

"Are you still thinking about joining that program?"

He nodded. "I'll probably leave after the first of the year."

His answer startled her. "I didn't know that."

"I thought my mom would have told you. She's told practically everyone else. She's worried I'll end up in a war zone," he said lightly, although it was not anything to be joking about.

"Is that a possibility?"

"There's always the possibility of war somewhere and, unfortunately, those are the areas that need the medical relief."

She frowned. "I thought you said you wanted to vaccinate children in the impoverished regions."

"I do, but if doctors are needed in more urgent situations…"

"How long will you be gone?"

"Six months to a year."

"Ohmigosh, you're kidding!" She stared at him as if in shock.

He smiled, wanting to erase the worry from her face. "From the way you're looking at me, I could almost believe that you're going to be sorry to see me go."

"Of course I am. I don't want you to go if you're going into a war zone." This time there was no mistaking the distress in her voice.

She'd never been one to hide her emotions and it was obvious she was upset. He wanted to think it was because she cared about him. But he also knew she had a soft heart and there was a good chance she would have the same reaction to hearing that any one of her friends was about to embark on a difficult assignment.

She shuddered and said, "Can we talk about something else?"

"Sure." It was too beautiful a night to talk about anything she found upsetting. "Is it my imagination or do the stars look brighter than usual tonight?"

She propped her chin on her hand and stared up at the night sky. "There are a lot of them tonight, but it's hard to see them with so many lights in the city. It's one of the first things I noticed when I moved here. Back home if you were to sit out on a night like this you'd see gazillions of tiny white dots in the sky. Here you only see the bigger stars."

"That's one of the advantages of small-town living. Better stargazing," he noted.

She chuckled. "Probably the only advantage, but don't say that in front of my mom."

"She likes it in Fergus Falls?"

"She'd like nothing better than for me to return."

"You don't think that'll ever happen?"

She shrugged. "I suppose it could, but St. Paul feels more like home to me now. There's just so much more to do here. One of the reasons I left Fergus Falls was because I was bored."

She needed excitement in her life. He'd known that about her from the day they met. She was like a sponge, ready to soak up as many things as she possibly could. Maybe that's what attracted him initially. She was so very different from him.

She snapped her fingers in front of his face. "Are you there? Why do you always do that?"

"Do what?" he asked.

"Disappear inside your head. Why don't you just tell me what's on your mind?"

"You really want to know?" he asked.

"Yes."

Before he could do just that, a tall figure came out of the shadows calling her name.

She jumped to her feet. "Roy! What are you doing here?"

"You need to ask me that?" he answered her question with a question as he stood directly in front of her. "I've talked to your mother."

Krystal's eyes widened. She looked from Roy to Garret and then back to Roy. Then she grabbed Roy by the hand. "Come with me," she ordered, pulling him into the house.

Garret felt as if someone had just thrown a blanket over the stars. He wanted to follow them inside and say, "Are you nuts? Have you forgotten what this guy did to you?" But he knew he couldn't. Because the only thing worse than seeing her drag Roy into the house would be if he were to follow them and she'd tell *him* to leave.

Ever since the night of the hospital ball he'd wanted to believe that she was finished with Roy Stanton. Now he could see that he hadn't been wrong to believe that she'd only slept with him because she'd been so distraught over Roy cheating on her.

Suddenly the corned beef sandwich tasted awful. He jammed what was left of it into the bag and tossed it in the garbage on the way to his car.

CHAPTER FOUR

KRYSTAL'S HEART BEAT so fast she could feel it in her throat. Why would Roy come to see her unless he knew about the baby?

I'll be there to help you. Her mother's words echoed in her ears. Was this her idea of help? Calling Roy on her behalf? She realized that, like everyone else, her mother had assumed he was the father of her baby. She should have expected it. There'd been no opportunity for Krystal to tell her he wasn't.

As she dragged Roy down the hallway past the kitchen, he called out, "Hi, Mrs. Graham. How's it going?"

Her mother glanced up from the sink and smiled, looking quite pleased with herself. "Oh, hello, Roy. It's nice to see you."

It's nice to see you? Krystal almost laughed out loud. If only her mother knew the absurdity of the situation.

"Would you like some cake and coffee?" her mother asked.

Krystal thought that it was a good thing she didn't have a sharp object in her hand, because she might have used it on her mother. She wondered if anyone had used gestational insanity as a defense for assault.

"Roy and I are going for a walk," she announced, realizing it was the only thing she could do with him. She couldn't risk anyone overhearing what he might say to her and she certainly didn't want him in her room. She didn't want him anywhere near 14 Valentine Place tonight.

She dragged him through the hallway and out the private entrance to the backyard. As she looked toward the patio, she noticed that Garret was gone. A glance at the driveway told her his car was missing, too.

It was just as well. His absence meant one less stress factor.

"You know I really don't feel like going for a walk," Roy said as she pulled him toward the sidewalk. "I came over to talk to you, not walk."

"Well, in order to do one, you have to do the other," she snapped at him.

"Fine, but could we at least slow down? This isn't a race, is it?"

Until he called attention to her gait, she hadn't realized she was practically running. She slowed, hoping the flow of adrenaline would ease as well.

"So are you going to talk to me or aren't you?" he asked irritably when silence stretched between them.

"Not in the middle of the street I'm not. We're going to the park." She really didn't want to take him there, because it held too many memories from their past—of romantic strolls on moonlit nights and promises made beneath the stars. None of that mattered at the moment. Tonight it was just a place where they could talk in private. Fortunately it wasn't far away.

"All right, we're here. Let's get this over with," he said as soon as they reached the tennis courts at the end of the park.

They could have sat down on any of the vacant benches, but Krystal's emotions wouldn't allow her to sit. She folded her arms across her chest and faced him.

"I don't know why you came over, Roy, but you shouldn't have. I have nothing to say to you and I made it perfectly clear that there is no way in hell there will ever be anything between us again." Her heart still raced and she struggled to control the trembling that had started the moment she'd seen him in the backyard.

"I came because I don't need your mother calling me and giving me crap." He pointed his finger at her for emphasis, which only fueled the anger she'd been trying to keep at bay. Seeing him again brought back the memory of the night she'd entered his apartment and found him with a naked woman.

"And what crap would that be?" she demanded, refusing to be intimidated by him.

"Don't play games with me." Again he used his finger for emphasis. "I know what you're trying to pull on me and it's not going to work."

"I'm not trying to pull anything. Look, I don't know what my mother said to you, but I told you the last time I saw you, that all I want is for you to be out of my life. I meant it then and I mean it now," she said firmly.

"Are you pregnant?" He looked repulsed by the possibility.

"That's none of your business."

"It is when your mother calls me and tries to guilt me into doing the right thing," he replied angrily. His eyes narrowed. "You are pregnant, aren't you?"

"Yes."

Gone was the charm he'd always managed to fall back on whenever he found himself in a tight spot. There was nothing even remotely attractive about him at this moment. He used an expletive and kicked the ground with his shoe, sending a divot of grass sailing in the air.

"There's no way I'm being a father to a kid that isn't mine," he yelled at her.

"Good, because you are the last man on this earth that I would want to be a father to my baby. I'm going home." She started to walk away, but he stopped her with a hand on her arm.

"So who is the father? Is it somebody I know?"

Suddenly she knew the true reason he'd come to see her. He wasn't upset that her mother thought she was pregnant with his child. What really bothered him was the knowledge that she had had sex with another man.

"You have no right to ask that." She jerked away from his touch and again started walking toward home, but he stepped in front of her.

"I think I have every right. We were supposed to be getting married…or have you forgotten?"

"You're the one with the short memory," she shot back at him. "You had trouble remembering to be faithful to me, your girlfriend."

"I wasn't cheating on you. I was having sex. There's a difference. And I wouldn't have had to go elsewhere to get it if you wouldn't have got it into your head that we should wait to have sex again until after we were married."

She was getting sick of him thrusting his finger in her face as if she deserved to be scolded. Her own hand shot up and she pointed right back at him.

"Just stop! You have no right to blame me for your inability to keep your pants zipped. The only thing I'm guilty of is being stupid enough to think you were a man who deserved a second chance." She pushed him out of the way, determined he wasn't going to stop her progress.

He didn't try. She knew he was behind her as she made her way back to 14 Valentine Place. She could hear his footsteps. Just before she reached the house, he caught up with her.

"I'd appreciate it if you'd tell your mother I'm not the one who knocked you up." His tone remained hostile.

"I will. I'm sorry she called you," she told him, which was the truth. She still couldn't believe her mother had done such a thing.

He nodded, then walked over to his car and drove away. She didn't bother watching the taillights disappear down the street, but went inside where she found her mother in the kitchen with Leonie, finishing the last of the dishes.

"Is everything okay?" It was Leonie who asked the question.

"Yeah, everything's fine," she lied, forcing a smile to her face.

"Your mom said Roy was here."

She nodded. "Yes, but he shouldn't have come here. It was all a big mistake." She looked at her mother as she spoke the words.

Her mother shifted uneasily and said, "I should probably get going. It's a long drive home."

"You're going to stay overnight, aren't you?" Leonie asked. "You shouldn't be driving that distance at this late hour."

Her mother glanced at the clock. "I didn't realize it was so late. Maybe I should stay…if it's all right with you?" She looked at Krystal, her brows raised in appeal.

"Or you could use the spare bedroom on this floor," Leonie offered.

As much as Krystal would have liked to have had her room to herself, she didn't trust her mother out of her sight, not after what she'd done. "You can sleep on my futon, Mom."

"Why don't the two of you go upstairs?" Leonie suggested. "I can finish down here."

"Are you sure you don't mind?" Krystal asked, not wanting to leave her landlady with the remainder of the cleanup.

Leonie gave her a gentle shove toward the door. "Not at all. You go have some quiet time with your mom."

Krystal knew that once they were back in her room their time would be anything but quiet. She thanked her landlady and took her mother upstairs, where she confronted her about the phone call to Roy as soon as she'd closed the door.

"Do you know how awful that was for me tonight?" she said, facing her mother with her hands on her hips.

"I'm sorry it didn't go well with Roy," Linda said.

"Did you think it would?" Krystal asked in disbelief. "Why did you call him?"

"Because I know how bullheaded you can be and I thought that if I gave you a little shove in the right direction, the two of you could patch things up and get on with the important things in life."

"Important things like marriage you mean." She made a sound of frustration. "You had no right to butt into my life like that."

"I'm concerned about my grandchild."

"That doesn't give you the right to call up my old boyfriend and tell him I'm pregnant!" She was too angry to stand still so she went over to the closet to get linens for the futon and began making up the bed.

"I was only trying to help." Her mother moved to the opposite side of the mattress to help her. "I know you and Roy have had your differences, but I thought…"

"Differences?" Krystal interrupted her. "He's immature, irresponsible and incapable of being faithful."

"Well, it would have been nice if you would have thought about that before you slept with him," she said, shaking out the top sheet.

"I didn't sleep with him," she blurted out.

"What are you talking about?"

"He's not the father of my baby."

The revelation stilled her mother's actions and took the color out of her cheeks. Krystal continued to make up the bed, tucking the corner under the mattress. When she straightened, her mother hadn't moved.

When she finally found her voice, she said, "Well, if he isn't the father, who is?"

"Just a guy I know," Krystal said, returning to the closet for a pillow.

"Just a guy you know?" her mother repeated in disbelief. "You do something as intimate as make a baby with a man and you call him *just a guy?*"

"It's not what you think."

"Then why don't you tell me what it is? How long have you been dating this man?"

"We're not dating."

She grimaced. "Oh, please don't tell me he was a one-night stand. I didn't raise you to be that kind of girl."

"I'm not that kind of girl." Her voice rose with the denial. "I may date a lot of guys but I don't sleep around, Mom. I never have and I never will."

"He's not married, is he?"

"No."

"Thank goodness for that. Then there's still hope."

"Hope for what? That he'll want to marry me?"

"I don't think you realize how hard it is to find a husband when you're a single woman with a child."

Krystal knew it would be a waste of time to try to tell her she wasn't looking for one. "Mom, don't you think we've done enough arguing about this for one night?"

Her mother wasn't about to let the subject drop, however. "I just don't understand you. I did my best to teach you and Carly to be smart when it came to men. I don't know how many times I told you that if a man truly loves you, he puts a ring on your finger."

Krystal could have told her it was at least a thousand times. It was always the same broken record when it came to the lesson about love.

"You're young, you're beautiful.... I don't understand why you have such trouble finding a decent guy," her mother said in consternation.

"Trust me, Mom, they're not easy to find," she said on a note of resignation.

"Your sister didn't have any trouble finding one and she didn't have to leave Fergus Falls to do it."

She should have known that sooner or later Carly's name would be mentioned. Her sister had fulfilled their mother's dream—met a nice boy, married well and had a family. Now she had the big fancy house in Fergus Falls, in-laws who were well-known around town and the ideal life as far as her mother was concerned. Krystal, on the other hand, had done exactly what her mother had told her not to do—she'd followed in her mother's footsteps instead of learning from her mistakes.

She knew it was a good thing that someone knocked on her door, because in her current state she was dangerously close to saying something she'd regret. When she opened the door, she found Dena, still wearing the paper veil they'd made for her to wear at the shower.

"I know it's late, but I wanted to tell you thank you again for the best bridal shower a girl could have." She gave her an exuberant hug.

"You're so very welcome," Krystal responded.

"Is everything okay?"

She nodded but had to bite on her lip to choke back the emotions threatening to spill forth in the form of tears.

"I could use some girl talk. How about you?"

It was late and Krystal was tired, but she needed to talk to someone who wasn't going to judge her about her pregnancy. "I'd like that."

"Your room or mine?"

"Yours. Mom's staying the night and I think she wants to go to bed."

She nodded in understanding. "Should I make tea?"

"Not for me." She stuck her head back into her apartment to tell her mother she'd be over at Dena's, then pulled the door shut and gave Dena's arm a squeeze saying, "Thank you for rescuing me. I so need to talk to someone other than my mom."

"Things aren't going well?" she asked as she led her to her room.

"I love my mother, but I wish she wouldn't have chosen today as the day she was going to fix what was wrong in my life," she said, sinking down on to the love seat. She curled her feet up underneath and faced Dena, who sat down beside her.

"Oh-oh, it was that bad, was it?"

"It was worse." She stretched her arms up over her head and rotated her neck, hoping to ease the stiffness tension had created.

"Want to talk about it?"

She did, but she wasn't going to spoil the end of what had been a very happy evening for her friend. "You don't need to hear me whine about my mother. This is your day to be happy."

Dena reached across and touched her arm. "I may have wedding jitters, but I'm not a basket case yet. Besides, I want to know what happened when Roy came here."

"You know he was here tonight?"

She nodded. "I saw his car out front when I went outside to say goodbye to one of the shower guests."

Krystal sighed. "It was not a pretty scene, believe me."

"What did he say?"

She hesitated only a moment. After everything that had happened that day, she needed a friend now. She relayed the entire story, leaving out the part with Garret on the patio.

When she'd finished, Dena gave her another hug. "You poor thing. That's horrible!"

"It's unbelievable is what it is," Krystal said, shaking her head. "I guess there is one positive that came out of all of this. I'm finally rid of Roy."

Dena threw up her hands in a gesture of triumph and said, "Yes! And that is reason to celebrate." She jumped up and went over to her compact refrigerator where she pulled out a bottle of grape juice. When she'd filled two paper cups, she returned to the love seat.

"It's not wine, but it's the next best thing." She lifted her cup in midair for a toast. "To my dear friend

Krystal, who had a frog pretending to be a prince, but she was smart enough to see his warts and kick his butt back into the pond."

Krystal grinned, then took a sip of the juice. "Mmm. This tastes good. I'd like to propose a toast, too." She lifted her cup. "To my dear friend Dena, who never made me feel I was crazy for wanting to get back together with the frog after he came home from his military duty."

"You weren't crazy. You just had to be sure of your feelings and now you are."

Krystal drained the remainder of her juice and said, "I am." She shuddered. "Just thinking about that guy creeps me out. But enough talk about him. Let's talk about something fun. The wedding. It's getting so close! Aren't you excited?"

"I am but I'm also scared."

"Scared? About what?"

"I love the thought of being married to Quinn, but don't forget that besides getting a husband I'm getting two kids. What if I'm a lousy mother? I mean, I've never done it before. How do I know I can do it?"

She shrugged. "I don't know. I've been asking myself those same questions."

"We're in the same boat in that aspect, aren't we? We're both going to be new moms. The only difference is my kids are going to be seven and twelve. You're getting a newborn."

"And you already know Sara and Luke like you."

"Your baby's going to like you, too," she stated with no uncertainty. "You're going to be a great mom."

"Both of us will be," Krystal added with conviction. "We'll help each other out, right?"

"Of course. And what's really cool is that Sara will

be old enough to baby-sit, so if we want to go out for an iced latte we can. We'll have our own little new moms support group.''

While Dena rambled on, thinking up all sorts of fun things for them to do as mothers, Krystal could only stare at her in disbelief. Finally Dena asked, ''Why are you looking at me like that?''

''Because I was just thinking what a unique friend you are. I've told you Roy isn't the father of my baby, yet not once while we've been talking have you asked who is.''

She shrugged. ''I figured if you wanted to tell me you would.''

That was so like Dena. Always listening but never prying. If there was one thing she'd never be accused of doing, it would be gossiping.

''The reason I haven't told you is I've been trying not to complicate your life,'' Krystal told her.

Dena reached out to take her hand. ''It's not going to complicate my life. You know that anything you tell me won't leave this room.''

''I know that. That isn't the reason why I haven't told you.'' She took a deep breath and said, ''It's Garret.''

''Oh.'' If she was surprised, she hid it well. ''I take it you haven't told him yet?''

She shook her head. ''I was waiting until after the wedding. For obvious reasons.''

''Leonie,'' she said in understanding.

She nodded solemnly. ''And Samantha lives upstairs.''

Dena grimaced. ''And she's been seeing Garret.''

''It's going to be really awkward around here when everyone finds out.''

"No one will find out until you're ready to tell them," she assured her.

Krystal leaned over to give her another hug. "Thank you. I want so much for you to have the perfect wedding."

"Don't worry. Everything will be fine." Then she wrinkled her nose. "I just thought of something. I paired you and Garret for the bridal procession."

"That's okay."

"Are you sure?"

"Yes. We're still friends." Or we used to be, she should have added, but she really didn't want to go into the details of her relationship with Garret. And Dena, being the kind of friend she was, didn't ask.

Krystal was grateful when she changed the subject, asking her opinion on what hairstyles would work with the veil she'd chosen. There was no more talk of babies or boyfriends, and by the time Krystal returned to her room, she felt much better.

But as she climbed into bed, all the upsetting things that had happened to her during the day came into her mind. And one refused to be ignored. It was Garret telling her he was going to be gone for six months to a year in the Doctors Without Borders program. Visions of him in a war zone haunted her until she fell asleep.

As DENA'S WEDDING DAY approached and 14 Valentine Place became a beehive of activity, Krystal felt more confident that she'd made the right decision to wait to tell Garret she was pregnant. She saw how something as minor as a delay in Maddie and Dylan's travel plans could upset the harmony in the house. She wasn't about to risk creating an even bigger upheaval with her news.

To everyone's relief, Dena's third bridesmaid did arrive on the Friday before the wedding. She'd missed the final fitting for the bridesmaids and their dresses, but to Leonie's relief, her dress was a perfect fit. Everyone saw it as a sign the wedding would go off without a hitch.

"I am so lucky this fits," Maddie said as she pirouetted in front of Krystal wearing the plum-colored bridesmaid dress. "I thought for sure when I missed that fitting we were going to be scrambling to find a seamstress at the last minute."

"You're lucky you're here. If the weather hadn't improved, you could still be sitting at the airport in Paris," Krystal pointed out.

"Yes, and we might have missed the wedding entirely. You want me to zip you up?" she asked as she watched Krystal struggle to get the back closed on her dress.

"Thanks." She turned around, lifting her hair off the nape of her neck.

"It's a little snug," Maddie said as she hooked the zipper in place. "I thought you said you had yours altered."

"I did. It was too big in the shoulders."

"Well, now it's a little tight in the bodice." She came around to Krystal's front side to peer closely at the dress. She pinched a layer of fabric under her arm, then down the skirt. "It appears that it's just the bodice. I think you're going to have to leave the padded bra at home."

Krystal didn't tell her that she wasn't wearing a padded bra. The fullness in the bodice was due to her swollen breasts, another of the changes her body had undergone during her early pregnancy.

"It doesn't feel tight," she told her, although it wasn't quite the truth.

"No? Well, then don't worry about it. I'm sure none of the men will care," Maddie said with a knowing lift of her brows. "You look lovely."

"So do you. It's a great dress. Don't you just love it?"

"I do. I was a little worried when I saw the picture, but now that I'm here—" she pivoted in front of the full-length mirror "—I can see that Dena did a great job of picking a dress that minimizes the tummy area, although nothing's going to hide this I'm afraid." She rested her hand on her slightly swollen stomach.

"Nothing should. You look beautiful," Krystal told her because it was the truth.

"I look pregnant." Maddie turned to the side. "I'm pretty big for twenty-two weeks, don't you think?"

"Mmm-hmm." Krystal wasn't sure what to say. It had been a shock to see Maddie walk through the front door of 14 Valentine Place wearing maternity clothes, because Krystal knew that in two months' time she would be wearing the same size and looking just as pregnant as her friend.

"At first the doctor thought it might be twins, but it's only one. Leonie told me all of the boys were over nine pounds, which means I'll probably have a big baby. I guess that's the price I have to pay for falling in love with a Donovan."

Krystal knew it was an opportunity to tell her friend that she was paying the price, too, but she hesitated because Maddie, besides being her friend, was also Garret's sister-in-law. Even though Krystal trusted her to keep her secret, she didn't want to put her good friend in the position of knowing something of importance and not being able to share it with the rest of her family. Krystal also knew that Maddie told Dylan everything and as much as she wanted to believe he wouldn't say anything to Garret, she simply didn't think it would be wise to tell any of the Donovans unless she was telling all of them.

"You're glowing, Maddie. You must be happy," Krystal remarked as Maddie stood in front of the mirror.

"I am happy. Dylan and I didn't plan to start a family so soon after we got married, but now that I'm pregnant, it just feels so right," she said.

"You're going to make wonderful parents. I wish you weren't going to be so far away when the baby's born. I miss you."

Maddie reached for her hand and gave it a squeeze. "Oh, I miss you, too. France is wonderful, but it's not home. It would feel more like home, however, if my friends would visit," she said with an appeal in her eyes.

"Oh, you know I'd love to, but…"

"If it's money stopping you from coming over, Dylan has a ridiculous amount of frequent flyer points."

She held up her hand. "It isn't that. This just wouldn't be a good time for me."

"Oh, come on. You're the one who always wants to travel someplace new and exciting. Paris is definitely exciting. And if you come before I get much bigger, Dylan and I can take you to the most fabulous places—"

She stopped suddenly and said, "Quick. Give me your hand." She took Krystal's palm and placed it on her stomach. "The baby's kicking. Can you feel it?"

Krystal shook her head because at first she didn't notice anything, but then she felt a tiny flutter. "Ohmigosh! I think I did!"

"There it is again. Feel it?"

Krystal giggled gleefully. "That is so neat!"

"I know. You should feel what it's like on my end." She rolled her eyes. "This little guy is either going to be a soccer star or a dancer. His feet never stop."

"Guy?" Krystal looked at her inquisitively. "Are you hoping for a boy?"

"It is a boy," she announced proudly.

"You found out?"

She nodded. "They did an ultrasound at twenty weeks, but don't say anything to Leonie. We haven't told her yet."

She shook her head. "Of course I won't. She's going to be so excited."

"I think she wanted a girl, but she'll just have to wait for her first granddaughter." She reached for her purse. "I have pictures in my bag. Want to see?"

Krystal nodded and Maddie pulled out an envelope. "It's amazing how much of the baby's anatomy you can identify." She named the different body parts as she pointed to them with her finger.

Krystal gazed in amazement at the grainy printouts. It was hard to believe that something very similar was forming inside her. "It's really a little person, isn't it?" she said as much for her own benefit as Maddie's.

"Look at the tiny little hands and feet! When I see these pictures, I get this lump in my throat and mist in my eyes."

Krystal understood why. "It's just so incredible to think that..." She didn't finish her sentence, because if she had she would have told Maddie that in two months she'd know if she was carrying a boy or a girl.

There was a knock on the door followed by Dylan's

voice. "Hey, don't take too much time in there. We have a wedding rehearsal to get to."

"We'll be down in a few minutes," Maddie called out, then said to Krystal, "We'll have to talk later. There's so much I want to tell you."

"The same goes for me. I've missed you," Krystal told her, her eyes filling with unshed tears.

"I've missed you, too. I wish I could have been here for Dena's shower. How is she holding up?" Maddie asked as she tucked the photos back into their envelope.

"She was fine until this morning," Krystal answered. "It's actually quite funny. You know how she's always trying to look as if she has everything under control...well today, she's the total opposite. She's running around like a chicken with her head cut off."

"That doesn't sound like the Dena I know," Maddie commented. "Back in college she was the one who kept me grounded."

"I know what you mean. We've become really good friends. I'm so glad you recommended her to Leonie."

"You become good friends with everyone who lives here."

"Yes, which makes it really hard when they move away. At least when you left Dena moved in across the hall. I don't know what I'm going to do if I don't like the next person who takes her place."

"That won't happen, because you know Leonie is very careful when it comes to choosing her tenants," Maddie told her.

"I don't think she's looked for a replacement for Dena—she's been too busy helping with the wedding plans.'' She sighed. ''Guess I'll just have to be alone for a while.''

''You're not alone. Isn't Samantha Penrose upstairs?''

''Oh, yeah. I forgot about her. I don't really know her.''

''She hasn't been down for any girl talk?''

''Uh-uh. I hardly see her around here at all.''

''She's a doctor and if she's anything like Garret, she works all the time,'' Maddie surmised.

''I think she's a lot like Garret. That's probably why they get along,'' Krystal pointed out.

''I was surprised when Leonie told me she'd rented a room to her. What's the deal with her and Garret anyway? Are they really back together?''

She shrugged. ''I don't know. You'd have to ask him.''

Maddie stared at her, her hands on her hips. ''Since when do you not know what's going on at 14 Valentine Place?''

She turned away so Maddie wouldn't see her face when she answered. If there was one thing she knew she couldn't do, it was lie to Maddie. They'd lived together too long and had become too close of friends.

''I told you why. I haven't seen her. Or Garret for that matter. And Leonie's been so caught up with the wedding....'' She trailed off, not wanting to say too much about Samantha.

''I'm looking forward to meeting her.''

''I thought you knew her. She and Garret dated in college.''

Maddie shook her head. ''They broke up before I moved to St. Paul. I remember Garret talking about her, though.''

Krystal wanted to ask her what he'd said about her,

but Dylan pounded on the door for the second time, reminding them they needed to hurry. Maddie disappeared with her husband, leaving Krystal to change out of the bridesmaid dress. Before slipping on the two-piece skirt and jacket she was wearing to the rehearsal, Krystal stood in front of the mirror in her bra and panties. Turning sideways, she tried to imagine Maddie's gently swelling tummy on her body. Then she placed her hand on her stomach, searching for some sign there was a baby kicking inside. There wasn't any.

Hearing Maddie so lovingly include Dylan's name when she talked about the baby made Krystal wish that she wasn't going through her pregnancy alone. She, too, had questions and concerns she wanted to share with the father of her baby. Only she couldn't. At least not yet.

Soon she would tell Garret he was going to be a father and then what? She wondered. His reaction was something she'd thought about often and each time she'd hoped that, after his initial shock, he would tell her he wanted to be a part of the baby's life. Until the night they'd conceived a child, they had been friends. Surely they could maintain a friendly relationship for the sake of their child.

She closed her eyes, not wanting to think about it. But she had to think about it. Because in a very short time there would be no more hiding the truth.

KRYSTAL KNEW DENA had planned for her to be escorted down the aisle by Garret. What she didn't expect was that she'd be seated next to him at the groom's dinner following the rehearsal. She had hoped to sit next to Maddie, but she found herself sandwiched between Dylan and Garret, and feeling very uneasy about it.

If she could have pleaded a headache and gone home after the rehearsal, she would have, but she knew Dena would suspect the reason she'd left. She'd spent the past six weeks trying to keep from letting her situation spoil Dena's happy occasion. She could get through a few more hours.

So she put on a happy face and acted as if she was enjoying herself. It wasn't as hard as she thought it would be. She was, after all, a people person and had no trouble making conversation. The difficult part was eating.

"Aren't you hungry?" Garret asked, glancing at her plate where most of her dinner sat untouched.

"I think I'm too excited to eat," she told him, not wanting to admit the true reason for her lack of an appetite. She usually became nauseous about this time every evening. Tonight was no exception.

He looked at the truffles next to her plate. "I've never known you to pass on chocolate."

Normally she didn't, but she knew that inside the chocolate confections was a boysenberry cream that killed any temptation she might have had. "There's a first for everything, I guess," she said with a weak smile. "Would you like them?"

He grinned. "It would be a shame to let them go to waste."

She shoved the plate in his direction. "Enjoy."

"Thanks." Before he could eat them, his five-year-old nephew went running past. Garret reached out to slow him down, grabbing him around his waist and lifting him onto his knee.

"Hey there, Mickey! Whatcha got, buddy?"

"Trucks," he said, proudly displaying two Hot

Wheels cars in his hand. One was a red pickup and the other was a yellow dump truck.

"Hey, they're pretty cool," Garret said.

"Do you like trucks?" he asked his uncle.

"I sure do. Can I try it?"

Mickey handed him the red pickup and Garret set it on the white linen tablecloth, moving it around his plate and glass and making zooming noises.

Mickey followed his example, pushing the tiny dump truck with his small fingers.

"We need to make a parking garage." Garret told him, then took his napkin and draped it over his water glass. He then pushed the red pickup under it.

More zooming sounds came out of Mickey's lips as he wheeled his tiny truck around the plate and under the linen tent. Then he spotted the uneaten truffles and reached for one. Garret's hand stopped his.

"Let's ask your mom first," he said, then glanced across the table at Jennifer Donovan for approval. "Do you care if Mickey eats another chocolate?"

"No, but he's going to make a mess of your clothes. Why don't you send him back over here," she answered, motioning to the chair next to hers.

"No, I want to sit by Uncle Garret," Mickey protested.

"He's okay," Garret said.

"He's pretty messy when it comes to eating chocolate," Jennifer warned.

"I don't mind." He gave his nephew the candy.

As his mother predicted, Mickey soon had chocolate on his hands and face. Krystal watched Garret take the napkin from the water goblet and wipe the boy's cheeks. The five-year-old protested, but only because he was using the makeshift garage to do the job.

"Uncle Garret! What about our cars?" he shrieked.

Krystal offered him her napkin. "Use mine. I'm finished eating." She watched the two of them play with the miniature trucks, noticing how patient Garret was with the young boy as they made roads using the silverware.

Gradually the dinner party began to break up. Guests left the table and began mingling and Mickey was sent back over to his parents.

Krystal thought about the scene she'd just witnessed. She'd always known Garret thought highly of family. All of Leonie's sons did. Only now she realized how important that was. In five years time it could be her son sitting on his knee.

When he flipped a penny on to her plate, she gave him a puzzled look. He said, "That's for your thoughts. You looked lost in them. I figured they must be good."

She didn't want to tell him that she'd been thinking he'd make a good father so she said, "You're really good with kids. You should be a pediatrician."

"I've thought about it, but I like family practice," he told her.

Dylan came over to stand beside him. "Hey, I have a question for you, little brother. It's about Maddie's pregnancy."

Krystal knew that was her cue to leave. She excused herself and joined Maddie and Leonie, who were discussing the plan for the morning. While they talked, her glance kept straying to the two brothers she'd just left.

As they stood next to each other it was easy to see the similarities. They had the same strong jaw with a hint of five-o'clock shadow, the same cheeks that dimpled when they smiled and the same brown eyes that held just a hint of mischief. Dylan's were less serious looking than Garret's, but they could play the same kind of havoc with a woman's heartbeat. She wasn't sure why she'd always thought Dylan was the best-looking of the four Donovan brothers. Garret wasn't hot in the sense that his brother was, but he had something that set him apart from the others.

He wasn't as broad in the shoulders as Dylan, but he was just as tall. Dylan definitely had more bulk to his frame, but Krystal knew that beneath Garret's loose-fitting jacket and slacks was a firm body. Heat spread through her as she remembered what he'd looked like lying next to her in bed, naked.

Until that night she'd always thought of him as being reserved and had expected that when he took a woman to bed for the first time he'd be a bit shy. But there had been nothing inhibited about his actions that night. Once she'd made it clear to him that she wanted him, he'd made love to her with an intensity that had had her begging for more. He'd been strong yet tender. In control yet unselfish. She had felt a sense of empowerment that she could unleash such passion in a man.

Just thinking about it made her tremble inside. Never had any man made her feel so desirable. "You don't know how long I've wanted to do this," he'd said, then called her a fantasy come true.

A fantasy. It was the one word that had ironically brought her back to reality. Maddie used to tell her she thought Garret had a crush on her, but she'd never paid any attention. She'd been too busy looking for love elsewhere.

Love. If only what she and Garret had shared had been love. It had felt so good and so right to be in his arms, yet she knew that they'd been together for the wrong reasons. She'd pretended he loved her in order to ease the pain of Roy's betrayal. He'd had a chance to make a fantasy a reality and hadn't passed on it.

They'd both agreed it had been a mistake. They'd parted and gone their separate ways, unable to return to what they once had—friendship. As she stood staring at him, she wondered if he ever thought about that night.

As if he could read her mind, he glanced at her. For one brief moment she thought she saw a glimpse of the man who had gazed so lovingly at her that night in May.

"Krystal, what do you think?" Maddie's voice broke into her thoughts and forced her to pull her eyes away from Garret's.

"I'm sorry. I didn't hear what you said."

"Quinn wants to take all of the wedding party to the reception. Leonie and I think just the two of them should ride in the limo."

"I agree with you. They ought to be alone," she answered.

"Of course they should," Leonie seconded. "I can ride with Shane and Jennifer and this way Krystal can go with you and Dylan," she said to her daughter-in-law.

"Why can't you ride with us?" Krystal wanted to know.

"Our rental car only holds five," Maddie explained. "Garret's coming with us, too."

"And Samantha," Leonie added.

Samantha. So he was bringing her to the wedding. Krystal quickly masked her disappointment, not wanting either Leonie or Maddie to see it.

"Why doesn't Leonie ride with you and I'll drive myself," she suggested brightly as if nothing was wrong.

"You are *not* driving yourself," Maddie insisted.

"While you two figure it out, I'm going to check on something," Leonie said, then disappeared.

"It's silly for you to drive alone when you could ride with us," Maddie said as soon as her mother-in-law was gone.

"And feel like a fifth wheel with you four? No thank you," Krystal stated in no uncertain terms.

Maddie flung her arm around her shoulder. "You could never be a fifth wheel with us. Besides, I don't think Samantha is actually Garret's date. Dena invited her to the wedding. She does live at 14 Valentine Place."

The last thing Krystal wanted was to be stuck in the back seat of a car with Garret and Samantha. Just thinking about the entire day tomorrow gave her a headache. With the exception of Sara and Luke, the junior bridesmaid and ring bearer, every other member of the bridal party was a part of a couple. She would be the only odd one out.

To her relief, Maddie said, "We can figure all this out tomorrow. One way or another, we'll all get to the church and the reception."

"Yes, we can. And as much fun as this groom's dinner is, we need to get our bride back to 14 Valentine Place so she can get her beauty rest," Krystal added.

"Good idea." Maddie looked in Dylan's direction. Without saying a word, he came toward her. He'd sensed she wanted to leave and had responded to the single glance she'd given him.

They knew each other so well, so intimately that they didn't need words to communicate with each other. Krystal wondered if she'd ever have that kind of a relationship with a man.

Her mother's words echoed in her ears. *Do you know how hard it is for a single woman with a child to find a husband?*

She couldn't think about that right now. She wouldn't think about it, especially not with Garret coming toward her. She glanced around, thinking he might be making his way toward someone else, but there was no one else nearby.

"Are you sure you're feeling okay?" he asked when he reached her.

She wished his voice didn't sound so impersonal. She wanted to hear in his voice the same tone she heard in Dylan's when he asked Maddie if she was feeling all right.

"Yeah, I'm fine," she replied. He looked uncomfortable and she asked, "Is anything wrong?"

"No." He rubbed his jaw, then said, "I just want you to know that I'm going to do whatever I can to make sure it won't be awkward tomorrow…you and I being paired together."

"Oh, me, too," she told him, wishing there was no need for them to even be bringing up the subject.

"It shouldn't be awkward. We've been friends for a long time."

"Yeah, we have," she agreed with a weak smile.

"Are you bringing a date to the wedding?" he asked.

"No. Are you?" She knew she shouldn't have asked, but she needed to know if he really was seeing Samantha again.

Krystal never heard his answer, because Dena interrupted them. "Sorry, Garret, but I need this woman," she said, looping her arm through Krystal's with an apologetic grin. "The car's leaving. You two can talk tomorrow."

Tomorrow. Krystal wished it never had to come.

CHAPTER FIVE

As PERSONAL ATTENDANT to the bride, Leonie appointed herself in charge of the bridesmaids and made it her duty to insure everyone was on time. She collected each and every one on Saturday morning and took them to the beauty salon, where Krystal had arranged makeup and hair appointments for the bridal party. After a light lunch catered by one of Leonie's friends, they headed for the church.

"Oh my gosh, it's hot," Krystal complained as she stepped out of the air-conditioned car into the bright sunshine.

"Happy is the bride the sun shines on," Leonie recited cheerfully.

"If that's true, then Dena is going to be one happy lady," Maddie noted, shading her eyes with her hand.

"Please tell me the church is air-conditioned," Krystal said on a moan as she lifted the large garment bag containing her bridesmaid dress from the back of the car.

"It must be. It didn't feel warm in there last night at rehearsal," Lisa Bailey remarked.

"No, but yesterday it wasn't this hot, either." Krystal could feel perspiration beading on her skin as she slammed the side door shut. "If I don't get inside soon my makeup is going to melt."

As they all made their way to the church entrance,

Maddie tugged on Krystal's elbow. "You seem a little on edge. Is everything okay?"

"Don't worry about me. I'll be all right," she answered, although today nothing felt right and she hated pretending it was, especially with Maddie.

When she stopped at a drinking fountain just inside the door, Maddie waited for her while the others went on ahead. "Are you sure you're okay? You usually love weddings, but if I didn't know better I'd say you don't want to be at this one."

Krystal should have known that Maddie would pick up on her mood. They'd been friends for a long time and not even distance could erase the intuitive bond that existed between them.

"I'm really happy for Dena and Quinn. It's just that..." She paused, wondering if she should simply be honest and tell her she was feeling lousy because she was pregnant. Then Leonie called out to them from down the hall and she knew couldn't. Not yet. So she said, "You know how my stomach gets when I'm nervous." It wasn't a lie. Anyone who'd lived at 14 Valentine Place knew she often had tummy troubles when she was anxious.

Maddie bought the explanation. "I thought maybe that was why you didn't come down for breakfast today. I have some antacids in my purse if you think they'll help."

"No, it's all right. I'll be fine."

But she wasn't fine and Leonie noticed a short while later when she helped her hook the clasp on her necklace. "You look a little pale, dear. I know you don't like to eat when you're nervous, but you really should have a bite of something," Leonie advised. "Why don't you have a piece of fruit?" She motioned to a small insulated cooler she'd packed with beverages and snacks.

Krystal nodded but didn't act on her suggestion.

Talk turned to the wedding ceremony and Krystal's queasy stomach was relegated to the same category as Dena's pacing—accepted as part of the prewedding ritual. Leonie fussed over the bridesmaids, smoothing wrinkles and pinning up errant curls.

Despite taking some of Maddie's antacid tablets, Krystal continued to have an unsettled stomach. It wasn't her only complaint. Her feet had swollen, making her specially dyed shoes uncomfortable. She did her best not to let her discomfort show, but Maddie noticed.

"You should have some fruit. It'll perk you up. Plus, it's delicious." She popped a fresh strawberry in her mouth. "I ought to know. I've eaten enough of it. You would not believe my appetite with this baby. I barely finish one meal and I'm planning the next."

Krystal couldn't imagine feeling that way. Lately she'd had to force herself to eat and then it was only accomplished out of sheer willpower because she knew that in order to have a healthy pregnancy, she needed nutritious foods.

"I thought you said you had morning sickness," Krystal remarked.

"At first I did. It was awful. Felt sick all day long. But then right before my fifth month…" She snapped her fingers. "Just like that it was gone. I've never felt as good as I do now."

Krystal hoped that meant she was getting close to being over her bout with the malady. Right now she'd give just about anything for it to go away for one day. She wondered if Maddie was right about the fruit and grabbed a small container of sliced cantaloupe from the cooler. To her surprise, it tasted good.

When she'd finished Maddie asked, "Feeling any better?"

"A little," she told her honestly. She'd learned that the best remedy for a queasy stomach was to lie down, but the bride's room had no cots or lounges. There were, however, padded bench seats in the hallway.

Telling Maddie she was going to take a walk, she slipped out into the corridor. It was empty, quiet and much cooler than the dressing room. She stretched out on a vinyl padded bench, her feet dangling over one end. With her eyes closed, she practiced a relaxation technique she'd learned at a one-day seminar for working women, letting her focus travel through her body. She was on her hips when a male voice broke her concentration.

"Had a late night, did you?"

She opened her eyes to see Garret standing over her. "Oh! Hi."

"Hi yourself. I thought maybe I was going to have to kiss you to wake you."

She knew it was said in a teasing manner for there was a smile on his face, but at that moment it was exactly what she wished he would do. Kiss her. She remembered how good those lips could feel on hers.

She quickly lowered her eyes so he wouldn't see what she was thinking and said, "I wasn't sleeping. I was meditating." She sat up, smoothing down the skirt of her dress. "This waiting can get to be a little nerve-wracking."

"The girls are jittery, are they?"

"Probably not any more so than the boys," she retorted. He offered her his hand and she took it. "Thanks."

"You look—" he paused as his eyes roved over her figure. "—fantastic."

She couldn't stop the blush that covered her cheeks. "Thank you." She looked him over and said with a teasing smile, "You don't look half bad yourself. Reminds me of the night of the hospital ball." As soon as she'd said the words, she regretted them. What neither of them needed was a reference to what had happened between them. She tried to make light of it by saying, "We were all dressed up, you in a tux, me in my 'night on the town' blue dress."

She wished they weren't in a corridor of the church with only minutes before Dena's wedding, because it could have been an opening for her to tell him the truth about what had happened that night.

Then he said, "We agreed we weren't going to talk about that night."

She felt like a fool. "We're not talking about it. Forget I mentioned it," she said abruptly, then started back.

"Krystal, wait." He grabbed her by the arm. "I'm sorry. I shouldn't have said that." He ran a hand over the back of his neck. "God, I hate what that night has done to us."

Her heart missed a beat. "What do you mean?"

"You know what I mean. We used to be friends."

She breathed a sigh of relief. For a moment she thought he'd somehow figured out she was pregnant. "We're still friends. You said we were last night."

"It doesn't feel like we are to me. It's more like we're acquaintances being pleasant to each other because it's expected of us."

She looked away, unsure what she should say. He hadn't said anything she didn't feel. Sex had ruined their friendship. She'd heard other women say sleeping with a guy you only regarded as a friend was a mistake. Now she knew for herself how true it was. Maybe some friends could continue on as if nothing had happened. It was obvious she and Garret couldn't.

"I'm sorry that night ever happened, Krystal, but it did and there's nothing we can do about it now except try to forget." There was a resignation in his voice that made her cringe inwardly.

He regretted sleeping with her. No, he didn't just regret it. He wished it had never happened. She hadn't lived up to his fantasy obviously. The thought cut through her, causing her throat to tighten with emotion. She didn't want to feel hurt, but she did.

"I guess fantasies are just never worth the price you have to pay for them, are they?" Her voice faltered with a combination of hurt and anger.

Before he could respond Shane's voice called out, "Hey, you two! It's time!"

Garret turned as his brother came striding toward them.

"You'd better get back in there." Shane jerked a thumb in the direction of the groomsmen's dressing room. "Quinn's so nervous I'm worried he's going to hyperventilate."

Krystal felt the same way. She watched Shane throw an arm around Garret's shoulder and drag him away. He didn't protest, giving her reason to believe he was relieved to be away from her. He'd said what he wanted to say. He'd told her he wished he could forget they'd ever slept together.

Krystal wanted to turn and run out the door as fast as her legs would carry her. Only she couldn't. She dropped down onto the padded bench seat and hung her head in her hands wishing she had never told Dena she'd be a bridesmaid. How was she ever going to get through the rest of the day?

The sound of heels clicking on the tile had her lifting her head to see Maddie coming toward her.

"You're still not feeling well, are you?" She sat down beside her.

She shook her head, trying to swallow back the emotion. "I shouldn't have told Dena I'd be in the wedding." A lone tear trickled down her cheek.

Maddie wrapped her arm around her. "Oh, don't cry, Krys. You want me to tell Dena you're sick? She'll understand. I know she will."

She was so very tempted to say yes, but then Sara, the junior bridesmaid, was at their side saying, "Ohmigosh! Dena is so freaking out because you two aren't in there. Come!" She waved with her hand. "The wedding coordinator is lining everyone up to start the processional. Hurry!"

"What do you want to do?" Maddie asked.

Krystal took a deep breath and willed her composure to return. "I think I can make it."

"Are you sure?"

"Yes." As she rose she wobbled on her feet. Seeing the look of panic on Maddie's face she said, "Relax. It's the shoes. My feet are killing me."

"Why don't you change them? I'm sure Dena wouldn't mind," Maddie suggested.

"No. I'm not going to be the only one in odd-colored shoes," she stated in no uncertain terms. "I'll make it."

"I think she'd rather see you with a different pair of shoes, then hobbling in those," Maddie pointed out.

"I'm not going to hobble. See." She demonstrated by taking a few steps without any difficulty.

When they reached the apse, Dena was already in

place, her father at her side. Krystal caught a glimpse of the inside of the church. It was full, as was to be expected considering Quinn was a professional hockey player. She also noticed that the large fans suspended from the ceiling were turning. She took a deep breath, willing her body to relax as she slipped between Maddie and Sara.

Just before the processional began, Maddie whispered over her shoulder, "Last chance to back out."

Krystal shook her head. She'd get through this day with sheer willpower because she wanted it to be special for Dena. She turned around and gave the bride a thumbs-up sign and a smile, then clasped her bouquet firmly. She waited until Sara was a third of the way down the aisle before stepping onto the white carpet.

True to the word she gave Maddie, she walked steadily even though her feet ached. At the altar she continued to gaze straight ahead, reaching for Garret's arm without actually looking at him. She felt him stiffen and hoped nobody noticed how uneasy they both were as they walked to their spots at the altar.

Krystal knew from rehearsal that all of the bridesmaids would be on Dena's left and the groomsmen on Quinn's right. Although Garret was her escort, the only time she needed to be next to him was during the recessional when they'd walk back down the aisle arm in arm.

As she stood waiting for Dena to make her grand entrance, she glanced out at the crowd. It was no wonder the church felt stuffy. It was packed with people, many of whom were fanning themselves with wedding programs. At the start of Mendelssohn's refrain, everyone rose to welcome the bride.

Warm air undulated with the crowd's movement. Krystal tried not to think about how stuffy it was inside the church, but it wasn't easy. She glanced at the minister and saw him wipe his brow with a handkerchief.

When Dena reached the altar and stood beside Quinn, the wedding ceremony began. The Donovan brothers had joked about how long-winded this particular minister could be, but Krystal hadn't expected he'd deliver a lengthy homily on such a warm day.

She briefly closed her eyes as she listened, thinking that if he went on much longer, she'd walk over and yank him off the pulpit herself. The only words she wanted to hear were *I now pronounce you husband and wife.*

As beautiful as the marriage ceremony was, Krystal was relieved when Quinn kissed Dena and the minister introduced the newlyweds to the crowd. The bells tolled and the recessional began.

Krystal grabbed on to Garret's arm when he extended it to her and started back down the white-carpeted aisle. The faces of the guests became hazy and she didn't understand why until all of sudden she felt a rush of light-headedness. Then her stomach lurched and she squeezed Garret's arm with both hands.

"I have to get out of here," she said in a frantic whisper.

He took one look at her face and said, "This way." Instead of exiting at the back of the church he led her out a side door. "There's a washroom to the left."

She thrust her bouquet at him and made a dash for it.

MADDIE HAD WARNED Garret before the wedding started that Krystal wasn't feeling well, but he'd seen nothing during the ceremony to make him think she was sick. If anything, she'd looked more beautiful than he'd ever seen her and he'd been happy to have an excuse to keep an eye on her.

It wasn't until she squeezed his arm and he saw the pallor of her skin that he realized she needed to get to the washroom quickly. Against her protest he went with her, waiting nearby to make sure she didn't need any assistance.

"Are you okay?" he asked when he'd given her a few minutes to be alone.

"Yes. Please leave," she called out from behind the stall door.

After their brief encounter right before the wedding, he thought, it was probably what he should do.

But he didn't want to leave her at a time like this. He couldn't leave her. So he waited quietly for her.

"This is a women's rest room," she said when she came out of the stall and found him still in the washroom. "You shouldn't have come in here."

"I was worried you were going to pass out. You were quite pale," he told her.

"I had an upset stomach. I'm fine now," she said, avoiding his gaze.

Because he was behind her, he had to look into the mirror to see her face while she washed up at the sink. She looked fragile and in need of someone to watch over her.

She made it clear that he wasn't going to be that someone. "Please, just go," she begged him.

He didn't, but watched in silence as she finished washing up and dried her hands on a paper towel. "You're still pale." He set her bouquet down on the small shelf over the sink and took her wrist to check her pulse.

She snatched her hand away from him before he

could finish. "Please. I am embarrassed enough the way it is."

He lifted her chin, forcing her to look him in the eye. "I'm a doctor, Krystal. You think I haven't been around sick people?"

"You're also..." she began, then stopped, flapping her hand in frustration. "Just forget it. It was too hot in church, but I'm fine now. It's amazing how good one can feel after doing...that...." Her fingers fluttered toward the stall.

"Do you have a headache?"

"No."

"Fever?"

"No."

"Blurry vision?"

"No!" She exhaled a long sigh. "Look. I don't need a doctor, Garret. I need a friend who understands that I suffered one of the worst embarrassments of my life. God only knows what Dena and Quinn must be thinking."

"Krystal, I doubt they even realized anything was wrong. They were already out of the church. So were Shane and Jennifer and Maddie. The only ones behind us were Sara and Luke."

"And about five hundred people!"

"You went out the side door. For all they know, you could have been taking care of a bridesmaid duty."

From the look she gave him he could see she wasn't buying into his rationalization.

"It could have been worse," he pointed out. "You could have keeled over at the altar or made your mad dash just as they were saying their vows." He stared at her, amazed at how beautiful she looked. Even at her worst she was more attractive than most women.

She wore her red hair piled up in a cascade of curls—
the same way she'd worn it the night of the hospital
ball. He remembered what it had been like to unravel
those curls.

"You're right. At least I didn't ruin the ceremony."
She glanced downward. "Or my dress." She looked
again in the mirror. "And I can touch up my makeup
once I get my purse from the attendant's lounge."

Her resiliency impressed him. If there was one thing
he'd always admired about her it was her upbeat personality. He'd noticed it right from the start, her ability
to be down one minute but bounce right back up the
next.

"You're not going to tell anybody about this, are
you?" she asked as she reached for her bouquet.

"Not if you don't want me to, although Maddie's
going to want to know what happened," he answered.

"I'll talk to her."

"You're riding with us in the car, aren't you?"

She shook her head. "No. Shane and Jennifer are
bringing me to the reception."

"Why? I'm your escort. I thought groomsmen were
supposed to accompany bridesmaids."

"I don't think there's room in Maddie and Dylan's
car for one more."

"There's only the three of us. Mom decided to ride
with the Sterlings."

"Three? What about Samantha?"

"She was called to the hospital." And at this moment he was glad. "So, what do you say?" He held
out his arm to her, but she hesitated to slip hers
through his.

"It could be awkward," she warned him.

"Maybe this is a good time to try to get away from
the awkwardness."

Again she hesitated, but then she linked her arm through his. "Thank you. It's very kind of you to escort me to the reception," she said politely.

Little did she know it had nothing to do with kindness.

KRYSTAL COULDN'T HAVE ASKED for a more attentive escort than Garret. He was the perfect date, except he wasn't a date and she needed to remember that. He was with her out of a sense of duty, a groomsman assigned to escort her. The woman he wanted to take to the wedding reception had been detained at the hospital.

Krystal was glad Samantha wasn't there. For just a few hours she was allowed to see what it would be like to be a part of the Donovan clan. It was a family that loved children and lavished attention on the one grandchild, five-year-old Mickey. As Krystal watched him romp between his aunts and uncles, the burden of her secret grew heavier. This baby she was carrying wasn't only Garret's son or daughter. He or she was Leonie's grandchild and a nephew or niece to Garret's brothers and sisters-in-law.

The baby was also Mickey's cousin.

Ever since she'd lived at 14 Valentine Place she'd admired the close-knit family Leonie had raised. Now as she watched Maddie strolling across the ballroom floor, one arm clinging to Garret and the other to Dylan, she felt a pang of envy. When the wedding celebration was over, Maddie would still be a part of the family. Krystal, however, would go back to being the tenant on the second floor.

She needed to tell Garret the truth and she need to do it as soon as possible. First, however, they needed to complete their duties as members of the wedding party. Pictures had to be taken and dinner had to be served. There was cake to be cut and champagne toasts to be made. The first few dances of the evening would involve the bridal party, but Garret didn't like to dance. That much she'd learned the night of the hospital ball. As soon as the obligatory wedding march was over, she'd ask him to step outside for a few minutes.

As the band warmed up, she rehearsed in her head what she would say to him. She knew it wasn't going to be easy, but it was something that needed to be done. For his sake as well as for her own.

When he came up behind her and leaned over her shoulder to say "Please tell me it isn't true," her heart nearly stopped beating.

She swallowed with difficulty before saying, "What isn't true?"

He slid on to the chair next to hers and wrinkled his nose. "We have to dance in the spotlight?"

She exhaled a sigh of relief. "It's only one dance and it's the entire wedding party."

He raked a hand over his neck. "You know how I feel about dancing."

She nodded and smiled. "It's the price you have to pay for being a groomsman. Have you forgotten Maddie and Dylan's wedding?"

"I was called back to the hospital before the dancing began."

"Oh, that's right. One of the ushers took your spot." She knew this would be a good time to suggest they step outside for some fresh air as soon as the wedding march was over. "Garret, do you think I could talk to you for a few minutes? I don't mean right now, but after our turn on the dance floor? There's something I want to discuss with you and..."

Before she could finish Samantha Penrose came swooping toward the table with a huge smile on her face. Krystal glanced at Garret's face to see his reaction, but as usual, it was the same old unreadable mask.

Samantha tossed a casual "Hi, Krystal" in her direction, then gave her undivided attention to Garret, explaining why she was so late. She monopolized Garret's attention, talking hospital business until Leonie came over to welcome Samantha to the party. The entire time Krystal felt out of place and wished she could quietly slip away.

"I'm sorry, Krystal. You wanted to tell me something?" Garret turned his attention back to her.

She shook her head. "It's all right. It can wait until tomorrow."

He pinned her with those dark brown eyes and she almost changed her mind. "Are you sure?"

She nodded.

"Are you feeling okay?" he asked.

She didn't want to snap at him, but she couldn't help herself. "Will you stop asking me how I feel? I'm fine!" She glanced around, hoping the others at the table didn't hear her. Fortunately the band was making enough noise that no one had caught their exchange.

His eyes darkened and before he could say another word, Krystal excused herself to go to the ladies' lounge. She was tired, her feet hurt and the nausea was back. She wanted nothing more than to go home and crawl into bed, but she knew she couldn't—at least not until the wedding party had danced.

She sat down on an upholstered chaise and kicked off her shoes, wiggling toes that were red and swollen. With canned music playing in the background, she leaned her chin on the crook of her arm, not wanting to mess her curls. That was how Maddie found her.

"So here's where you disappeared to. Garret's looking for you."

"Why?"

She shrugged. "I don't know. He said something about wanting to talk to you. You look tired," she observed.

"I am. I wish I could go home and go to bed," she said candidly.

"You want to go home when there's a party going on in the next room?" Maddie repeated in disbelief.

Krystal managed to give her friend a weak smile. "I'm just not in the mood for a party." She reached for her shoes and tried to slip them on, but it was impossible to get her swollen feet into them. "Oh, this is just great. Now I can't get my shoes back on!" she said on a note of frustration.

Maddie looked down. "Oh my goodness. Your poor feet. What did you do? Buy the wrong size? I thought my feet were bad, but I have an excuse. I'm pregnant."

It wasn't the time or the place to tell Maddie about her pregnancy, but Krystal was tired of keeping the secret. And she needed an understanding friend.

"I guess I need to watch my sodium intake more carefully," she said, watching Maddie's face for her reaction.

"You always did like the salty stuff, but I don't remember you ever swelling in the summer because of it."

"I've never been pregnant before, either," she said quietly.

That caused Maddie's eyes to widen. "What did you say?"

"I'm pregnant. The reason I disappeared after the wedding ceremony is because I had to rush into the ladies' room. Garret was with me."

Maddie dropped down beside her, her face pale from the shock of the news. "You're going to have a baby?"

Krystal nodded. "I'm due in February, so I'm still in that feeling awful stage."

Shock was replaced by understanding as Maddie wrapped her arms around her and gave her a squeeze. When she released her Krystal noticed the moisture in her eyes.

"Are those tears of happiness or pity?" she asked.

"Neither. I feel like such a fool. Ever since I got back all I've done is carry on about how wonderful it is to be married to Dylan and having his baby. And here you are pregnant and..." She broke off, shaking her head.

"Not married and not babbling about how wonderful life is," Krystal finished for her. "Maddie, you're happy and you have every right to be."

Her eyes still reflected her bewilderment. "No wonder you didn't want any champagne. And that's why you weren't feeling well before the ceremony. And why you hardly touched your food at dinner."

"You noticed I didn't have an appetite."

"Of course I noticed. I'm pregnant. I notice what everyone's eating," she said with a grin. "And you will, too, once you get over the beginning phase. How are you feeling now?"

"Lousy."

"You have morning sickness in the evening, too, right?" she asked with a sympathetic grimace.

Krystal nodded. "And I'm tired all the time and I cry buckets for no reason."

"Well, you always did that," Maddie said with a teasing grin. Her smile faded. "I should have been there for you at the church."

"It's all right. You didn't know."

"But you could have used a friend."

"Garret was with me."

"I asked him to keep an eye on you."

Krystal smiled weakly. "Thanks.

"I have to admit. This is quite a shock."

"For me, too," Krystal admitted.

"How did it happen?" She quickly apologized. "I'm sorry, Krys. Please forget I asked that. It's none of my business."

"Yes it is. We've been too good friends for there to be secrets between us. I want to tell you everything, but I can't…at least not here."

"No, of course not. There'll be plenty of time for girl talk after this is all over. Dylan and I aren't going back to France until the fourteenth."

The door opened and two women Krystal didn't recognize entered the rest room. "I wanted to tell you yesterday, but there never seemed to be a right time." She glanced around. "Not many people know. Leonie doesn't."

"Why not? She's a dear and she is so understanding. You know that better than anyone who's lived at 14 Valentine Place."

"Yes, but…" She paused, as again the door opened admitting more women. "It's really complicated,

Maddie. I'm going to tell Leonie...soon, but until I
do, I need you to not say anything.''

She reached for her hands and gave them a squeeze.
"You know you can trust me to keep your confidence.''

The door swung open again and this time Krystal
recognized the woman's face. It was one of Quinn's
sisters announcing that the dancing would soon begin
and all bridesmaids were wanted in the ballroom.

"Tell her we'll be right there,'' Maddie instructed
her, and the woman disappeared out the door again.
"We'd better go.''

Krystal nodded, dabbing at the moisture in her eyes.
"Thank goodness for waterproof mascara, huh?''

Maddie grinned and wiped her eyes, too. "I just
can't believe we're both having babies!'' As Krystal
bent to pick up her shoes she asked, "Are your feet
going to be okay?''

"Yeah. I'm not even going to try to put on these
shoes. I'll dance in my stockings.'' As they walked
out the door, Krystal placed her hand on Maddie's
arm. "I'm sorry I couldn't tell you sooner. I wanted
to, but...''

Maddie gave her another quick hug. "It's all right.
I understand.''

As Krystal knew she would. "Thanks. I'm thinking
of leaving early. You don't think Dena will mind, do
you?''

"Maybe I should go home with you. We could say
I wasn't feeling well and you were going home to keep
me company. No one would question my reasons for
leaving.''

Krystal shook her head. "Dylan would insist on going with you and then there'd be two bridesmaids

missing. I'll be just fine. You don't need to worry about me.''

''But I do worry. Do you want Dylan to give you a ride home?''

''No, I'm going to call Shannon.'' And with another deep breath she headed back to the ballroom.

GARRET KNEW THAT everyone in his family—especially his mother—thought Samantha Penrose was a good match for him. He understood why. Even he had to admit they had a lot in common. They were both dedicated doctors, wanting to make a difference in the world.

What his family didn't understand was that Samantha—like him—wasn't looking for a mate. She'd made it perfectly clear that she'd be willing to pick up where they left off three years ago. At one time he would have jumped at the opportunity. But not now, which was why he was relieved when she was called back to the hospital that night.

''We're thinking about stopping for coffee,'' Dylan said as the last of the wedding guests filed out of the reception hall. ''Want to join us?''

The us referred to Maddie and Leonie, since Shane and Jennifer had taken Mickey home and put him to bed earlier in the evening. Garret was tired himself, but he wanted to spend time with his brother and Maddie so he accepted their offer.

''Why not just come back to the house?'' Leonie suggested. ''We can get pastries on the way at that new twenty-four-hour deli over on Snelling.''

''That'll work for me. I left my car at Mom's this morning,'' he told everyone.

''Yeah, and this way if Samantha gets back, you

can pop upstairs and see her,'' Dylan said with a sly grin and a nudge in his brother's rib cage.

"Or she can join us for coffee. We'd love to get to know her better,'' Maddie said.

Samantha, however, wasn't home when they got back to the house, but Garret noticed Krystal's light was on in her second-floor window. She'd left the party several hours earlier saying she was tired, yet she hadn't gone to bed.

"It's too bad Jason wasn't able to come home for the wedding,'' Leonie said as the four of them sat at the round wooden table. "I do believe that was one of the most beautiful weddings I have ever seen.''

"Mom, you say that about every wedding you attend,'' Garret reminded her with an affectionate grin.

"I do not. This one was special.''

"I agree,'' Dylan said, "but I'm not sure our baby brother would have appreciated it. He wasn't too fond of having to come home from California for Maddie's and my wedding,'' Dylan reminded her.

"When you're twenty, weddings are not on your list of important social events,'' Garret added.

"I think he would have had a good time had he been home,'' Maddie commented. "I know I had a wonderful time. What about you, Garret? Did you have fun?''

He grinned. "Let's just say it wasn't as bad as I thought it was going to be.''

"Bad?'' Leonie tapped his wrist lightly in reprimand. "How could you even use that word about such a lovely party?''

"Because it was a party,'' Dylan said with a chuckle. "You know he hates any gathering where there are more than four people—not counting family, of course,'' he added with a grin.

Garret raised his coffee cup in salute. ''True.''

''You're like your father that way. He hated weddings.''

''I don't hate them. I just feel more comfortable when there aren't a couple of hundred people crowding around me.''

''There were actually five hundred at the wedding,'' his mother pointed out. ''That's what made it fun. All the energy and excitement of people celebrating Dena and Quinn's marriage.''

''You really love going to those things, don't you?'' Garret noted.

''Yes, and so do a lot of others,'' his mother stated. ''You noticed how many people groaned when the band announced the last number.''

''And what a way to end a celebration,'' Maddie noted. ''Doing the conga.''

''It's too bad Krystal wasn't there,'' Leonie mused. ''She loves a good conga line.''

The mention of Krystal's name had Garret thinking about the way she looked when she'd been sick after the wedding ceremony. Fragile and vulnerable. When Maddie had told him that she'd gone home because she wasn't feeling well, he'd wanted to phone her to see if she was all right, but he knew she wouldn't welcome such a call. She'd made it perfectly clear earlier in the day what she thought of his concern for her well-being.

''I'm a little worried about her,'' his mother said. ''It's not like her to leave any party early.''

''She's fine,'' Maddie insisted. ''I think she was just tired.''

"She's been tired a lot lately. I hope she's not run-down. I'd hate to see her catch one of those viruses going around. There are so many right now. It happens every year at this time. Kids go back to school and germs spread," his mother continued, her brow creased with concern. "I wonder if I should check on her."

"Do you want me to go up?" Maddie offered.

Dylan got up from his chair and came around to place his hands on her shoulders. "You, my sweet, lovely pregnant wife, should be in bed. I'm sure Krystal is fine and is more than likely sound asleep. You can talk to her in the morning. Right now, I'm taking you back to the hotel and putting you to bed."

"I should get going, too," Garret said rising to his feet, trying not to think about Krystal and how tanta-lizing she'd looked in her purple dress. "I'll walk you to the car."

They'd all parked in the back. Dylan had just opened the door for Maddie and tucked her inside the rental car when he patted his pockets. "Oops, forgot my keys inside." He looked at Garret and said, "Watch my girl while I run back in and get them."

Garret nodded and glanced back at the house, once again noticing the light on in Krystal's window. Mad-die saw the direction of his gaze and said, "Is that a professional concern or friendly concern in your eyes?"

"Both."

"She told me you were with her when she got sick at the church."

"Yes, but she wasn't happy I was. She didn't want anyone to know about it—not even me, a doctor."

"No, I don't imagine she would. No woman wants anyone to see her in that condition."

"I'm also her friend."

"Yes, thank goodness you are. For some reason she didn't feel as if she could tell me about the baby. I guess she didn't want to spoil Dena's big day."

Garret frowned. Baby? Krystal?

"I think she thought she could get through the day without any problem," Maddie continued. "I can relate to that. Morning sickness is so unpredictable. You can be sick one minute and feel fine the next."

Morning sickness? The reason Krystal had been sick at church was because she was pregnant? He was too stunned to say anything, not that it mattered. Maddie kept talking.

"I know they teach you about that stuff in school, Garret, but unless you're a woman and you've suffered from it, you have no idea how terrible it can be. You feel so miserable." His expression must have revealed his shock for she suddenly gasped. "Oh, my gosh! You didn't know, did you?" He didn't need to answer her question. "Oh, please don't tell her I told you. I thought since you were with her that she would have told you..."

"Are you sure..." he began, but Maddie cut him off.

"Shh. Here comes Dylan and he doesn't know yet," Maddie warned him just seconds before he came into view bouncing a set of keys in his hands.

"Hey, I got 'em." He patted Garret on the arm. "We gotta go. We'll see you tomorrow morning for brunch, right?"

"Er...yeah, if I can make it," he said absently, his

mind still trying to comprehend what Maddie had just told him. Krystal was pregnant?

Maddie tossed a goodbye in his direction, doors slammed shut, and the car pulled away. Garret didn't move. He simply stood there staring up at Krystal's window.

It all made sense—now. How come he hadn't seen the signs himself? He was a doctor for crying out loud.

Maybe because she'd worked very hard at not letting him see any of the symptoms. He tried to think back to what she'd worn the last few times he'd seen her. Silky-type cargo pants that were baggy. A dress that hung loose over her slender frame.

He wondered just how pregnant she was. It was something he was going to find out. Instead of getting in his car, he went back inside 14 Valentine Place.

CHAPTER SIX

WHEN GARRET LET HIMSELF back into the house he found his mother at the sink rinsing out the coffee cups.

"What are you doing back? Don't tell me you forgot your keys, too?" she asked.

"No, I'm going upstairs. I want to leave a message for Samantha." He told the white lie because he couldn't tell her the truth. Right now he wasn't sure he knew the truth. "Don't worry about me, Mom. I'll let myself out. You go on to bed."

"Okay, dear. Good night," she called as he headed for the stairs.

When he came to the second-floor landing he stopped. He could see the sliver of light beneath Krystal's door. He raised his fingers to the wood and rapped.

She didn't answer right away and he knocked again, this time with more force. The door flew open and there she stood, mouth open, wearing nothing but a pale blue nightgown. Her hair was mussed, her eyes half-shut. As usual, she looked beautiful. And also as usual, his body reacted.

"Were you asleep?" he asked.

"Of course I was asleep." She glanced over her shoulder to the clock. "It's two o'clock in the morning."

"I saw your light from downstairs."

"I must have fallen asleep with it on. What's happened? Is something wrong with Leonie?" Panic replaced the sleepy look in her eyes.

"No, Mom's fine," he reassured her.

"Then what is it?" She obviously was confused as to why he would be at her door in the middle of the night.

"I need to come in."

"Sure." She stepped aside and he walked past her.

It had been a while since he'd been in her room, but it looked the same. It reminded him of a sexy boudoir with its large brass bed draped in peach chiffon as the focal point. Satin pillows lay scattered across the floor and the bed linens were in a tangle. The one light that was on had a peach-colored scarf draped over the shade giving everything a rosy glow, and the room smelled the way she did—of a floral fragrance that had just a hint of wildness to it.

"Do you want to sit down?" She gestured toward the futon.

"No, I'm not staying long."

"If you came here to check on me, it's not necessary," she said. "I'm not sick."

"I know. You're pregnant."

That stunned her into silence. She looked at him the way his patients did when he had a syringe in his hand, her face growing paler by the minute. With the thin cotton nightgown the only thing covering her body, he could see the gentle swell of her belly. Aware of his eyes on her, she reached for her robe and pulled it on.

"It's too late. I've already seen it," he said as she tied the sash.

He waited for her to say something, but nothing came out of her mouth. For the first time since he'd known her, she appeared to be at a loss for words.

"It's true, isn't it?" he said.

She moistened her lips with her tongue, then said, "Yes. I'm sorry."

He frowned. "For what? You don't need to apologize to me, Krystal."

"I feel I do. I feel this is all my fault. If I hadn't practically begged you to take me bed, we wouldn't be in this—"

"Wait a minute!" he cut her off. "Are you saying that I'm the father?"

Her eyes darkened and her voice rose. "Of course it's your baby. Nobody else could be the father." When he didn't say anything, she cried, "You think it's Roy's?"

"You were back together…" He didn't finish when he saw the look on her face, which wasn't much different from the one that had been there when she'd been sick in the bathroom at the church.

"For three days!"

He ran a hand across his forehead. This was getting him nowhere.

"Think," a small voice inside him whispered, but it was hard to do when he felt as if he'd just stepped off the planet and was falling into a black hole in space.

"I don't understand how this could have happened. We used protection." He stated the thought foremost in his head.

She shrugged. "It must have failed. Condoms aren't the most reliable form of birth control."

"Weren't you on the pill?"

"No, I was not," she stated with a hint of indignation. "I didn't plan to go to bed with you, in case you've forgotten."

How could he forget? She reminded him every

chance she had. "I am aware of that but I thought—"
He stopped abruptly, realizing he'd never asked her
about the pill. He'd assumed she was on it and they
would have double protection.

"You thought what? That I take it regularly so
whenever I pick up a guy I can sleep with him?" Her
cheeks colored. "I wasn't planning to have sex with
anybody that night. Not you or Roy. For your information, Garret, I don't go to bed with every man who
buys me dinner and pays me compliments." He could
hear the tears in her voice and it made him feel like a
first-class jerk.

"I didn't say you did," he said quietly.

"You didn't have to say it. It's there in your attitude," she accused him on a muffled sob.

The only attitude he had right now was one of disbelief. Ever since he'd been a child he'd mapped out
what he wanted for his life. Become a doctor, make a
difference in the world. Having a child with a one-
night stand had never been in his plan.

"How do you think I feel? I'm the one who did the
good deed here. I went out on that date with you as a
favor and I'm the one who ends up pregnant," she
reminded him. "And now you stand there and treat
me like I'm cheap." She burst into tears.

He raked a hand over his head. "For God's sake, I
don't think you're cheap, Krystal. I'm trying to understand how this happened."

"What's there to understand? We had sex. I got
pregnant."

Yes, that about summed it up. He'd gone and done
exactly what his father had warned him not to do when
he was a teenager. He'd gotten a girl pregnant. Only
Krystal was no girl—she was a woman and he was a

man. They were two adults who should have known better.

But he'd wanted her. Ever since the first day he'd met her he'd fantasized as to what it would be like to be her lover. The night of the hospital ball he'd been given a chance to fulfill that fantasy and he'd taken it. It hadn't mattered that she was only with him because she'd been hurt by the man she loved. It had been a night of passion for pleasure's sake only. A night they both agreed they would forget ever happened.

Only now there would be a permanent reminder. No matter how emotional she was, he needed to be rational. "Okay. What's done is done. Let's not dwell on that. Can we try to discuss this calmly?"

She nodded and he mentally calculated how long it had been since the hospital ball. "So you're what? Fifteen, sixteen weeks?"

"Sixteen," she confirmed.

He tried to look at her as if she were his patient, but he couldn't. She wasn't someone who'd come to the clinic to see him. She was the woman who'd conceived his child.

"Are you sure about the conception date?"

That raised her hackles again. "Do you think I'm lying to you?"

"No, I don't," he said on a note of frustration. "Would you stop reading something into my words that isn't there?"

He hated how adversarial their relationship had become in such a short time. "I'm trying to think but it's difficult to do with you throwing accusations at me."

"I'm sorry," she said on a sniffle.

"I'm in shock here. You've had some time to get used to the idea. I've had about ten minutes."

"I'm sorry," she repeated on another sniffle.

"It's all right," he said, raising his hands. "I would appreciate it if you could try not to cry quite so much. I know this is a difficult situation for you, but you getting so emotional that we can't have a rational discussion isn't doing us any good, either."

"It's my hor-hormones," she said on a hiccup. "They're wacko."

Seeing her looking so vulnerable made him soften his tone. "I know they are." He led her over to the bed where he sat her down. "Just sit there quietly for a minute while I think, okay?"

She nodded and didn't say a word. All he heard was an occasional sniffle.

His insides were churning, his body begging him to run. It's what he usually did to relieve stress—take a run either at the gym or on the street. He paced the narrow confines of her apartment.

He should have known she couldn't sit quietly for very long. "I'm sorry I didn't tell you before now."

"Why didn't you tell me?"

"I didn't want to spoil Dena's wedding. You can imagine what this kind of news would have done to the atmosphere in this house. I wanted it to be a happy time for her."

"We could have kept it between us."

She nodded and bit down on her upper lip. "Maybe I didn't want you to be your usual analytical self and present all my options to me."

"There is only one option, right?"

She nodded. "I'm having this baby."

It was what he wanted to hear. What he'd expected to hear from her. "Who knows you're pregnant?"

"No one in your family except Maddie."

He didn't think it was necessary to reveal that Maddie had accidentally told him.

"What about your family?" he asked.

She nodded. "Carly and my mom both know. Oh, and Dena and Quinn found out by accident and I told Shannon."

All of them knew before he did. It didn't make him happy.

"Other than the morning sickness, have you had any problems?"

"Mmm-hmm. My feet are swelling, my back aches, and look at my skin." She thrust her chin up so that he could get a closer look at her face. "I have acne."

He moved closer to her to get a better look. "That's not acne. It's a couple of pimples."

"They look awful. Luckily Shannon is a makeup artist and could cover them for the wedding. The worst part though is that I'm emotional."

"You're always emotional."

"Not like this."

"No, never quite as bad as this," he agreed. He paced some more, his mind trying to absorb what she'd told him. With two words his well-planned, orderly life had been thrown off course and he wasn't sure it would ever be set straight again.

"Now what happens?" she asked.

"I don't know," he answered the only way he could. "This is the last thing I ever expected would happen to me."

"I know. I feel the same way."

He wanted to go over and take her in his arms and hold her, but something stopped him. Maybe it was the knowledge that sympathy wasn't the sole motivation for wanting to be close to her. Ever since they'd made love he'd been having trouble forgetting how good it had been between them. Knowing that she was carrying his child only made her more desirable.

"It's late," he said on a sigh. "I'd better go."

She nodded, her arms wrapped around her midsection. "I am truly sorry that whole night backfired on us, Garret. I only wanted to help a friend."

He didn't need to be reminded of why she'd gone out with him. Or why she went to bed with him. She couldn't have Roy so she'd settled for him, and he, in seeking his fantasy, hadn't hesitated to take advantage of the situation. The irony of it all was enough to make him want to grab a stiff drink.

"None of that matters now, Krystal." He walked over to the door, pausing before he opened it to say, "I'll call you when I've had time to process all of this."

She simply nodded and showed him the door.

KRYSTAL AWOKE THE following morning and stared at the ceiling. Before she even lifted her head she reached for the soda crackers next to her bed. She didn't need them, however. No queasy tummy, just hunger. She carefully climbed out of bed and padded about her room. Still nothing.

She closed her eyes and said a brief prayer of thanks. Lately she had no clue as to when or where she'd have an attack of morning sickness. She wondered if she dared hope that her bout with it was coming to an end. It would certainly make life a lot easier.

Not that she expected her troubles would disappear with the absence of morning sickness. It was trivial compared to some of the issues facing her. Like what was going to happen now that Garret knew she was pregnant.

A knock on her door raised the hairs on the back

of her neck. Her first thought was that Leonie had heard she was pregnant and had come to confront her about it. She glanced at the clock and saw it was after ten. She knew Leonie had arranged to meet her children for brunch this morning. The house should be empty.

The knocking became louder and steadier. Krystal could feel her heart pounding in her chest. She took a deep breath and pulled the door open. "Carly!" She stared at her sister in disbelief. She looked as if she'd been up all night and had left the house in a hurry. Next to her was four-year-old Emily, who didn't look much better. Her hair hadn't been combed and both looked as if they'd slept in their clothes. Behind them were two of the biggest suitcases Krystal had ever seen.

"What are you doing here?" A sinking feeling in her stomach warned her she wasn't going to like the answer.

"You said I could always come to you in a time of need." There was no emotion in her sister's voice. She looked as if she could collapse any moment, her face pale, her eyes rimmed with dark circles.

"Of course you can. Come on inside." She smiled at Emily and ruffled the little girl's hair as she said hello. Then she gave each of them a gentle shove, urging them to step inside the apartment while she dragged the suitcases in behind her.

As soon as they were all inside and the door was closed, she said,

"If I didn't know you were so happy with Joe I'd think you'd left him."

"I did leave him," Carly said quietly.

The sinking feeling in Krystal's stomach plunged all the way to her toes. "But you love him. So does

Emily.'' She glanced at her niece, who stood clutching a soft furry pig close to her chest.

''But he doesn't love me.''

''Of course he does. Look, if you've had a fight…'' she began but her sister interrupted her.

''It wasn't a fight. He doesn't want me anymore.'' Her voice was a hollow echo of its usual cheery tone. ''It's over. Everything. Our marriage…my life…'' she said despondently, paying no attention to the fact that Emily was wide-eyed and taking in every word she said.

''You look awfully tired. Why don't I make the futon into a bed and you can lie down for a while,'' Krystal suggested, putting her hand on her arm.

She shook her head. ''It's no good. I can't sleep. I have to think.''

''Carly, you need rest.''

''What I need is Joe but I can't have him,'' she said on a frantic whisper, then burst into tears, flinging herself facedown on the futon. It was the worst crying Krystal had ever heard from her sister. Before she could console her, Emily let out a wail and began to cry at the top of her lungs, too.

Krystal scooped the four-year-old into her arms and comforted her. ''Shh. It's okay, Emily. Don't cry. Your mommy's going to be okay.''

The little girl hiccuped. ''N-No, she's not. She hates my daddy.''

Krystal carried her over to her bed and set her down. ''She doesn't hate your daddy. She's just angry at him, but everything's going to be okay. Now can you sit here for a few minutes and let me talk to your mommy?''

The little girl shook her head and bawled even louder. ''I want to go h-home.''

"I know you do and you will, but first everybody has to stop crying...including your mommy. I'm going to help her do that, but I need you to be a big girl and put on a happy face. Can you do that for me?"

She nodded but continued to cry.

Krystal walked over to the portable TV and turned it on. "Look. You can watch a movie. I have *Shrek*. You like *Shrek*, right?" She put a DVD in the player.

The little girl nodded but continued to cry.

"What if I told you I'd paint your fingernails if you could sit quietly for a few minutes." She held up her hands. "Wouldn't you like to have pretty polish on them?"

Krystal could see she was interested. "Do you have purple?" Emily asked on a hiccup.

"Yes, and it has sparkles in it. It's really pretty. Does your mom ever paint your toenails?" When she shook her head, Krystal went on, "I can do both your fingers and your toes, but only if you have a smile on your face. What do you think?"

The weakest of smiles slowly appeared, accompanied by several sniffles.

Krystal kissed her on the forehead. "Beautiful. Now you hold on to that smile and I'll see if I can make your mommy feel better, okay?"

She went over to the futon and sat down beside her sister. "Carly, you've got to pull yourself together. You're upsetting Emily," she said in a gentle but firm tone.

Her sister continued to sob. "I can't help it. It hurts so bad."

"I'm sure it does, but this isn't just about you. It's about Emily, too." She deliberately kept her voice low as she talked. "You're frightening her. You don't want to do that, do you? Try to keep your voice down.''

As if suddenly aware of the emotional impact she was having on her daughter, Carly sat up, swiping at her tearstained face with the backs of her hands. ''I don't know what I'm going to do,'' she said softly. ''He doesn't want me, Krys.''

''I think you're wrong, Carly. Joe's crazy about you. He always has been.''

She shook her head. ''He wants someone else.''

Anger toward her brother-in-law erupted inside Krystal. ''Are you sure about that?''

She nodded miserably. ''He's been cheating on me. He admitted it.''

Krystal felt sick and it had nothing to do with being pregnant. She didn't understand how her brother-in-law could be unfaithful to her sister. They had always seemed so happy together.

''What a no-good, low-down...'' She almost uttered an expletive until she remembered her niece was sitting not more than ten feet away. ''How could he do such a thing?''

''It's my fault. I should have watched my weight more carefully. I knew fat was a turnoff for him.''

The notion that her sister felt responsible for his sordid behavior sparked Krystal's anger. ''For Pete's sake, Carly, you are not fat! And even if you were, that doesn't give him the right to cheat on you. He's your husband and he took a vow to be faithful.''

''Every man wants a wife he can be proud of.'' Her voice had a defeated tone Krystal had never heard before. Usually her sister was the steady, confident one in the family. It was one of the reasons why, even though Krystal was older, their roles had reversed, with Carly acting like the big sister.

"There's no reason why Joe shouldn't be proud of you," Krystal insisted. "Carly, you are a lovely person and you're a good wife and mother. I'm not going to let you take the blame for this," she said on a fierce whisper.

She might as well have been talking to the wall. It didn't matter what she said, her sister had already accepted the blame for her husband falling in love with another woman.

"He wanted me to take golf lessons, but I didn't think it would be any fun," she said in this tiny voice that sounded nothing like the Carly she knew.

"What does golf have to do with anything?" Krystal demanded.

"*She* golfs. And she's skinny."

"You've seen her?"

Carly bit down on her lower lip and nodded. As her eyes pooled with tears, she looked up at Krystal and asked, "What am I going to do?"

Krystal hugged her. "The first thing you're going to do is get some rest. You need sleep."

"Mommy, are you crying again?" Emily's little voice could be heard above the sound of the TV.

Carly managed to swallow back the tears, but she couldn't stop the trembling in her shoulders. "Mommy's okay, sweetie," she called out in a broken voice. She forced a smile that Krystal thought was the most pathetic excuse for a grin that she'd ever seen, but Emily didn't seem to mind.

She climbed down from the bed and came running over to throw herself at her mother. "Can we go home now, Mommy?"

"Not just yet," Carly said gently, meeting Krystal's gaze over the small blond head.

"But I'm hungry," the four-year-old whined.

Krystal reached for a box of tissues and shoved it on to her sister's lap. "Mop up and we'll go downstairs. I could use some breakfast, too."

Carly looked at her daughter. "Emily, you already ate breakfast."

"She can have more." Krystal looked at her niece and asked, "What do you like to eat?"

"Froot Loops."

Krystal frowned. "Oh, we don't have any Froot Loops. But I can make you pancakes. Would you like that?"

"Yes, please," the tiny voice answered. "Can Mommy come, too?"

"Mommy's not going to go with you," Carly answered, then looked at Krystal. "I don't want to see anybody. I look a mess."

"You don't need to worry. The Donovans all went to brunch this morning," Krystal assured her. "We'll have the kitchen to ourselves."

Carly shook her head. "It doesn't matter. I'm not hungry and I couldn't eat anything even if I tried."

No, Krystal didn't suppose she could. Seeing how pale and exhausted her sister was, she decided not to press the issue. "All right. You stay up here and get some rest. We won't be long. Promise."

She knew it was a promise that wouldn't be difficult to keep. Krystal wanted to get in and get out of the kitchen before any of the Donovans returned. She shivered as she thought about their family gathering together, wondering if Garret was telling them the news this very minute.

It was an unsettling thought. One that was so unsettling she found her appetite had vanished by the time she'd made the pancakes. She fed Emily and hurried back upstairs.

GARRET WAS RESTLESS. The others had noticed and commented on it, but he'd allowed them to believe the reason he'd left the table four times was to check in on a patient of his in the hospital. The truth was he'd gone outside to pace the parking lot. He did his best thinking when he was alone and he definitely needed to think.

He wouldn't have come to the family brunch if it wasn't for the fact that Dylan and Maddie would only be visiting a short while before they returned to France. He would have preferred to eat a stale piece of toast in the privacy of his own apartment where he could pace the floor and try to figure out what the best course of action was regarding Krystal.

Every time he thought about her his insides became all jumbled. He still couldn't believe she was carrying his child, yet he knew it was true. Krystal was not the kind of woman to lie about such a thing. And if she were going to lie about the paternity of the baby, she would have said it belonged to Roy. He was, after all, the man of her dreams. The one she'd been trying to forget the night she'd slept with Garret.

"You're awfully quiet," Maddie broke into his thoughts. "You're not just a little bit hungover, are you?" she asked with a twinkle in her eye.

"No, you saw how little I had to drink last night," he answered.

"Then it must be those phone calls you made to the hospital. You're worried about a patient, aren't you?"

Before he could answer, Dylan leaned closer and said, "Maybe he wasn't calling the hospital because of a patient. Could be he was speaking to one lady doctor who has his stomach all tied up in knots?''

Maddie elbowed her husband. ''Stop teasing.'' To Garret she said, ''Tell me more about this Doctors Without Borders program. Have you heard when you'll be leaving?''

''I'm not sure.'' It was one of the things that was on hold at the moment—as well as the rest of his life. If he left in January to go overseas to work, it meant he'd be gone when Krystal had her baby. He frowned.

''Not soon enough for you, eh, bro?'' Dylan misread the gesture. ''I bet it's soon enough for Mom, though.''

Leonie heard his comment and said, ''It's only natural for mothers to want their children close by. But you, Dylan, know better than any of your brothers that I never interfere with your career goals.''

Dylan lifted his coffee cup in salute. ''You're the best, Mom.''

An echo of ''hear, hear,'' could be heard as the other family members agreed.

''Shane's the only one of us who hasn't spread his wings and flown off to distant parts,'' Dylan remarked.

''No, I leave that to my brothers. Me, I'm happy right here in good old Minnesota with this little guy,'' he said, wrapping his arms around his son. ''You're smart, Garret, to go after what you want. You might as well travel and do the kind of work that interests you. Once you marry and have a family, you won't have the choices you have now.''

Garret felt as if his choices had already become restricted. When Leonie and Maddie excused themselves to go to the ladies' room, five-year-old Mickey announced he needed to use the facilities, too. Shane took him by the hand leaving Dylan and Garret alone at the table.

"One day that'll be me," Dylan said as he watched their brother and nephew walk away hand in hand. "I still can't believe I'm going to be a father."

"You're happy about it, aren't you?" Garret asked.

Dylan chuckled. "Isn't it obvious?"

Garret smiled. "Just checking." He was glad his brother had brought up the subject of fatherhood, because it gave them the opportunity to talk. "Did you and Maddie plan to have kids so soon after you were married?"

"No, and to be honest, at first I felt a little cheated. I thought we would have a couple of years with it being just the two of us. Then wham! We're married one month and she gets pregnant."

Garret could understand that sentiment—it was what had kept him tossing and turning last night. He too felt cheated. He'd missed out on the chance of falling in love with a woman before discovering he was going to be a father.

"I should have known better though," Dylan continued. "The same thing happened to Shane and Jennifer." He wagged his finger at Garret. "So be forewarned. When that time comes and you meet the right woman, it could be wham!"

Garret nodded and looked away, not wanting to give him any indication the warning came too late. He took a sip of his coffee, then asked, "So what got you past that feeling-cheated stage?"

"Seeing how happy Maddie was," Dylan answered. "She told me the minute she found out. Plus the knowledge that the baby inside her is a part of me. It's my son." He shook his head in amazement. "I'm telling you, Garret, it's an incredible feeling. I can't explain it. I guess you're just going to have to experience it yourself someday to know what I'm talking about.''

Garret almost told him about Krystal. He thought about it, but before he could actually do it, Dylan was reaching into his pocket and pulling out an envelope. He handed it to him.

''It's an ultrasound of the baby, but I guess I don't need to tell you that, do I?'' he said with a proud grin.

''Actually, this printout is called the sonogram,'' Garret corrected him. ''Ultrasound is the procedure.''

''Can you see? It's a boy!'' Dylan boasted.

Garret smiled as he gazed at the printout. ''Yup. Looks like a Donovan to me. Big head, big feet.''

''You've probably seen hundreds of these, but it's the first one I've ever seen,'' he said, looking at it once more before tucking it back into his pocket. ''Technology is amazing, isn't it?''

Garret nodded in agreement. ''You're going to make a good dad, Dylan,'' he said sincerely.

''Thanks. It means a lot to me to hear you say that. I know we haven't always seen eye to eye on things.''

Garret shrugged. ''Does that surprise you? We're brothers.''

''We're a lot alike,'' he said, tucking the sonogram back into his pocket.

''You think so?''

''Yup. You're very protective of the people you care about. That's why you were so upset with me when Dad and I weren't getting along.''

It was the one time in their family history where there had actually been a rift that had caused heartache. Garret was glad it was in the past. ''I wasn't trying to protect Dad,'' he felt obliged to say.

''No, you were trying to protect Mom. So was I.''

Garret leaned back, thinking about his father, wondering what he'd say if he were still alive. What advice would he give him regarding Krystal? "I miss Dad."

"So do I. He did some things I didn't like, some things I'll never understand, but he was still my father. And I'm sad that I don't have the chance to share this time of my life with him. Remember how excited he was when Mickey was born?" His eyes clouded at the memory. "He was a grandpa for only a short time, but he loved it."

"Yeah, he did," Garret concurred with a sigh. He eyed his brother thoughtfully, then said, "Marriage has changed you, Dylan."

"Why? Because I realized that Mom was right?"

"About what?"

"Remember when we were kids and one of us would get mad at Dad, we inevitably would say, Dad just doesn't get it. She'd always tell us, Oh, he gets it all right. And one day, when you're a father, you'll understand just how much he gets it. I think I'm beginning to understand. Fatherhood changes a man's life."

Garret agreed with him silently. It had been less than twelve hours since Krystal had told him about her pregnancy and already his life had changed. Only right now it didn't seem to be the positive change it was for his brother.

Again he was tempted to tell Dylan about Krystal, but he couldn't. Not yet. Not when he wasn't sure what he was going to do. Or what she was going to do for that matter.

It was something he hadn't given much consideration until now. He'd spent most of his time thinking about the impact this baby would have on his life. Now he realized he hadn't given any thought as to what it would do to hers. Like him, she had decisions to make.

"Listen to me, rambling on about fatherhood like this. I'm probably boring the socks off a single guy like you," Dylan said with a brotherly pat on his shoulder.

Garret shook his head. "No, not at all," he said honestly.

"I'm just so excited about this baby," he told him. "I'll tell you what. When the day comes and you're in my shoes, I promise I'll let you talk my ear off."

Again Garret was tempted to tell him that day had come, but Maddie was coming toward them. "Bet I can guess what you two are talking about," she said.

"I had to show him the picture." Dylan hugged her before she sat back down, his hand on her slightly bulging stomach.

It was such a loving gesture Garret couldn't help but be envious. Little did Dylan know that Garret *was* walking in his shoes. The problem was, he couldn't fill them. He didn't have a happy marriage, or a loving wife. He didn't even live with the mother of his child. Maddie had told Dylan the minute she suspected she was pregnant. Krystal had known about her pregnancy for months before she even told him.

No, he would not be walking in Dylan's shoes. He was going to have a pair all to himself. He only hoped he knew what to do with them.

CHAPTER SEVEN

AS SOON AS EMILY HAD finished eating her breakfast, Krystal took her back upstairs. Carly wasn't asleep, but was on her cell phone. From the look on her face and the tone of her voice, Krystal knew she wanted privacy and suggested she finish her conversation in the hall.

While she was gone, Krystal made good on her promise to Emily to paint her fingernails and toenails. When that was accomplished, she braided the little girl's long blond hair, then read her a story. As she suspected, her niece fell asleep before she'd turned but a couple of pages.

It wasn't much later that Carly came back into the room wearing the same weary, downtrodden look she'd had when she'd arrived on her doorstep that morning.

"Are you okay?" Krystal asked.

She nodded. "That was Mom, in case you couldn't tell. She gave me the usual 'you don't solve problems by running away from them' speech."

"She ought to know." Krystal knew it was a catty remark, but she couldn't help herself.

"Yeah. How many times did we move because of some guy she no longer wanted in her life?" She dropped down on to the futon. "I feel sick."

Krystal sat beside her. "You're exhausted. I wish you'd try to get some sleep."

"I can't sleep. I keep seeing him…with her." She shivered, then rubbed her hands on her arms. "Everyone in town knows about it. I'll never be able to face anyone ever again…not even Sofie."

Sofie was her best friend. She also was Joe's cousin. "It's probably not as bad as you think." Krystal tried to be optimistic.

"Yes, it is." She wrapped her arms around herself. "I don't care what Mom says. I'm never going back, Krys. I can't."

Krystal knew at this point it wouldn't do much good to tell her sister it was unrealistic to think she could run away from the situation forever. Instead, she said, "What about your house?"

"I don't want it. It's his anyway."

"He built it for you."

"Doesn't matter. I don't want it anymore. He can keep it." There was no emotion in her voice, just a flat resignation that told Krystal how deeply hurt her sister was.

"You don't need to make that decision now. How you feel today might not be how you feel tomorrow, and you have to remember that even if you don't reconcile with Joe, you're going to need a place to live," she stated pragmatically.

Carly didn't appreciate her attempt to be rational. "Look, if you don't want me here, just say so. I'll leave."

"I do want you here. You're my sister and I love you and I want to help you in any way I can. All I'm saying is that at some point, you're going to have to sit down with Joe and get this all straightened out." She worked at keeping her voice even, not wanting this to disintegrate into an emotional argument.

"Maybe you didn't hear me. It is straight as far as

Joe is concerned. He doesn't want me for a wife. He wants Miss Bathing Suit. There's nothing left to think about.'' Carly's voice rose in frustration.

Krystal raised her hands in surrender. "All right. I'm sorry. I didn't mean to imply you hadn't thought this through. But I have to tell you, Carly, that it doesn't seem right to me that he's the one who cheats on you, yet you're the one who moves out. Do you know how many times I've heard you say that house is your dream home?''

"That was before he brought *her* there.''

"He didn't...'' She trailed off in disgust.

Carly nodded. "That weekend Emily and I went with Mom to visit Aunt Lois? She was there at the house, eating in my kitchen, taking a bath in my whirl-pool tub, and sleeping with my husband in my bed!'' Again the tears ran down her cheeks.

"Why, that big zero! Who does he think he is?'' Anger coursed through her. "You should have kicked his butt to the curb, Carly. He doesn't deserve you or Emily.''

Carly looked at her with woeful eyes. "He told me he built the house for me. He said it was a gift of love, that it would be the house where all our dreams came true. Then he turns around and does *that*...with *her*.''

Seeing the pain of betrayal on her sister's face made Krystal want to smack her brother-in-law. Carly was far from perfect, but she was a good wife to Joe and a good mother to Emily. She didn't deserve to suffer such a humiliation. Krystal wrapped her arms around her sister and tried to comfort her.

"Oh, Carly, I'm sorry. No wonder you're so upset. That is unforgivable.''

"That's what I told Mom. She thinks I should just go back home, but I can't forgive him, Krys.''

"I don't blame you."

"Then you don't think I'm wrong for leaving?"

"No! How could you be wrong for walking out on someone who's done that to you?"

"Mom said all men make mistakes and that before I do anything I'll regret, I should think about Emily," she said between sobs. "She needs a father."

"She also needs to see her mother treated with respect," Krystal pointed out.

Just then Carly's cell phone rang. Glancing at the caller ID, she whispered, "It's him."

For one moment Krystal saw a spark of hope in her sister's eyes. It was enough to tell her that no matter what Carly said, she still cared for Joe.

Again Carly went out into the hall for privacy, but this call was significantly shorter than the one she'd had with their mother. When she returned, the hope that had momentarily brightened her eyes was gone.

"He only called because he wanted to talk to Emily," she said, tossing her cell phone on to the futon. "I told him she was sleeping, but I don't think he believed me." She groaned in frustration. "I wish I could run far away where he'd never be able to see her again."

"Mom's right about one thing, Carly. He is Emily's father and, no matter what happens between the two of you, that's not going to change."

"I don't want him in her life," she said bitterly.

Krystal didn't think it was a good time to remind Carly of Joe's responsibilities toward his daughter. Her sister was too distraught to have any perspective on Emily and Joe's relationship.

"I don't blame you for feeling that way. It's only normal for you to be angry right now. He's done a terrible thing and I know you only want what's best for Emily.''

Carly looked up at her with gratitude in her eyes. "I knew you'd understand. You don't want Garret in your baby's life, either, do you?"

She shifted uncomfortably. "Carly, I never said I wasn't going to tell Garret I'm pregnant."

"If you were smart, you wouldn't," she advised her.

She didn't tell her that it was too late. Garret already knew. Instead she moved the conversation back to her sister's situation. "Did Joe give you any money when you left?"

"He doesn't have any."

"What do you mean he doesn't have any? His parents own half of Fergus Falls."

"I know, but they stopped giving him money a long time ago. They knew it was ending up in the casino."

"He has a gambling problem?" Krystal frowned. "How long has this been going on?"

Carly shrugged. "Since he got bored being with me, I guess. I'm a boring person, you know." Self-pity laced her words.

"You are not boring. And even if you were, it wouldn't give him the right to gamble away your household money. How bad is your financial situation?"

"Bad enough."

"You do have some money, right?"

"Yeah, yeah, I have some." She got up and began to pace the floor, rubbing her forehead with her fingers. "I can't believe he had that woman at the house when he was talking to me."

"Carly, would you forget about the other woman? You need to think about what you're going to do. How much money do you have right now?'' She tried to steer the conversation back to the practical.

She shrugged. ''I don't know. A couple of thousand, I guess. There should be some money in my savings account.''

''Don't you know?''

She shook her head. ''Joe was the one who took care of the bills.''

''Obviously, he didn't take care of them very well if he's broke,'' Krystal said with disdain.

''Can we not talk about him?'' Carly pleaded.

Krystal sighed. She knew they would not have a rational conversation at this point. Krystal knew it was up to her to get things under control.

''We need to talk about you and Emily. You need a place to stay until you figure out what you're going to do,'' she told her sister.

Carly interpreted that statement as a sign that she wasn't welcome as Krystal's houseguest. ''I knew you didn't want me here.''

''I do want you here, but look at this place.'' She waved her arm in the air. ''It's not big enough for three people.'' Although her room was quite large for an efficiency-size apartment, she had no kitchen and she had to share a bath with the other second-floor tenant.

''All right, all right, I get the message,'' Carly said impatiently, jumping to her feet. ''I'll get out of your way and you won't have to be bothered by me.''

Krystal groaned. ''Will you stop?'' She reached for her sister's hand. ''How many times do I have to tell you I want you here?'' She let out a long sigh of frustration. ''If you would let me finish what I have to say, I'd tell you that I am not going to send you home or to Mom's. I'm going to ask Leonie if you can use the apartment across the hall. It's about the same size as this one.'' It was not a request Krystal wanted to make—not after what she'd told Garret last night, but she didn't see any other option at the moment.

A ray of optimism brightened her sister's face. ''You think she'll say yes?''

''I'm not sure what Leonie will say,'' she answered honestly, knowing her relationship with her landlady could have changed dramatically since yesterday. She didn't tell Carly that but said, ''We're not supposed to have children in this building, but she's made exceptions in the past so she might now.''

''Do you want me to come with you?''

Krystal glanced at her niece asleep on the bed. ''No. You stay here with Emily.'' As she headed toward the door, she said, ''Wish me luck. I'm going to need it.'' And for more reasons than one, she added silently.

WITH EACH STEP KRYSTAL TOOK down the stairs, her anxiety increased. She knew Leonie was home because she could hear voices. The sound wasn't coming from the kitchen, however, but the great room.

As she stepped into the entry, she saw that most of the Donovans were gathered there. All heads turned in her direction at the sound of her footsteps. Conversation ceased and from the way everyone stared at her, Krystal thought it could only be for one reason. Garret had told them she was pregnant with his child.

''Good morning...or I guess I should say good afternoon,'' Leonie greeted her. ''How are you feeling?''

''I'm fine. Thanks,'' she replied, wishing she wasn't the center of attention.

''When you left the wedding last night I was worried you were coming down with the flu that's going around.'' Her landlady eyed her in a motherly way.

She shook her head. ''No, no flu.''

Krystal's eyes met Garret's in an unspoken question. They gave her no indication what he was thinking. She quickly glanced at Maddie and saw sympathy and understanding.

''Come join in the celebration,'' Dylan said. It was then that Krystal noticed the open bottle of champagne.

''What are you celebrating?'' she asked cautiously.

''Donovan babies,'' he said with a grin.

Babies. Plural with an *s*. Krystal conveyed her panic to Maddie with a glance.

''We hope there will be more than one coming in the near future. Shane told us he and Jennifer would like to have another baby.''

Krystal didn't realize she was holding her breath until she let it out in a rush. ''That's great!'' she finally managed to squeak out.

Shane looked at Maddie. ''Thank you for not saying we're *trying* to get pregnant or else I never would have heard the end of it from this guy,'' he said, jerking a thumb in Dylan's direction.

''It was only yesterday that I was telling Garret the Donovan men have never had to work hard at that particular project,'' he said with a grin.

Maddie playfully punched him on the arm. ''You shush.''

''Hey—it's a good kind of work, isn't it?'' Dylan added. ''All kidding aside—'' he lifted his champagne flute ''—I'm looking forward to the third Donovan grandbaby. This way our little guy will have another boy cousin to keep him company.''

''Or a little girl cousin,'' Leonie spoke up.

"We all know Mom would like a granddaughter," Shane said with an affectionate grin aimed at his mother.

"Well, I've had four boys, so it wouldn't surprise me if I had four grandsons," Leonie told them all with a shrug of her shoulders.

Krystal knew her face was red and hoped no one else noticed. She tried not to look at Garret, but she couldn't help casting a glance his way. His face had the same unreadable mask it always had. She didn't know how he could keep his emotions hidden. Worried that she wouldn't be as successful at hiding hers, she said, "I'm going to leave and let you have your family moment together."

"Don't be silly," Leonie said, pulling her by the elbow into the room. "You're like one of the family, isn't she?" she said to no one in particular and a chorus of yeses answered. "You must celebrate with us."

"I'd like to, but I have company. My sister's here. Actually, she's the reason I came down here. Leonie, I need to speak with you for a few moments—if you don't mind?"

"Of course, dear. Why don't we go into the kitchen?"

Dear. She hardly felt worthy of the affectionate title. She followed her landlady, listening to her chatter happily about how wonderful the wedding had been.

When they were alone, she asked, "What is it you need to talk to me about?"

Krystal gave her an abbreviated version of what Carly had told her, ending with, "So she really could use a place to stay until she figures out what she's going to do."

"You want her to take Dena's room?"

"If it wouldn't be too much of an inconvenience for you."

"It's not an inconvenience at all," Leonie insisted. "I haven't had time to find a new tenant. Tell Carly she's welcome to use the room."

"She'll pay you…" she began, but Leonie cut her off.

"There's no need for her to pay. Once she's back on her feet we'll talk about it. Dena moved everything out of that room except the bed. I'll send up some fresh linens and she may need some hangers for the closet."

Her generous spirit only made Krystal feel more uneasy about her own situation. "Thank you. That's very kind of you."

Leonie brushed aside her compliment. "It's what family does in a time of need. They take care of one another."

Krystal gave her a smile of gratitude, then went back upstairs. She could only hope Leonie would feel the same once she learned Krystal was expecting Garret's baby.

KRYSTAL SPENT THE remainder of Sunday taking care of Emily. While Carly slept, she took her niece to the park, where they flew a kite and had a picnic lunch. Being with four-year-old Emily made her realize that, for the past few months, she'd been focusing on how difficult her life had become because of her pregnancy. Stress and uncertainty had overshadowed the fact that one day she would be blessed with the greatest gift a woman could have—a child.

Playing with Emily and watching her mimic her mother's behavior made Krystal hope she was carrying a girl. "A son is your son till he takes his wife, but a daughter's your daughter all of her life.'' How many times had she heard her mother say those words? She wasn't sure they were true. After all, Leonie had four sons and they were all very close to her, yet Krystal found herself hoping for a daughter.

Normally Krystal ate her meals in the kitchen, but on this particular Sunday evening she decided it would be much easier to order pizza and eat in her room. Carly slept most of the day, getting up to take a couple of bites from a slice, then returning to the futon.

Krystal marveled at how resilient kids could be. Emily, with all the innocence of a typical four-year-old, hopped and sang as Krystal brushed her teeth and got her ready for bed.

As Leonie had promised, she'd sent up fresh linens to Dena's old room. She'd also put a vase of fresh-cut flowers on the small bedside table and a message of welcome.

''If there's anything else you need, please let me know.'' It was signed, ''Love, Leonie.''

''She's very kind, isn't she?'' Carly said when she read the note.

''Yes, she is.''

''Have you told her about…'' her sister began but Krystal cut her off, not wanting her to mention the baby in front of Emily.

''No, and it's important that she hears it from Garret. You understand?''

Carly gave her a cross look. ''Of course. What do you think I'm going to do? Blab?''

Krystal wasn't sure what Carly would do in her present emotional state. She didn't bear much resemblance to the sister she knew. ''I hope you don't.''

Carly just rolled her eyes. ''I'm tired. I'm going to

bed,'' she said, pulling back the covers. ''Get in, Emily.''

The little girl looked around. ''I don't want to sleep in here.''

''Why not? There's nothing wrong with this room,'' her mother said.

Big eyes surveyed the nearly empty apartment. ''It's scary.''

Krystal could see Carly didn't have much patience. ''It won't be. I'm going to be in bed with you.''

The little girl looked as if she were going to cry. ''Why can't we go home?''

''Because we can't,'' Carly said wearily.

''Maybe Emily wants to sleep with me?'' Krystal suggested. ''Would you like that?'' she asked her niece.

The little head nodded, her lower lip still pushed out.

''What do you think?'' Krystal looked to Carly for approval.

Carly looked as if she wanted to protest but was simply too worn-out to say anything. ''Go ahead. Most of her stuffed animals are in there anyway.''

So Emily took Krystal's hand and headed across the hall where the four-year-old climbed up onto the bed, positioning her plush pig on one side of her and her bunny rabbit on the other.

''Are you going to pull the shade?'' she asked, pointing toward the window.

''Sure am.'' Krystal walked over to the window. As she reached for the shade pull, she glanced outside and saw Samantha standing next to Garret's car.

She quickly lowered the shade, not wanting to stare at them. She wondered if he had told her about the baby.

As she climbed into bed, she tried not to think about Garret and Samantha. What he did or didn't say to Samantha was none of her business. Right now she had more important things to worry about. Like helping her sister and Emily get through the next few days.

She glanced at her niece. "There. Is that better?"

Emily nodded. "Are you coming to bed now, too?"

Normally Krystal would have said no, but she was exhausted. Emotionally and physically. She took off her robe and slid in next to her niece. She was about to turn off the light when Emily sat forward.

"Can you leave the light on for a little bit?"

"I'll tell you what," Krystal said climbing back out of bed. "How about if I plug in a night-light for you? I have one I think you'll like." She dug through a drawer until she found a tiny light in the shape of a rose. She plugged it in next to the bed. "There. How's that?"

"I like it," Emily said, then lay back down against the pillow.

After more hugs and good-night kisses, she thought maybe her niece would finally go to sleep. First, however, she had to say her prayers. Krystal listened while Emily went down her list of people to bless, which included her aunt. It was the last line, however, that weighed heavily on her mind long after she'd fallen asleep.

She said, "And please make Mommy and Daddy stop fighting."

THE NEXT FEW DAYS Krystal felt as if she were walking through a minefield, waiting for any one of the several explosive situations in her life to detonate. She waited for Garret to call or come see her, but he didn't. She waited for Leonie to confront her about the baby, but she didn't. She waited for her mother to come riding in on her high horse because Carly was still at her place, but so far she hadn't. About the only place Krystal could feel any sense of comfort at all was at the salon, where at least listening to other people's stories took her mind off her own problems.

She had told her boss of her pregnancy, but none of her co-workers, with the exception of Shannon, knew she was having a baby. Since it was nearly impossible to fit into any of her clothes, it was only a matter of time before everyone knew. She took advantage of the large bib-front aprons provided by the salon, wearing them with the hope they would hide her weight gain. It also helped that the heat wave had broken and fall had arrived, bringing cooler temperatures and a reason for her to wear dusters and sweaters.

If it wasn't for the fact that Leonie was a client at the salon, she would have made her pregnancy public knowledge by now. What she didn't want, however, was for her landlady to hear from someone else that she was pregnant, which was why, when she saw that Leonie had scheduled an appointment for later that week, she called Garret.

As she suspected, he was unavailable, which meant she had to leave her name and number and wait for him to return her call. To her surprise it wasn't a long wait. She was in the middle of cutting a client's hair when the receptionist announced over the loudspeaker that she had a call on line three.

Krystal excused herself and hurried into the employee lounge. She pressed the button next to the blinking light. "This is Krystal."

"It's Garret."

She swallowed to ease the dryness in her mouth.

"I..." she began. "I need to know what you're planning to do."

"Krystal, I don't know what I'm going to do. It's only been three days since you told me."

"I mean about your mother. I feel guilty keeping this from her."

She heard him sigh and imagined him raking his hand over the back of his neck, the way he always did when he was stressed. "I know. I feel the same way and I'm going to tell her soon."

"She's coming in on Friday to get her hair done. It wouldn't be good if she heard the news from someone other than you or me."

"No, you're right." Again there was a sigh. "I'll take care of it before then. Is that it?"

She wanted to say, *No, that's not it. In about five months we're going to be parents and I don't have a clue as to how you feel about it.*

But she couldn't tell him that right now. He was an overworked doctor with a long list of patients demanding his time, and she had a client with one side of her hair shorter than the other waiting for her to finish the job.

"Yeah, that's all I wanted." She tried to make her voice as impersonal as his, but knew she failed.

"All right then, we'll talk soon," he told her and, before she could utter another word, he'd hung up.

Soon? When is soon? she wondered. She thought it might be that evening. When she arrived home, she saw his car outside 14 Valentine Place. Butterflies danced in her stomach at the thought of him inside with his mother. She used the tenants' entrance to the house rather than walk through the main dining area.

When she reached the second floor, she found Emily on the flight of stairs leading to the third floor.

"I'm playing with my Slinky. Mommy bought it for me today. Watch." She climbed several risers then let the metal spring toy flop down, giggling as it tumbled from stair to stair.

"Where's your mommy?"

She pointed to Krystal's room. "In there. Want to play with me?"

"In a minute, sweetie. First let me talk to your mommy, okay?" She went into her apartment and found Carly inside reading a magazine.

"Why is Emily playing on the stairs?"

"She has a Slinky. Where else would she play with it?"

"This is a boardinghouse that's not supposed to have any children living here."

"So? Leonie doesn't mind. She told me it was okay."

"And Samantha?"

"She said it was okay, too."

"You asked her?"

She nodded. "If you don't believe me, you could have asked her yourself. You just missed her. She left a couple of minutes ago. Does she know about..." Her glance moved down to Krystal's stomach.

"I don't know but I'm wishing you didn't," she snapped.

"I told you I wouldn't say anything and I haven't."

Krystal knew stress was causing her to be short with her sister. "I'm going to change my clothes and then we'll go get some supper. There's a good coffee shop over on Grand that has a kids' menu."

"I don't feel much like going out. Can't we just eat downstairs?"

"We could but Maddie and Dylan are still here. They're probably having dinner with Leonie."

"No, they aren't. They all went out to eat."

It seemed that her sister knew more about what was going on in the house than she did. "Anything else you want to report happened while I was gone?" she asked dryly.

"Mom called, like, three times."

"She didn't say she was coming to visit, did she?" Carly shook her head.

That was one land mine she could sidestep for today anyway. "Are you sure I can't talk you into going out for something to eat? We could go to the cinema café. There's an animated feature playing there that Emily would enjoy. We could get a bite to eat."

"I don't feel much like sitting through a movie."

"You don't feel much like doing anything, Carly. Why not do it for Emily?" Krystal urged her.

Just when she thought she'd have to take her niece by herself, Carly agreed. The evening turned out to be a better experience than Krystal expected. The film may have been rated G for kids but much of its humor was intended for adults. For the first time in three days her sister actually laughed.

When they got back to the house, however, her mood turned sullen once again, when Emily asked if she could call her daddy and tell him about the movie. Carly told her daughter her cell phone needed to be recharged before they made any more calls. Krystal's offer to use her phone drew a nasty look from her sister, but she didn't try to stop Emily from calling her father.

To Emily's dismay and Carly's relief, Joe wasn't home. Emily left a message in her tiny voice, which had Krystal looking at Carly in sympathy.

Long after they'd all gone to bed, Krystal was still awake. Not only was she restless, she was hungry. For the first time since she'd been pregnant she had a craving. It was for the root-beer-flavored Popsicles she'd purchased for Emily. She tried to ignore it, but all she could think about was sucking on that ice-cold treat.

She glanced at the clock. It was after midnight. Normally Leonie would be in bed at this hour, but with Dylan and Maddie visiting, there was a good possibility she might still be awake. The question was, did Krystal want to risk running into her?

The craving refused to go away and she gently slid out from beneath the covers, not wanting to disturb Emily, who still refused to sleep with her mother across the hall. She pulled her robe from the closet and headed for the kitchen. The house was quiet as she made her way down to the first floor, the only light the glow of a lamp that was always lit in the hallway.

On tiptoe Krystal padded into the kitchen. She didn't turn on any lights, simply went straight for the refrigerator. She stood with the freezer compartment open, searching for the Popsicles when the overhead light came on. Startled, she let out a gasp.

"You're caught."

It was Dylan dressed in a pair of khakis and a polo shirt. Krystal looked behind him, expecting to find Maddie, but she wasn't there.

"I didn't expect to find you raiding the refrigerator," he said.

"I'm hungry. I thought you and Maddie would have gone back to the hotel by now."

"You know how Mom is. She likes to stay up late and talk. What are you after?"

"Popsicles." She pulled one from its box and held it up.

"Maddie wants some yogurt. I thought she'd be

sending me out for pizza or ice cream, but she craves yogurt.'' He shook his head in disbelief.

''At least it's a healthy craving.''

He opened the lower part of the refrigerator. ''And Mom has some here in the house. I could have been out pounding the pavement looking for an all-night diner if she had asked for a pastrami on rye.''

She smiled at him. ''You're a good man, Dylan Donovan. Not many men would go out past midnight to satisfy a wife's cravings.''

''Not many men have a wife like Maddie.''

''I'm glad to hear that marriage agrees with you.''

He grinned. ''Garret tells me I'm like a smoker who's quit the habit. Now that I'm smoke free, I want everybody else to be.''

''You think everyone should get married?''

''Not everyone, but my brother could use a good woman.''

''And does he agree with you?'' She couldn't resist asking.

''Net yet, but I still have a few days left to work on him,'' he said with a wink. ''You know Garret. Work always has been his number-one priority and with this Doctors Without Borders assignment he's accepted, he isn't making it any easier.''

They were interrupted by the appearance of Leonie. ''I came to see what was keeping you,'' she said to Dylan as she entered the kitchen.

''I take it Maddie's looking for her snack,'' he said, holding up the yogurt carton.

''Yes, and I need one more cup of coffee. I'll be with you in a minute,'' she told her son before he left. Then she turned to Krystal. ''Couldn't sleep?'' she asked as she refilled her coffee mug.

''I was a bit restless,'' Krystal admitted.

"You're worried about Carly, aren't you?" She unwrapped a sugar substitute and poured it into her coffee. "I'm sorry we haven't had much time to talk lately. There's been so much activity going on around here."

"I've been really busy, too. I haven't even had much time to spend with Maddie."

"She and Dylan are so happy." She sighed. "It does a mother's heart good...you know what I mean?"

Krystal nodded. "They're a good match."

"I've been lucky. My two elder sons have married lovely women. Now if I could get Garret married, I'd have only Jason to worry about."

"I thought Garret was going overseas."

She took a sip of coffee, then said, "He is. That's why he needs someone who understands his dedication to his profession. Someone who'd be willing to wait for him while he's gone."

Krystal swallowed with difficulty. She knew by the tone of Leonie's voice that she had someone in mind. Samantha.

"You sound like you're taking a professional interest in his personal life," she remarked.

Leonie raised one hand. "I plead guilty. I know I said I would never interfere in my sons' personal lives, but Garret is the one of the four I think needs a little nudge."

"And in which direction do you want to nudge him?" she asked.

"Samantha's perfect for him. She's smart. She's independent. She has a good sense of humor." She used her fingers to enumerate her many good qualities. "And most importantly, she understands his world."

Leonie wasn't saying anything Krystal hadn't already said to herself. As much as she hated to admit it, Samantha Penrose was a much better match for Garret than she would ever be. It was not something she wanted to tell her landlady, however.

Unfortunately, Leonie asked her opinion. "You've had some time to get to know her. Don't you think she's a good match for Garret?"

She took a lick of her Popsicle to get rid of her dry mouth. "It doesn't really matter what I think, does it? I mean, isn't Garret the one who should be deciding?"

Leonie reached over to give her a hug. "You are absolutely right, but you can't blame a mom for trying, can you?" she said with an endearing grin. "Besides, I have a feeling he may not need a push when it comes to settling down and having a family."

Krystal didn't want to ask the question, but it refused to stay unanswered. "What makes you say that?"

"Dylan told me he and Garret had a man-to-man talk the other day about marriage and children. One thing I have been pretty accurate on is recognizing when a man is looking for someone to spend his life with and I do believe Garret is ready."

And there was Samantha, just waiting to pounce, Krystal thought. She didn't want to think about Garret...or Samantha. She looked at the clock and said, "Oh! I didn't realize how late it is. I'd better get to bed." She forced a smile, mumbled something about wishing Garret all the best and then said good-night.

"Good night, dear," Leonie said in her usual sweet voice. "And try not to worry. Carly will get through the bad times."

Maybe Carly would, but the question was, would she? Until now she'd been thinking about the baby in terms of it belonging exclusively to her and Garret.

Her conversation with Leonie had reminded her of the possibility that he could marry and bring another woman into the equation. And Samantha could be that woman. She could become a stepmother to her child.

Krystal couldn't let that happen. She wouldn't let it happen. Unfortunately, it wasn't her call to make. It was up to Garret. And he hadn't told her anything about what he'd been thinking.

Was it any wonder she couldn't sleep?

CHAPTER EIGHT

KRYSTAL ENDED UP getting very little sleep that night. The following morning she felt tired and blue. Her mood worsened when she discovered she had nothing left in her closet that fit her pregnant body. She borrowed a pair of slacks from her sister, who wore a larger size than she did, and headed for the salon.

The first thing she did when she arrived was find her friend Shannon. "Did you mean it when you said I could borrow some of your maternity clothes?"

"Of course I meant it, but I'm not sure they're going to fit you. You're welcome to come over and try them on though."

"I'd better do it soon. Look." She lifted her shirt to reveal two large safety pins holding her slacks closed.

"I'm surprised you made it this long. I was in maternity clothes by the end of my third month. Why don't we go shopping after work? There's a new place over on Grand Avenue that specializes in clothing for the expectant mother."

Krystal grimaced. "I suppose I don't really have a choice, do I?"

Shannon gave her a sympathetic shake of her head. "I'll call the sitter and tell her I'm going to be a little late."

"Thanks. I could use some time with a friend."

"Are things getting you down?"

She told her about her conversation with Leonie the night before and her worry that Garret might marry someone like Samantha.

"Are they dating exclusively?"

She honestly didn't know. "I'm not sure, but it doesn't really matter, does it? I mean, if Samantha isn't the one, there will probably be another woman like her who captures his heart."

"That doesn't mean he'll ignore his obligation to his son or daughter."

"That's not what's worrying me. What if he gets married and decides that he and his wife should be the baby's full-time parents?"

"What you need to do is to talk about this with Garret. Tell him your concerns," Shannon urged her.

They were concerns that kept her on edge all day long. When she met Shannon after work the first thing her friend said to her was, "Don't frown. It causes wrinkles."

"In that case by the time this baby arrives I'll be a prune."

Shannon squeezed her arm. "Oh, it's not that bad."

Krystal didn't see how it could get much worse. Shannon attempted to cheer her up on the short walk to the clothing store, but her efforts were wasted.

When Krystal stepped inside the shop full of maternity clothes and accessories, she groaned. "I don't want to be doing this." She attempted to turn around and leave, but Shannon wouldn't let her.

She put her hands on Krystal's shoulders and pushed her toward the rack of matching tops and slacks. "You don't have a choice in the matter. You need clothes for work." Shannon dove into the rack, pushing aside hangers, critically eyeing the garments before pulling out a dark green pantsuit. "This is cute. You can't even tell it's maternity."

Krystal pulled open the jacket and grimaced at the sight of the elastic insert in the front of the slacks. "What do you call this?"

"Comfortable," Shannon answered. She pulled out several more items, then said, "Go try them on."

Krystal hesitated until Shannon gave her a gentle shove. "Go."

"Here. Hold my purse for me," she said, then went into the curtained dressing room. When she had the first of the outfits in place, she stepped back out into the store to get Shannon's opinion.

"I'm never going to fill this out," she said, tugging on the elastic insert in the pants.

"Trust me, you will. That jacket would be a good choice because it will go with practically anything. Green's always been a great color on you because of your hair."

She glanced at the price tag. "It's affordable, too. It's a possibility." She went back into the dressing room, pulling the curtain shut behind her, stripped off the clothes and tried on several more outfits. Shannon suggested she give them all to the salesclerk and decide when she was finished which ones she could afford.

It was while she was in the middle of changing that she heard the electronic Mexican hat dance song ringing on her phone.

"That's your cell, Krys," Shannon called out from the other side of the curtain.

"It's in my purse. Will you get it for me?" she asked, poking her arm through a slit in the curtain. Shannon placed the phone in her palm and Krystal pulled it into the dressing room and flipped it open.

When she saw it was Garret calling, her heart began to race.

"Hello."

"It's Garret. I'm at the salon," he told her. "Mom thought you worked until six today but they said you'd already gone home for the day. I noticed your car's still in the parking lot."

"Yeah. I'm with Shannon. We're shopping."

"We really need to talk and I don't have much time. How far away are you?"

"Not far. I'm in a clothing shop over on Grand."

"I'll come there then, unless you want to come back here."

Neither option sounded particularly exciting at the moment. She stared at her reflection in the mirror. Dressed in only her bra and underpants, she could see the changes pregnancy had caused. Her body was getting wider, more rounded. Although she was alone in the changing room, she felt exposed and vulnerable.

"Krystal, which would be better? Should I come to you or do you want to come to me? We need to talk," he said for the second time, his voice urgent.

"You can come here, but I'll need about fifteen minutes."

"All right. I'll wait for you outside. Just tell me the name of the store."

"It's Motherhood Fashions," she told him. "Just go over to Grand Avenue and take a right. You can't miss it."

He said, "I'll be there shortly" and hung up.

She stuck her head outside the dressing-room curtain. "That was Garret. I guess I'm going to find out what he plans to do."

"Maybe Leonie's wrong about him and Samantha."

"She's a romance coach. She's seldom wrong about these things."

"Yes, but it's different when it's your own kids. You lose your objectivity."

"Maybe." As she struggled to get back into Carly's slacks. Shannon's arm shot through the curtain. Dangling from her fingers were bras and underpants.

"I don't need underwear," Krystal told her.

"Trust me, in a few weeks' time, you will."

"But those are huge. You have the wrong size."

"No, I don't." She wiggled them in front of her. "Do you want them or not?"

She sighed. "I guess." When she couldn't get the pin closed to hook Carly's slacks, she called out, "Bring me a pair of jeans from out there, will you?"

Shannon did as she was requested. Krystal was in the middle of pulling them on when her friend announced, "Garret's out front."

Krystal fumbled with the buttons on her blouse as her heart skipped a beat. "Will you do me a favor and tell him I'll be out as soon as I've paid for this stuff? And tell the clerk I'm going to wear this pair of jeans home." She ripped off the tag and handed it to Shannon.

Krystal finished buttoning her shirt, then pulled on the coat-length sweater she had worn to work, appreciating that it covered the elastic insert on the maternity jeans. She took a brush from her purse and ran it through her hair, then powdered her cheeks and applied a lip gloss.

When she stepped outside the dressing room, Shannon asked, "Do you want me to wait for you?" Her eyes went to the sales counter where Garret stood staring in her direction.

She shook her head. "No, you go home to Josh. I'll call you later, okay?"

Shannon nodded and slung a "see ya, Garret" in his direction as she left. Krystal walked over to the sales counter and handed the clerk her charge card.

"It's already taken care of," she told her, smiling in Garret's direction.

Krystal's mouth dropped open. "You paid for my clothes?"

"Yes, he did." The clerk handed him the bundle of clothes wrapped in plastic, then gave a smaller bag to Krystal. A look passed between the very attractive salesclerk and Garret. For a brief moment, Garret's smile reminded Krystal of the way Dylan grinned at women. Dylan the flirt. Had Garret been flirting with the salesclerk?

As he walked away she realized that he wasn't even aware of the effect his smile had on women. The salesclerk said, "Have a nice day now," in a tone Krystal was certain she never used on women.

"Why did you pay for my things?" Krystal asked him as they left the store.

"Because I wanted to," he answered simply, then paused to hold the door open for her.

"I wish you wouldn't have. It makes me feel obligated."

"Why? I'm the reason you need these clothes," he pointed out. He walked over to the car and opened the rear door. He laid the bundle on the back seat then slammed the door shut again. "I'm on my dinner break. You don't mind if we go someplace where I can grab a quick bite to eat, do you?"

She shook her head. "There's a Chinese place on the next block that has a buffet."

"It'll do," he told her. "Should we walk or drive?"

"We'd better walk. Parking's limited."

As they started up the street, he asked her if she was hungry.

"A little," she answered, which was quite an understatement. She was starving. Her appetite had definitely picked up the past couple of days.

"How are you feeling today?"

She shrugged. "Okay."

They walked the rest of the way in near silence, with the exception of small talk about the weather. It wasn't until they were seated in the restaurant that he brought up the reason for them being together.

"I'm sorry this had to be so last-minute, but my schedule's been impossible lately. I'm glad you were able to meet with me because the sooner we get this taken care of, the better."

She assumed *this* meant what they were going to do about the baby. The arrival of a waiter postponed their discussion. They each ordered tea and were told they could visit the buffet whenever they were ready. It was obvious he was ready. He stood and held her chair for her. If there was one thing Leonie had done, it was to teach her sons manners. Garret's were impeccable.

They made their selections at the buffet, then returned to the table. He looked at her plate, which was barely half-full. "You should be eating more than that."

"I'm trying to eat more often and have smaller meals. It's supposed to help with the morning sickness."

"You're still bothered by it?"

"Not as often, but it hasn't disappeared completely."

"It should just about have run its course."

"So everyone tells me. I've also heard that some women have it their entire pregnancy."

"Some do."

He ate his dinner as he did most things in life—very deliberately. As his hands moved from his utensils to his napkin to his teacup, she noticed how beautiful they were. Most of the guys she dated had rough, callused hands with thick fingers. His hands were large but they were smooth and graceful. She remembered what they'd felt like on her skin and a warmth spread through her.

She looked down at her food, wishing she was anywhere but here in this restaurant waiting for the man across from her to tell her what his plans were for their unborn child. She knew he had to have given it considerable thought, otherwise he wouldn't be here with her. She also knew that when he was ready, he'd tell her what was on his mind.

She remembered when she moved into 14 Valentine Place, and attended her first house party given by her landlady. Maddie had told her about spending a summer with the Donovans when she'd been a teen and how it was Garret who'd made her feel welcome.

At the time Krystal couldn't understand why Maddie regarded him as her favorite among the brothers. He didn't say more than two sentences to her the entire evening. Actually, she didn't think he'd said more than two sentences to anybody except Maddie.

Later that night, when Krystal had remarked on how different he was from the rest of the family, Maddie had said, "Don't let his quietness fool you. He's brilliant and he's a great guy once you get to know him." At the time Krystal wasn't looking for brainy men who seldom spoke. But as she'd gotten to know him, she'd realized that what Maddie had said was true. Although he seldom told you what was on his mind, you knew it was always churning with thought.

Right now she wished she knew what thoughts were running through his head. With each minute of silence that passed, she became more anxious. Maybe he thought it was more important to eat first and talk later, but she was tired of waiting for him to find the right moment to speak. She needed to know what his plans were and she needed to know now.

"You said you don't have much time," she reminded him.

He looked up at her. "I never have much time."

"Then don't you think we should talk about the baby? That is why we're here, isn't it?"

"Yes." He set down his fork and gave her his undivided attention. That was another thing she'd discovered about him. He always made her feel as if everything she said was important.

"I've been doing a lot of thinking on the subject," he began.

"I figured you were. It's been five days."

"Decisions of this importance aren't arrived at overnight, are they?" It was a rhetorical question for which he expected no answer. "It's a situation I never expected to find myself in."

"Me neither."

"First I want to apologize to you. I'm sorry that my actions have led to this. I should have used better judgment."

"Garret, you don't need to apologize. It was just as much my fault as it was yours."

"I guess it really doesn't matter whose fault it was. It doesn't change the fact that we're now in a situation where the decisions we make will affect the life of another person." He stared into her eyes as he talked and she could see a strength that she found comforting. "I want to do the right thing, Krystal."

"So do I."

"Legally I have responsibilities toward this baby and you know I'm not the kind of man who would ever try to deny those responsibilities. But I don't want my obligations to only be financial."

She swallowed back the dryness in her mouth. "What do you want them to be?"

"You know my family background." She nodded and he continued. "There was no divorce, no blending of families. My brothers and I had two parents there for us every day."

"You were lucky. That isn't always the reality for kids nowadays."

"But I want it to be the reality for my kids."

This is it, she thought. Leonie was right. He was considering settling down and who would be more appropriate for him than Samantha? Her hands tightened around her napkin.

"I want my children to be raised in a two-parent family the way I was. I want them to go to bed each night knowing that their mom and dad are in the same house and will be there for them no matter what happens. Don't you agree it would be better for this baby to have two parents who live together instead of being shuffled back and forth between single-parent homes?"

"Yes, but..." She wanted to tell him what was on her mind, but emotion clogged her throat. Yes, she knew that he would make a good father and even though she didn't know Samantha all that well, she didn't think she needed to fear that she'd be a bad mother to her child. Together the two of them would be able to give her baby a very good life. They certainly had the financial means. But the thought of relinquishing full-time custody of her child…it was too painful to even consider.

"I want to be a full-time father," he continued. "To have my son or daughter with me every day, not only on weekends or whatever time some judge determines I'm allowed to visit. People have married for reasons not nearly so important."

She took a drink of water to get rid of the dryness in her mouth. "Then you're definitely considering getting married?"

"I've never believed that cohabitating is a good idea and in this case it would involve not only two adults but a child as well." He shook his head. "It would send the wrong message. I've given this a lot of thought and marriage seems like the only solution."

"For you, maybe. But what about me? What about what I want?" She struggled to maintain her composure, not wanting her emotions to lead her astray, but at the moment her insides were trembling.

"What do you want?" he asked.

She took a deep breath, then as calmly as possible said, "I'm not sure, but I know I don't want Samantha Penrose raising my child."

He frowned. "Samantha? What does she have to do with this?"

"You said marriage appeared to be the only solution…" She suddenly realized she'd been listening through a filter shaped by Leonie's perception.

"I'm not planning to marry Samantha," he told her, his brown eyes darkening as they stared at her intently. "What makes you think I am?"

"You've been seeing her."

"We work together and we've gone out a few times, but I'm not going to marry her."

"Then who—" She stared at him in disbelief. "You want *us* to get married?"

"We are the baby's parents."

"Yes, but..." His suggestion caught her totally off guard. Never would she have suspected he'd offer marriage to her as a solution to their baby dilemma. "But we're not in love."

"Not everyone marries for love, Krystal."

"Maybe not, but it's important to me."

"As important as giving your baby a father? You said you wouldn't want Samantha to raise your child. Well, I don't want another man to raise mine, either, and I especially don't want someone like Roy Stanton doing the job."

"You can be sure I am never going to marry Roy," she stated in no uncertain terms.

He raised one eyebrow. "Can I?"

"Yes! I'm not in love with him!"

"Then there is no reason why we shouldn't marry...unless there's someone else in your life?"

"No. I just don't see how we can get married considering the circumstances," she told him.

"Our circumstance should be what convinces you marriage would be the best thing," he argued.

At a loss for words, she could only stare at him.

"We've been friends for a long time," he told her, leaning forward and holding her gaze with his own. "And there's some chemistry between us, Krystal. Otherwise that night after the hospital ball wouldn't have happened."

She very rarely blushed in front of men, but this was one moment when she couldn't prevent the red that warmed her face. "Then you expect..." She stared down at her plate.

"Only if it feels right between us."

She kept her eyes downcast and nodded.

"I think it could work for us. You know my family...they all love you... Mom already thinks of you like a daughter."

"Those are not reasons to get married."

"No, but that baby you're carrying is." An alarm sounded and she realized that it was his watch. He clicked it off and said, "I'm sorry, but I have to get back to the hospital." He motioned toward her half-eaten plate. "Do you want a box for that?"

She shook her head. "It's all right."

He signaled for the waiter and paid the check, then escorted her to the car. They drove the short distance to the salon in silence. At her car, he transferred the bundle of maternity clothes from his car to hers, then opened her door for her and waited for her to get in.

"Think about what I said, will you?"

She nodded and he added, "I'll stop by this weekend for your answer. No matter what you decide, we need to talk to my mother. It's probably easier on both of us if we do it together, don't you agree?"

It was one of the few things he'd said today with which she did agree. "Thank you for dinner...and for the clothes."

"It's the least I can do," he told her, then tapped on her window. When she rolled it down he said, "Drive safely, won't you?" She nodded and he went back to his car and drove away. Krystal watched the taillights disappear down the street, then reached for her cell phone and frantically dialed Shannon's number. She needed her best friend.

Only her best friend wasn't there. All she heard was her recorded voice-mail message asking her to leave her name and number.

"Shannon, it's me. You're not going to believe what's happened. Call me."

WHEN SHE ARRIVED at 14 Valentine Place, Krystal discovered that she had a visitor. Her mother's car sat in the parking lot. Just what she didn't need tonight of all nights. She groaned, closed her eyes and rested her head on the steering wheel, wishing she didn't have to go inside.

The next thing she knew a woman's voice was calling to her. "Are you all right?"

Samantha had opened her car door and was leaning in, giving her a very thorough appraisal.

Krystal lifted her head. "Yes, I'm fine."

She looked as if she didn't believe her but didn't pursue the line of questioning. "You shouldn't be driving if you're tired."

"I'm not tired and I'm not driving," she told her. "I'm just sitting here thinking."

Samantha didn't waste any more words. She simply nodded and said, "If you're sure you're okay, I'll go inside."

"I'm fine. Thank you."

She walked away and Krystal wondered what she thought. Did she know that she was pregnant? Garret had said they were friends, leaving her to wonder just how much Samantha Penrose did know about her relationship with him.

Krystal climbed out of the car, dragging her maternity clothes with her. She went through the private entrance, not wanting to run into any of the Donovans. When she reached her room, the door was open. As she expected, her mother was inside sitting on the futon flipping through the pages of a fashion magazine. Emily was asleep on the bed.

"Oh, you're finally home. We wondered what happened to you. The salon said you left at five-thirty," Linda said in a soft voice.

"Yes, but Shannon and I went shopping." She left out the part about having dinner with Garret. "Why didn't you tell me you were coming?"

"I thought you'd tell me not to come."

Krystal sighed. "I'd never do that."

"No, but Carly would. I was hoping she would have come to her senses and gone back to Joe by now."

Krystal took a deep breath and counted to ten. She didn't want to have words with her mother over Carly's situation. "She needs time to think things through," she told her, hanging her garments in the closet.

"Well, I'm worried about her."

"I am, too, but she is an adult and we have to respect that she has to do what she thinks is best for her."

"In her confused state I'm not sure she knows what's best," her mother said, setting the magazine aside.

"Maybe not, but if she makes a mistake, she'll figure out a way to fix it, I'm sure."

"Kryssie, the longer she stays away from Joe, the less likely it is they're going to get back together."

Krystal raked a hand through her hair. "Mom, we've been over this a dozen times on the phone. If Joe doesn't want the marriage to continue, there's nothing Carly can do."

"She can fight for her man," her mother stated vehemently.

"Maybe she doesn't think he's worth fighting for."

Linda made a sound of disgust. "Do you know how many women would love to be Mrs. Joe Benson?"

"Obviously too many, which is why he thinks he can go to bed with whomever he pleases and whenever he pleases."

"He had one affair," her mother corrected her.

"He was supposed to have none. Doesn't it bother you that he cheated on your daughter?"

"Of course it does, but I also know that marriages survive infidelity. They have a child together." She glanced at the sleeping Emily.

"I know. For her sake I'd hate to see them divorce, too."

"But you think their marriage is over, don't you?"

"I don't know, Mom," she answered honestly. "All I know is two people who I thought had everything going for them are now separated and contemplating divorce."

"They seemed to be so much in love, didn't they?" Linda said wistfully.

Krystal nodded soberly. "I remember their wedding day, standing next to Carly at the altar, watching the way they looked at each other. I thought they were two of the luckiest people in the world. So in love, so happy to be starting a marriage together."

"I thought the same thing. When I saw the looks on their faces as they came down that wedding aisle, I said to myself, 'I may have failed miserably in the love department, but my baby girl got it right.'" She shook her head. "I guess sometimes love isn't enough."

That caused Krystal to jerk her head up. "Why isn't it?"

Her mother shrugged. "If I knew the answer to that, there'd be a lot fewer divorces." She chuckled. "Maybe that's the mistake we all make. We fall in love and we get married thinking love is all we need."

"It might not be all that we need, but it has to be there to make the marriage work," Krystal stated, more for her own reflection than her mother's.

To her surprise, Linda didn't agree. "I'm not so sure."

"How can you say that?"

"Because I have friends who didn't marry for love and they have happy marriages. If I hadn't been so idealistic, I could be in such a marriage right now."

Krystal frowned. "What are you talking about?"

"You were barely three. I was seeing this man named George. He was crazy about me, but I didn't have the kind of feelings for him that I'd had for your father. I liked him. He was a good man, but it wasn't that all-consuming, intense physical kind of emotion that happens when you fall in love. He told me it didn't matter, that in time a better kind of love would grow between us, one based on friendship, mutual respect, his love for my children." She sighed. "I didn't think it would work, so I said no."

"And you regret it?"

Linda simply looked at her and said, "Yeah, I really do."

"It might not have lasted," Krystal said.

"No, you're right. It might not have, but I'll never know. I do know that the man I did love with my whole body and soul didn't stay, either."

"You're talking about my father, aren't you?"

As usual, whenever the subject came up, she was quick to close the door on it. "There's not much point in talking about him. I didn't drive all the way down here to discuss water over the dam."

"Why did you come?"

"Because I'm worried about you and your sister.

You seldom call. How am I supposed to know if you're all right?''

"We're both fine."

"I don't know how you can say that when your sister's marriage is falling apart and you're expecting a baby with no marriage prospects in sight," she said irritably.

Krystal could have corrected the latter statement but chose not to bring Garret's name into the conversation. "Some people might think we're both lucky. Marriage isn't for everybody. You did just fine without a husband. Carly and I will, too."

Linda sighed in exasperation. "We'd better change the subject or we'll end up fighting again. Are you hungry? Have you had dinner?"

"Yes, I stopped and had a bite before I came home. I hope Carly fed you. By the way, where is she? Did she go to bed already?"

"No, she went to drop her car off at the garage. It wouldn't start this morning and she thought she was going to have to have it towed, but then Leonie asked one of her sons to take a look at it and apparently he got it going for her."

Krystal could just imagine Dylan being asked to help out. "Oh, I wish she hadn't done that."

"Why not? He was able to get it running and save her the expense of a towing fee. He followed her to the garage just to make sure she wouldn't have more trouble with it stalling on her."

"Still it was an imposition on Dylan's time."

"Dylan? I thought Carly said it was Shane who helped her."

"Shane?" Krystal frowned. "I'm surprised he was around."

"It's a good thing he was." Linda glanced at the

clock radio next to Krystal's bed. "I thought she'd be back by now."

"What time did she leave?"

"About an hour ago. I'm not sure how far away the service station is though."

"If it's the same one I use it's only about twenty minutes from here."

"Then she should be back shortly," her mother said, and changed the subject. "So tell me how you're feeling? Have you felt the baby kick yet?"

She shook her head.

"With both you and Carly, I felt life around the fifth month. I'm surprised you've made it this far without having to wear maternity clothes."

Krystal opened her sweater to expose the jeans. "I just got them."

"Ah." Linda eyed Krystal's still-slender figure. "Are you eating properly?"

"Yeah, of course."

"What about the father. Does he know yet?"

So they were back to that square. "As a matter of fact he does."

Her mother regarded her suspiciously. "And?"

"Nothing's changed, Mom, if that's what you're getting at. And if you don't mind, I'd rather not talk about me and the baby. Tell me what's new in your life. Are you still taking those ceramic classes?"

To Krystal's relief, her mother took the hint and went on to talk about life in Fergus Falls. When an hour had passed and there was still no sign of Carly, Krystal said, "I wonder what could be keeping her?"

"Maybe she waited for them to fix the car."

"I thought that was the point of Shane following her over there...so he could give her a lift home."

"Call her on her cell phone."

Krystal tried but could only connect to her voice mail. After leaving a message, she said to her mother, "Are you planning to stay the night?"

"It would be nice to spend some time with Emily."

Tonight, Krystal didn't feel like having another guest. She needed time alone to think about Garret's proposal. Not that her mother leaving would give her any privacy. She glanced at her niece asleep in her bed.

"You can sleep on the futon," she heard herself say.

"Are you sure you don't mind? I don't want to get in your way."

She shook her head. "You won't get in my way, Mom. I'm just going to take a shower and go to bed anyway. I'm really tired and I need sleep."

"Yes, you do. I remember what it was like at your stage of pregnancy. Maybe I should go downstairs to wait for Carly."

"Someone should probably sit with Emily until I get out of the shower," Krystal suggested. "If you're hungry, I could get something delivered from the deli."

"No, I'm fine."

"You can make yourself a cup of coffee." She motioned to the small cart on wheels in the corner where she kept a hot plate and a one-cup coffeemaker for those times she didn't want to go downstairs to cook.

"That sounds good." Linda gave Krystal a gentle shove. "You go take that shower and don't worry about me."

But Krystal did worry about her mother. And she worried about Carly who still hadn't returned. But most of all she worried about Garret and what she was going to do about his proposal of marriage.

CHAPTER NINE

"DID YOU HEAR ABOUT Gladys Lingenfelser?" the salon receptionist asked Krystal the following morning when she arrived at work.

"No, what about her?"

"She had a stroke. They moved her to the nursing home yesterday."

Tears misted Krystal's eyes. "That is so sad. Thanks for telling me."

"I figured you'd want to know."

Krystal nodded and headed for the employee lounge, dabbing at her eyes with a tissue. It always upset her to hear that misfortune had struck one of her elderly clients. Being pregnant only made her emotional response more dramatic.

Gladys Lingenfelser was in her thoughts often that day, so much so that by the time she'd finished working, she'd made up her mind to go visit her. After calling Carly to say she wouldn't be home for dinner, she stopped in at the flower section of the grocery store and bought an African violet and a package of gingersnaps, then headed over to the nursing home.

Her distress was eased somewhat when she saw Gladys sitting up in bed. Although she needed help eating her dinner, she was able to talk and seemed in good spirits considering the circumstances. Gladys smiled when she saw the violet and told Krystal she was the nicest hairdresser she'd ever had in all of her eighty-seven years. Krystal promised to stop by on Tuesday when she came to wash and style the hair of several of the other residents.

After a short visit with Gladys, Krystal headed over to see another of her favorite clients. Expecting she wouldn't be in her room, she went straight to the recreation center, where she spotted the white-haired woman playing bingo.

"Win anything?" Krystal asked as she slid on to a chair.

Dolly Anderson grinned from ear to ear when she saw her. "Kryssie! What are you doing here on a Saturday night? You should be out with one of your boyfriends instead of visiting old ladies."

"I don't have a boyfriend and you're not old."

"Oh yes I am," she said with a wag of her finger. "And what do you mean you don't have a boyfriend?"

She spread her hands in frustration. "What can I say? I went from having too many to having none."

"Sounds to me like your romance train has stalled."

"I think it's derailed. Permanently," Krystal told her.

Dolly laughed.

Krystal took one of the round plastic disks and placed it on her bingo card. "He called B-twelve."

Dolly waved her hand. "It doesn't matter. If you win it just means you get to pick the movie for tonight. I've seen all the ones they have."

Krystal reached into her tote and pulled out the box of gingersnaps. "I brought you something."

"Well, aren't you just the sweetest thing," Dolly gushed, gazing at the cookies as if they were a pot of gold.

"How's your hip?"

"Oh, it could be better, but it hasn't kept me from taking care of my garden. The harvest is almost over."

Krystal nodded. "Thank you for those wonderful tomatoes. They were delicious."

"You are most welcome. If I were still in my house, you'd have so much more, including a pumpkin."

Krystal placed another marker on the bingo card. "Look. You have four corners."

Dolly's hand shot up. "Bingo" she called out in a shaky voice.

Krystal applauded enthusiastically. "Good job."

"You brought me luck."

As soon as the numbers had been confirmed, Dolly was given a coupon good for one free movie rental and Krystal said, "There. Now you get to choose the movie for tonight."

"Want to stay and watch with me since your romance train is stalled?"

Krystal thought about it. She could go home and listen to Carly and her mother, or she could watch a movie with Dolly. She chose the movie.

"Good," Dolly said with a satisfied grin. "I know just the one I want to watch. It's one of your favorites, too. Might put you in the mood to get back on the romance train."

Krystal doubted it, but she didn't tell Dolly that. She just smiled and helped the older woman to her feet.

GARRET GLANCED AT HIS WATCH. His mother had said dinner was at seven-thirty and it was now ten-fifteen. He couldn't even say he was late. He'd missed it completely. Not that his mother would be upset. She understood what it meant to be a doctor and knew that his schedule was as unpredictable as the Minnesota weather.

But he had several reasons he didn't want to miss this dinner. It was Dylan and Maddie's last night in town before they went back to France. There were things he hadn't said to his brother, things he should have said. He checked his watch again, hoping he would get that opportunity.

He had hoped that by tonight Krystal would have made a decision regarding his marriage proposal, because he could get everything out in the open. He knew, however, that whether or not she accepted it, he needed to tell his family about her pregnancy.

He'd already decided tonight was to be the night. He'd wanted to discuss it with Krystal first but had been unable to reach her all day. His only choice had been to leave her a voice-mail message telling her he planned to make the announcement this evening.

As he stepped into the house, he heard voices coming from the great room. He hung his raincoat on a hook. From the hallway he could see Dylan and Shane were at one end, Maddie and his mother at the other. Krystal was nowhere in sight. Disappointment seeped through him. He'd hoped that she'd be there.

"Sorry I missed dinner," he said as he made his entrance into the great room.

His mother got up to give him a hug. "Better late than never. Are you hungry? I saved you a plate. All I have to do is put it in the microwave." She looked at him as if he were ten again and needing her attention.

"Thanks, Mom, but you sit. I'll do it later. Right now I'd rather spend some time with Dylan and Maddie," he said, looking at his brother.

"We can do that in the kitchen. We haven't had dessert," Maddie told him. She gave her husband's arm a tug. "Come. We're going to eat your mother's apple pie. Let's move the party there."

"Isn't the party missing a couple of people?" Garret asked Maddie as she ushered everyone out of the great room.

"Jennifer stayed home with Mickey because he has a cold," she answered.

"What about Krystal? I thought she was coming for dinner."

"Oh, she's around. I think she went upstairs to check on Carly and Emily."

"She's coming back down, isn't she?"

"She'd better. We haven't said our goodbyes." Maddie changed the subject, asking him about his work at the hospital while his mother fussed over getting him something to eat. He wished she would simply sit down and that Krystal would return so he could make his announcement.

But his mother continued to move about the kitchen and Krystal didn't appear. Garret grew more uneasy.

Finally he heard footsteps on the stairs and Maddie said, "There's Krystal now."

He looked toward the doorway and saw her come in wearing a two-piece gray slack set that Garret remembered seeing in the selection of maternity clothes the clerk had rung up for him. It was the only time he'd ever seen her in gray. Usually her clothes were bright and colorful and fun. This outfit made her look demure—so very unlike Krystal.

"Oh good, you're back." Maddie was the first one to speak to her. "I was worried we weren't going to get to say our goodbyes."

"That would never happen," Krystal said, coming into the kitchen.

"Is Emily okay?" Maddie asked.

She nodded. "Actually, tonight's the first night she's slept with Carly. She's been sleeping with me in my bed."

Krystal's eyes met his, revealing an uncertainty he had come to expect whenever he looked at her lately. Her red hair framed her pale cheeks and immediately he wondered how she was feeling. As if she could read his mind, she gave him a weak smile of reassurance. His heart missed a beat. She had a vulnerable look that made him want to protect her.

Dylan pulled out a chair for her, placing her directly across from Garret. "Would you like a piece of apple pie?" he asked her.

"Ah…no…no pie for me, thanks," she answered, and Dylan turned his attention to helping Maddie serve dessert. When Shane excused himself to make a phone call, it left only Garret and Krystal seated at the table.

"Did you get my phone message?" he asked.

She nodded.

"Then you're okay with me being here tonight?"

"Not really," she admitted, shifting uneasily. She lowered her voice to a whisper and asked, "Are you sure you want to do this now?"

He nodded. "It needs to be done. Trust me. I know my family. They'll understand."

If he could get everyone to sit back down at the table, that is. The way Krystal's eyes kept darting back and forth, he could see she was just as uneasy waiting for everyone to return to the table. He took a couple of bites of the leftover pot roast his mother had re-heated for him, then shoved his plate aside.

"I'm really glad everyone—or almost everyone—is here," he began. "I have some news I want to share with the family."

He saw his mother's eyes twinkle as she nudged Maddie. "Does it concern your trip overseas?"

He took a deep breath. "Actually, I've decided not to take part in the Doctors Without Borders program."

There was a silence as all eyes stared at him in bewilderment.

"But why not?" His mother asked the question he knew all of them were thinking.

"Well, my plans have changed." He didn't want to look at Krystal, but he couldn't help himself. She sat with her hands squeezed so tightly together he could see the whites of her knuckles.

"I don't suppose there's a woman involved in these changed plans," Dylan said with a sly grin.

"Actually, there is," Garret admitted. From the look of agonizing anxiety on Krystal's face, Garret knew he needed to get to the point. "The reason I'm not going to accept the responsibility of working in the Doctors Without Borders program is because I have a more important responsibility to take care of here. I'm going to be a father."

Stunned silence greeted his words and then his mother said, "Oh, my goodness! Samantha is pregnant?"

He rolled his eyes. "No, Mom, not Samantha," he snapped impatiently.

"Then who?" His mother's voice was almost a whisper.

Before he could tell her, Krystal spoke. "It's me, Leonie. I'm pregnant with Garret's baby."

This time the silence was deafening. He wished someone would say something. Anything. He was grateful when Dylan jumped to his feet and offered him a handshake and then a hug saying, "Congratulations, little brother.'' Shane did the same thing, but his mother said nothing.

She sat with a look of bewilderment on her face, staring at Krystal. ''You slept with my son?'' she finally said.

''I'm sorry,'' Krystal's apology crackled with unshed tears.

''Mom, don't blame Krystal. I'm equally responsible,'' Garret said, but it was as if his mother didn't hear him.

''I treated you like a daughter,'' Leonie said to her in a voice that wobbled uncharacteristically.

Maddie came to Krystal's defense. ''Leonie, Krystal is like a daughter to you and she's like a sister to me. This doesn't change that.''

Then his mother turned to Maddie and asked in an accusing tone, ''Did you know about this?''

Krystal jumped to her feet. ''If you're going to be upset with anyone, it should be me, Leonie,'' she said, her body trembling. ''And this is exactly why I was afraid to tell any of you—I knew this would happen.'' Then she burst into tears and ran out of the room.

Maddie called out after her and would have followed her, but Garret stopped her.

''I'll go.'' Before he left, however, he turned to his mother and said, ''You didn't react this way when Dylan told you he was going to be a father.''

''You can't expect me not to be shocked, Garret,'' she told him.

''No, but I did expect you to be fair,'' he said before turning to leave the room. He climbed the stairs to the second floor. When he reached the landing, Krystal's door was closed. He knocked lightly, saying, ''Krystal, it's me.''

She opened the door and he saw her tearstained cheeks. "She hates me," she said on a hiccup.

"No, she doesn't." He pulled her into his arms. It seemed like the natural thing to do. It was also the first time she'd been in his arms since the night of the hospital ball. She felt warm and soft and she clung to him, quietly sobbing into his chest.

"I'm sorry," she finally said, straightening. "I'm superemotional because of the hormone thing." She motioned for him to come inside, then closed the door behind him.

"My mother could have reacted a little less emotionally herself."

She hiccuped. "At least she didn't slap me, like my mother did."

"Your mother slapped you?"

She nodded. "It's hard for mothers to hear that kind of news." She reached for a tissue to blow her nose.

"That doesn't give them the right to behave the way they did. We're adults, Krystal, not some fifteen-year-old kids who need supervision."

She dropped down on to the futon. "Apparently we needed it that night."

"No, what we needed was better birth control protection."

She looked at him briefly, then buried her head in her hands. "Don't remind me."

He pulled her hands away from her face. "You can't hide from the facts, Krystal. Don't you think it's about time you stopped beating yourself up for something that you can't change?"

"You sound as if you're okay with all of this," she said, allowing him to pull her into the crook of his arm.

"I've accepted that I'm going to become a father...if that's what you mean." Her hair smelled like oranges and her body was warm as it rested against his. "We can't go back and change what's already happened, so we might as well go forward, right?"

"It isn't that easy."

"I didn't say it was going to be easy." She sighed and he wished he knew what she was thinking. "I'm sorry I didn't tell my mother ahead of time in private. It would have given her time to get over the initial shock. Maddie's right. She does think of you like a daughter."

"Well, at least she did at one time."

"And she will again. She's just not thinking clearly right now. I'm sure that I'm the last of her four sons she expected to be in this position."

"She wouldn't be so upset if it were Samantha who was pregnant. She thinks she's a good match for you and she's right." She shook her head. "It's just plain stupid to think that you and I could make a marriage work."

He didn't like the sound of that. "That sounds like a rejection of my marriage proposal."

She cast a sideways glance at him. "I'm sorry, but I just don't see how it would work. I mean, I know that marriages based on friendship can work. I have plenty of clients who married for that very reason."

"So why wouldn't ours work?"

She shrugged. "I don't know. Maybe it would. Do we have to decide this tonight?"

He shook his head. "No, we don't. The important thing is we told my family."

"Yeah. And you saw the way your mom reacted. So now what do we do?"

"Give her some time."

"That's easy for you to say. I'm the one who lives

in her house.'' She leaned her head back and closed her eyes. ''What a mess I made of things.''

''You didn't do it alone,'' he said, pulling her closer to him. ''I did my part.'' He liked the way she felt in his arms. It made him feel as if they were a team in this mess. He also liked the way she touched him when she talked, even though it was that aspect of her personality that was partly responsible for their situation.

Suddenly her eyes flew open and she reached for him, her hand grabbing his leg. ''Oh my gosh.''

''What is it?''

''I think the baby kicked.'' She grabbed his hand and placed it on her tummy. ''Right here.''

They sat in silence, waiting for some sign that it had been the baby that had moved.

''There. Did you feel it?'' she asked him, a look of wonder on her face.

When he shook his head, she lifted the gray fabric and placed his hand under it. His palm met silky-smooth underwear.

''Try right there,'' she said, excitement lighting up her already beautiful eyes.

He soon discovered she was right. He felt the tiniest of movements beneath his fingertips. His eyes met hers and he smiled. ''You're right. She kicked.''

''She? How do you know it isn't a he?''

Because all he could think about was having a daughter who looked exactly like her. But he didn't tell her that. ''I don't, but we'll know soon enough. You must be scheduled for an ultrasound.''

She nodded. ''Next week. I heard they can't always tell the sex though.''

''That's true,'' he confirmed. ''I'd like to be there with you.''

''During the ultrasound?''

"Yes, that won't bother you, will it?"

"No." There was a knock on the door, startling her. She pushed his hand away and got up to see who it was.

"Can I come in?" he heard Maddie's voice say. "I'd like to talk to you and Garret."

Krystal let her in and as soon as the door was opened they went into each other's arms. "I'm sorry. I tried to help, but I'm afraid I only made things worse," Maddie said.

As soon as she'd finished hugging Krystal, she turned to Garret and wrapped her arms around him, too. "This can't be easy for you, either."

"We could have handled it differently," Garret admitted.

"He's right," Krystal seconded. "I should have told everyone a long time ago."

"None of that matters," Maddie said with her familiar smile of understanding. She reached out to touch Krystal's arm. "Hey—everything will work out. I only wish I could be here to help you. I hate the thought of you going through this alone."

"She's not alone. She has me." Garret said. He could see the unasked question in his sister-in-law's eyes. "Why don't I let Krystal tell you what her plans are. I should probably go downstairs." He looked at Krystal and asked, "Are you going to be okay?"

"Yeah, thanks."

"Call me if you need anything," he told her.

Maddie reached for his arm to give him another hug. "You're a good man, Garret. If that husband of mine gives you any trouble, let me know."

"Dylan's the least of my worries," he said, then reluctantly went back downstairs to the kitchen. As he expected, his mother sat at the table with his brothers.

The way the three of them stared at him when he entered the room, he knew they'd been discussing only one thing.

"All right, get it off your chests. I can see you're dying to ask me how it happened," he said, plopping himself down on a chair.

"How did it happen? You're a doctor for crying out loud," his mother said, obviously still upset with the news.

"I didn't realize that doctors were exempt from unplanned pregnancies," he answered.

"I think she means you should have known better," Dylan said in an aside that his mother heard.

"You *should* have known better," she repeated. "And what about Samantha?"

"What about her?" he countered.

"Were you just using her as a smoke screen to hide your affair with Krystal?" his mother wanted to know.

"There is no affair with Krystal," he stated emphatically. "And you ought to know me well enough to know that I don't use people."

"Yes, I do know you, which is why I'm having trouble understanding how something like this could have happened," his mother went on.

"It just did, so can we drop the fact that it did and move on to what's going to happen next?"

"I think that would be smart," Dylan stated.

"How far along is she in her pregnancy?" Leonie asked.

"The baby's due in February," he replied.

Again his mother's mouth dropped open. "How long have you known she was pregnant?"

"About a week."

"So she kept it from you, too?"

He ignored that question. "Mom, I know this isn't

what you expected from me, but it's happened and I can't change it. Now you can either choose to be happy that you're having another grandchild or you can spend your time finding fault with me and Krystal. I mean, I am going to be a dad. Wouldn't you rather spend your time giving me advice on that subject?''

She smiled then and reached across to cover his hand. ''You're going to make a wonderful father...just like your brothers.''

''I'm going to try, Mom, and Krystal will be a good mother. You ought to know that.''

She sighed. ''Yes, I do know that,'' she admitted quietly. ''Have you discussed how you're going to raise this child?''

''Yeah, we have, but nothing's settled yet, except we both know that we want to do the right thing.''

''The right thing...what do you consider the right thing?'' she asked cautiously.

''I'm a Donovan, Mom.''

''Then you mean marriage.''

''I want my child to have the kind of home I had,'' he admitted.

''Then you need to marry for love, not convenience,'' she advised him.

''Mom, you said you'd never wear your romance coach hat with us boys,'' Shane reminded her.

''I'm not trying to give him advice. I just want him to think very carefully before he makes a decision as important as marriage. It's a commitment that should be based on love, not convenience.''

''That sounds like advice, Mom,'' Dylan rebuked her gently.

She gave Garret an apologetic smile. ''I just want what's best for you.''

''I know you do, Mom, but you have to trust me to

do the right thing,'' Garret told her. ''I created the problem and I'll find a solution to it.''

''He's always been the brains in the family,'' Dylan said with affection.

''I can handle this, Mom. You don't have to worry about me.''

Her face remained skeptical.

Later that evening, after goodbyes had been said, Garret walked with Shane out to their cars. He was surprised when his brother said, ''You know, as much as I hate to admit it, Mom has a point. You don't have to get married to do the right thing by Krystal.''

''Whose side are you on anyway?''

''Yours. Always yours, but what if the marriage doesn't work out?''

''I'll make it work.''

''Yeah, that's what I said, too.''

Garret frowned. ''What are you talking about? You and Jennifer announced last week that you're thinking about having another baby.''

''It turns out that I was a bit premature with that idea. She doesn't really want another child. I found that out this evening before I came over here. She's been taking the pill and I didn't even know it.''

''What's going on?''

He shrugged. ''Who knows? Maybe we're just going through a rough spell.'' He leaned up against his truck. ''All marriages do.''

''Are you saying your marriage is in trouble?'' Garret could hardly believe it could be true.

''We don't spend enough time together, that's all. Ever since she went back to school, it's been that way.''

''So make time for each other.''

He shrugged. ''That's easier said than done.''

"I've got next weekend off. You want me to take Mickey so you two can go away for a couple of days?"

He shook his head. "It's not going to happen. She's got classes every weekend."

"What about a nice dinner then?"

"I'll let you know." He clapped him on the arm. "Thanks for the offer."

"Thank you for sticking up for me in there." He jerked his head toward the house.

"You kind of threw us a curve ball. None of us realized you and Krystal were seeing each other."

"We're not." A car passed through the alley and he realized that the things he wanted to discuss with his brother were better said someplace other than in his mother's backyard. "Look. How about if we stop at Al's and I'll tell you all about it?"

KRYSTAL AWOKE to find Emily at her bedside saying, "I get to go to Sunday school today."

Krystal propped herself up on one arm as her sister appeared in the doorway. "You're going to church?"

"Yes. I'm not sure when we'll go back to Fergus Falls and Emily's used to going to Sunday school," Carly answered. "Leonie suggested we go to the one where Shane and Jennifer take Mickey."

"Is Mickey going to be at Sunday school?" Emily asked.

"She knows Mickey?"

"They've played together a couple of times when Shane's been over visiting his mother," Carly said, then held out her hand for her daughter. "Come on, Emily. We don't want to be late."

"Can Aunt Krystal come?"

"I don't think she feels well." Carly looked at Krystal and asked, "Do you?"

Krystal had the distinct impression she didn't want her going to church with them, which was silly. What difference would it make—unless she thought Krystal would make them late.

"No, I'd better stay here," she told Emily. "I'm not feeling very good."

Carly nodded, saying, "We'll close the door on our way out."

Emily blew her a kiss. "Hope you feel better."

Krystal pretended she caught the kiss, then blew one back. "See you later." She lay back against the pillows, thinking that it had been a long week—a week during which she'd managed to avoid seeing her landlady. Garret had suggested she give Leonie some time to come to terms with what had happened.

Upon reflection, she thought it was a bad idea. For Garret it might work to do a lot of thinking, but all it had done was to create more anxiety in her. The time had come for the two of them to clear the air. If Leonie wasn't going to come to her, Krystal would go to her.

She climbed out of bed and was about to head for the shower when there was a knock on the door. She called out, "Come in," and Leonie stepped into her room.

"Is it too early for me to be here?" she asked.

"No, not at all." She reached for her robe and slipped it on as she climbed out of bed. "Actually, I was just thinking about coming down to see you."

She didn't miss the way Leonie's eyes traveled to her stomach. She knew she'd caught a glimpse of just how pregnant she was before she'd covered up with the robe.

"I bet you miss Maddie and Dylan." Krystal knew

it was a dumb statement, but it was an awkward situation and she felt she had to say something. Anything.

"Yes, I do." Leonie didn't move from her spot in front of the door.

"I hope they had a smooth flight back." She focused her attention on tying her robe, avoiding Leonie's eyes.

There was an awkward silence and Krystal knew she couldn't avoid the reason her landlady was in her room. "I'm sorry I didn't tell you I was pregnant."

"You've always been able to tell me anything."

"Yes, but this was different."

"I suppose you're right," she said thoughtfully. "Have you made any decisions?"

"You know that Garret thinks we should get married."

"Oh yes, he told me that. How do you feel about it?"

Krystal could see she was doing her best to remain detached, to act as if she were coaching one of her clients.

"I'm really confused right now...about a lot of things," she admitted.

"Krystal, you know that I have an agreement with all my tenants. I don't give unsolicited advice on anyone's love life."

But Krystal had a feeling she was going to make an exception and she was right.

"You're like a daughter to me and I don't want to see you make a mistake."

Krystal didn't doubt for one minute that the advice was given with the best of intentions. She knew Leonie too well to suspect she had any other motive.

"Maybe it wouldn't be a mistake," she said quietly.

"Are you in love with Garret?"

"No."

"Then it would be a mistake."

She wasn't saying anything Krystal hadn't already said to herself. How could she marry Garret when she didn't love him with her whole heart and soul?

"Babies need two parents," she stated with conviction.

"And this one will have two wonderful, good people as its parents. Whether or not you're married to Garret, your child will be a Donovan and he'll be a part of this family. You both will be part of our family. You know Garret. Can you imagine him having it any other way?"

She couldn't, but she also knew that eventually Garret would probably marry. If not Samantha, then someone like her. Probably another doctor who Leonie would consider to be another good match like Samantha.

Krystal tried not to feel hurt, but a pain rifled through her. How quickly their relationship had changed. Leonie had treated her like a daughter, yet when it came right down to it, she didn't want her in the family. Krystal wanted to tell her how much it hurt her to hear those words, but she couldn't.

She bit down on her lip and fought for control of her emotions. "I only want to do what's best for the baby."

"I know you do, that's why I'm here. I wouldn't be your friend if I didn't try to help you through this situation."

Krystal realized their definition of help was not one and the same.

"I'm not trying to tell you what to do, Krystal. I just want you to think carefully about all of your options. Don't rush to make any hasty decisions. You have some time to think things through.''

Krystal nodded, not trusting herself to speak.

''I want you to know that I will support whatever decision you make.''

Krystal wondered how true those words were. Would she welcome her into the family even if she and Garret went against her advice?

''Thanks, Leonie. That means a lot to me,'' she managed to say.

''If there's anything I can do to help you, I want you to let me know.'' She opened her arms and Krystal went into them. ''Let's make today a new beginning, all right?''

''Okay,'' Krystal agreed, and gave her a smile as she left.

But as soon as the door had closed behind Leonie, tears fell down Krystal's cheeks. She didn't like that their relationship had changed. It was as if Leonie didn't have a clue as to how terrified she was being a single woman about to have a child. She wanted things to be the way they used to be, where Leonie had been her friend, her confidante, her mother.

Krystal crumpled on to her bed in a heap of self-pity, feeling very much alone. No one understood what she was going through. Not her mother, who thought that above all, getting married should be a priority. Not Leonie, who thought it would be in everyone's best interest if she didn't marry Garret. Not Carly, who was so wrapped up in her own marital problems that she couldn't expend any emotional energy on her sister. And certainly not Garret.

Or did he? Maybe it was time she found out.

CHAPTER TEN

GARRET WAS A LIGHT SLEEPER and woke immediately when the phone rang. "Yes."

"It's me—Krystal."

She wouldn't have needed to identify herself. He could never forget her voice and on the phone it had an even sexier sound than it did in person. It was one of the things that had attracted him to her the first time they met. He pushed himself up on one elbow.

"Good morning."

"It's nearly afternoon," she told him.

He glanced at the clock. "You're right. It is."

"You were sleeping. I'm sorry."

"No, it's all right."

"I shouldn't have disturbed you. You were probably up half the night with a patient."

"No, I wasn't." It was true. The reason he had trouble sleeping was that he had been unable to stop thinking about her. "I'm glad you called."

"Really?" She sounded doubtful.

"Yes, really." He sighed. "If we're going to have a child together, we need to work at being comfortable together, don't you agree?"

"We never used to have to work at that," she reminded him.

"No, we didn't."

"I miss the way things were between us. We used

to talk…and laugh…" He could hear the sigh in her voice.

"I miss that, too,"

"That's one of the reasons why I called. I thought that if we spent some time together and we made it a rule that we weren't going to talk about the baby, then maybe we could become friends again."

"I'd like that."

"You would? Good. Maybe we could do something today…if you're not busy?"

She wanted to spend time with him. It was a tantalizing thought. "No…no, I'm not busy," he answered, relieved that he hadn't scheduled anything for his day off. "Have you had breakfast…or maybe I should say lunch?"

"I can do either one. Name the restaurant and I'll meet you there."

He knew she made the suggestion to avoid another confrontation with his mother. "There's a café right around the corner from me that's good. Why don't you come to my place and we'll go from here?"

"I can do that, although I must warn you my estrogen levels are high. Are you sure you want to take the risk?"

He chuckled. "I think I can handle it."

"All right. I think I'll be okay as long as we stick to the rules."

"Rules?"

"No baby talk."

Which he knew meant she didn't want to talk about his marriage proposal, either. "Okay. Give me about thirty minutes to shower and take care of a couple of things, will you?"

The couple of things involved the state of his apartment. It was its usual disorganized mess and he groaned at the thought he had only thirty minutes to get it in order. He moved as quickly as he could, picking up clothes, straightening tabletops, stuffing glasses and cups into the dishwasher.

She hadn't been there since the night of the hospital ball when they'd had little time for anything except satisfying their hunger for each other. As usual, his body reacted to the memories and he went straight to the shower for relief.

She arrived forty-five minutes later and apologized for being late. "I had trouble getting my hair to behave. Being pregnant has made it extremely unruly," she said, pointing to her red tresses, which did look a bit unruly to him. They went in every which direction, but he had a hunch it was an effect she'd created.

She wore a light jacket, which she kept on while giving his place a quick survey. "It looks different from when I was last here."

"Yes, well, we didn't spend much time in this room, did we?" If he thought he could get her to blush, he was wrong. To his surprise, she lifted one eyebrow provocatively and smiled.

"I don't think I've ever had my clothes off that fast." There was a sparkle in her eye telling him that she, too, remembered how oblivious they'd been to everything but each other. Then she spread her arm in a gesture that encompassed the entire room. "This definitely looks like you."

"Why do you say that?"

"There are books everywhere." She picked up one that was on the top of the stack next to his favorite chair and read the title aloud. *"The First Nine Months?"* Then she sifted through the rest of the pile. "I think you have all the bases covered when it comes to babies."

"It's new territory for me."

"Me, too." She rolled her eyes. "Oops, already broke the rule." She pulled a face, then looked around and spotted his chess set carved out of wood. She fingered several of the pieces saying, "A game for thinkers. Maddie says you're really good at it."

"What? Thinking or playing chess?"

She grinned. "Both."

"Maddie plays a pretty mean game of chess herself. What about you?"

She shook her head. "I never learned how."

"I could teach you," he offered.

She wrinkled her nose. "I don't think so."

"It might be good for the baby," he said in a tempting tone.

"Why do you say that?"

"You know how they say reading to the baby in utero stimulates the brain? Well maybe hearing her mom and dad discussing chess moves will give her an edge intellectually. As you said, this is a game for thinkers."

"But what if I'm horrible at it?"

"You won't be."

"You sound pretty sure about that."

He shrugged. "Just a hunch I have."

"We're doing it again," she told him.

"Doing what?"

"Breaking the rule."

He gave her a weak smile. "Sorry. But as long as it's broken, let me add very quickly that I've arranged to be at your doctor appointment next week. You did say you didn't mind if I was there, right?"

"No, I want you to come. We'll find out whether you're right."

Puzzled, he asked, "About what?"

"Always referring to the baby as a girl."

"That's because it is a girl."

"We'll see," she said with a playful grin.

Then her stomach growled and he said, "We need to get you something to eat. Should we walk or drive?"

"Walk. I need the exercise."

It was a beautiful autumn day with temperatures unseasonably warm—so warm the restaurant's patio was open for dining. He was pleased when she said she'd like to sit outside. Although they sat in the shade of an umbrella, when she tipped her head a certain way her red hair caught the sunlight.

She'd always been stunningly beautiful, drawing the attention of many male eyes. Today was no different. He didn't miss the looks of envy that came his way when they'd walked in together. She was by far the most beautiful woman he'd ever escorted anywhere and, like the night of the hospital ball, he found himself wishing that she wasn't with him out of a sense of duty.

Then he had to stop himself. He didn't need a beautiful wife. He needed a woman who loved him.

When he glanced across the patio he noticed Samantha at one of the tables. She wasn't alone. She sat next to a man he recognized as a lab technician from the hospital.

Krystal noticed something had distracted him and asked, "What's wrong? Is your mother here or something?"

He shook his head. "It's nothing."

She dropped her napkin on purpose so she could turn around and see what it was that had captured his attention. When she sat back up she said, "That's hardly nothing. It's your girlfriend with another guy. We can leave if you want.''

''There's no need to leave. She's not my girl-friend.''

''Because of me. I'm sorry.''

''You don't need to apologize, Krystal.''

''Yes, I do. If I hadn't…if this hadn't happened, you'd be with her right now. It just seems like a cruel twist of fate. I mean, the reason we went to the ball together was for you to get her attention and then you did and now this…'' She shook her head in regret. ''How can I not feel bad about that?'' A tear escaped, trickling down her cheek.

He reached across the table to stop it with his finger. ''You don't need to cry for me, Krystal.''

''I can't help it,'' she said on a broken voice. ''It's so sad.''

''What's sad is you crying over nothing. The reason Samantha and I aren't together has nothing to do with you or the baby.'' Although that wasn't quite the truth. He'd often found himself thinking about Krystal when he was with Samantha. He signaled for the waiter. ''We'd like our food to go,'' he told him when he appeared, then said to Krystal, ''We'll eat at my place. It'll be much more comfortable for both of us.''

''I don't know why I bother with eye makeup,'' she said as she dabbed at her eyes with a tissue.

''I don't know why you do, either. You certainly don't need it.''

''Yes, I do. My eyelashes are so light you can hardly see them.''

''That's what makes your face so interesting. You have red hair yet your lashes are blond.''

''Interesting?'' She looked at him as if he'd just told

her he liked her shoes because one was for the left foot and one was for the right.

The waiter came with their order, boxed and ready to go. Garret settled the bill, then ushered Krystal from the restaurant, grateful they didn't need to pass by Samantha and her companion.

For the first time since the night they'd spent together, he felt as if their relationship was back to where it had been before they'd made love. Instead of being uncomfortable around him, she seemed to enjoy his company. It was a good sign and gave him hope that by the time the baby arrived, they might actually be very good friends instead of acquaintances.

After they finished eating they took a walk down by the river, where they sat on a park bench and watched the barges slowly navigating the water. When a paddle wheeler went by with a load of passengers who waved at them, they waved back.

"That's the *Jonathan Padelford*. I haven't been on that since I was a kid and we went with our Cub Scout troop," he remarked.

"I've never been on it," she told him.

"You're kidding."

"No. You're forgetting I didn't grow up here. Where does it dock?"

He pointed to his left. "Over there at Harriet Island."

She shaded her eyes with her hand. "There's another paddleboat there now." She continued to gaze at the landing. "It looks like people are getting on. Do you need to buy tickets ahead of time?"

He shrugged. "I don't think so."

She jumped to her feet and stretched out her hands to him. "Then let's go take a ride."

"Now?"

"Sure, why not?" When he hesitated, she pleaded with him, "Come on. I've never been on a paddle wheeler. Please?"

The smile she gave him reminded him of the one she'd lured him to bed with. He knew he shouldn't respond to it, but he couldn't help himself. He had thought that because he'd slept with her, he'd destroyed the fantasy. Now he knew it wasn't true. She would always be a temptation for him.

"It's a bit of a hike," he warned. "And we might get there just as it's leaving."

"Then we'll have had a walk on a beautiful day." She tugged on his hands. "Please say yes."

He couldn't disappoint her. "Sure. Why not? There probably won't be many more September days like this."

They walked the short distance and discovered that the *Harriet Bishop* would be making one more trip on the Mississippi that afternoon and there were still tickets available. Garret thought Krystal was like a little kid, nearly jumping up and down with excitement at the thought of getting on the boat.

"Let's sit on the top," she said, then led him by the hand up the narrow staircase to the upper deck.

"It'll be sunny," he warned.

"I know but I don't want to be indoors." She found two chairs at the back of the boat where they could see the big wooden paddle wheel turn. "Isn't this great?" she said as the engine started and the wheel began to spin.

"Great," he agreed, and he didn't mean the boat ride.

It was the most pleasant hour and a half Garret had spent in a long time and he was sorry when the boat returned to the dock. He wanted to prolong their time together and suggested they get an ice-cream cone on the way back to his apartment. As they walked he told her he couldn't remember the last time he'd had such a relaxing afternoon.

"You work too much," she told him, licking chocolate from her fingers. "I know you're a dedicated doctor, but you need to make time for the fun things in life. You're far too serious."

"Doctors aren't supposed to be clowns, Krystal."

"Patch Adams was and his patients loved him."

He smiled. "That was a movie."

"Based on a real person."

"You love movies, don't you?"

"Mmm-hmm. Now that I'm pregnant my ideal job is being a taster for Ben & Jerry's ice cream. But when I was a kid I used to dream about directing movies. I wanted to travel all over the world and say, 'Lights! Camera! Action!' " There was a wistful gleam in her eyes.

"How come you never went to film school?"

"When you grow up in Fergus Falls, you don't think about going to film school."

"So you became a stylist instead of a cinematographer?"

"Mom said it was more practical than trying to make movies."

There was no regret in her voice and he knew it was because she liked styling hair. She'd told him that when she'd cut his hair for him that day of the hospital ball. No matter how hard he tried, he couldn't keep his thoughts from returning to that night. But then, why shouldn't they? With the wind blowing the fabric of her shirt against her body, he could see the gentle swell of her stomach where his baby was growing.

"Did I tell you I like that outfit on you?" he asked.

She looked down, as if she'd forgotten what she'd put on. "I guess the one nice thing about my pregnancy no longer being a secret is that I can now wear my maternity clothes and be comfortable." Her hand flew to her mouth. "I did it again, didn't I?"

"Considering we've been together all afternoon and there have only been a handful of references to—" he deliberately omitted the words "—I'd say you've done quite well."

She grinned. "I have, haven't I?"

"Want to talk about it now?"

She shook her head. "Why spoil a good day?"

He stopped and had her face him. "I don't want it to be a negative in my life, Krystal."

"I'm sorry. I shouldn't have said that. I don't want it to be a negative, either. It's just that lately I feel talked out on the subject."

He wanted to remind her that it was probably because she'd had over four months to talk about it. He'd only known about the baby for a few weeks.

He decided to let the subject rest. There would be plenty of time for them to discuss the issues that needed to be resolved. For now it was enough that the awkwardness between them was now gone. Because of the baby, their lives were forever going to be entwined. They needed to be friends. He wanted them to be friends. Not just for the baby, but for himself as well.

It was Monday morning and Krystal's first appointment of the day was Ida Longley. Wash, blue rinse, set, dry and comb out. Krystal had the routine down. Ida had been one of her first clients when she'd started at the salon. Like her friend Gladys, she was more than a customer to Krystal. She was like the grandmother

she no longer had, and Krystal took great care to make
sure she was satisfied each time she came in for a wash
and set.

"So tell me the news. Is it a boy or a girl?" Ida
asked the minute she saw Krystal.

"I don't know. They couldn't tell."

"What?" she squawked. "I thought that's why they
did an ultrasound."

"Actually, they do it to check to make sure the
baby's developing as it should. Getting to know the
sex is just a bonus. And in our case, we did get the
good news that the baby is right on schedule, but no
bonus information. The legs were crossed."

"Have you noticed anything unusual about your
breasts?" Ida asked her.

From anybody else it might have been an embarrassing question, but Krystal had become accustomed
to hearing off-the-wall remarks from her. "They're
larger, which is to be expected."

"Yes, but is one bigger than the other?" Ida asked
as she handed Krystal her walking stick.

Krystal frowned. She hadn't really noticed. "Is that
normal during pregnancy?"

"Oh yes," she said with a wave of her fingers.
"And if it's the right one that's larger, it means you're
having a boy. If the left one is bigger, you're having
a girl."

From the way Ida was staring at her, Krystal was
relieved she had put an apron on over her regular
clothes and her breasts were well hidden. "I'll have
to remember that," she said, helping her into the styling chair.

"Personally, I think it's more fun when you don't
know the sex of the baby. You get a big surprise."

"That's true, but it would have been nice to know.

Want me to take that for you?'' She reached for Ida's
purse so she could set it on the counter.

"Yes, but before I forget, I have something for
you.'' She reached into her bag and pulled out a small
plastic bottle. "They're papaya tablets. I read they're
good for indigestion and they're all natural.''

"Why thank you. That is so sweet of you,'' she
said, examining the label on the jar. She opened her
cupboard and set them inside.

Now that most of her regular clients knew about her
pregnancy, she'd been getting advice on everything
ranging from how to prevent stretch marks to what
drugs to take during delivery.

"I don't know if they work or not, but I thought it
was worth a try. I know how you like taking natural
remedies,'' Ida told her.

"I'll give them a try,'' Krystal told her, draping the
plastic cape over Ida's shoulders.

"Did you buy the support hose I told you about last
week?''

Krystal lifted her long skirt to reveal a length of her
leg. "Got them on today.''

"Good. You don't want to have trouble with vari-
cose veins.''

"I try to sit with my legs up during my breaks,''
she said, snapping the cape in place.

"You must be taking good care of yourself. You
look great. You've got that healthy pregnant glow.''

Krystal glanced in the mirror and knew what her
client said was true. She did look good and, to her
amazement, she felt even better. It was as if she'd
crossed the midway point in her pregnancy and a
switch had been flipped. She went from feeling terrible
to feeling fantastic practically overnight.

"I'm doing all right.''

"What about that feller of yours?"

Although it was no secret that she was a pregnant single woman, only a handful of people knew Garret was the father. Ida was one of those people. That's because on Monday mornings there was seldom anyone else around and she was a good listener.

"You know I don't have a feller, Ida," she gently chastised her.

"When a man wants to marry you, he's your feller," Ida told her with a wag of a finger.

"Yes, but if he's in love with someone else, he's *her* feller," she argued.

"But he didn't ask *her* to marry him. He asked you."

"Only because of the baby. I don't want a man marrying me out of a sense of duty," she said as she backcombed Ida's curls.

"Why think of it as a duty? Why not think of it as a gesture of love—love for a baby? You said he's a good man."

"He is."

"And that you trust him."

"I do."

"And he's very concerned about the baby."

"He is."

"So what's the big obstacle?"

She sighed. "His mother for one."

She flapped her hand. "Don't pay any attention her. She'll get over it."

"You think I should accept his proposal, don't you?"

"Hell, yes. Good men are hard to find. At my age, they're practically extinct. I'd settle for one that was alive," she said with a chuckle.

Krystal smiled and handed Ida a mirror, then swiv-

eled her around so she could see the back of her hair.
"What do you think of that?"

"Perfect, as always." Ida handed the mirror back
to her. "Now I feel as good as you look."

"You look good," Krystal told her, handing her the
walking stick and the purse.

"Thank you, dear, and I'll see you next Monday,"
Ida said, pressing money into her hand. "Take good
care of yourself until then and try not to worry. Things
have a way of working out for the best."

Krystal hoped she was right.

ALTHOUGH KRYSTAL KNEW that one of the things she
needed to work out before the baby was born was
housing, she hadn't given it too much thought until
she came home after work one night and found Carly's
suitcases in her room.

"Are you leaving?" she asked her sister.

"We're going to Grandma's," Emily answered.

Krystal looked at Carly. "Are you?"

She nodded. "First thing in the morning. I think
we've overstayed our welcome."

"Did Leonie say something to you?" She couldn't
believe that her landlady would do such a thing, but
she needed to ask.

"Well, she's not exactly kicking us out. Apparently
she has a tenant for that room who'll be moving in
the first of November. When she told me I took it as
a hint that I should find another place to live, like
ASAP, which is just as well. I really don't feel comfortable here anymore anyway."

Krystal heard the implication in her tone. "I suppose you think that's my fault."

"Well, she was a lot friendlier before she found out
about you and Garret, but I'm not blaming you. It's

time Emily and I found our own place anyway.'' She shoved a manila envelope toward her. ''This came today.''

Krystal opened it and found a petition for a divorce. ''Carly, I'm sorry.''

She shrugged. ''I knew it was coming. Now you see why I need to find a place of my own.''

''Have you looked through the classifieds?''

She nodded. ''I couldn't find anything in my price range, so I phoned a rental agent who's going to take me to look at some places this evening. I was hoping you'd come with me.''

Emily tugged on her hand. ''I'm going to have a lot of room to play.''

''That'll be fun, won't it?'' Krystal said with a smile.

''You can live there, too, if you want. Mommy said so.''

Again Krystal looked at her sister. ''I thought it might make more sense for us to share a house. I mean, you're not going to be able to stay here much longer, are you?''

It was something that had been on Krystal's mind, especially since Carly's arrival. She knew the three of them were an imposition on Leonie's generosity when she'd been on good terms with her landlady. Now that Leonie's attitude toward her had changed, there was an even greater incentive to move.

At one time she hadn't been able to imagine wanting to live anywhere but 14 Valentine Place. Now she knew she really had no choice. She was going to have a baby and even if Leonie wanted her to stay, it wouldn't be practical.

''No, I need to find another place, but...'' But she hadn't given any thought as to living with her sister.

Financially, it was a good idea, but would it be good for their relationship?

"I think it would work out really well for us, Krys." Carly did her best to persuade her. "Soon we're both going to be in the same situation—two single moms trying to raise kids. And it's not like we don't know how to get along. We shared a bedroom when we lived with Mom. We certainly could share a whole house, don't you think?"

Krystal had her doubts but didn't express them. "Are you sure there's no chance of you getting back together with Joe?"

"Believe me, Krys. It's over. Why don't you come with us to see the rental agent tonight? Emily would like that, wouldn't you, Emily?"

"Uh-huh." The four-year-old gave her a big grin.

Krystal knew it would be a solution to her housing problem, but then so would marriage to Garret. For weeks she'd been thinking about his proposal. At times she thought it was a realistic solution, and other times she thought she had to be crazy to even consider the idea.

"First I need to make a phone call," she told her sister.

"Are you worried about what Garret will say?"

"He is the baby's father."

Carly stared at her, hands on her hips. "Don't tell me you're actually thinking about marrying him? Krys, you're the one who told me that you would never settle for anything less than the right man. And believe me, marriage is tough enough the way it is without starting with one strike against you already."

"And what strike would that be?"

"Another woman in the picture? Everyone knows Garret's been seeing your neighbor upstairs."

"He told me he wasn't."

"And you believe him?"

"Yes, I did. Even if I don't marry him, I still need to tell Garret what I plan to do as far as housing goes."

She walked across the room to the small alcove where her dressing table was and dialed Garret's number. Getting his voice mail, she left him a message, then said to her sister, "I'll go with you to look at houses tonight, but I'm not going to make a decision just yet."

"But I need to find something soon, otherwise I'm going to end up staying here with you. Krys, you can't have the baby here."

Krystal knew she had a point. "How long are you planning to stay with Mom?"

"As short a time as possible. She said she'd go with me to get furniture from the house. Emily needs her own bed. I need the rest of my clothes among other things."

"Have you talked to Joe about taking stuff out of the house?"

"Yes, he said I could take what I need."

"And what about moving it all down here?"

"Mom knows a guy who has a pickup and a trailer."

And if he was like most of her mother's friends, he wasn't necessarily the most reliable person in Fergus Falls. Krystal sighed. "This has all happened pretty fast. Are you sure you're ready to make such a move?"

"Yes. I need a new start." She waved the divorce papers under her nose.

Krystal could see by the set of her sister's jaw that she wasn't going to be able to talk her into taking some time to think about it. "What about a job? Do you want me to ask at the salon and see if they need a receptionist?''

"You don't have to. I found one on my own," she boasted.

"Doing what?"

"Helping out in an office. It's a small company, on the bus line and the best part is, I'll have a great boss." She had a cagey grin on her face. "Want to know who it is?"

"Is it someone I know?"

Carly nodded. "It's Shane. He needs someone to help out…you know, answer phones, do some paperwork, that kind of stuff."

"I thought Jennifer did that for him."

"Apparently she doesn't have time for that anymore, now that she's gone back to school. Sounds as if she doesn't have time for much of anything when it comes to Shane and Mickey."

"Who told you that?"

She shrugged. "No one had to tell me. I have eyes and ears."

A hint of uneasiness narrowed Krystal's eyes. In the short time Carly had been staying at 14 Valentine Place she'd undergone quite a dramatic change. The first few days she hadn't bothered to even get dressed. She hadn't fussed with her hair or makeup, too caught up in her unhappiness to care about her personal appearance.

Today she wore an emerald sweater that highlighted the green in her eyes and a pair of slacks that showed that although she'd gained weight since she'd had Emily, she still had a nice figure. Her blond hair fell in gentle curls around her face, a face that was beautifully made up. Even her nails had been recently manicured. She looked good—almost too good for someone recovering from a broken marriage.

Suspicion had Krystal asking, "How did Shane know you were looking for a job?"

"I told him. Mickey's in Emily's Sunday school class."

Which could explain the reason her sister had decided the past few Sundays she needed to get her daughter to church. The uneasiness grew in Krystal's stomach.

She'd thought she'd noticed something different about her sister recently and now she knew what it was. There was a sparkle in her eye. When she'd first come to stay she'd been depressed, sleeping away most of her day, uninterested in life. Now she had color in her cheeks, enthusiasm in her voice. Krystal only hoped Shane Donovan wasn't the reason.

There was enough tension at 14 Valentine Place because of what had happened between her and Garret. Krystal could only imagine the fireworks that would fly if Shane were to show any interest in her sister.

The thought of moving was getting more attractive by the minute.

BEFORE THEY MET with the rental agent, Krystal warned her sister she was not going to make an immediate decision that evening. Although she knew Carly wanted to get on with her life, she also knew that her emotional state wasn't the most reliable at the moment. She told Carly it was always best to sleep on important decisions and to sit down and do the math to make sure the house was what they could afford.

After seeing the first two homes, Krystal didn't think she needed to worry about her sister rushing into any deal. It was a shock for her to see how expensive housing in St. Paul was compared to rental rates in Fergus Falls. After living in an upscale two-story with an interior designed by a professional decorator, Carly found it hard not to find fault with the rental properties the agent showed them. The rooms were too small, the carpets the wrong color, the appliances too old.

Krystal was tired and ready to call it quits for the evening, but the rental agent insisted they look at one more place that had a great location and was perfect for kids. The only problem was that it was out of the price range Carly and she could afford. However, once her sister saw it, she quickly forgot that money had anything at all to do with her decision.

Krystal could understand why her sister wanted the bungalow. It was perfect for a small family. The rooms were painted bright, cheery colors, the floors polished to a shine. The backyard was fenced with a swing hanging from a large oak tree. The kitchen had been recently remodeled with brand-new stainless-steel appliances and an eating counter as well as a breakfast nook.

"Look, Krys. There's a nursery!" Carly told her as the real estate agent flicked on a light in one of the bedrooms.

It was painted a soft yellow with nursery rhyme characters stenciled around the edges. Krystal could imagine a rocking chair in the corner, a crib along the inside wall.

"I think we should take this place," Carly urged her.

"It's nice, but..."

"Ooh, please don't say but. This house is perfect for us. You can have the room next to this one and I'll take the smaller bedroom next to Emily's."

It *was* nice. Krystal chewed on her lip, trying to

figure out how she and Carly would be able to afford it. She pulled her aside to talk finances.

"Are you going to be making enough to pay half of the rent on this place? Don't forget we have utilities, food, upkeep...." She rattled the items off on her fingers.

"I'm going to be getting child support for Emily," she told her.

"Do you know that for a fact? I thought you said Joe was broke."

"He is, but his folks will make him pay for Emily. They told me they will." She tugged on Krystal's arm. "Please say you'll go in on this with me."

"It's a lot of money."

"I know, but it'll be worth it."

Krystal was tempted to sign the rental agreement, but finally said, "I think we should sleep on it."

It wasn't what Carly wanted to hear. She moaned and groaned and pleaded with Krystal to have a heart and warned her that if they didn't act tonight, tomorrow it might be gone. She used every argument she could think of, including the fact that it would only get more uncomfortable at 14 Valentine Place the further along she was in her pregnancy.

It was that last argument that nearly had Krystal agreeing. Then her cell phone rang. It was Garret.

"Is everything okay?" There was concern in his voice and she realized that her message had alarmed him.

She stepped into one of the empty rooms to have privacy. "Everything's fine. I just wanted to tell you that I was going with Carly to try to find another place to live."

"Did Mom ask you to leave?" His voice resonated with disbelief.

"No," she quickly reassured him. "But I'm going to need a bigger place eventually and Carly's looking for something for her and Emily so we thought we might share a house. Actually, we're in one right now that looks as if it would work for us."

There was a silence, then he said, "I see."

"It's small, but there's a nursery. And it's in a good neighborhood."

"Is that what you want? To live with your sister?" Before she had a chance to answer, he said, "Excuse me a moment."

Krystal could hear muffled sounds in the background, mainly a woman's voice. It was a familiar one and she realized it belonged to Samantha. She felt a twinge—something like jealousy. She shook her head. Why would she care if Garret still saw Samantha?

"I'm sorry, Krystal. What were you saying?"

Apparently what Samantha had to say was of more interest. Again the tiny jab of jealousy surfaced, which she knew was ridiculous.

"I think this house might be a good solution for now," she told him.

"It sounds as if you've already made up your mind. I take it marriage is no longer an option."

It wasn't what she'd decided at all, but the woman's voice in the background reminded her of Carly's words earlier that evening. Did she really want to consider marriage to a man who was attracted to another woman?

"No, it isn't, and I need a place to live, Garret, and so does Carly. Before I make a decision I thought I should let you know."

"Thank you for that at least," he said a bit tersely. "I'd like to take a look at it. Give me the rental agent's name."

He wanted to make sure it was an appropriate place for his child to live. She knew it was what she'd want to do if she were in his shoes. If he were looking for housing for her baby she'd want to see where he planned to live.

Later that night she couldn't help but wonder if he hadn't been relieved when she'd told him she wanted to move in with Carly. It was a thought that kept her from falling asleep that night. And one that was on her mind the next morning when she awoke. In fact it bothered her all morning long. It wasn't until she glanced out the window and saw Samantha walking toward her car, smiling as she talked on her cell phone, that she realized why.

The reason she didn't want to see Garret with Samantha had nothing to do with the kind of stepmother she'd make. It was because she didn't want to see Garret with another woman.

She was jealous.

CHAPTER ELEVEN

THE FOLLOWING MORNING when Krystal left for work she ran into a rumpled Samantha coming home. Her clothes looked as if they'd been thrown on in a hurry, her hair, which was normally pulled back in a chignon, hung loose around her shoulders and she had a look about her Krystal recognized as one that said, *I'm sneaking in after spending the night somewhere I hadn't expected to be.*

"Hi. How are you?" Krystal greeted her with the standard neighborly greeting.

"I'm great, thanks," she said with a grin that could only be described as *If you only knew how great, you'd be so jealous.*

"Good," Krystal said pleasantly.

"And you?"

"Oh, I'm great, too," Krystal replied, which was hardly the truth. She hadn't slept much and her back was bothering her.

"I'm glad to hear that. Have a nice day," Samantha said, and continued up the stairs, humming to herself, definitely pleased about something.

Krystal could only imagine what...or whom. Memories of her phone call with Garret last night flashed in her mind. Samantha had been in the background. Laughing.

Throughout the morning at work, Krystal's mind drifted back to her conversation with Garret. She wished she knew what was going on in his head. Had he been disappointed that she wanted to move in with Carly or had he been relieved?

But that was the trouble with Garret. One never knew what he was thinking. When she first met him she thought he was simply shy. Now she knew it was more a case of him not talking about what was on his mind. It wasn't that he didn't want to share his thoughts with people. He simply wasn't in the habit of doing it.

Which was why Shannon suggested that Krystal ask him what he thought about her plan to live with her sister. It did no good to make assumptions about his feelings.

When he called her on her cell phone she was determined to do just that. She was in the middle of cutting a client's hair but excused herself, knowing that if she didn't talk to him she might not get another chance.

Before she could bring up the subject of marriage, however, he said, "I only have a minute, Krystal, so I need to talk fast. I saw the house. It's great. I don't see any reason you and Carly shouldn't rent it. In fact I ran into Carly there and I told her the same thing. She said the two of you had talked last night and that you had already decided to take the place if I approved, so it looks like you have a house. Carly can fill you in on the details. She has the lease."

Krystal gulped. "The lease? You mean it's a done deal?"

"Yes, I thought I just said that." He sounded a bit impatient and once again she could tell he was preoccupied.

"What about the rental deposit?" she asked, knowing her sister didn't have the money to cover it.

"It's taken care of," he answered.

"What do you mean it's taken care of?"

"I paid it."

"You shouldn't have done that!" she protested.

"Krystal, I have an obligation to this baby. Part of that obligation is to provide housing. This is a nice house. I wanted you to be there."

So she hadn't been imagining things last night. He *was* relieved that she'd decided to share a house with her sister.

"But the money—" she began but he cut her short.

"We can figure out the financial details another time. I really can't talk right now. I'll call you later." And with a quick goodbye he hung up.

She slowly clicked her cell phone shut and put it back in her pocket. Hearing Samantha's voice in the background during their phone conversation last night, seeing her on the steps this morning, and now hearing Garret's eagerness to have her rent the house all fed her suspicion that despite what he said, he was still interested in Samantha.

"Is everything okay? You look a little troubled," her client said as Krystal went back to her workstation.

"No, I'm fine. I'm just a little surprised at how quickly things happen, that's all. It looks like I'm going to be moving out of 14 Valentine Place."

KRYSTAL TRIED CALLING Carly numerous times that afternoon, but she had her cell phone turned off. After leaving a message three times and not getting a return call, she decided her sister was ignoring her. And rightly so. Carly had led Garret to believe that all that was needed for them to rent the house was his approval. It still angered her to think about it.

When she got home that evening she went straight

238   A BABY IN THE HOUSE

up to her room to tell Carly exactly what she thought of her methods. Only her sister wasn't there. She'd left a note saying she'd gone back to Fergus Falls to get furniture for their new place.

Krystal crumpled the note and threw it in the trash, then dialed her mother's number. She should have known better than to make that mistake. First of all Carly was not there and, secondly, her mother wasted no time telling her what she thought of her new living arrangements.

"Are you crazy?" her mother screeched in her ear.

"No, but I have a feeling I will be by the end of this conversation," Krystal said dryly, in no mood to be criticized by her mother.

"I can understand Carly not thinking clearly. She's devastated by what Joe's done to her, but you...you should know better."

"Well, Mom, this might come as a news flash, but I am not responsible for that house getting rented," she retorted.

"I can't believe you let a terrific guy like Garret Donovan slip through your fingers."

Krystal sighed. So that's what her mother was upset about. Not the fact that she and Carly would be living together, but that she hadn't accepted Garret's marriage proposal.

"For your information, Mother, I never had him in my fingers."

"Carly told me he wanted to marry you," she said in an accusing tone.

"Well I didn't want to marry him," she snapped back, although that wasn't exactly true. She wasn't sure what she wanted. Lately she'd been having feelings toward Garret that confused the issue, especially now that marriage was no longer an option.

"What is wrong with you?" her mother continued. "He's a doctor. Do you realize the kind of lifestyle he could have provided for you?"

Krystal knew it was pointless to argue with her mother so she changed the subject. "It's spilled milk, Mom. Give it a rest, will you? I need to talk to Carly."

"I told you she's not here. She went over to the house."

"Would you have her call me when she gets back? And while you're at it, ask her where the rental agreement is. I want to see what she's gotten us into."

"Don't you know?" The question was loaded with criticism.

"No, she went ahead and signed it without my knowledge. See how your 'always right, always perfect' daughter behaved?" She knew it was childish to attack Carly, but she'd had a lifetime of "you should be more like your sister" comments and she didn't need her mother acting as if she were once again the big sister leading the younger one astray.

"I gotta go, Mom. There's someone at my door," she told her even though it wasn't true. All they were doing was upsetting each other. She needed to end the conversation before things were said that they both would regret.

CARLY DIDN'T CALL HER BACK that night. Or even the next day. Krystal got tired of waiting for her to phone and went to the rental agent to get a copy of the agreement herself. It was only after she read it that she realized Garret had not only paid the damage deposit, but her portion of the rent. The lease was for a one-year period.

Now she knew why Carly had left town so quickly and why she didn't return her phone calls. Her sister

knew Krystal would be upset with the way she'd mis-
led Garret into thinking that the only reason she hadn't
signed the contract was because she'd wanted him to
see the house.

Krystal doubted she could feel any worse about the
situation. She had lived with Leonie long enough to
know that although Garret had finished his residency
and had a position at the clinic, he also had the burden
of a huge student debt from medical school.

Shannon laughed when she expressed her concern
about his financial status. She told her that no matter
how much student debt he had, he was still a doctor
with a good income.

That didn't matter to Krystal. She hated being indebted to Garret, which was exactly how she felt.
Again Shannon told her that she shouldn't look at it
as being in his debt. He did, after all, have a financial
obligation to his baby. To Krystal, that obligation
hadn't been defined clearly and until it was, she would
not be comfortable accepting anything from him.

That's why she decided to call him and ask him to
meet her. He told her he would be at 14 Valentine
Place that evening. As she hung up the phone she
wondered if he was coming to the house to see Samantha or his mother.

When she arrived home from work she saw his car
parked out back. Samantha's Volvo was not next to it.
Krystal used the private entrance. The fewer people
she saw, the better, which was why she'd brought dinner home to eat in her room.

She hadn't finished when there was a knock on her
door. She opened it to find Garret standing outside.

"Oh, you're home. I didn't see you come in," he
said as he stepped inside.

"I came up the side entrance," she told him.

"Still avoiding Mom?"

She shrugged. "It just seems easier."

"I just spoke to her. I didn't realize you hadn't told her about the house and I mentioned it. I'm sorry."

"It's okay. I'm sure she's relieved to hear that I'm moving."

"I think you're wrong about that."

He hadn't heard the conversation she'd had with Leonie and Krystal didn't see any point in telling him about it. "Maybe it would be better if we didn't discuss your mother."

"Probably," he agreed. "But I think you should know that you and I aren't the only reason she's unhappy. Shane told her today that he and Jennifer are having problems."

Uneasiness spread through Krystal like water on a flat surface. "You don't mean marital problems?" She hated to even ask the question. Seeing his nod, the uneasiness got stronger.

"Apparently Jennifer's been unhappy for a while," he said quietly. "They're thinking about trying a trial separation."

"But when Dylan and Maddie were here they announced they were going to try to have another baby," she said in disbelief.

"It turns out that was Shane's idea not hers. He hasn't said very much except that she told him she feels trapped and that she needs some space. Shane's frustrated."

And probably feeling lonely and hanging around Carly, who's emotionally vulnerable. Krystal didn't want to even contemplate the volatility of such a situation. "You don't think there's a third person involved, do you?"

"Shane says there isn't."

Krystal hoped he was right. She hadn't forgotten how her sister's face had glowed when she'd talked about Garret's brother. This did, however, explain why Jennifer was no longer Shane's assistant in the accounting firm.

"I hope they can work out whatever problems they're having," Krystal said sincerely.

He nodded, then pulled a card from his pocket. "There's something else I wanted to talk about with you." He gave her the card. "This is my insurance information. As soon as the baby is born, she—or he," he quickly added before she could protest, "will be covered under my policy."

"But I have health insurance," she told him.

"Yes, I know you do, but I'd like you to use mine."

First it was the clothes, then the rent, and now the health insurance. He was taking care of things she should have been taking care of herself and it bothered her. She didn't want to feel indebted to him, even if he was the father of her child.

She folded her arms together saying, "I appreciate you letting me know about this, but I would rather use mine."

"It doesn't make any sense to pay for yours when you can use mine. Besides, I have better coverage."

"How do you know you do?"

"When I went with you to your appointment I asked the claims rep at the clinic to look into it for us."

He was making decisions and taking control of things that should have been her responsibility. Intellectually she understood why he felt the need to do it, but emotionally she had trouble accepting it.

"I think we need to come to some kind of agreement as to just how much responsibility for this baby is yours and how much is mine," she said in a tone she hadn't meant to sound antagonistic, but she could see by the way his eyes narrowed that that was exactly the way he'd heard it.

"Why do you have so much trouble accepting help from me?"

"I don't. It's just…" She paused, wondering how to explain feelings she herself didn't understand. "I'm used to taking care of myself."

"Don't think of it as me doing things for you. It's for the baby. You're not telling me you're uncomfortable with me wanting to provide for my child, are you?"

She wasn't, so why was it so difficult to accept his help? "No."

"Then what is it you want me to do?"

She wished she had an answer to that question herself. She wanted him to be a father to her baby, yet when he made any sort of gesture that indicated he was acting in that role, she became uncomfortable. "I'm not sure how people handle a situation like this."

"We don't need to do what other people do. We can handle it any way we choose."

"Maybe it would be better if we waited until after the baby is born to discuss this." She could see by the look he gave her that he didn't like that suggestion.

"I'm sorry if you feel I'm forcing myself into your life, but you might as well get used to it, because I'm going to be there for my child, Krystal." He looked at his watch. "Now I have to go. If you need anything, call me."

He started for the door and she called out to him, "Garret." He turned to look at her. "Thank you…for putting the deposit down on the house—'' she waved the health card ''—and for thinking of this.''

"You're welcome," he said, and left.

As soon as Garret left, Krystal went downstairs to find her landlady. She found her in the great room, where she sat in the flickering light from the fire crackling in the fireplace. The rest of the room was in darkness.

"Leonie, could I talk to you?" she asked, walking into the room.

Her landlady glanced up and for just a moment Krystal caught a glimpse of sadness, but it was quickly replaced by a smile. She motioned to her, saying, "Come sit down and enjoy the fire with me."

It was the overture Krystal needed and she didn't hesitate to accept her invitation. "Thanks, I'd like that," she said, taking a seat on one of the chairs close to the fireplace. "This feels good. It's awfully cold for October."

"Yes. I've been chilly all day, but finally I'm warming up. I love the smell of birch when it burns, don't you?"

"Yes, it's nice."

There was silence except for the crackling of the fire as the dry wood snapped and popped in the flames. Krystal wished they could turn back the clock to the last time they'd sat and talked in front of a fire. It had been spring and life had been so uncomplicated back then. Her biggest worry had been how she was going to juggle dating three different guys. Now she was trying to figure out how she was going to juggle a baby and a career.

Leonie must have been having similar nostalgic

thoughts for she said, "This has always been a popular spot in the house."

"Yes, it has. It's a good thing those bricks can't talk. We've had some pretty wild discussions in this room."

"It has seen its share of girl talk, hasn't it?" she said with a faint smile.

"Yes. I'm going to miss it," she said quietly. "I know Garret told you that Carly and I have found a house to rent."

"Yes, he did."

"I'm sorry you had to hear the news from him. I was going to tell you myself, but it all happened rather suddenly."

Leonie held up a hand. "You don't need to explain, Krystal."

"Yes, I do. And not just about the house. If I had explained things a long time ago, maybe these past few months wouldn't have been so miserable for me and maybe I wouldn't have hurt you."

"You didn't hurt me, Krystal."

"I disappointed you."

Leonie sighed. "Well, that's true. A mother doesn't want to hear that her grandchild is coming into the world without the benefit of having two parents who love each other. But I've talked with Garret and I realize that although it's not a perfect arrangement, it's the best possible one for right now."

They were words Krystal needed to hear. "Thank you for saying that."

"You don't need to thank me. This is the era of blended families. I advise my clients to be open to family situations and I guess I should apply that advice to my own situation."

"One thing you can count on, I'm going to do my

best to be a good mother,'' Krystal stated with conviction.

''I know you will and I know that Garret will make
a good father.''

''I think so, too.''

''He's a fair man, Krystal. You know that no matter
what the future holds for either of you, he'll never
make unreasonable demands when it comes to custody
arrangements.''

The word *custody* made her shiver. It reminded her
that no matter how much she didn't want to think
about the baby in such terms, it was inevitable. She
and Garret wouldn't be living together and the possibility existed that both of them could marry other people.

''And as long as you're both willing to try hard to
make this arrangement work, that's all anyone can
ask,'' Leonie continued. ''It'll help that you and Garret are friends.''

''We are and I want it to always be that way.''

''I'm sure he does, too. Now tell me about this
house,'' Leonie said, switching topics. ''Garret says
it's nice.''

''Oh, it is. And it's not far from here. Maybe a
fifteen-minute walk. So I'll be able to bring the baby
over here or you could go there...if you want.''

''I'd like that. When do you plan to move?''

''The house is available the first of November,
which is when Carly will move in, but I want to give
you a sixty-day notice, so I probably won't move in
until you find someone to take my room.''

''You don't need to worry about your lease with
me,'' Leonie said.

''Yes, I do. It's not fair of me to leave you on short
notice.''

"I don't think I'll have any trouble finding a replacement for you. Garret told me Samantha may
know a couple of nursing students at the hospital who
are looking for housing."

Garret and Samantha. Again Krystal wondered
about their relationship. Were they seeing each other?
She was tempted to ask Leonie, but she couldn't bring
herself to do it.

"I should get to bed. I have to work in the morning," Krystal said, rising to her feet.

Leonie got up. "I'm glad we had this talk."

"Me, too."

"It's important to keep the lines of communication
open."

"I agree. There's one other thing I wanted to tell
you, and that's thank you for all the kindness and understanding you showed Carly while she was here,"
Krystal said with a heartfelt sincerity.

"I'm glad she's going to be all right. I was worried
about her when she first arrived."

"I know. So was I, but she's slowly getting back
on her feet." Krystal wondered if Leonie knew that
Shane had offered Carly a job. Considering what Garret had told her earlier that evening, she decided it
might be better not to mention it, as she was fairly
certain it would be Jennifer's place Carly took at the
accounting firm.

"Emily's a sweet child," Leonie remarked. "I hope
she can get through this without any emotional trauma.
Divorce can be devastating on children." Again the
sadness came into her eyes. "I don't know whether
Garret told you, but Shane and Jennifer are having
problems."

The fact that she brought up the subject gave Krystal hope that in time they would be as close as they

had been before her pregnancy had put a rift in their relationship. "I'm so sorry, Leonie. That's not the kind of news anyone wants to hear. I hope they can find a way to resolve them."

"I do, too," she said quietly.

Later, as Krystal lay in bed thinking about their conversation, she knew she needed to talk to her sister about Garret's brother. It would be very easy for Carly and Shane to be attracted to each other. They were both vulnerable. Each had a spouse that had rejected them. It was a prescription for trouble and Krystal only hoped that her sister would think before jumping from the frying pan into the fire.

IN THE FOLLOWING DAYS, neither Garret nor Leonie mentioned anything about Shane offering Carly a job. Although Garret did tell Krystal that Shane had hired someone from a temp agency until he found a permanent replacement for Jennifer, he gave no indication that Carly was in line for that position.

The last thing Krystal wanted was for Carly to be Jennifer's replacement in Shane's personal or his professional life. The tension in her relationship with Leonie was slowly easing and she didn't need her sister to complicate everything by getting involved with Shane. Each time she tried to warn Carly to be careful when it came to Garret's brother, however, her sister told her to mind her own business. Krystal thought if it was a preview of how they would get along once they were sharing the same house, they were in trouble.

Because Krystal knew Carly would need help with the move, she rearranged her work schedule so that she could drive up to Fergus Falls a day early and help with the packing. She knew it would be a little cramped staying at her mother's with Carly and Emily there, but it would only be for one night.

When she arrived at the trailer park, her mother looked startled to see her. "You must not have gotten Carly's message."

"What message?" Krystal had a feeling she wasn't going to like the answer to her question.

"There's been a change in plans."

Krystal shrugged out of her coat and tossed it over the arm of the sofa. "Why? What's happened?"

"Carly went with Joe to the Cayman Islands."

Krystal shoved her hands to her hips. "Is that where they went to get a divorce?"

Linda grimaced. "She didn't tell you, did she?"

The niggling doubts of suspicion that had been with her ever since she'd arrived at her mother's became one big concern. "Tell me what, Mother?"

"They're trying to work things out. That's why they went to the Cayman Islands. They want to see if they can recapture some of the magic. It's where they spent their honeymoon," she reminded her.

Krystal's mouth dropped open. "Magic? The last I heard he was planning to marry another woman."

"Oh, that's over," her mother said with a flap of her hand.

"Really." Krystal had trouble believing that one. "And where did they get the money to go to the Cayman Islands? I thought he was filing for bankruptcy."

"Apparently his parents are going to help him and Carly get back on their feet."

"Are they going to put a choke collar on him so he can't go to the casino?" She shook her head in disgust. "How many times are they going to bail him out?"

"They're good people, Krys."

She didn't comment. "Where's Emily?"

"She's with her other grandparents."

"The good people," Krystal stated dryly.

"I know you wanted Carly to come back to the city so you'd have someone to live with you in that house you rented—" she began, and Krystal cut her short.

"*I* rented? No, Mom. *Carly* rented the house, not me. She wanted *me* to live with *her*. And now she's left me with a one-year lease on a place I can't afford."

That silenced her mother.

Krystal paced the small space in the trailer home, rubbing her brow. "I can't believe Carly did this."

"You don't want her to try to save her marriage?"

"Yes, but…" She also wanted her sister to be responsible for her obligations and one of those was a house in St. Paul that Krystal was now going to have to occupy by herself. "I can't believe she did this to me!" she repeated, although it really wasn't quite true. What she meant was she couldn't believe she'd been so foolish to even contemplate setting up house with her sister when her life was in emotional turmoil.

Krystal should never have taken her to look at rental houses until Carly had worked through her problems. She should have waited until the divorce was final, until Carly could at least make decisions without weeping.

"I'm screwed," she said in frustration.

"Watch your language in this house, young lady," Linda said in a stern voice.

"Well, what would you call it? Mom, I'm six months pregnant, I have no furniture other than the few things in my room at Leonie's, I have bills piling up, I don't know what I'm going to do for day care, and now my sister runs off with her ex-husband to some tropical island and leaves me footing the bill for her mistake!''

"I have some money saved. How much do you need?'' Linda offered.

Krystal knew her mother saved very little money and what she did have was for those rainy days when illness kept her from working. She couldn't take away the small bit of security her mother had.

"It's all right, Mom. I'll figure something out,'' she said. "I'm going to go.''

"You're driving back to the city at this time of night?''

She nodded. "I can't stay, Mom. Please don't ask me to.''

"Don't be angry at your sister, Krystal. She's got a child to think about.''

"You know what, Mom? So do I,'' she said, and walked out the door.

"WHAT ARE YOU DOING HERE?'' Shannon asked her the following day. "I thought you were helping Carly move today.''

"I was supposed to be but she went to the Cayman Islands with Joe.''

Shannon was as shocked as Krystal had been. "You're kidding, right?''

"No, I'm not.''

"They're getting back together?''

"It sounds as if they might be, but with my sister, who knows? All I know is I no longer have a room-mate.''

"Oh, Krys, I'm so sorry. What are you going to do?''

Krystal shrugged. "I don't know. Maybe get a part-time job and see if I can swing the rent on my own.''

"There has to be another solution than for you to work two jobs. I mean, you can do that for now, but what about when the baby comes? If I hadn't just renewed my lease, Josh and I would move in with you."

She waved her hand. "It's all right. I'll manage somehow. I'll have to."

"Maybe if you talk to your landlord and explain the situation he'll let you out of the lease."

"Maybe," she said thoughtfully. "I'm still going to have to find a place to live. I've given Leonie my notice and she already has another tenant who has signed a lease. Anyway you look at it, I have to move."

"Maybe Garret can help you. Have you discussed this with him?"

"I can't ask him for help. Everything is going good right now. Leonie and I are talking again and I don't want money getting in the way and messing things up. Besides, I don't want to look like a charity case."

"From what I know about the Donovan family, I don't think any of them would think of you in that way."

"Probably not, but I do have my pride."

"Are you sure that's all it is?" Shannon folded her arms across her chest.

"Why are you looking at me like that?"

"Krys, are you sure you haven't fallen for Garret?"

"No!" She was quick to deny the accusation. "He is so *not* what I'm looking for in a guy."

"Are you sure?"

She wasn't, but she didn't want to admit that to Shannon. "You can't honestly think that I'm falling in love with him? We're friends for Pete's sake."

"Friends who went to bed together," she reminded her.

"Yes and you know why."

"Oh Roy shmoy. You were never in love with him."

"Shannon! How can you of all people say that?"

"Because I don't think you were. Krys, haven't you ever wondered why you could go to bed with Garret so easily that night of the ball? I mean, Roy had cheated on you before, yet you never went to bed with another guy to get over the pain."

Shannon wasn't saying anything Krystal hadn't already said to herself, but she didn't want to be having this discussion. "There's no point in talking about this. Roy's gone and out of my life for good and Garret's attracted to another woman."

"Again I ask you, are you sure?"

She sighed. "Yes. You saw how fast Roy bolted when he discovered I was pregnant."

"I meant are you sure about Garret. Looks like he's your man, to me."

"Didn't you hear what I just said? He's attracted to another woman." She made a sound of exasperation. "Can we not talk about this?"

"I'm sorry, Krys. I didn't mean to upset you."

Krystal sighed. "It's all right. The trouble is, this isn't getting my housing problem solved."

"Maybe Carly will come back from the Cayman Islands and tell you she and Joe gave their marriage one last chance and it didn't work."

"Maybe." There was still that possibility, Krystal realized. But long after she and Shannon had gone back to their workstations, it wasn't the housing dilemma on Krystal's mind. It was Shannon's suggestion that she could be falling in love with Garret.

Yes, he was different from any man she'd ever known. And they were having a baby together. It was only natural that she'd have some feelings for him. But love? It just wasn't possible. Or was it?

CHAPTER TWELVE

THE FOLLOWING WEEK Krystal applied for several part-time positions at various department stores, but she knew that even if she worked the extra hours, it was going to be difficult to earn enough to afford the house. Every time she went over her budget figures she ended up drawing the same conclusion. Without Carly, she couldn't make the rent.

When her sister phoned her after her trip to the Cayman Islands, she tried to keep her emotions under control, but it wasn't easy, especially when Carly's voice held a hint of petulance. "Mom warned me you were going to be angry,"' she told Krystal.

"Can you honestly blame me, Carly? Why didn't you at least call me and tell me what was going on?"

"Because I knew you'd be upset! You know how awful my life has been these past couple of months. And I didn't know if you'd try to talk me out of going with Joe."

Krystal knew her sister had a point, but didn't comment.

"Would you have been able to be objective at that time?" Carly didn't expect an answer and continued on. "I went with Joe because I needed to make sure I was doing the right thing for me and for Emily. St. Paul is a long way from Fergus Falls."

"I know it is, Carly, which is why I suggested we not rush into getting the house in the first place," she reminded her. She sighed, knowing that it did no good to bring up the reason they were in this mess. It wouldn't change anything.

"I'm really sorry, Krys. Truly, I am."

"So are you and Joe getting back together?" Krystal had a feeling she already knew the answer, but she needed to ask the question anyway.

"Yes. I know you're upset about the house. Mom says you're worried about the legal ramifications, but you don't need to worry. I'll call the landlord and explain the situation. The worst thing that will happen is we'll lose our deposit."

"Carly, that money's not ours. It's Garret's. Do you realize what an uncomfortable position you put me in because of this?"

"I know and I'm sorry, Krys, but if you could have seen how Emily cried when she saw Joe. It just broke my heart. For her sake, Joe and I have got to try to make this work."

As frustrated as Krystal was by Carly's behavior, she knew that more was at stake than a rental deposit and a lease agreement. "I understand that and I'm not criticizing you for wanting to save your marriage. It's just that your actions have put us—and especially me—in a big financial mess."

"And I told you—I'm going to get the mess with the house straightened out," she insisted.

"How?"

"Don't worry about it. I've talked to Joe's dad and he says there's no lease that can't be broken. He's amazing when it comes to straightening out financial messes."

Krystal wanted to say he must be if a near-bankrupt Joe had been able to take Carly to the Cayman Islands. "Will you do it today?" she asked, needing the peace of mind of knowing that it was resolved without Garret's involvement.

"Yes. Trust me. It'll be fine."

Krystal had her doubts but decided there was no point in worrying until she heard from her sister that there was a problem. To her surprise, Carly called a short while later with the news that the original lease agreement had been voided. Since there was another party interested in renting the house immediately, the landlord agreed to only deduct a cancellation fee from the damage deposit.

"I hope you told him to take it out of your check?" Krystal told her sister.

"Of course I did," she replied. "It was my fault we didn't take the place. You can relax. No one lost any money and everything's fine."

"It's not quite fine, Carly. I still need to find a place to live."

"If you want me to come down and go looking with you, I will," she offered.

"No, it's all right," Krystal said in resignation.

"You were there for me when I needed you, Krys, and I really appreciate it. I only hope you can understand why I went back to Joe and try to be happy for me."

"I do want to be happy for you, Carly and I hope that this reconciliation with Joe works—for your sake and for Emily's," she said sincerely. She didn't add that she wasn't convinced it would work. She wanted to believe that her brother-in-law could make changes in his life and be the husband and father Carly and Emily needed, but she'd spent the past five years wanting to believe that Roy could change into something he wasn't.

"You should be happy I'm not going to be living

in St. Paul,'' Carly continued. ''At least now you won't have to worry about anything happening between me and Shane Donovan.''

''I wasn't worried about that,'' she lied. ''I knew you were just being friends during a time when you both were going through some problems.''

''Yes, we were. How are things between him and Jennifer?'' Carly asked.

''I'm not sure. I haven't seen Shane recently,'' Krystal answered, not wanting to discuss Garret's brother and his wife. She changed the subject, asking her sister about Emily. By the time they said goodbye, the tension that had been in their relationship at the start of the call was gone.

Carly's last words were, ''I'm glad everything's okay between us, Krys.''

Krystal expressed the same sentiment and hung up the phone, relieved that Carly had taken care of the problem involving the house. It was one less worry for her and meant she wouldn't have to feel indebted to Garret. She only wished that the rest of the issues she had with him could be resolved so easily.

GARRET WASN'T ONE to surprise people. He himself didn't appreciate getting caught unaware so he seldom sprang anything on anyone. Only sometimes the surprise was warranted, which was why he was on his way over to 14 Valentine Place with a trunk full of moving boxes to give to Krystal. It was not what she would be expecting to have dumped on her doorstep on a Monday morning.

Actually, she wouldn't be expecting to see him, either. It had been a while since he'd last seen her, and not because busy schedules had kept them from running into each other. He was fairly certain she had deliberately been avoiding him. Why else wouldn't she have told him about Carly wanting out of the house lease?

If it hadn't been for the fact that his name was on the rental agreement, he doubted that he'd even know there had been a problem. That made him all the more determined that today she would be the one getting the unexpected news.

When he pulled into the alley behind 14 Valentine Place, he parked next to her car, then opened his trunk and removed the cardboard boxes he'd stowed there last night. When he went inside he found Krystal and his mother in the kitchen eating breakfast.

"Well, good morning," his mother called out when she saw him. "This is a surprise."

"A good one, I hope," he answered.

"Of course," she said with a smile. Seeing the startled look on Krystal's face, he was fairly certain she didn't share his mother's opinion. "We're having muffins and coffee. Want to join us?"

"Sure, but first I need to get rid of these." He raised the boxes slightly. "They're for Krystal." Seeing the quizzical look on her face, he added, "My neighbor was going to toss them but I thought they'd make good moving boxes."

"They're the right size—not too big so that you won't be able to lift them once they're full," Leonie commented. She looked at Krystal and asked, "Do you want him to take them upstairs right away or should I put them in the storage room until you're ready to use them?"

"I should probably take them upstairs," Garret answered for her, then gave her a pointed look. "Now that Mom's found a tenant for your room, you're probably going to want to move before the weather turns nasty and cold.''

She looked reluctant to take him up on his offer, but she finally said, ''You can put them in my room.''

He followed her up the steps, admiring how slender she looked from the rear. Unless she turned to the side he couldn't even tell she was pregnant. She held her door open for him as he carried the stack of boxes into her room and set them on the floor.

''Looks like you could use some help. You haven't started packing,'' he said, glancing around.

She bit on her lower lip, then said, ''It's probably a good thing you came over this morning. I need to tell you something. Carly and I aren't moving into the house.''

He feigned innocence. ''Why not?''

''Joe convinced Carly they should give their marriage another chance. She decided to stay in Fergus Falls, so she won't be needing a place to live here.''

''Well, maybe she doesn't, but you still do,'' he pointed out.

''An apartment maybe. Not a whole house. But you don't have to worry about the money you put down. Carly called the landlord and explained the situation. He was very understanding and let us out of the lease agreement.''

''Is that right?''

She nodded eagerly. ''He said you'll get your damage deposit back within ten business days.''

He shook his head. ''I don't think so.''

Krystal looked puzzled. ''Sure you will. I told you, Carly was able to cancel the lease.''

''No, she was able to get her name off the lease because I was willing to keep my name on it,'' he told her.

He had definitely surprised her with that information.

"What are you talking about?" She eyed him suspiciously.

"When Carly called the landlord and asked to get out of the lease, he called me. I assured him that even though Carly didn't want to live at the house, I knew someone who did." He wiggled his brows. "You."

"But I can't afford that place!" she protested.

"Maybe not, but I can."

"Are you saying the reason Carly was able to get out of the deal was because you absorbed her responsibility?" He could see she was flustered. Her cheeks had more color than he'd seen in a long time.

"Yes. So you'll still be able to move in next week. The only thing that's changed is that you won't have Emily and Carly as housemates."

He expected her to smile and say thank you, that it was a very thoughtful thing for him to do, but she frowned and looked at him as if he'd done something to personally offend her.

"I wish you hadn't done that," she said stiffly.

"I thought you wanted to live there? Carly said you especially liked the place because it had the nursery for the baby."

"It's a great house for a baby, but I can't afford to pay that kind of rent."

"And I told you I would take care of the rent for you."

She was more than flustered. She was upset. She folded her arms across her chest in a defiant stance and shook her head. "No, I can't let you do that!"

"Why not?"

"Because it makes me feel indebted to you."

"Why should it? I'm the reason you need to move.

It's my child you're carrying which makes me responsible for both of you.''

"No, you're not responsible for me," she stated adamantly.

The outburst of emotion surprised him. "What's with your attitude anyway? Do you realize how many women in your situation would be grateful to have the fathers of their babies behave in a responsible way?''

"I am grateful," she insisted. "It's just that I'm used to taking care of myself and if I let you pay half of the rent even though we're not..." She paused, as if searching for the right words. "Involved in any type of relationship, it wouldn't be right.''

"We have a child together. Isn't that a relationship?" he asked.

"Yes, but..."

"And aren't we equally responsible for that child?"

"Yes, but..."

"So you agree it's a fifty-fifty deal.''

"Yes, but..."

"Then I'll pay half of the rent and you'll pay the other half." It was said with an authority that dared her to challenge it. He expected she would and he wasn't wrong.

"I can't let you do that. You'd be paying rent on two places," she protested with indignation on his behalf.

"Not if I sublet my apartment and move into the house I won't be." It was an argument he had been prepared to use should the need arise. He was fairly certain she didn't want him to pay double rent. "I know you don't want to be married for the baby's sake, but we could be roommates—for the baby's sake, of course." She didn't have a response to that suggestion and he wasn't sure if it was because she was shocked or if she was trying to think of a way to tell him what an awful idea she thought it was.

He decided to use the silence to argue the advantages of such an arrangement. "Carly backing out of the deal could be the solution we've been looking for when it comes to figuring out how we're going to share parenting duties. You know I hate the thought of being a part-time parent and, with the hours I work, it's going to be difficult to arrange a visiting schedule. If I were living in the same house as you and the baby, it would mean I'd get to see her every day instead of whenever our schedules would allow it."

She still didn't say anything, which was unusual for Krystal. She normally reacted immediately and emotionally to everything he said.

"Was Carly wrong? Didn't you like the house?" he prodded.

Finally she spoke. "Yeah. I liked it a lot. But are you sure this is what you want?"

"I wouldn't be suggesting it if it wasn't," he answered.

"You told me you didn't believe in couples living together outside of marriage," she reminded him. "That it wouldn't be a good example for a child to see."

"We wouldn't be a couple, Krystal. We'd be roommates."

That brought more color to her cheeks. "Oh."

She appeared to give his suggestion some consideration, chewing on her lower lip as she mulled it over. "We'd have to agree to some things."

"Like what?"

"How we handle our private lives. Whether guests can stay the night. That type of thing."

Was she referring to her having men friends over?

He didn't think she'd been dating. "We can say no overnight guests without consulting each other."

She nodded. "What about *special* friends?"

"Are you talking about me wanting to bring women home?"

"You don't think it'll happen?"

"No. I told you. I'm not seeing anyone. Are you seeing anyone?"

Her hand pointed to her tummy. "With this?"

"You're every bit as beautiful pregnant as you are when you're not." It was the truth. He'd hoped that his physical attraction to her would wane with time, but it only grew stronger. "Actually, I think you're more beautiful now than I've ever seen you."

That caused her to blush and she looked away from his gaze. "I wish you wouldn't say things like that."

"Why not?"

"Because it—" she glanced around the room as if looking for the words "—it's distracting us from the issue here. We're talking about rules for being room-mates. Having guests can be a serious problem."

"Not for me it won't be. I'm not having any."

"Me neither," she said, then quickly added, "—unless my sister or my mom come for a visit."

"Relatives aren't a problem. In case you haven't noticed, I have a few myself." He grinned, trying to lighten the mood. It didn't work.

Her brows drew together and she asked, "What about your mom? Do you think she'll object to us living in the same house?"

"Does it matter if she does?"

She hesitated only a moment before shaking her head.

"We have to do what we think is best for the baby, Krystal." He paused a moment, then said, "I'm not suggesting a lifetime arrangement here. Just one year until we get the hang of this parenting stuff.''

She hesitated only a second longer, then said, ''Okay. We'll give it a shot and see what happens.''

He smiled and thought surprises weren't so bad after all.

''SO ARE YOU ALL SETTLED in your new place?'' Most of Krystal's regular clients knew she'd moved out of 14 Valentine Place so the question came as no surprise to her.

''I'm getting there.''

''And how do you like it?''

''It's great having so much room,'' she said as she applied color to the woman's hair.

''Then you don't miss the boardinghouse?''

''I miss having people around all the time. It's so quiet.''

''What about your guy? He must make some noise, doesn't he?''

Garret wasn't her guy, but she didn't correct her client's mistake. She knew it was impossible to hide the fact that she was pregnant and single, but she didn't need to divulge the details of her relationship with Garret.

''I hardly ever see him. I think he works even more than I do.'' She didn't realize how many hours he did put in until he'd moved in with her.

''Last time I was in you said you'd signed up for the prenatal classes. Is he going with you for that?''

''He said he would, but last night was our first one and he had an emergency so Shannon went with me. Not that it matters. Being a doctor, he probably knows all the information they give at those classes anyway.''

"It's still nice that he wants to go with you," she remarked.

It was nice and Krystal appreciated that he'd made the effort to enroll in the classes. She only wished he was doing it for a different reason. Last night there'd been several couples in the course who were obviously very much in love and happy to be having a baby. For Krystal it had almost been a relief not to have Garret there. She didn't want anyone to see that he wasn't in love with her.

"Have you picked out any names?" her customer wanted to know.

"We both like Emma."

"What if it's a boy?"

"We haven't been able to agree on a boy's name. He's convinced it's a girl."

"Show me your hands," the client demanded.

Krystal set down the color and brush on the counter, then shoved her hands out in front of her.

"He's right. It's a girl," she declared on a note of glee.

"What makes you say that?"

"You showed me your hands with your palms up. If you'd had palms down, it would have meant you're having a boy."

Krystal chuckled. "I have a client who's convinced it's a boy because when I drink my tea I lift my mug by the handle."

"I haven't heard that one before, but I know the palm test works. It's been right twenty-three times in a row so far. You'll see," she said with a knowing nod of her head.

"So you're saying I don't need to worry that I haven't a boy's name picked out?" Krystal asked with a dubious grin.

"Nope, you won't need it. You're lucky your guy wants a girl. Most men want a son the first time around," she remarked.

It was true that Garret often referred to the baby as she, but Krystal honestly didn't know if he was truly hoping it was a girl, because he hadn't told her his preference. Garret kept most of his thoughts about the baby to himself. Unless she asked him specific questions, he seemed content to go about daily life without much conversation at all.

Being a people person, she found it frustrating to live with someone who was perfectly content to keep to himself. She could have been living alone. When they were home together Garret closeted himself in his room with the door shut. Krystal wasn't sure what he did in there at night. Judging by the number of bookcases he owned, she figured he was probably reading.

That's why she was surprised when she arrived home from work one evening and found him in the kitchen cooking. She didn't think he did cook. He seldom left dirty dishes in the kitchen.

"Something smells good," she commented.

"It's chili."

Noticing the size of the pot, she asked, "Are you having guests?"

"As a matter of fact I am. I hope you don't mind?"

She shook her head. "No, go ahead," she told him, wondering whether they were male or female. "I'll make myself scarce."

"You don't have to do that. It's only Shane and Mickey."

"Not Jennifer?" she asked.

He shook his head. "No, they're still separated." He lifted the lid on the pot and stirred the contents.

"So you invited your brother and nephew over for supper. That was nice of you," she remarked.

"I have an ulterior motive," he admitted with a sheepish grin.

"And what would that be?" She rose to the bait.

"Look in the nursery."

She hung up her coat in the closet before walking down the hallway to the small bedroom connected to hers. It had been empty ever since she'd moved in, but now there was a bookcase filled with children's books along one of the walls. It was what was in the middle of the room, however, that had her mouth gaping. Scattered on the floor were various parts of what appeared to be a crib. She went back to the kitchen.

"Where did that come from?"

"I thought it was time we got that room ready. You never know when a baby's going to decide to arrive early." He clanked a lid onto a pan and faced her, a wooden spoon in his hand. "Bookcases I know how to put together. Cribs are another thing, which is why I called Shane. He knows his way around nuts and bolts much better than I do."

They hadn't talked about buying a crib yet. Although she and Shannon had looked at nursery furniture when they'd been at the mall, it was a purchase she thought she could delay until she was closer to her due date. It was also something *she* wanted to buy for her baby. Once more she had the feeling that he was making decisions and taking control of things that were her responsibility.

"I wish you had told me you were going to buy it," she stated as evenly as she could and trying not to sound unhappy.

"I thought I did tell you. It's been on my mind for quite some time."

"But that's just it. It was on your mind. You didn't tell me because you don't tell me anything!" To her dismay her voice rose, making it sound more like an accusation than a plea for understanding. It was exactly what she didn't want to have happen.

He put the spoon down and looked at her. "I'm sorry you feel that way," he stated calmly. He didn't speak immediately and she could see that he was carefully measuring his words before he did tell her what was on his mind. "We're in a situation that is new to both of us and, naturally, it'll take some time to adjust."

At that moment Mickey burst through the door like a whirlwind of energy. "We brought something for my cousin!" he boasted, his cheeks red from the brisk November wind.

Following behind him was Shane carrying a wooden cradle. "Since you're getting the baby's room ready I thought I might as well bring this over."

He set the cradle down in the middle of the kitchen floor and looked at Krystal. "This thing has been in the Donovan family for generations. Mickey here left his mark on it with a few crayons, but I sanded off his artwork and refinished it," he said, mussing his son's hair affectionately.

"Didn't Great-Grandpa Donovan carve this himself?" Garret asked, admiring the antique. "I thought Mom said you were going to ship it over to Dylan?"

He shook his head. "Maddie didn't want to risk anything happening to it in transit so Mom said I should give it to you and Krystal." He looked at her then and said, "I know Jennifer liked having it because she could keep it next to the bed at night."

When she didn't comment immediately, Garret said, "If you don't want it, I'll put it in my room."

It was an awkward moment and Krystal wished she had worked late instead of coming home. She wondered if she would ever stop feeling uncomfortable about her relationship with Garret.

"We probably don't need to decide what to do with it tonight, do we?" she said weakly, then added, "If you'll excuse me, I've got things to do."

"Aren't you going to have supper with us?" Shane wanted to know. "Garret makes a pretty mean chili...but you probably already know that. You live here."

She didn't know about the chili, but she was learning a lot about Garret that she hadn't known until she'd become his housemate. Like the fact that he worked the crossword puzzle every day in the paper while he ate his breakfast, which usually consisted of cold cereal and fruit. And he occasionally sang in the shower and he left his shoes in the same spot next to the door every night. And he did his own ironing and often forgot to take his clean clothes out of the dryer.

She'd always known he'd be a good doctor, but until she'd overheard him returning a phone call to one of his patients after hours she hadn't realized just how good he would be. He was dedicated to his work and passionate about helping people. It was why he was so solicitous of her health, so concerned for her well-being. He had a good heart, which was why she was living with him and not in a tiny apartment barely big enough for one person let alone a mother and child. It only made her feelings toward him grow stronger each day and wish that his actions weren't motivated out a sense of duty.

"You're welcome to join us," Garret seconded his brother's invitation.

Welcome to join us. Krystal noticed he didn't say,

Please stay. I want you, too. She tried not to let her emotions get the better of her, but she couldn't stop the self-pity. She felt like a big albatross around the Donovan family's neck. They tolerated her because they were good people and they wanted to do what they could to make everything go smoothly for the Donovan baby she carried.

But as she stood there in the kitchen looking at the Donovan heirloom cradle and thinking about the crib in the other room the two brothers were about to tackle, she didn't want him doing all those things for her because she was the mother of his child. She wanted him to do them because he loved her.

Mentally she shook herself. She stared at Garret and saw the same face, the same eyes, the same smile she'd seen every time she'd looked at him in the past three years. Only something was very different. Before, when she'd stared into those dark eyes, she'd seen a friend. Now she saw the man she loved.

It was an overwhelming realization, one that had her staring at him in bewilderment, wondering when it had happened. How could she have fallen in love with him and not been aware of it?

"Krystal, are you okay?" Garret asked.

She swallowed nervously. "Yeah, I'm fine," she mumbled, then excused herself and hurried to her room before either he or his brother saw on her face what was in her heart.

WHEN GARRET ARRIVED at the nursing home, he found Dolly Anderson in the solarium seated in a chair next to the window. She looked perfectly content as she gazed at the snow falling at a steady pace.

"So this is where you are," he said, walking into the glass-enclosed room.

"Isn't it lovely, Dr. G.?" she said, referring to the scene outdoors. "I know it's early to be getting this heavy a snowfall, but it's so beautiful." Her sigh was one of contentment. "They told me you might not be coming today. I should have known a little snow wouldn't stop you from doing your work."

"It's a little sloppy out there, but the road crews are doing their job and keeping the streets clear," he told her. "You ought to know by now, Dolly, that nothing can keep me away from you." He produced a box of gingersnaps from his bag.

Her eyes twinkled. "That is so sweet of you," she cooed. "I suppose now you want to take me back to my room so you can get me out of my clothes."

"The thought did cross my mind," he said with a flirtatious grin.

She giggled and struggled to her feet with his assistance. "A handsome doctor like you... I can't believe you're still single. Have I told you about my little gal who does my hair?"

"I believe you have," he said, helping her as she navigated toward the door using her cane.

"She's the sweetest thing," she said, her tone one of amazement. "And other people think so, too. I'm not the only one who thinks she's a gem."

"I'm sure she's very nice."

"Oh, she is. She listens to what you have to say. I mean really listens. I think you'd like her if you met her."

"I'm sure I would," he said with an indulgent grin.

"It's too bad you weren't here earlier this morning. She was here. You two could have met."

Sometimes being behind schedule wasn't such a bad thing, he thought as he helped her back to her room.

"You said she's pretty. She probably has a boy-friend."

"Uh-uh. She likes this one fella, but she said he's all wrong for her. Who knows? Maybe you'd be the right one, now that you're not going to the Doctors Without Borders program."

"I still don't have time for women, however," he told her.

"You need to make time," she advised him. "You should come to the party next week. She's going to be there. When she found out they needed someone to help with the entertainment, she volunteered." She sighed again. "Wasn't that sweet of her?"

"Very."

"What I like about her is she always has a smile on her face."

"Sounds like you, Dolly." They'd reached her room and he led her over to her favorite chair. "Now you sit right there. I'm going to close your curtains so no one sees what's going on between you and me," he told her with a wink.

"But the snow is so pretty,'" she protested.

"It'll just take us a minute."

"Boy, you are good, aren't you?" she quipped.

He grinned and wagged his finger at her. "Ah, Dolly, you are one sharp lady." As he reached for the cord on her drapes he automatically glanced outside to where his car sat in the parking lot. Although he'd arrived a short while ago, it was already covered with snow.

He had started to pull the drapes shut when he saw a familiar red head. It was bent over the windshield of a car, clearing away the snow. Its owner wore a dark green jacket, black slacks and a pair of chunky-heeled shoes that were totally inappropriate for the weather.

"Dolly, what did you say the woman's name is who does your hair for you?"

"You mean Kryssie?"

"Kryssie, huh?" he said, closing the curtain.

"It's really Krystal but she lets me call her Kryssie. Isn't she sweet?"

"You know what Dolly, I do believe she is." And with a smile on his face he got to work.

TUESDAYS WERE LONG DAYS for Krystal, because she spent her morning at the nursing home then went straight to the salon for a full day of work. Today she had brought her lunch, which she ate in the employee lounge while she balanced her checkbook and went over her monthly budget.

She and Garret had lived in the house well over a month, yet so far they'd had no utility bills arrive in the mail. Concerned, she made several phone calls during her lunch break and discovered the accounts were paid in full. When she asked to verify the billing addresses, she learned that although both of their names appeared on the accounts, the bills were mailed to Garret at his clinic address.

Without consulting her, he had assumed responsibility for the payment of the heat, electric and telephone bills. So much for his fifty-fifty division of expenses, she thought. As usual, when she tried to call him she reached his voice mail. She decided not to leave a message, but was determined she would talk to him about the matter that evening.

It continued to snow all afternoon and she was relieved when her final two appointments of the day canceled, meaning that as soon as she finished with her afternoon clients, she could go home. By the time she left the salon, many businesses had closed because of the winter storm. As she made her way through the parking lot to her car, she nearly fell, her feet sliding around on the ice and snow. After scraping her windshield and brushing off the car, her fingers were as cold as her toes.

Driving was difficult, but she managed to make it to within a couple of blocks of the house before she had any serious problems. Trying to avoid a collision, she ended up in a snowbank. The man driving the car behind her stopped to make sure she was all right and offered to call a tow truck, but she knew it was unlikely that on such a night anyone would respond to the call.

She decided to leave her car and walk the remaining distance since she was so close to home. As she climbed out she wished she had worn a different pair of shoes, but the severity of the storm had caught many people by surprise, including her.

She had trudged about half a block when she saw Garret's car at the corner. When he saw her, he got out. He didn't speak but came toward her with an intense look on his face.

Before she could say a word to him, he scooped her up into his arms and began to carry her toward the car.

"What are you doing?" she demanded.

"Rescuing you."

"You don't have to carry me. I can walk. I'm pregnant, not crippled," she told him.

He paid no attention. "Haven't you heard of boots?" he asked, looking at her platform shoes.

"It wasn't snowing when I left this morning." He stumbled and she thought they would both go tumbling to the ground, but he managed to stay on his feet. "Please put me down. I'm perfectly capable of walking."

He ignored her pleas and kept slogging through the snow until he got to his car, where he managed to open the passenger door and dump her inside. When he'd come around and sat in the driver's seat, he asked, "Where's your car?"

"Not far from here." She explained how she was forced off the road to avoid an accident. "How did you know where to find me?"

"I called the salon and they said you left for home an hour ago. I figured you'd be somewhere between here and there."

"Thank you for coming to find me," she said gratefully.

He didn't appreciate her thanks, however. "Why didn't you leave when they issued the winter storm warning?"

"Because I had clients with appointments."

"The salon didn't close?"

"Did the clinic?"

"Yes. Most businesses did."

"Well, mine didn't."

They had reached the house and the car skidded as he pulled into the snowy driveway. He turned off the engine and, without another word, he came around to her side to open the door. When she got out, he picked her up again and, despite her protests, carried her into the house, once more mumbling about the inappropriateness of her footwear.

It was warm inside and she kicked off her wet shoes and padded in her wet stocking feet across the kitchen floor. She was thirsty and hungry and went straight for the refrigerator.

When she opened it, he said, "You need to get out of those wet clothes."

Something in his tone set her off. "I don't need to be told what to do. I'm perfectly capable of taking care of myself."

"Oh really? Is that what you were doing when you ran your car off the road? Taking care of yourself?"

"That could have happened to anyone in this kind of weather."

"And how far do you think you would have made it in those shoes if I hadn't come along? For crying out loud, Krystal. It's a snowstorm out there. Don't you own a pair of snow boots?"

"And I told you, it wasn't snowing when I left this morning," she said, unwrapping her scarf from around her neck.

"It doesn't matter. Someone who's pregnant shouldn't be wearing shoes that look like they have Mickey's building blocks for soles," he shot back at her.

"The kind of shoes I wear is none of your business," she retaliated.

"Everything you do is my business. You're carrying my child."

She shoved her hands to her hips. So that's what this was really about. The baby. He wasn't worried about her health or her well-being. He was worried that she might do something that would harm his child.

When she'd first seen his car, she'd felt a rush of warmth at the thought he'd come looking for her. But now she realized the only reason he had was because of the baby.

Everything was for the baby. The house, the clothes, the food, the bills...at the thought of the utility bills, a fresh stream of anger rose in her. "And there's something I want to talk to you about. Since when did it become your responsibility to pay all of the utility bills for this house?''

''I do live here,'' he said calmly.

''So do I and we agreed everything would be fifty-fifty. Now I find you've paid the gas, the electric and the telephone bills without telling me!''

He stared at her in disbelief. ''You're angry because I'm paying the utility bills?''

''I told you I didn't want to feel indebted to you.'' The quivering of her voice told her she was dangerously close to losing control of her emotions, but she continued on anyway. ''I know that doesn't matter to you. You don't care how I feel about anything! You just want to be in control.'' She shrugged out of her coat and threw it in the corner in frustration.

He stared at her, wide-eyed, then went over to pick it up. When he would have hung it up in the closet for her, she grabbed it from his hands.

''I don't want you hanging up my coat! I'll do it myself,'' she cried.

''You're obviously overwrought. Maybe you should go lie down,'' he suggested.

''I am not overwrought,'' she denied strongly. ''What I am is tired of you treating me like a child. You keep doing all these things for me without even taking into consideration I might not want you to do them. How do you think that makes me feel?''

He didn't say anything for several seconds. He just stood staring at her. Finally he said in a quiet voice, ''I do them because I care about you, Krystal, but I can see that's a misspent emotion. What does a man have to do? Walk out on you before you think he deserves your attention? Well, I can do that.'' And before she could utter a single word, he was gone.

Krystal found it difficult to swallow. Her body began to tremble, from emotion as well as from cold. She stumbled down the hallway to her bedroom, where she went inside and slammed the door. She peeled off the layers of clothes and hopped in the shower, needing the warmth of the water to chase away the chill in her bones. As she let the steam envelop her, there was only one thought running through her mind. How could she have been so stupid to fall in love with a man who saw her as nothing but an obligation?

CHAPTER THIRTEEN

IT HAD ONLY BEEN one week since the first snowfall of the season and already it had melted. Garret wished he could say the same thing about the tension in the house, but ever since that night when Krystal had made it perfectly clear what she thought about his efforts to make life easier for her, they had hardly said more than ten words to each other.

He'd tried to give her a peace offering—bringing home a book on breast-feeding. She'd interpreted it as a sign he was worried about her baby's IQ. He simply didn't know how to handle her mood swings and decided he might as well give up. It was easier not to have any contact with her than to get his head snapped off for trying to do something nice for her.

They were like two strangers living in the same house. Not a good environment for a child. And certainly not the way he wanted to live his own life. At least when he'd lived alone he was comfortable. Now he could hardly sleep nights and he knew that she felt the awkwardness, too. They were avoiding each other as much as possible and that was no way to live.

He'd been contemplating solutions to the problem and so far hadn't been able to come up with one. He'd sublet his apartment—not that he wanted to move back into it, because he didn't. He liked the house. And he liked living with Krystal in the house. The problem was she didn't like living in the house with him. Any way he looked at it, it was a mess.

He glanced at his watch. It was barely four. She wouldn't be home from work yet. He knew her schedule because she wrote her hours in red on the calendar in the kitchen. Today she worked until five. She also had karaoke tonight.

Karaoke. He didn't even want to think about her hanging out in some bar singing on a stage. But she had a different life than he did. She liked to have fun. How many times had he heard that from her? Too many, as an image of her in a smoky bar played in his head. She should have known better than to expose her unborn baby to all that secondhand smoke. She also should have known better than to go out in a snowstorm in platform shoes.

As he pulled up in front of the house he saw his mother's car out front. A glance in the driveway told him Krystal was home, too. Uneasiness filled him. Why would his mother be over unless something was wrong?

He quickly parked and went inside. Seated at the kitchen table were the two of them, laughing and having a jolly good time, as if the past couple of months had never happened.

"Garret! I didn't expect to see you so soon," his mother remarked when she saw him.

"It's my early afternoon," he told her, noticing how Krystal's laughter came to an abrupt halt. She averted her eyes, pretending to be fussing with the teapot sitting on the table.

"You look tired. You must be working too hard," his mother commented.

"I'm fine," he answered. He was about to excuse

himself and go into his room, but Krystal beat him to it.

"If you'll excuse me, Leonie, I'm going to change my clothes," she said, and made a hasty departure.

"Cavorting with the enemy, Mother?" he asked, shrugging out of his overcoat.

"Krystal's not my enemy, dear...or did you mean I was cavorting with *your* enemy?" she asked with a perceptive lift of one brow.

"What are you doing here?" he demanded.

"I was having tea with Krystal until you walked in and scared her away," she remarked.

He couldn't believe it. His own mother was looking at him as if the icy tension that existed in the house was his fault.

"Krystal doesn't frighten quite that easily," he retorted, then went to hang his coat in the entry closet. His mother let that comment slide.

"I thought you would be happy to see me here. You're the one who's been encouraging me to set aside my disappointment and try to look at the positive side of your situation. Now I have and you look annoyed."

He sighed. "I'm not annoyed. I'm glad...for your sake and for Krystal's. You are, after all, the baby's grandmother."

"And I'm Krystal's friend." She got up to clear away the cups and saucers from the table. "She needed both today."

He frowned. "Why was that?"

"Because she was upset."

"About the baby?"

"No, not about the baby," his mother said with a reassuring pat on his arm.

"Then what?"

"If you want to know what it is, why don't you go ask her and find out for yourself?"

He shrugged. "I will later. I thought she worked until five today."

"No, she had the afternoon off so we went shopping. You'll have to have her show you what I bought for the baby."

Leonie's cell phone rang and she excused herself to take the call. He could hear that it was a client by the tone of her voice, so he stepped into the living room to give her privacy. Spread out on the sofa were tiny little undershirts and nightgowns. Some were pink and some were blue.

He was standing over them when his mother walked in. "Aren't they tiny? I'd forgotten how small those things can be. It's been quite a while since Mickey was that size."

Just then Krystal reappeared. She'd changed out of a white T-shirt and jeans and into a black dress that sparkled when she walked. For a change her hair was worn in a rather simple style, brushed away from her face. She'd never looked sexier to him.

"Oh, you look lovely." His mother said what he wished he could have. "They make the cutest maternity clothes nowadays. Nothing at all like what I had in my day."

Garret hardly thought the dress should be described as cute. Elegant maybe, and much too nice for some bar. Again, the thought of her being with a bunch of people drinking beer and whiskey in order to get up the courage to sing into a microphone made him irritable.

"Garret, doesn't she look lovely?" his mother prodded.

He met Krystal's eyes then, and what he saw there

made him want to take her in his arms and hold her close to him. She quickly looked away as he said, "Yes, very nice."

"I'd better get going," she announced. "Dinner's early."

Leonie nodded in understanding. "I wish I could be there to see you perform."

"I'm sure it'll be fun," Krystal said as she pulled her coat from the closet.

There it was again. That word. *Fun.*

His mother gave him one of her looks which he knew meant he should do the gentlemanly thing and help Krystal with her coat. As he did he caught a whiff of the scent she wore and he had to fight the urge to wrap his arms around her and hold her close to him. Memories of the night they'd made love flashed in his mind. Before he knew it, she was out the door, eager to be away from him, as usual.

That's when his mother turned on him. She faced him with hands on her hips and said, "All right. What is going on with you two?"

"I'm sure Krystal's already answered that for you."

"If you mean did she tell me that you won't talk to her, yes, she did."

Leonie sounded angry with him. "Do you think maybe that *she's* the one who won't talk to *me?*" he asked.

That caused her to chuckle. "No, because I know better. Krystal cannot not talk to anyone. You, my son, can go for days without speaking and see nothing wrong with it."

"Well, thank you, Mom, for the compliment," he drawled sarcastically.

She slung an arm around his shoulder and gave it a squeeze. "That's not a criticism. It's just the way it is. She's a talker. You're a thinker. It's one of the reasons you're attracted to each other.''

"I'll let that slide.''

"What? The talker-thinker stuff or the part about you being attracted to her.''

"Well, it would be pointless to deny that I'm attracted to her, not with my sofa covered in baby things,'' he said dryly.

"You know I try not to interfere when it comes to your personal life.''

He held up his hands in supplication. "Then don't say anything, Mom. I thought renting a house together would be a good solution to our problem, but you know what? It's not working and I'm not sure I can do this…not even for the baby's sake.''

She grimaced. "That's what she said, too.''

A knifelike pain went through him. She didn't want to live with him. It shouldn't have come as a surprise. He'd only been fooling himself if he thought she was going to suddenly appreciate his interest in her. The phone rang and he went to answer it.

"I'm looking for Krystal,'' a man's voice said.

"She's gone.'' Garret was rather terse but he didn't care.

"Oh, shoot. I missed her. All right. I guess I'll just have to tell her when she gets here. Thanks.'' And the voice was gone.

"I take it that was for Krystal?'' his mother said.

"Just another guy. We both know there's been no shortage of men in her life,'' he said irritably.

His mother frowned. "I didn't think she'd been dating since she broke up with Roy. Not that it would matter to you,'' she added, scrutinizing his face closely.

"No, it doesn't matter,'' he lied.

"The same way it wouldn't matter to Krystal if I told her Samantha asked to be let out of her lease so she could move in with her latest boyfriend."

"Did you tell Krystal that?" he asked with interest.

"No, I thought I'd let you share that piece of information with her since she seems to think you're still interested in Samantha."

"That's ridiculous. I've told her half a dozen times that Samantha means nothing to me."

"Then if that's the case, just what is it that's keeping you and Krystal apart?"

"You make it sound as if we've had a lovers' quarrel and all we need to do is kiss and make up. We share a house, Mom. We're not lovers."

"Maybe that's the problem," his mother said, reaching for her coat, which had been slung over the kitchen chair. "Romance is my business, Garret. I know the look of love when I see it and it's in your eyes whether you want to see it or not."

"You think I'm in love with Krystal?"

"Yes. Now what do you plan to do about it?" She pulled on her coat and began buttoning it up.

"Nothing, because you're wrong. I'm not in love with her," he stated for his own benefit as much as hers.

"All right, so you're not." She gave him a kiss on the cheek and started toward the door. "I've got to get home. See you, dear."

"Mother, wait!"

She paused near the door. "What?" she asked impatiently.

"You don't think Krystal thinks I'm in love with her, do you?"

"Oh, good heavens, no. She thinks you're only living here because of the baby, that you treat her the way you do because of a sense of duty. She's given up hope that you'll ever fall in love with her.''

''You make it sound like she would want that to happen.''

''Why Garret, are you pumping your mother for information about a woman?'' she asked with a reproving look. ''There's only one way for you to find out what Krystal wants. Go ask her. You saw how pretty she looked tonight. Why don't you do something impulsive—like get in your car and go after her.''

''Oh yeah,'' he drawled sarcastically. ''Like I want to go to some smoky bar where she's singing karaoke to find out if we're a good match.''

His mother frowned. ''Bar? What are you talking about? Krystal's not at a bar. She's at the nursing home.''

''Nursing home?'' He frowned, suddenly remembering Dolly Anderson telling him about Krystal volunteering to help at a party.

''It's their party night and she's hosting the karaoke for the seniors. Not that you'd want to go. I know how you hate parties.''

And with a wave and a bye-bye tossed over her shoulder, Leonie walked out, leaving Garret's mind racing with possibilities. Was Krystal hoping he'd fall in love with her? Or would he look like a fool if he showed up at the nursing home?

He paced for several minutes, unable to stop thinking about her. ''You need to have more fun in your life.'' How many times had she told him that? Maybe it was time he showed her what a fun guy he could be. He grabbed his coat and keys and headed out the door. One of them was going to be in for a big surprise this evening. He could only hope it was Krystal.

"Oh, my! Don't you look beautiful," Dolly crooned when she saw Krystal. "All those spangles! It's too bad Dr. G. isn't going to be here tonight to see you."

Personally, Krystal was relieved he wasn't. For months Dolly had been mentioning her favorite doctor, who just happened to be single. Krystal was in no mood to have anybody matchmaking for her and she'd had enough of one particular doctor that she didn't care if she never met another one.

She couldn't think of Garret without her heart feeling as if it were being squeezed in a vise. When she'd first moved in with him she'd been determined to make their living arrangements work—for the sake of the baby. But ever since their huge fight last week, she'd been seriously thinking of looking for her own place.

She blamed herself. If she hadn't fallen in love with him, she wouldn't care that he ignored her. It wouldn't matter that he came home at night after she was in bed and was gone in the morning before she got up. But she did love him and she did care.

That's why today had been another painful reminder of why it would never work between them. When he'd come home and found her in the kitchen with his mother, she hadn't missed the surprise on his face. For one brief moment she had thought that maybe he was happy to see her, but then he'd looked away, as if he didn't need any reminders of his obligation.

"I made sure that you're seated at my table for dinner," Dolly told her, pulling her by the hand to where six other senior citizens already sat around the circular table. Introductions were made with Dolly bragging that Krystal would be in charge of entertainment after dinner.

The kitchen staff had just started to serve the food

when Dolly grabbed her by the arm and exclaimed, "Well, isn't that nice! He was able to come after all." She stared past Krystal in the direction of the exit.

Krystal assumed it was one of the older gentlemen residents until Dolly said, "It's Dr. G.—you know, the one I want you to meet, but he's sitting way across the room at a corner table. Maybe I can get him moved over here with us," she said, glancing around for a staff member.

"No, it's all right." Krystal pulled her hand down, in no hurry to be the recipient of Dolly's matchmaking attempts. "Let him eat. I'll meet him after dinner."

Dolly didn't protest, but Krystal noticed she glanced frequently in the doctor's direction throughout dinner. Krystal, however, kept her attention on the hot dish, green beans and gelatin salad on her plate, hoping that as soon as she was finished, her duties as a volunteer on the entertainment committee would keep her busy.

"Krystal, there's someone who wants to see you," Dolly said when they were on the final course—a scoop of ice cream.

Krystal knew the inevitable moment had come. She had to meet Dolly's doctor friend. She turned and was surprised to see Gladys Lingenfelser in a wheelchair.

"Oh, good! You're out of bed," Krystal said, giving the elderly woman a hug.

"I have something for you," Gladys said. She reached into her pocket and pulled out a beaded bracelet. "I made it for you."

"Why, thank you." Krystal's eyes misted with tears as she slipped the bracelet over her wrist. "That is one of the nicest gifts anyone has ever given me."

The elderly woman grinned and patted her hand. "You're such a sweet thing."

"Isn't she though?" Dolly seconded.

Then Krystal heard a male voice say, "I think she just might be the sweetest thing I've ever met."

Startled, she looked up to see Garret standing over her shoulder. Before she could utter a word, Dolly tugged on his sleeve. "I'm so glad you came to the party. Now you can meet my friend Kryssie."

Krystal looked from Dolly to Garret. "This is Dr. G.?"

Dolly beamed. "Yes, didn't I tell you he was good-looking?"

"You did."

"And wasn't I right?"

Krystal looked at Garret when she answered. "Yes, you were right."

Dolly again pulled on Garret's coat sleeve. "Say hello to Kryssie. Didn't I tell you she was pretty?"

"Yes, you did," he answered, amusement dancing in the eyes that gazed into Krystal's. "Hello, Kryssie."

"What are you doing here?" she whispered to him.

"Looking to have some fun," he answered.

"Here?" she squeaked.

He glanced around. "There are a few more people than I like to see at a party, but I certainly can't complain about the guest list. And I hear the entertainment is worth the price of admission in itself." His eyes stared into hers as he finished his sentence.

"Kryssie, it's time to get started," Dolly interrupted them, pointing to the front of the room where the other volunteers now stood.

From the program that had been at her place at dinner, Krystal knew the entertainment consisted of three parts. A flutist, a magician and a karaoke specialist. She was the karaoke specialist, although she didn't want to admit to anyone that the only time she'd actually stood up in a bar and sung along with karaoke, she'd been a few sheets to the wind.

The flutist went first, followed by the magician. Both were received warmly by the elderly audience. When it was her turn, she took her place next to the karaoke machine, microphone in hand.

Dolly volunteered to sing "White Cliffs of Dover" because it reminded her of her husband. Music from the forties was very popular and Krystal was surprised at how many didn't need lyrics to sing along. When it appeared that everyone who wanted a turn had sung a favorite tune, Krystal was about to put the microphone away when Garret stood up.

"What about me. Don't I get to try?"

She stared at him in disbelief. He wanted to sing in front of an audience? She whispered close to his ear, "Are you sure? This isn't the shower."

He took the microphone from her and made his song selection. Before he started, he said, "Dolly, you know how you dedicated your song to your husband? Well, I'm dedicating this song to your Kryssie."

Krystal knew her eyes bulged. She couldn't imagine what it was he could possibly sing to her. Then he began and she nearly fell off her chair. The song was "Baby, I Need Your Lovin'."

Dolly nearly swooned over with joy. The rest of the audience grinned and applauded. Krystal couldn't do a single thing but cry.

She couldn't believe that quiet, unemotional Garret was belting out his love for her in a roomful of strangers. She knew how much he hated large groups of people. She knew how hard it was for him to shed his reserve and do something out of his comfort zone. Yet he was going on and on and on...

Suddenly she leaped to her feet and grabbed the

microphone from him and turned off the karaoke machine. She stared into eyes that were as dark and as rich as chocolate. "I need your lovin,' too."

Then she kissed him.

"So, Dr. G., what happens next?" she asked provocatively when they were the only two left in the cafeteria of the nursing home. "Do you have any other fun things you can show me?"

He pulled her into his arms and gave her a lingering kiss that would have continued a lot longer had they not been in a public place. "I've been wanting to do that for a long, long time."

"I wish you would have. It could have saved us a lot of misery," she said on a sigh.

He lifted her chin and stared into her eyes. "Have you been miserable?"

"Yes. Haven't you?"

"Yes." He brushed another kiss across her lips.

"I thought you wanted to be with Samantha and were only with me out of a sense of obligation to the baby."

"And I thought you wanted to be with Roy and were only with me because of the baby."

"He was never the right man for me and subconsciously I think I knew it all along. It's why one of the conditions I made when we got back together was that we'd have no sex until I knew it would last."

"But it didn't last."

She made a face. "Roy Stanton is such a loser compared to you...no, he's *nothing* compared to you." She smoothed her fingers across his brow. "You are good to the bone, Garret Donovan, and I can't think of anyone I'd rather have as a father to my baby."

That earned her another long kiss that ended with a

groan. ''You don't know how many times I've fantasized about hearing you say that.''

She stiffened and pushed away from him. ''Then maybe I shouldn't have said it.''

''Why not?'' He gave her a puzzled look.

''Because that night we made love you said that's what I'd been to you—a fantasy. Then the next morning you told me it's all I'd been.''

He pulled her back into his arms. ''Because that's what it was for me. I've been a little in love with you since the day we met. For that one night you were the woman of my dreams. Then I awoke and found you crying and you told me it was all a mistake.'' He shook his head.

''I cried because I thought I'd disappointed you. That the reality of being with me hadn't lived up to the fantasy.''

''It was so much better,'' he said, then kissed her in a way that convinced her she'd been wrong. A little breathless, he said, ''I should have listened to Dolly sooner. She told me you would be perfect for me— only I didn't know you were the Kryssie she kept mentioning to me.''

''I know. She kept calling you Dr. G.,'' Krystal said with a smile. ''Is she the reason you came down here tonight?''

''Yes and no. She had told me about the party, but I also had a little help from a romance coach,'' he said with a grin.

''Your mother? But how did she know I was in love with you? I didn't say anything to her.''

Garret grinned. ''She knows her business. She also told me you were upset and that's why she'd come over.''

''I was. I had some questions about becoming a

mother. And then she asked me how things were going between us and I said a few things I probably shouldn't have said.''

''So you did tell her you were in love with me?''

''Not in so many words, but...''

He kissed her again. ''I told you she thinks of you as a daughter.''

''Yes, we're lucky she's going to be our baby's grandmother,'' she said, placing her fingertips on his lips so he could kiss them. ''I never wanted you out of my life, but it was hard letting you in, especially when I knew that because of me you were going to have to sacrifice one of your dreams.''

''You're talking about going overseas.'' She nodded and he said, ''That wasn't my only dream, Krystal. And there are other humanitarian projects I can become involved with right here in the States.''

''I admire you for wanting to help people.''

''Why? You're the same way. I've seen how you are with the residents here.''

In his arms she found a strength and a sense of rightness she'd never known before. ''We're alike in some ways, but we're pretty different in a lot of ways, too.''

''Don't tell me you're trying to figure us out?''

She shook her head. ''Uh-uh. I just want to hold fast to it and never let it slip away.''

He kissed her again. ''That's exactly how I feel. It doesn't matter why you slept with me that night. What matters is that from our time together, something wonderful happened...and I don't just mean the baby.''

''Garret, I think we need to talk about that night.''

This time he put his fingertip to her lips, to quiet her. ''It's not necessary.''

''For me it is. I know you think that night happened

because I was hurt. And when I went back to your apartment with you, I did want to be with a friend, but once I looked into your eyes, what I saw there made me want you in a way I'd never expected. Maybe it was because when I looked into your eyes I saw someone who really cared about me. Whatever the reason, it made loving you feel right.''

"Why didn't you tell me any of this before now?"

She shrugged. "I can think of a few good reasons...like Samantha, for one."

"I told you she was not my girlfriend," he said with a hint of impatience.

"Believe me, she wanted to be."

He lifted her chin and planted another kiss on her lips. "There's only one woman for me and now I'd like to take her home with me."

"I think that's an excellent idea. Dolly says you could teach me a few things about love."

"Dolly said that?"

"Mmm-hmm, but I have to warn you. It might take you a while."

"And why is that?"

"I'm a slow learner."

"Don't worry. We have a lifetime ahead of us."

EPILOGUE

KRYSTAL AWOKE to find she was alone in bed. On the pillow where Garret's head should have been was a single red rose and a small book of poetry. She reached for the rose and inhaled its fragrance.

She'd been married exactly one week and she didn't think she could be any happier. Judging by the dedication Garret had written in the book of love poems, he shared her sentiment.

"I hope that smile means you like my valentine." The sound of his voice had her glancing toward the doorway.

"I do, but what are you doing out of bed so early on your day off?" she asked as he came toward her carrying a tray.

"Making breakfast for you." He sat down beside her, setting the tray in front of her. On a pink heart-shaped plate were two heart-shaped eggs, heart-shaped toast covered with raspberry jam, and a small red dish filled with freshly cut fruit.

She took his face in her hands and kissed him. "You are such a romantic and I love you, but I thought I was going to treat you to a Valentine's Day breakfast at that wonderful new French café."

"It's too cold this morning to be going out. Besides, I rather like the idea of spending the entire day inside with you," he said, stroking her hair.

"It works for me," she said with a grin.

Only it didn't work for either one of them. Before she'd taken a single bite of her breakfast, she felt a sudden warm sensation beneath her. "Ohmigosh!"

She didn't need to say another word. Garret could see what had happened.

"Is this…?" she asked.

He nodded. "You, my lovely wife, are going to have a baby."

"But…but I'm not ready!" she exclaimed as he calmly removed the tray and helped her out of bed.

With the onset of contractions, however, she changed her mind. She definitely was ready to give birth. She allowed her husband to drive her to the hospital, where she labored long and hard all afternoon to hear three little words.

"It's a girl."

As the doctor placed her baby on her bare abdomen, Krystal stared in disbelief at the tiny arms and legs flailing about. "I did that!" she said to Garret.

He kissed her. "Yes, you did. Thank you for giving me the perfect valentine."

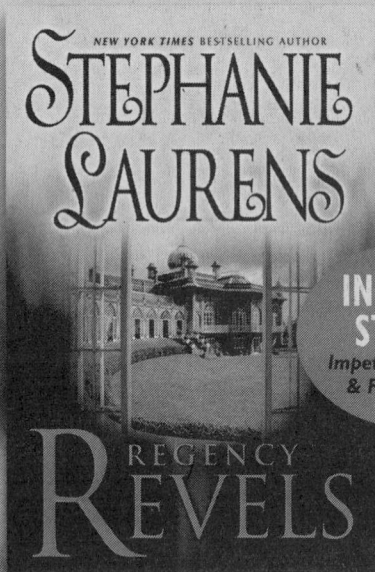

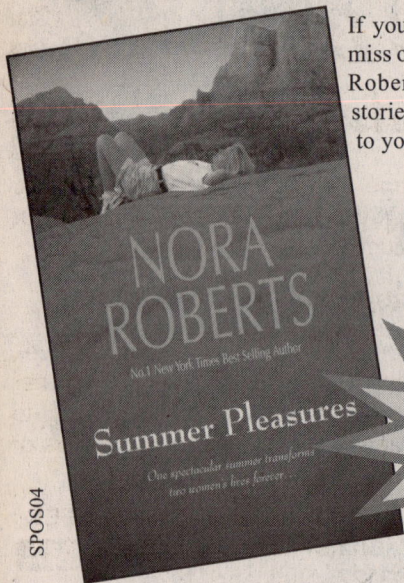

Send in for a
FREE BOOK
today!

How would you like to escape into a world of romance and excitement? A world in which you can experience all the glamour and allure of romance and seduction?

No purchase necessary - now or ever!

To receive your FREE Harlequin Mills & Boon romance novel, simply fill in the coupon and send it to the address below, together with $1.00 worth of loose postage stamps (80 cents in NZ) to cover postage and handling (please do not send money orders or cheques). There is never any obligation to buy!

Send to: HARLEQUIN MILLS & BOON FREE BOOK OFFER
Aust: Locked Bag 2, Chatswood, NSW, 2067
NZ: Private Bag 92122, Auckland, 1020

Harlequin
Mills & Boon
Direct to you

✂ ---

Please send me my FREE Harlequin Mills & Boon Sexy romance valued at $5.75 (NZ$6.95). I have included $1.00 worth of loose postage stamps (80 cents in NZ). Please do not stick them to anything.

Name: Mrs / Ms / Miss / Mr: _____

Address: _____

_____ P/Code _____

Daytime Tel. No.: (_____) _____

FBBP03/ZFBBP3

This offer is restricted to one free book per coupon. Only original coupons with $1.00 worth of loose postage stamps (80 cents in NZ) will be accepted. Your book may differ from those shown. Offer expires 31st December, 2004 or while stocks last. Offer only available to Australian and NZ residents over 18 years. You may also receive offers from other reputable companies as a result of this application. If you do not wish to share in this opportunity please tick the box. ☐